THE PARANORMALS BLOOD WORLD

BOOKS 1-4

TAMSIN BAKER

AMELIA SHAW

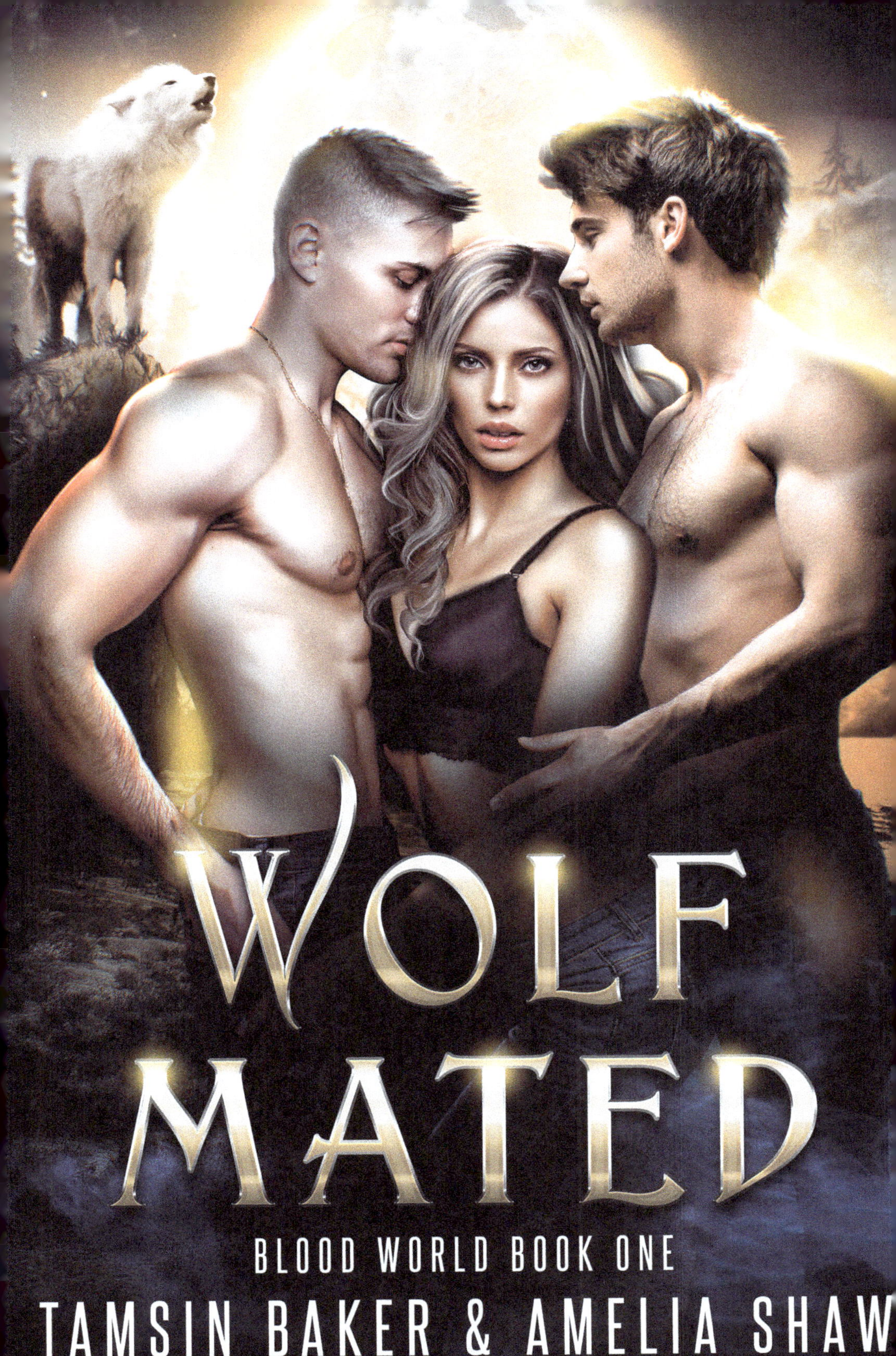

WOLF MATED
BLOOD WORLD BOOK ONE
TAMSIN BAKER & AMELIA SHAW

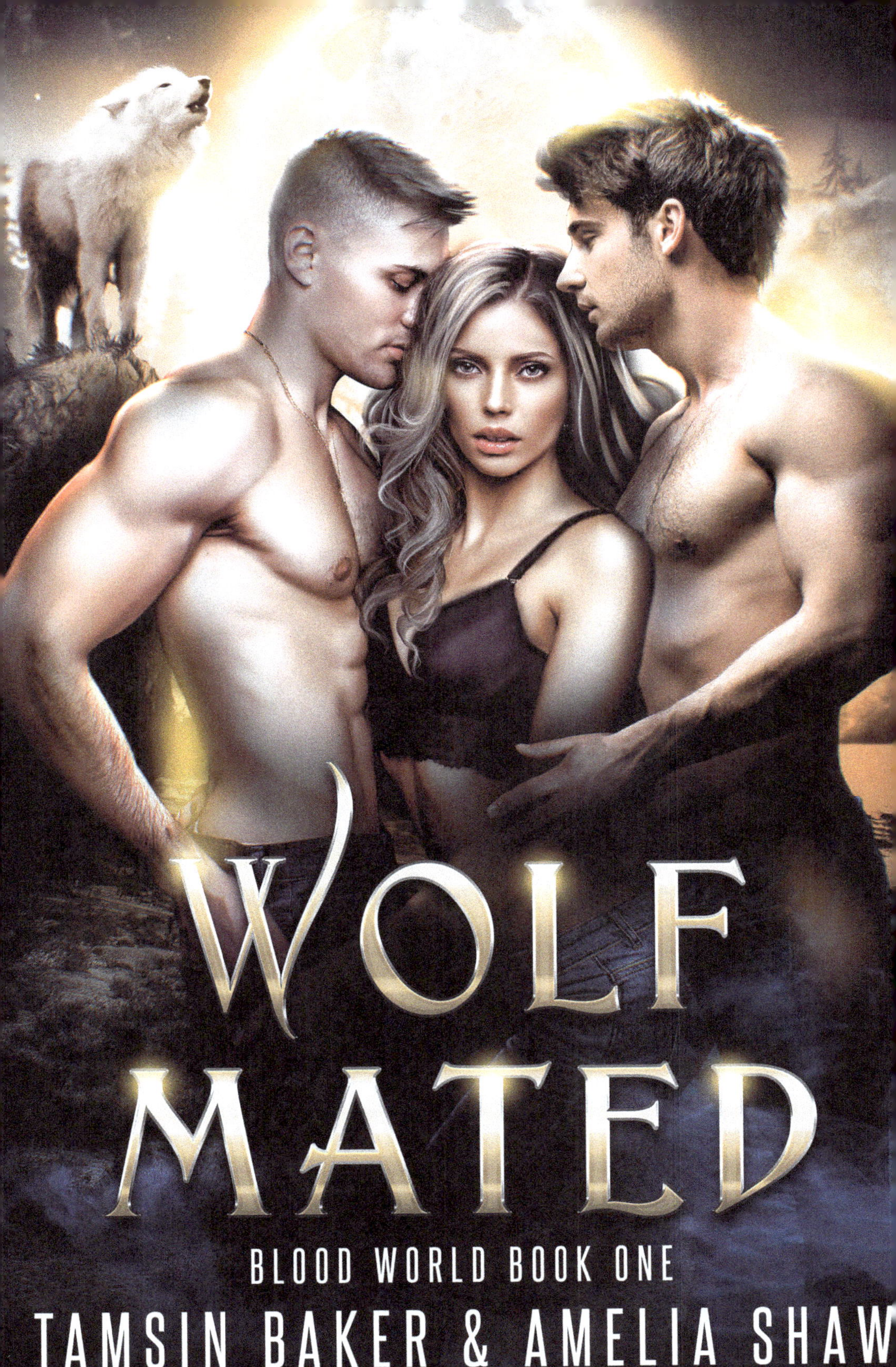

WOLF MATED
BLOOD WORLD BOOK ONE
TAMSIN BAKER & AMELIA SHAW

WOLF MATED

THE PARANORMALS BLOOD WORLD BOOK 1

CHAPTER 1
SADIE

The day my father was murdered started off like any other day. No inkling of what was to come.

Metallic grating sounds of a new knife—Dad's weapon of choice—being sharpened reached my ears as I walked into the kitchen with my briefcase in hand.

Being a corporate lawyer was fast-paced, high stress and extremely intense. But perhaps not when compared to my father's line of work. He was a bounty hunter, feared by all. He ate bad guys for breakfast. All I did was send them emails.

I grinned at him as I set the briefcase down. "Morning, Dad."

"Mornin' Sadie." He glanced up at me, his gaze running over my work attire, and sighed. "All that talent with a knife, and you'd rather go to court and work for the corporate shills, huh? Wouldn't you rather use your natural skills to catch the bad guys?"

I rolled my eyes. My father had never been one to hold back on telling his truth. He'd always hated my job, but this morning the hatred seemed to come with an unusual amount of gusto.

My suit jacket was hanging over the back of one of the dining chairs. I reached for it and pulled it on. Then I picked up my briefcase again. "I'm good at my job, Dad. And I like it. You know that."

The clanging slide of the large knife being sharpened echoed around the room.

Slice. Slice. Slice.

"Yeah... but you're even better at *my* job," he said with a grin.

I decided to ignore that jibe and glanced at my watch. I grimaced. "Damn, I'm late."

I strode over to where he sat at our kitchen counter, sharpening a beautiful new Bowie. I couldn't help but stop and admire it before I kissed him goodbye. "Oh, that's nice."

He held the weapon up and turned it from side to side so I could see it at its best advantage. The silver blade glistened in the light of the bright kitchen, making me ache to reach out and touch it.

"It's new," he said, as if aware of the effect of the knife on my senses.

I shook my head, mentally pulling on my professional hat and tamping down my natural inclination to curve my fingers around the knife handle and feel its weight in my palm.

I am a lawyer. A good one. And my weapon of choice is the law.

I kissed the only man in my life on top of his bald head. "Love you, Dad."

"Love you too, sweetie. See you tonight?"

"Yeah... I have a pretty intense day, but if things go better in court than I expect, I'll swing by your workshop later and take you out for dinner."

His eyebrows flicked up. "Any particular occasion?"

I shook my head. I never needed a reason to spend time with my dad. He was the funniest, most hard-working, most kickass and awesome person I knew. The fact that he happened to know how to kill a person in a thousand different ways just made him even cooler.

"Nope. But there's a new Italian place I want to try that just opened up."

He frowned. "Is that the one on Main Street? It's owned by vampires."

I shrugged as I grabbed my coffee off the counter, checking the lid was tight and sealed.

I glanced at the large, modern silver clock on the wall. *Now I'm really late.*

I slid my keys into my pants pocket and headed to the door.

"The vampires own everything, Dad."

If you wanted to eat at a place that *wasn't* owned by vamps, then you'd never eat. Not out at a restaurant, and not food from a supermarket.

You wouldn't work, either.

Even my corporate law firm was owned by vampires. They were immortal, super-intelligent, and had mastered the art of day-walking decades ago.

"Not *my* shop they don't," Dad threw back at me, pride evident in his tone.

Unlike practically everyone else we knew, Dad outright owned everything he had. His business, and this apartment we lived in.

I opened the door, smiling back at him. "I'll call if I'm going to be late, but otherwise see you for dinner!"

"Okay, sweetie." He waved, and I couldn't stop myself from taking one final look at my dad before I left.

He was quite an unusual man to behold. His bald head shone beneath the fluorescent lights. He had a graying beard, and today he was wearing a tight leather vest and his muscles flexed with each movement. His shoulders and arms were covered in full-sleeve tattoos and he looked like a man you wouldn't want to run into in a dark alley at night.

And in truth… he wasn't. Not if you were a bad guy.

But if you were a good guy, or a good girl, this was a man you could trust and rely on. And I was the luckiest girl in the world to have him as my father.

"Bye!" I waved back and rushed off, really late now.

Time to use the brain I'd inherited from both my parents, and use my powers for good instead of evil.

~

AFTER SECURING a multi-billion-dollar deal for my bosses much quicker than I'd expected to, there was no question what I was doing tonight. I was definitely taking Dad out for dinner and indulging in a massive carb overload.

"You going home already, Sarah?" Nikki asked from her seat at her desk, just outside my office as I packed up my briefcase.

"Yeah, why not?" I asked. The people at work knew me by my real name, Sarah. It was only usually Dad who ever called me Sadie.

I'd barely had lunch, and I never ate breakfast, beyond coffee. And with all the extra work I'd put in to pull this deal off, I'd earned myself a huge serving of lasagna, garlic bread, and a glass of red wine.

"Because you never leave early," she said, throwing her hands up like I was an idiot for not already knowing that would be her answer.

I laughed. I'd graduated from law school a few years ago and worked my ass off pretty much ever since. Going home early was definitely not my 'normal'. She was right there.

"I'm starving and I told my dad I'd take him out for dinner."

Nikki shivered, though I knew she didn't mean to show it. I giggled to myself as I locked my briefcase and walked over to her desk, cell phone in hand.

Nikki was half-human, half-wolf shifter, just like my dad. They had an unusual connection, like most of their breed. I knew she was attracted to him. I barely had to mention him and she was instantly a shivery, hormonal mess.

But he was my dad and twice her age, and her constant blushes and defensive behavior indicated that she didn't want to be so affected by him.

It was *hilarious.*

"What's wrong, Nik? Wanna come?" I grinned at her. "You hungry too?"

For more than dinner, I'm sure!

She turned back to her computer, her cheeks coloring with a blush. "You know I can't help it."

"Yeah... because my dad's *so* hot," I teased.

Nikki flipped me the bird, her long, manicured fingernail capturing my attention. I'd always wanted pretty nails like that, but the way I trained with my dad five days a week, long nails were beyond impractical. They were *impossible.*

I waved at my gorgeous friend and headed out the door. Most women with any wolf shifter blood lusted after my father, and he could have pretty much anyone he wanted. They apparently found all that strength in him hot. I mean, to me he was just Dad, but I guess he was still a man.

Since Mom died, he hadn't dated anyone. Not openly, anyway. Which I was grateful for. If he was sleeping with someone, I didn't want to know about it.

What daughter did?

I stepped through the double doors of my office building and walked along the sidewalk. It wasn't dark yet, as the sun was only now dropping out of the sky.

I glanced down the street and assessed my choices. Cab... or walk? I glanced at my watch. Dad would probably still be doing paperwork. I had time to get some fresh air. His workshop was only six blocks away from my office, and I rarely had a moment to relax like this, where I wasn't jumping from my office, to a meeting, to court, and back to the office.

Why not take advantage and simply stroll for once?

As I walked, I enjoyed the loud noises of bustling traffic and the people around me. I loved this city, even with its lack of pretty parks, and overly-clogged, smoky air.

It was home. Always had been. Always would be.

I strolled all the way to Dad's workshop, which was what he called it. Like it was some tiny garage where he tinkered with toys.

In reality, it was a huge business, housed in an impressive building, with over fifty employees and raking in millions of dollars a month.

I glanced up at the sign over the doorway. *Hunters.*

A shorter version of the full business name, Bounty Hunters. My dad trained killers. Thrill-seekers. Perfectly legal, of course.

They hunted bad guys.

Bad guys who had very expensive price tags on them. In this city and in many others.

He trained his guys, he booked their jobs, and basically he ran the whole show. He was a one-man juggernaut.

I glanced up at the building, admiring the beauty of the heritage-listed architecture. So much more attractive than the brand-new office building in which I worked.

I put my hand on the glass door, noticing the closed sign had already been put up, and pushed.

I inhaled sharply, my wolf shifter senses delighting in the change of scents from outside to inside the building. Outside there was smog and gas, and a strange, artificial sort of smell.

Inside Dad's workshop there was a feast for the senses. The smell of the hardwood floors, the heady mix of cologne, sweat, and leather punching bags that had recently been oiled.

The scent of my youth. After all, I'd grown up in this place.

Unfortunately, once I turned sixteen, I hadn't spent much time here. I'd been too obsessed with going out with my friends, meeting boys, and trying to exert my independence by doing the opposite of everything my dad wanted me to do. But I'd missed this place.

I should come by more often.

I headed up the stairs to my dad's office, a nostalgic smile on my face.

All the other staff had gone home from the looks of it. The lights were mostly off, and all was quiet.

"Dad? You up here?" I called into the silence.

Usually, when he was closing up for the day, he played some old, classic songs that floated around the hallway. The silence was unusual, and for some reason the hairs rose up on the back of my neck.

"Dad?" I called out again as I hit the landing and kept walking past his receptionist's empty desk and pushed open the door to his large office.

He wasn't there.

Huh. Weird.

I checked my cell phone. No message. No missed call.

He knew I was coming to pick him up for dinner. He wouldn't leave me hanging like this without a good reason.

But then again, the front door had been open, not locked. So, he had to be here.

Was he doing inventory or something in the gym?

"Dad?"

There was a sudden noise downstairs. A squeak, then a heavy thud.

I turned, a shiver coursing down my spine.

What the hell was that?

It sounded like something heavy had been dropped. A punching bag, maybe?

"Dad? Is that you?"

The sound of a door swinging open followed, the metallic creak a bit freaky in the otherwise silent building.

That's the back door.

I started forward, then thought better of it. Instead, I stepped around my dad's desk, opened the top drawer where I knew I'd find some kind of weapon, and pulled out his new Bowie knife.

It was cold and heavy in my hand and I gripped it hard enough my knuckles turned white. I'd grown up throwing knives and could use one like this with deadly efficiency if necessary.

If someone had broken into my dad's business, they'd regret it.

A grim smile quirked my lips. I didn't think there'd be a person in the city stupid enough to do that. No human, shifter, or vamp.

My father had a reputation, and it wasn't one that made him sound soft and fluffy.

I crept down the stairs, listening for any sign of movement, but there was nothing.

I made my way through the massive training hall for the bounty hunters, and headed for the back door. It was the only metal door in the whole building, and that metallic squeak had been a dead giveaway.

A smell began to permeate my nostrils and I stopped dead in my tracks as my stomach dropped through the floor. *Blood!*

"*Dad!*"

Adrenaline pumped into my legs and I raced forward, almost tripping as I reached the prone figure on the wooden floor. I knelt, dropping the knife beside me as I identified my dad. He was face down and not moving.

"No. No. No." I tried to roll him over, pushing on his heavy shoulders. "Dad! Wake up. Please."

Tears began to stream down my face, hot and persistent.

This couldn't be happening.

I pushed and pushed, but he was too heavy. I had no chance of moving him. He weighed almost three hundred pounds, and he was a dead weight.

I put my fingers to his neck, feeling for a pulse.

There was nothing but slippery wetness.

I brought my hand away so I could stare at my trembling fingers.

Dark red blood.

My stomach lurched. Oh, God… it must have been a vampire.

The front door swung open then, the characteristic thunk making me jump to grab the knife.

"Jimmy! You still here?" a man called out from the front of the building.

Someone was looking for my dad. Probably one of his employees. Cold relief washed over me as I began to shake.

"Please!" I shouted. "Come quickly! We're near the back door! Dad's hurt!"

Footsteps pounded through the building and two huge men burst into the back room, looking around wildly.

I hadn't realized I'd picked up the knife again. I was holding it in a defensive grip as the men ground to a halt in front of me, eyeing me suspiciously. I'd never seen either of them before, and they didn't appear to recognize me. Not surprising, given how little time I'd spent here in recent years.

"What's happened?" the smaller one asked, dark curls falling over his eyes.

"I came to pick Dad up for dinner. He's not breathing. There's no pulse. I can't… turn him over."

The two men looked at one another then bent down, grabbing my father's arms and shoulders, and flipped him over while I jumped up and skittered back out of the way.

I gasped at the morbid sight of my father's white, pain-filled expression, and turned away so I couldn't see anymore. *God.* Was there any actual blood left in his body?

Breathe. Breathe. I had to swallow the urge to scream, tears clogging my throat.

Oh, my God.

"It was definitely a vamp," one of the guys said from behind me.

I shook my arms out over and over as I gulped at the air. I had to calm down, I had to think.

Fuck!

Fuck!

What the hell was I going to do?

I turned around to face them. If two virtual strangers could help my father in this moment of need, then I could, too.

I looked down at my dad's once handsome visage. Bile rose in my throat, but I forced it down. His face was contorted in pain, his eyes open but not seeing.

"So, he's... ah... is he?" I swallowed, unable to say the word out loud.

The taller guy, a large blond man, looked up at me from his crouched position next to my father. He had piercing green eyes. Definitely some sort of shifter. Not wolf, though.

"Yes. I'm sorry. Jimmy's dead. You're his daughter?"

I nodded. I'd known he was dead as soon as I saw him, but it hadn't seemed real.

I had to be sure there was no bringing him back.

"Is he... drained?"

There was little to no blood around him, other than the sticky patch on his neck. That alone indicated this was more than a random feeding. A man my father's size had more than enough blood to survive a normal vampire pull. Two of them, even.

The dark-haired man stood up. His gaze was sympathetic. "We'll have to wait for the autopsy, but yes, judging by his appearance, I think so."

I inhaled sharply. "Okay."

The blond one moved to his feet and I was suddenly dwarfed by the two men.

Shifters. Both of them.

Beneath all my grief, anger, and shock, an attraction simmered to life.

The dark-haired one was a wolf shifter, and the little bit of wolf shifter inherited from my father could feel it. But there was something stronger than that... I just couldn't put my finger on it.

Not now.

I took a deep breath, a strange calm falling over me. I had to be strong now. I had to do what my father would want, and take charge.

"We need to call the cops," I said. "Can you stay with him while I grab my phone?"

The men nodded at me and I walked off unsteadily, not feeling my legs as I made my way up to my dad's office where I'd left my bag and phone, and called the police.

Unfortunately, I knew what they'd find when they arrived to investigate.

No evidence of a break-in. No struggle. Just my father's dead body and two puncture wounds from the animal who'd killed him.

CHAPTER 2
ROGAN

"Thank you for your co-operation," the old male cop said, his nose still stuck in the air.

The police in the area hated us bounty hunters. They always had.

But I tried to be reasonable. There was no reason to have them as enemies, even if half of them were owned by the vampires. Then again, what wasn't under vamp control in this town?

"Have you got a card?" I asked him. "If I think of anything else, I'll let you know."

The cop handed me his business card and stalked away.

I sighed as I stared down at the email and phone number. They weren't going to find the perp. They never did when this type of paranormal was the killer and it was obvious from the puncture wounds and Jimmy's complete lack of remaining blood in the body, that a vampire had drained him.

The problem was, there was no physical evidence to be found except for his body. Vampires left no DNA. No identifying trace of who they were. It was impossible to distinguish one vampire bite from another. Even if it was determined that a vamp killed him, there was no way to identify which of the many vampires in this area had done the deed.

Fridge ambled up to me. "You done?"

I nodded. "Yeah. Not that it's gonna help."

Fridge grunted and shoved his hands into his jean pockets. "Yeah. I know. Fucking shame."

I nodded. Understatement of the century.

Jimmy's death was worse than a shame. It was a tragedy. Jimmy was like a father to Fridge, and to me. He had been our mentor. A great man. A brilliant boss. And a friend.

I wasn't sure what we were going to do without him.

"Pretty brutal," Fridge said, lifting his chin to gesture to Sarah Williams, Jimmy's adult daughter, who was still talking to one of the female cops.

Her face was pale and tear-stained.

"Yeah. Imagine finding your father dead in that way," I said.

Fridge shrugged. "I can't." Rogan knew Fridge wasn't close to his father.

But for Jimmy's daughter to have found him first... there couldn't be a worse way to find out someone you loved was gone.

"You think we should head home? Or..." I let my voice trail off.

Fridge and I were friends from school. Roommates for, well, forever. Home was a two-bedroom apartment ten minutes' drive out of the city.

"I think we should hang here a bit longer," Fridge said, gazing over at Jimmy's daughter once more.

I nodded, looking at Sarah, then back at Fridge.

I'd never seen him look at anyone—especially not a woman— like that before. Like he didn't dare look away in case she disappeared.

Even as my brows rose, I realized I didn't blame him. Despite the tragedy of the circumstances, the male part of me—and definitely the wolf part of me—recognized a beautiful female with shifter genes when I saw one.

In fact, there was more to it than that. Something deeper. But I couldn't put my finger on it right now, and with my grief over Jimmy rising up like a wave to swallow me, I didn't think I could work it out tonight.

Maybe tomorrow, after some sleep.

"I agree," I said, and grabbed a few chairs for us to collapse into. "Let's see if she wants a ride home when she's done with the cops."

"Yeah." Fridge huffed, still staring at her. "The vamp might still be around. And until we find out what happened to Jimmy, she may be a target, too."

I could see the protector in my huge dragon shifter friend come to the fore-front. Dragons were notoriously narcissistic. Vain and self-centered. And although Fridge did look in the mirror more than most women I knew, he also had a loyal streak a mile wide. I trusted him with my life.

I settled onto my chair and took a good look at Jimmy's daughter. I could see so much of him in her, and yet she was so different.

She had long, dark hair, dark eyes and spectacularly red lips. She had an innate strength to her that I recognized as being like Jimmy. The way she stood, the way she held herself—everything about her screamed "don't mess with me", a vibe that I was sure put off a lot of guys.

But those city clothes didn't suit her. That corporate suit and frilly crap wasn't her. I could already tell.

And despite the beautiful face and badass posture, I could sense the softness beneath. Her femininity, but even that didn't detract from her strength.

Despite the ugly suit and clothes that covered far too much flesh, her rounded tits and firm ass were obvious.

Strong, yet feminine. But also sexy as hell.

Hard, soft *and* sexy.
Kinda... perfect.

SADIE

The police came quickly and interviewed all three of us.

It was all a complete blur. I just wanted their questions to end, but they kept asking more. My brain hurt, and my throat ached from holding in my tears.

After what felt like hours and hours, the police finally left, and someone was handing me a hot mug with steam rising off the top.

"It's a hot chocolate, in case you don't drink coffee."

I glanced up and wrapped my hands gratefully around the mug being offered to me. It was the wolf shifter. I didn't know his name.

I sat in my dad's chair, in his office, trying to piece together what was left of my life.

I huffed out a strained laugh. "Ah... I'm a lawyer, so I usually take coffee via IV drip, but you made the right call, considering the time of night." I sighed. "Not that I'm going to get any sleep tonight." I put the mug to my lips, vaguely remembering that I'd been hungry before I arrived.

Dinner. I'd been going to have dinner with Dad. I tamped down the grief that threatened to swamp me. I could manage the hot chocolate. Just. But food was the last thing on my mind now. "Thank you," I said, belatedly.

I drank, registering the intense sweetness but not really caring.

He glanced at the door, then at me. Did he want to leave?

I waved my hand at him. "Please don't let me keep you. I'm sure you have a life to get back to."

Whereas, my life as I'd known it was over.

My father had been the center of everything, for so long. I didn't even know how to contemplate living without him.

"Ah... we don't really," he said.

"We?" I repeated, just as the big, blond guy walked in. I perked up, addressing them both. "Oh, hey. I should thank you both for your help tonight." My brain skittered away from the image of them turning my father over to expose his pale, dead face. "I'm not sure I would have handled everything without you," I added, hoping my voice sounded normal.

The coroner had taken my dad's body away to the morgue, and now that the cops had left, these guys probably wanted to get out of here, fast.

The wolf shifter sat down in one of the chairs opposite the desk. "We didn't get to actually introduce ourselves before. I'm Rogan, and this is Fridge. We work... err... worked for Jimmy."

"Fridge?" I asked, glancing at the blond. I kind of got the reference; he was bloody *built*. I hoped it was a nickname, though.

Amazingly, the blond guy flushed, his cheeks pinkening. "My real name is Travis. But I hate my given name."

I smiled. "Yeah, I get that. I'm Sarah. Sarah Williams. But my dad always called me Sadie."

My eyes and nose tingled with tears at the reference, but I wasn't going to stop talking about him just because it made me cry.

Not now. Not ever.

"So..." Rogan glanced at Fridge and back to me. "Sadie?"

I blinked away the tears and attempted a smile. "Yeah, you can call me Sadie."

Only my corporate-life people called me Sarah, and I'd never really liked it. The name was too proper; too English. It ignored that part of me that my father had cultivated.

The part that could gut a man with precision and speed.

I glanced at the blond guy with the nickname "Fridge". "What sort of shifter are you? I haven't been able to work it out."

Rogan laughed. "You know what I am, then?"

I nodded. "Yeah. That was easy."

I glanced back at Fridge, the man with blond, spiky hair, bright green eyes, and muscles bulging out of every part of his black tank top. He was extremely fit. Exactly the sort of guy my father liked to hire.

And that I usually liked to look at. Normally it would be a *wow* moment. Tonight, I banked the knowledge that these guys were hot, but that was as far as it went.

"We don't generally tell people..." he began.

I nodded in understanding. In the city, the paranormals I knew tried to ignore their genetic make-up.

Myself included.

We all held tightly to our human sides and, other than enjoying the speed and stamina that came with shifter blood, very few of us actually indulged our animals and let them out to roam.

It was too uncomfortable. Too beastly.

I still wanted to know what he was.

Then an idea occurred to me and I couldn't stop the smile that spread over my face.

"I totally understand," I said, running a hand over the edge of my father's desk. "I'll just look it up in my dad's files. I know he'll have your information around here somewhere."

I made a show of checking through the top drawer of Dad's desk and Rogan laughed. "She's got you there."

Fridge grunted. "I guess. I'm a dragon."

I slid to the edge of my seat. I knew those emerald eyes of his indicated something strong. "A purebred?"

Pure dragons were as rare as hen's teeth nowadays, with everyone breeding with humans in order to assimilate. I knew a few powerful men with some dragon in them but it was usually a quarter blood strength or less.

Dragons were powerful, but they could also be temperamental and flighty.

Fridge froze for a moment, as though considering his options, then nodded.

I shivered in sympathy for the emotions and pheromones he was emitting into the room. He was nervous, tense, as if he believed I might use the information against him.

I stood so that I wasn't looking up at them quite as much as I was while seated.

"I know you guys trusted my dad, and I know that without even asking because he was the best man on the planet. So, please trust *me* when I tell you I will take your secrets to the grave, just as my father would have done. I may look like a"—I gestured down to my plain black pencil skirt and white blouse—"stuck-up corporate chick, but I was raised by my father. I promise... you can trust me."

The atmosphere relaxed immediately, like a balloon deflating.

"Okay," Fridge replied, and I think he believed me.

And if he didn't... well, I couldn't worry too much about that. If it came down to a fist fight with the guy, I would lose. Most people would lose a fight with a purebred dragon. They were strong and fierce, and super protective of those they loved. Did he have someone special in his life? Someone he would protect with his life?

Why did my mind go there?

I shook myself. "Anyway, thank you both again for sticking around, but you can go home now."

Rogan tapped on the desk. "Will you be running the show from now on?"

I stared at him for a minute, trying to understand what he'd just asked. My brain still felt sluggish with shock. "What do you mean?"

"The business. Are you going to sell it? Take it on yourself? Or close it down, which I wouldn't recommend. It's a great business."

I sat down again in my dad's executive chair and motioned to them to do the same. "Sit. Please."

They did, then Rogan grimaced. "I'm sorry, I should have left that question until another time. You already have so much to process, and deal with."

I waved my hand at him. "No, it's a relevant question, and I don't mind being distracted at a time like this. Ah... to be honest, I haven't even considered..."

I trailed off. I'd never even thought about my father *not* working.

Both men waited, giving me a moment to gather myself.

"Um, well... I'd never close it down. Dad loved this business. Built it up from nothing. But finding someone to replace him..." I whistled through my teeth and shook my head. How was I ever going to get through this?

Fridge chuckled softly, and there was sympathy in the sound rather than mirth. "Yeah, we know. That would be impossible. Jimmy was one in a million."

I managed a smile. "That's understating it."

In a city of five million people, he was far rarer than one in a million.

"I know this is a weird question..." Rogan began and I turned to look at him, my heart kicking out again in recognition of another wolf shifter. And something else underlying that pull, that I hadn't worked out yet.

I certainly hadn't had this reaction to any other wolf shifters I'd met.

I shrugged off the strange thoughts and feelings. "Ask away. What weird question?"

What else was I going to do tonight? Go home to our empty apartment and cry for the next week? I set my jaw, determined not to fall apart.

"We all always wondered how he was so strong. You know, as a half-human, half-wolf shifter combo. He could beat almost any full shifter in a fight, and technically, that *should* be impossible..."

He trailed off and I leaned back in the leather chair, letting a moment of happiness trickle over me.

"Well... that's a bit of a secret," I said, relaxing back in the chair.

The two men's close proximity was making me feel strange, almost like nothing was worrying me, or nothing else mattered. Which was odd, given the circumstances.

Probably the shock of the evening's events. Maybe I was running out of adrenaline and about to crash and burn.

I cocked my head to the side and stared at the men. "But I've asked you to trust me... so I suppose I need to do the same in return."

They leaned forward.

"But you can't tell anyone else," I said, making sure both of them nodded in agreement before I began.

I really shouldn't have told them this, but what did it matter now? The two people this secret involved—my parents—were both dead.

I was officially an orphan.

"Are you going to tell us that he just trained more than anyone else? Worked harder? Wanted it more? Because that's what he used to tell everyone," Fridge said with a grin.

I shook my head. "No. A witch gave my dad a gift a long time ago. A spell to increase his shifting powers to that of a full shifter. *Then* he worked his ass off, of course, to be the best he could be. That was just his way."

Add in his intelligence and cunning, and my dad was unbeatable.

Well, he *had* been unbeatable. I swallowed, forcing the image of his body out of my mind.

Both men stared at me like I was crazy. "But witches are—"

"All but extinct. I know," I finished for them. Then I shrugged. "It's the truth."

"But how did he…"

A shiver of warning and unease moved over my neck, making the hairs stand on end. That was the part of the story I couldn't reveal.

"Let's just say he was pretty convincing when he was younger. Of course, it all happened before I was born, so I can't give you the full details."

I could. I knew the story, but the complete truth endangered my life and I'd promised never to reveal it to anyone.

Ever.

Rogan chuckled. "I didn't think it was possible, but my respect for Jimmy just went up a notch."

Fridge nodded. "Yeah, me too."

I couldn't help but laugh at the surprise on their faces. I let the happy feeling roll through my grief-stricken body. It felt good, for a few seconds, to experience enjoyment.

I wiped at the tears that had fallen onto my cheeks. "Yeah, well, I already knew he was amazing." I stood up, swaying on my feet. "I think it's time we all headed home." I squinted at the clock on the wall. It was after midnight.

"We'll walk you home," Fridge said as both men got to their feet.

I gaped at him. *Seriously?*

"I'm fine," I said, gathering my belongings. "Trust me."

Fridge shook his head and Rogan said, "Either we walk *with* you, or ten feet behind you. Those are your only two options I'm afraid, Sadie."

A part of me hated the whole caveman routine. Especially when I knew how well I could look after myself.

But the logical part—my mother's contribution to my DNA—

realized that the trauma of losing Dad had probably not quite kicked in fully yet. I was better off not arguing.

"Okay," I said. "But it's not far."

Dad had purchased an apartment property and a good commercial building within a short distance of each other.

"That's fine," Rogan said.

I looked at him for a moment, noticing the set of his jaw and the tension in his shoulders. He had been expecting a fight, but he didn't need to worry.

I wasn't in the mood for fighting tonight.

"I'll just lock up and meet you downstairs then," I said.

The men nodded, and then clomped down the stairs and out toward the front door.

I sighed as the silence settled around me. What *was* I going to do with the business? With all the men who worked for Dad? *I* couldn't replace him... could I?

Although I could easily run the business side of things, and some of the training, I'd need to hire some specialized staff if I wanted the same, high-quality advantages my father had provided.

Was there any reason why not? I could sub-contract some of the work out, and do the rest. Couldn't I? If I wanted to. What about my career? The one I'd busted my butt for.

I shook myself and started walking around the building, locking doors, turning off lights.

My gaze was drawn to the place on the floor by the back door where I'd found my father's body. Why? Why had a vampire killed him?

It made no sense. My father was a respected man in this city. A large and intimidating force. Why take him out?

Just... why?

I sighed as I moved to the front of the workshop. I had a key to the main door and the code to the alarm. I'd always had those.

But as I armed the security, then pulled the front door shut and locked it, it somehow felt like the end of an era.

I wasn't here, locking up for my dad as I had done on occasion in the past. I wasn't going home to see his bright face, alight with stories of his day.

My dad was gone, and he wasn't coming back.

I still couldn't wrap my head around it.

Not properly. Not yet.

"I feel so numb," I said aloud, leaning my forehead against the door for a moment.

Rogan and Fridge were standing on the street, shuffling uncomfortably on their feet as they watched me.

I glanced up. Damn. Men. I forgot. Not great with feelings.

"Shit, sorry. Didn't actually mean to say that aloud."

Rogan cleared his throat. "It's all good. I just wish there was more we could do for you."

I smiled. That was a beautiful thing to say, really. It felt... genuine.

"You've already done more than enough, but thanks." I indicated that we should walk up the street, and together we began to move.

"Do you guys live together?" I asked, though I was pretty sure they did. From the way they moved and spoke, their connection was obvious. And I was pretty sure it wasn't because they were lovers.

There was something in the way they both looked at me that gave the impression they were very definitely hetero when it came to sex.

"Yeah," Fridge answered as they flanked me, one on each side.

"Isn't that unusual?" I asked, glancing up at one, then the other, my heart beating un-naturally fast.

Wolves usually stuck with their own, and dragons were solitary creatures. Or so I'd been told.

When neither of them answered, I looked pointedly at Rogan,

who shrugged then shoved his hands in his jean pockets. "What do you mean?"

"I mean… I know no one really shifts anymore, but don't a wolf and a dragon clash?"

Fridge chuckled on my other side. "Yeah, like crazy, but we've been friends since school, and I haven't had a reason to get rid of him yet."

Rogan moved behind my back, and from the sounds of flesh thudding and a few grunts, I assumed they were playfully fighting.

I kept walking, shaking my head and smiling at their antics. It was only five blocks to my apartment, and the night air was clearing my head a little, which was good.

The guys jogged to keep up with me, chatting about a case they were currently working on together.

I let their chatter settle around me, and it was nice, for once, not to have to talk.

They must be a good team to live and work together. That was often the biggest test of any relationship, romantic or otherwise.

Often, the time together had you growing together, and other times, it split you apart.

We arrived at my building and I glanced up, tension catching in my throat. I was going home to an empty apartment, for the first time, ever.

"Ah, this is it. Thanks for the escort home."

"We'll walk you up," Fridge said and I put a hand out to stop him.

"It's really fine."

Neither of them said anything to rebut me, but neither of them moved away, either.

I waited, but soon realized they weren't going anywhere.

Stubborn asses.

I rolled my eyes and reached forward to pass the key card over the entrance door. "Fine. But you're both being silly."

I stomped into the building and they quickly followed as I moved to the stairs. "We live on the first floor. It's just one flight up."

"Great," Rogan said, waiting patiently for me to go ahead of them.

"Argh. You guys are being way over-protective. But considering the night I've just had, I guess it's not a terrible thing. Thank you."

I marched up the stairs and froze on the landing.

The entry door to my highly secure apartment was wide open, and I was one hundred percent certain that my dad wouldn't have left it like that when he headed out this morning.

The hairs on the back of my neck stood up, causing a shiver of fear to pulse down my spine. "What the fuck?"

CHAPTER 4
SADIE

"**I**s that door supposed to be open?" Rogan asked, though from the dark tone in his deep voice, he already knew the answer.

I shook my head.

For the past twenty years, since I was three years old and my mom died, my dad and I had lived alone.

Dad was currently on his way to the city morgue and I was standing on the first-floor landing feeling stupefied.

The two men who'd escorted me home moved in front of me with practiced stealth. Fridge leaned down and pulled a concealed weapon from his ankle, a lovely-looking sharp knife.

Rogan had a pistol in his hand, though I had no idea where he'd pulled it from.

"Let's go," Rogan said.

They walked in before me and I was glad they were armed. If there was a bad guy still in there, I bloody hoped Fridge or Rogan got him.

I crept in after them and went straight for the kitchen. My dad had knives hidden all over the apartment, but my favorite was under the table.

I reached under the large, dark wooden tabletop and pulled the weapon out of the box mounted to the underside, the deadly piece finding a comfortable place in my palm. Suddenly, I felt less helpless. I hefted the weapon. It was nicely balanced.

"Sadie," Rogan called out from the other room and I followed the sound of his voice.

There didn't seem to be much damage done to the apartment. No flipped couches, no pulled-out or upended drawers. This was obviously not a normal burglary.

THEN I STEPPED into my dad's study, his home office, and the sight that met my eyes there was a completely different story. Dad usually kept this room locked.

What the hell? I stared at the mess that was my father's home work space.

The door hung off its hinges, splinters of wood all over the carpet. The filing cabinets had been completely emptied. Every organized drawer and shelf was a mess, the contents all over the ground. Papers and ledgers were strewn everywhere and his small laptop was missing.

Someone had been looking for something... but what were they looking for?

Is this why Dad locked his office? Was there something extremely precious inside?

Dad was a bit of a luddite. Hated modern technology. Phones. Computers. But he had accepted that they were an integral part of running a business. So he had his one small laptop at home, but kept paper files of everything as well.

"What the hell were they looking for?" I said aloud, although I suspected the two men who were now standing beside me didn't have an answer.

I looked at them, and they both shrugged.

"No idea," Rogan said.

I frowned. "In over twenty years in the game, he's never had an issue with theft of information."

Not that I knew of, anyway. But that was definitely something to check.

Rogan moved toward the door. "I'm going to secure the apartment entrance."

Before I could stop him, he hurried out of the room, leaving me alone with Fridge.

A moment later, the front door shut and the locks clicked into place.

Good idea, I should have done that.

Fridge began to lift furniture back up, righting the room.

I put my hand out to stop him. "Wait. Should we leave it? Call the police?"

Fridge shook his head. "I don't think they're gonna get any fingerprints or DNA."

I cocked my head at him. Interesting assumption. "How come?"

"Can't you smell it?"

I inhaled sharply, but couldn't smell anything out of the ordinary. I was only one-quarter wolf shifter. My senses weren't *that* strong. "No... should I?"

"No. And that's the point. All shifters leave a scent, as do humans. Whoever was here was as sterile as a hospital room."

Our gazes met with a clash of intensity.

"Vampire," we said at the same time.

Shit.

"So, you think the same person who killed Dad came here and tried to find whatever he, or she, was looking for?" I asked as I tried to put together the few pieces we knew.

Fridge shrugged. "Maybe... but it could be multiple people, not just one. Perhaps part of an organization and they hit both places at once. You never know. The question is though, what *were* they looking for?"

I had a headache. One that had begun hours ago but was now pounding to the point that seeing straight was becoming a problem.

I tugged at my hair, pulling the pins and elastics out of my bun until my dark hair fell in waves down to my shoulders.

I sighed with relief, and ran my fingers along my scalp, massaging the tender skin. The pain from my rigid hairstyle that was now released made me wish I'd removed the pins earlier.

Fridge wasn't moving and as my gaze swung over to him, I found him staring at me as though he would swallow me whole if he had the chance.

I could feel it in my gut, in my veins, between my legs. The connection, the attraction... the... what the hell *was* this thing?

I cleared my throat, suddenly uncomfortable, and it wasn't because Fridge's stare repelled me. Quite the opposite, in fact. I had to fight the urge to flick my hair and smile flirtatiously, which was so inappropriate in the circumstances it made my stomach ache.

I couldn't understand what was happening to me? Was this urge to get closer to Fridge the result of stress?

"You okay?" I asked him. My wolf's ability to scent, which wasn't that impressive, had suddenly picked up on the mating pheromones he was now emitting into the room.

"Ah, yeah, sorry. I was just thinking about your dad and who might have done this," he said. I knew it was a lie, but I let it slide. "He was so above board. I mean, he had so many opportunities to deal drugs, bribe the cops, work with the worst of society just for financial gain, but he didn't. He had an impeccable reputation in every way. Your dad garnered respect, not enemies. I don't get this at all." He gestured to the room and shook his head.

I gaped at him. That was the most he'd spoken in one go, and I was glad they were all positive and focused on my father.

But how should I respond?

"I didn't realize all that... but I appreciate the sentiment."

I knew my dad was a good guy, but we'd never really discussed how easy it would have been for him to slide into the dark side of the law. I thought being a bounty hunter walked the line enough, anyway.

Rogan appeared in the doorway, gun in hand. He glanced between us, and then slid the weapon into a concealed holster on his back.

He grinned. "Don't worry. I've got a license to carry."

I smiled. Not that I cared at this point, but it was nice to know.

"But do you have silver bullets?" I asked, only half-joking.

It was one of the only things that stopped vampires. Silver didn't kill them, but it slowed them down long enough to be staked.

He grinned, his smile as devastating as the scent of Fridge's pheromones.

My belly quivered and my pulse sped up.

Shit! This is not what I need right now.

Rogan nodded. "Of course. All my bullets are silver. Expensive, but they take down all manner of paranormal creature. Wouldn't want to come up against a vampire with lead only." He cocked his head at me. "You all right, Sadie?"

Not really.

I hadn't dated anyone in... forever.

I compared every man to my dad, and they were always found lacking.

But the last thing I needed was to find *two* guys I wanted. Especially on the day of my dad's murder. It was just too much.

My dad's.... *what?* My dad's...

"Oh, my God," I said, my knees giving out from under me. I staggered sideways and only just managed to get to a chair and collapse into it. "It just hit me," I said, staring off into the distance. My eyes blurred as darkness threatened around the edges of my vision.

"What? What's happened?" Rogan rushed over and knelt down so he was eye to eye with me.

Fridge hovered near by.

I forced my eyes to focus, to see the face of the wolf shifter before me.

"It just sunk in. Dad was... murdered." That sounded so much worse than if he'd just *died*. "And the police aren't going to be able to find the killer, are they?"

I looked straight at Rogan.

He swallowed hard. "Ah, probably not. Vamps are exceptionally hard to track. They have no blood. No DNA, no fingerprints."

"Fuck." I couldn't let this stand. *I couldn't.*

The person or corporation responsible for my father's death had to pay for what they'd done.

I got up out of the chair and began to pace the small room, my heart beating harder and my mind racing. "I'll take a month of leave from work and investigate this myself."

I had to work out what to do with Dad's company anyway, since I had no idea about the bounty hunter business. I was sure I could find someone to help me run it for a month, even if it was one of the men in the room with me. Or both of them.

Rogan pushed to his feet. "We'll help you."

"Fuck, yeah," Fridge said, moving to stand next to Rogan.

I stopped pacing and turned to them, feeling guilty for imposing on them. "You don't need to do that. Although, I could use some help sorting Dad's business out in the interim."

Rogan and Fridge's jaws set in an identical way that indicated matching stubborn streaks.

I almost laughed.

Fridge narrowed his eyes at me. "We're investigating this, no matter what, Sadie. We can either do it together with you, or set up a separate investigation."

I opened my mouth to tell him where to go, then shut it again. Wouldn't a couple of bounty hunters who were used to finding people be an advantage to me? Sometimes being stubborn wasn't the smartest way to get things accomplished.

"Okay," I said softly. "Thanks, but I'm gonna need assistance with the business side of things as well."

Rogan nodded. "That's fine. We'll be here for everything you need."

I studied him, surprised by the vehemence in his tone. "Not that I'm ungrateful, but why are you guys so interested in helping me?"

My dad was their boss, not blood. Surely, they didn't feel any strong loyalty to him? Perhaps it was their jobs they were trying to protect?

"Jimmy was a great man," Fridge declared in an emotional way that had his voice husky before he cleared it with a rough cough. "He's helped me out of more scrapes than I can tell you."

"He helped us find an apartment when we moved to the city. Made sure we kept our jobs even when there was little or no work," Rogan added.

I stared at them. Did my dad really inspire people outside of my family, the way he did me?

Rogan shook his head, continuing his speech. "He did *not* deserve to go down like that, and we're gonna catch the assholes who did it, and make them pay."

Something shifted in the air around us, and I shivered. It was the witch in me that sensed it. The magic, the bond, the promise.

Oh, no. Please, not that. Not now. It's not the right time.

I swallowed hard and focused on the conversation. I told myself it wasn't true what the voices inside my mind were whispering to me. *It wasn't!*

It had to be something else they were talking about. A binding contract between us all, perhaps? Yes. That must be it.

I clenched my hands in front of me. "So, you're saying you'll help me? With the business, finding Dad's killer, and everything?"

Of course, I'd have to deal with his estate and the funeral, and so many other terrible things. But if I had two allies, then navigating those tumultuous waters would be so much easier. Less daunting.

They both nodded, and I shivered again. I wasn't casting a spell, and as shifters, they had no power to do so. But I could feel the promise of something special teetering on the edge of a true casting, and I had to see it to completion.

"I need to hear you say it," I said.

Rogan clenched his hands into fists. "Yes, I'll help you. With everything you need."

Fridge nodded. "Of course. Anything for Jimmy's daughter."

And there it was.

My eyelids fluttered and a shiver of magic worked over my skin, through my core and into my heart.

The blackness that had begun at the edges of my vision a few minutes earlier was now beginning to consume me. I was going to pass out.

Damn it...

I couldn't open my eyes, couldn't find anything to grip onto. I staggered forward, toward the worried sounds of the men in front of me, and I fell into the darkness.

CHAPTER 5

FRIDGE

I dove forward and scooped Sadie into my arms. She weighed even less than I'd anticipated. She was so tiny in comparison to us, but clearly had an underlying toughness. She'd have to, if she'd been raised by Jimmy. Which made her sudden collapse all the more surprising.

I hoisted her up against my chest and held her tightly. "What the hell happened to her?" I demanded, glancing over at Rogan. Maybe he'd know.

"I have no idea," Rogan said, his voice angry and frustrated. "I wouldn't have thought she'd be the type to faint easily."

Neither would I. "Where should I put her?" I asked, looking around for a safe space. Should I try to find her bedroom?

I shuddered. That wouldn't send the right message, and we wanted her to trust us.

"I don't know. The couch, maybe?" Rogan said.

Good a place as any.

I placed her as gently as possible down on the massive leather couch. Jimmy had been a big guy, and the furniture showed it.

I stepped back and stared down at the sleeping beauty before me.

But I was no prince, and neither was Rogan. "How are we going to wake her up?"

"I have no idea." Rogan sat down on the couch and gently lifted her head and placed it on his thigh. "Carefully, I guess."

I glared at him and sat down at the opposite end of her, putting a hand on her leg.

She wasn't Rogan's, and she certainly wasn't mine, and yet I was feeling extremely possessive toward her. I didn't want Rogan to touch her, but I also had no right to stop him, either.

But I couldn't withdraw my hand. It felt… wrong to be disconnected from her.

Rogan stroked the side of her face gently and a soft sigh fell from Sadie's lips.

Was she still unconscious? Or was she playing us?

When she didn't stir, I assumed she was indeed asleep.

I glanced up at Rogan. "So how are we going to catch a vampire killer? You know it's practically impossible."

Rogan shrugged. "Someone had to order the hit. We can call Shadow. Get him on the case."

I raised an eyebrow. "You wanna call in help?"

Since when did Rogan want to outsource? Though if he felt he had to, I guess Shadow was a damn good option.

"Why not?" he asked. "Anything to find Jimmy's killer."

I nodded. "True. Then we take them down. Together."

Rogan gazed down on the woman between us and sighed, running a hand softly over her dark hair. "Yep. Together."

Something twanged inside my chest and I clenched my jaw against it.

I could feel the call of family. Of a bond I'd avoided for as long as I could remember. But I couldn't work out where it was coming from.

From Rogan?

From Sadie?

From this apartment where the man I loved like a father had lived for so long?

"I think she's waking up."

CHAPTER 6

SADIE

I woke up with my head in someone's lap, and the cool leather of the couch beneath my fingertips.

"I think she's coming around," a voice said. *Fridge*. The timbre of his voice deep and mellow.

"Sadie? You okay?" That was Rogan, and he was whispering to me for some reason.

I blinked a few times, gathering my brain cells back together, then forced myself to open my eyes. A part of me wanted to stay blissfully passed out, being held. Safe and oblivious.

When I finally pried my eyelids open, I found that my head was resting in Rogan's lap. Strangely, I wasn't surprised. There had been something about him that suggested a softer side, though I suspected most people would never see that part of him. Though how I could deduce that when the guy was probably six foot two and two hundred pounds of muscle, I wasn't sure.

"Yeah... I'm okay." I tried to sit up, but my body felt like it was made of jelly. I fell back onto Rogan's lap. "Can you help me up?"

Fridge was standing beside us. He reached down, grabbed my

hands and gently pulled me up into a sitting position. My head still spun but it was better to be upright. "Whoa."

I blinked quickly multiple times.

Fridge handed me a glass of water he must have gotten from the kitchen while I was passed out. "You okay? Need something to eat?"

I quirked a brow at him. "You cook?"

He choked out a laugh and pulled out his cell phone. "I order Uber Eats with the best of them."

My stomach growled in response, and despite the fact there was food in the fridge, something greasy and hot sounded perfect. "Can you please get me a burger or pizza? Or both?"

Rogan laughed. "You certainly have some shifter in you."

I smiled and leaned back against the headrest. I did, of course, have shifter genes. But even so, I didn't usually eat junk food. I couldn't count on my shifter metabolism like a lot of full-bloods, or even half-bloods, could. But tonight, I was going to make an exception.

Fridge tapped away on his phone then lifted his head and grinned. "It will be here in about fifteen minutes."

"Perfect," I said, smiling, though all my energy had drained away.

Rogan was still sitting next to me on the massive sofa and Fridge took a seat in my dad's recliner opposite us.

I opened my mouth to tell him not to sit there; that it was my dad's chair. No one else was allowed to sit there.

But I clamped my jaw shut. My dad was gone, and that was the last thing I should be saying to a man who hadn't left my side since the worst trauma of my life had occurred.

Especially since I had realized he was my fated mate.

I groaned and hung my head. *Of all the timing...*

"What's wrong?" Rogan asked, running a hand over my arm. I shivered with longing.

He retracted his hand and I couldn't stop the bitter laugh that bubbled up and out. Why did this have to happen now?

I'd hoped the little whispers of magic were wrong. They'd been getting stronger all night, telling me these men were important. But I'd hoped it was only the bond of a shared purpose that would connect us.

No, it was so much more than that.

I'd fainted, and while I'd been passed out, the magic had woven even tighter inside me. Now that I was awake, I knew the truth as clearly as I knew my own name.

I didn't have just one fated mate. I had *two*.

And they were both currently sitting in the living room with me.

The only question was, should I tell them?

Tonight was not the night for lies or omissions of fact, because they were certainly going to find out soon enough. The bond was too strong to deny.

"Why did you faint, Sadie? Are you unwell? Or is it just because of shock, and everything that happened tonight?" Rogan's tone was gentle.

I looked from one hot man to the other. Why—and how—did I have two fated mates? I couldn't conceive of such a thing. No one had told me it was even possible to have more than one.

"I have so much to tell you guys..." I began.

Fridge leaned back in my dad's dark leather recliner. Surprisingly, the urge to tell him not to sit there had receded. "We've got all night," he said. "Hit us with it."

"Well..." Should I divulge the long-hidden secret of my witch abilities? How could I tell them about the promise without revealing who I was, though? "Do you believe in... fated mates?"

The men recoiled like I was a snake about to strike.

The temperature in the room dropped about twenty degrees.

Damn, that was fast.

I laughed. I couldn't help it. Freaking men and their fear of commitment. "I'll take that as a no."

How was I going to explain that they were *both* my fated mates, if they weren't open to the possibility, let alone the concept?

Rogan cleared his throat. "Well, ah…"

"No. I don't," Fridge said, his voice booming like it was amplified on purpose to make sure I knew exactly how he felt about that topic.

I shrugged. "Okay."

There was a long, drawn-out pause.

"Okay? That's all you're gonna say?" Rogan asked.

I turned to him. "What do you want me to say? You answered my question. I'm not pushing my thoughts on you. I barely know you."

And if you fuckwits aren't smart enough to realize that there's more to our connection than animal magnetism, then the joke's on you.

The doorbell rang and Fridge got up to answer it.

I stumbled to my feet and pulled out some glasses and plates from the kitchen, not sure exactly what he'd ordered.

When he came back in, I was arranging the plates on the table.

He dumped pizza boxes next to the dinner plates along with a plastic bag. Despite still being frustrated with them, I wasn't going to let it get in the way of my very late dinner.

We'd have our whole lives to deal with the ramifications of our fated mate bond.

"Whatcha get?" I asked, peering into the bag.

"What you asked for. Burgers and pizzas. And Coke, of course."

He pulled a couple of bottles of soft drinks out from under his arms and we all sat down to a high-calorie feast.

"Thank you," I said.

We chowed down on the food, my ravenous body loving the greasy burgers, extra cheesy crust, and sweet bubbles to wash it all down.

We barely talked while we ate, but chomped away in companionable silence.

When I'd finally gotten my fill, I pushed the plate away and covered my mouth while I burped, and the men snickered. "That was so good. I have cash in my bag."

Fridge waved his hand. "My treat. Can't have you fainting again."

I rubbed my bulging belly and sighed. "Well, I certainly feel better. Thank you."

I cleared away the plates we'd barely used and closed my eyes, swaying on my feet. Damn I was tired. *Beyond tired.*

"I think I need to go to bed." I glanced at the guys, who were still sitting on their chairs staring at me. Didn't they understand that meant it was time to leave?

They looked at each other but didn't say anything.

They wanted to stay with me? Seriously?

I sighed. We had a massive apartment for two people, so if they wanted to, they could certainly sleep over.

"There's a spare bedroom and the couch is comfy, if you guys wanna crash," I said, leaning against the doorway. "Dad always liked having space for people to drop by."

Not that we had a lot of visitors, but Dad's family was huge, so he made sure we had room for them to stay when they did call in.

There was a pull-out couch in his study too, but that wasn't habitable at the moment.

"That would be great," Rogan said, putting the lids back on the two pizza boxes that still had slices in them. "I'd feel more comfortable staying, in case anyone comes back."

"Me too," Fridge said, collecting the rubbish. "Where do you want this?"

I crossed into the kitchen and opened the closet where the trash can resided. "Here, please."

When everything was put away, the guys lingered around me, watching and waiting.

I could barely keep my eyes open. I wondered if it was my body's way of coping with the grief. If I was asleep, I wouldn't feel the hollow emptiness every time thoughts of my dad popped into my head.

I had better organize where the guys were going to rest before I ended up sleeping where I fell.

"Okay, who wants the bed?" I asked.

Fridge said, "I'll take the couch."

He glanced at the front door as though he'd rather be closer to the entrance of the 'cage'.

Classic dragon.

"Done. I'll get you some blankets. Rogan, come with me."

Rogan followed me down the hall to the end, where I pushed open the door to the rarely-used guest room. "The bed's comfy, or so I've been told."

He walked into the room and glanced around. "This is great. Thank you."

He stood next to the bed, his intense blue eyes staring at me, his dark locks tumbling over his forehead. My breath caught in my throat and my chest tightened.

There was something so forceful about this man. I wasn't sure if it was the fated mate link, his wolf shifter genes, or his personality, but my whole body shivered with need whenever he was nearby.

Sadness flowed through me at the notion he'd rejected any such attraction before it had a chance to shine.

"Well, goodnight," I said, unable to think of anything more coherent. "I suppose I'll see you in the morning."

He nodded and began to undress, pulling at the buckle on his belt. My body reacted with a twist and jolt deep inside.

I pulled the door shut before I said or did anything stupid.

I walked over to the blanket closet and rested my forehead on the door.

Why? Why now?

I should be bawling my eyes out, an utter mess about my father's death. But instead, I had two fated mates willing to fight by my side while we made those who were responsible pay.

If this was my dad's—or Mom's, for that matter—idea of a good way of distracting me from the fact my life was irrevocably changed, they were doing a good job of it.

Get a move on.

I pulled open the door to the closet, grabbed a spare pillow and a couple of blankets, and headed back to the living room.

Travis—Fridge—was different to Rogan. Even though my genetics didn't recognize him the same way they did Rogan, the fated mate link was still there.

In fact, the connection was almost stronger, simply because it *was* so different.

Our attraction was so deep I could barely think straight, and I had an intense desire to watch him shift, then tuck myself beneath his wings and never leave him.

I shook my head just before I stepped back into the living room. I was usually stubbornly independent and had never felt this way about a man before.

This need to be protected, to feel safe, was the way I had always assumed it would feel with a mate. To want to give him babies and allow my mate to protect them as well as me.

Oh. My. God. Just stop it!

When I stepped back into the room, Fridge had disposed of his jeans and tank top, standing about in only a tight pair of black, cotton boxer briefs. He was every woman's wet dream, with massive shoulders, ripped abs, and sparkling green eyes in a beautiful, rugged face.

My pussy practically melted as I staggered forward, throwing the pillow and blankets that I held in my arms at him. "Here."

He caught them and, instead of holding them in front of his body in a modest manner, he tossed them onto the couch.

"You okay?" he asked, his brow furrowing.

I kind of wanted to smack him in the face.

Well, not really. Actually, I wanted to fuck the shit out of him, but that was hardly the way to start a lifetime relationship, nor deal with the grief that shadowed my heart.

"I'm fine." My voice was a little strangled, but what the heck? I'd managed *words*. "Goodnight." My frustration was running high, and I didn't want to take it out on Fridge. That wouldn't be fair. I turned away, determined to pull my rarely-used vibrator out of its hiding spot in my nightstand as soon as I got back to my bedroom.

Desire and lust clawed at my insides like a wild animal and I wasn't sure how I was going to cope with any of this.

Especially if these oblivious men were determined to ignore the bond. If they continued to do that, they'd probably end up driving us all insane.

Fridge's hand snaked out and grabbed my arm, turning me back to face him.

I glared at him and shook off his arm, my skin tingling and heating at his touch. I wanted him; desired him. Need clawed at me. And yet, he had already rejected me. So, I needed to get away, before my body exploded in the most embarrassing ever spontaneous orgasm.

"What is it?" I said, though I was struggling to breathe with his hot skin and gorgeous face so close.

"You look... strange." His nostrils flared, and his eyes widened.

So, he could smell my desire, huh? *Welcome to the club, buddy.*

Then his brilliant green eyes darkened and shifted so that his pupils changed to slit-like diamonds. His true dragon eyes were suddenly on show.

I shivered as he pulled me close, wrapping his other arm around my waist.

I couldn't fight his strength, and I didn't want to.

He dragged me in until our thighs pressed together and I had to crane my neck to look up at him.

"What... is this?" he hissed, in a voice I had to assume was his shifter's tone.

Almost snake-like, the sound was as creepy as it was lustful.

"It's the fated mate link," I whispered. "Whether you believe in it or not. Will you please kiss me, Fridge?"

Recognition flared in his eyes. Then anger and disappointment warred with his natural need to take me. Mate with me. Devour me whole in the best way possible.

His eyes flickered from human to dragon, and back again. He was clearly struggling for control. His jaw clenched, his arms shook, and he snorted as though he were in a real fight.

But finally, the human side of him won, and he stumbled backwards, falling down onto the couch.

He shook his head, growling softly, apparently conflicted.

I used Fridge's rejection to cool the lust pouring through me.

"Sleep well, dragon," I said, lifting my chin and storming out of the room.

Anger overpowered my frustration and began to build as I made my way to my room, so I slammed the bedroom door just to see if it would make me feel better. It didn't.

Why had he rejected me? *Again.*

Was it just because he didn't want to believe that the Universe had a plan for us all? That the concept of fated mates was true?

Well, he could fucking wait now! My cheeks heated as I leaned back against the door. I couldn't believe I had begged him to kiss me. That should have been the last thing on my mind right now. And yet, I had given in to the urge and let the connection pull me in. Believing in it. Believing in *us.*

Until humiliation had won, over desire and a magical bond.

He was going to have to beg on bended knee before I offered myself so blatantly again.

Fated mate bond, or not.

CHAPTER 7

FRIDGE

I felt like I'd been smacked sideways. But in this case, I'd been slapped down onto my ass.

I sat on Jimmy's large couch, staring off into space, the room now empty and cold. Devoid of the hot little woman who'd just been my whole world.

For a few fleeting seconds I'd known how amazing it felt to have her in my arms.

But it wasn't meant to be. It couldn't be.

What she was saying was bullshit. It simply wasn't true.

Why did I know that? Because fated mates were a myth. A fallacy. A way of driving people together who simply weren't meant to be together for more than a fleeting minute.

Sure, we had some amazing chemistry. And damn, did I want to fuck her. But that was my shifter calling, running the show. And I wasn't going to allow that. Not tonight.

Not ever.

I was more than my beast.

And I wouldn't allow the rules of the shifter world to determine my future.

No matter how much I wanted Sadie in my arms, and my bed.

CHAPTER 8
SADIE

Dreams of wolves, dragons, witches, and knives tormented my night. I woke up too many times to count —sweaty, scared, aroused and annoyed.

When daybreak came, I was so relieved to see the end of the dark, I finally fell into a restful sleep.

Why the men didn't wake me, I had no idea, but it was close to lunchtime when I opened my eyes and glanced at the clock.

Damn, it's late!

"Gah..." I groaned and stretched, reaching for my cell phone that lay on the bedside table. It was totally dead.

Of course. No wonder I slept until noon. No alarm. No frantic calls from work wondering where the hell I was. No police, wanting to interview me further in relation to my dad.

I rolled out of bed and stumbled straight into the shower. Dad had made sure we each had our own private bathrooms, as well as a powder room for guests. It was one of the best features of this apartment.

I scrubbed myself clean of the stench of my fitful night's sleep, sweat and arousal nauseatingly intertwined.

I even washed my hair. Today was going to need all my energy just to survive. Better to start the day fresh and clean.

When I got out of the steamy, hot bathroom, I felt deflated and tired, but my head was clearer, the cloud of depression lifting enough so that I could see myself getting through the day in one piece.

I pulled on a pair of panties and a plain t-shirt bra, scowling as I deliberately chose un-sexy underthings out of spite.

Damn men.

Then I stood in front of my closet, dismissing all the plain, corporate gear I wore every day. I was having a month off work, at least. If I went back at all. No need to wear any of that boring crap right now.

Through the night, my dad's voice had haunted me. The countless times he'd taunted me about my career not suiting me.

How he wished I'd chosen to work alongside him.

I'd never really taken him seriously when he mentioned it. Even yesterday morning, he'd said it again. After all, his comments had been made in jest, hadn't they? What man wanted his daughter to become a bounty hunter?

Well, whether he'd meant to drag me into his world or not, I was jumping in now. With both feet.

My dad had spent over twenty years building his business, and I wasn't about to let it go under. Not to mention the fact that his work, or one of his bounties, had to be the reason that he'd been killed.

That was no random killing. No unintentional over-bleeding.

We'd all seen them on the news. A young vampire arrested for over-feeding. It was always messy, and stupid, and an accident.

Vampires didn't need to drain a person to survive. A weekly meal for most vampires was barely a quart of blood.

To drain a man the size of my father... I shivered. That took not only an incredibly ravenous appetite, but precision and deliberation.

It also just wouldn't have been possible for a young, ravenous, inexperienced vampire to get the drop on my father.

Thanks to his natural predispositions, and my mother's magical enhancements, his hearing and protection instincts were exceptional. He'd hunted all manner of beasts, including vampires, with success.

The person—the creature—that had killed him was a professional. And more than likely, extremely old. The older a vampire got, the stealthier and stronger they became.

But they did not necessarily get any hungrier. In fact, quite the opposite. Control over their appetite came with age. So why drain him? For his blood, which was not a rare type at all, or to make sure no one brought him back?

I added that question to my long list.

I stepped into my walk-in closet, looking for an outfit appropriate for battle.

I flicked through my pale sweaters, my skin-tight jeans.

What did I have... "Ah-ha!"

My old motorcycle leathers. Perfect. I hadn't worn them since college, but fingers-crossed they still fit. I was pretty much the same weight I was five years ago.

I pulled out the outfit and tossed it on my bed. I grabbed a white tank from the drawer, tugged that on, then set about pouring myself into the leather pants.

By the time I'd moaned and groaned my way through getting them up my thighs, they looked great, though I was pretty sure I'd need a new pair. Something comfortable to train in.

These were strictly for intimidation purposes.

The jacket was too big; it always had been. So I just layered up with a see-through mesh black top over the white tank.

I'd usually do my hair and apply makeup.

Not today. I was dealing with men who didn't want to see me as anything other than Jimmy's daughter. Plus, the tears would come sooner or later. I'd held them in, and now I felt almost numb when I thought of Dad. I knew that wouldn't last, though. And when the dam finally burst, I did not want to look like some horror oil painting.

I threw my hair up into a ponytail and opened my bedroom door. Now for coffee and a plan for the day.

In the kitchen, Rogan sat at the counter, tapping away on his phone.

When he heard me, he turned with a smile on his face. "You're awake."

I frowned. "You're still here."

His smile fell and I felt a moment of regret for snapping at him.

"Sorry." I gave him a small apology-smile, hoping to soften the mood.

It wasn't Rogan's fault that his douche bag friend had rejected me so spectacularly last night.

Rogan shrugged. "Looks like you're in the same sort of mood that Fridge was in this morning. Something happen between you two last night?"

The question surprised me, and I didn't have time to put my normal neutral lawyer face into place. "Ah..."

Rogan lifted a single eyebrow.

I walked forward, heading straight to the fridge. "What do you mean? What was he like this morning?"

I rummaged around for something to eat. Not that I usually ate breakfast, but I felt like I'd need the sustenance today. I chose yogurt and my favorite juice.

When I came back out, I plastered a fake smile on my face, trying to keep my attitude light. Or at least, to give that impression to anyone on the outside, looking in.

"He was in a shit mood. Grouchy, short-tempered, and couldn't wait to get out of here. I thought it was because he'd slept on the couch and had a sore back, but seeing you... I don't think that was it."

I shrugged, opening the yogurt and finding a spoon. "We had a disagreement before bed. That's all."

"Mm... hmm."

I poured my juice and gestured to him. "You want something?"

He shook his head. "I'm all good. When you're ready, I'll escort you wherever you want to go."

I frowned. "*Escort* me?"

"Yeah. We're not leaving your side until this guy—or guys—are caught. They could be after you, too."

I huffed out a laugh. "I doubt it. I didn't even work with Dad."

I had nothing to do with my father's business, and therefore I knew nothing. Plus, if they wanted to use me as leverage to obtain something, who were they going to threaten? There was no one left.

Rogan gestured to my outfit. "Are you planning on stepping in to take over Hunters?"

I glanced down, wondering how he'd figured that out so fast. *Smart guy.*

"Yeah, why?"

"Then you definitely need our help. I'm sure Hunters is the reason they went after him."

"Hunters? You have an idea who it is, and why?" I sucked on the spoon and continued eating the yogurt, though my heart was beating uncontrollably.

Hopefully, the unsettled feelings would stop, especially if Rogan rejected the bond as well.

I needed to get back to feeling normal. Whatever my new normal would look like, without Dad in my life.

Rogan set down his phone and gave me his full attention. "Hunters, because of the kind of cases we all work on. And why? Because Jimmy was a rare man, even among rare men. He had standards and integrity. He couldn't be bought. And that pissed a lot of people off."

I knew he had enemies. Dad had always lived like he had a target on his back. Our apartment was full of hidden weapons and alarms.

Strangely, none of them seemed to have been triggered last night... something else to sort out.

"Yeah." I dipped my head. "He often told me of run-ins with cops, and even lawyers who were trying to get their clients off by paying people. They tried to bribe him to stop the hunt; erase the bounty. He would never do that."

"No, he wouldn't," Rogan said. "He always got the bad guy. And he held all of his staff to the same high standards."

"Really?" I asked. I'd always assumed Dad would only hire the best, but hearing it from someone on the inside was so much better. "Tell me more."

One side of Rogan's mouth quirked up. "His interview process was vicious, in both physical combat testing and psychological drills. His contract stated that if you were caught taking bribes or didn't report illegal activity, he'd arrest you himself."

I could feel my eyes widen and my eyebrows rose high on my forehead. "Wow."

Rogan laughed. "Oh, yeah, he was one tough motherfucker. But he paid really well and made sure we all got along, Because of that, we were all loyal to him. All of us would have fought beside him. Done whatever he asked. Any day of the week."

He sighed, as though he'd had his heart broken too, yesterday.

I felt a pang of sympathy for Rogan, and Fridge, and all Dad's staff. They'd definitely be hurting, and even though I'd already decided to step up, I knew it wouldn't be the same. Not with the way they'd all obviously liked and respected my father.

The logical part of my brain was already firing with the new information. "Okay, well, if he was that tough, do you think it's possible it was a former employee, or someone who didn't make it through the training, who might have wanted him dead? A more personal grudge, maybe?"

My dad could piss people off like no other. He had a heart of gold, but he was a tough man, in a tough world and he didn't tolerate weakness or stupidity.

"I suppose that's possible. But I doubt it."

"How come?"

"Your dad didn't hire vamps."

Hmm.... Interesting. I knew he had disdain for the species as a whole, but I had just assumed he'd use their skills to his advantage in some way.

"That surprises me." I tossed the yogurt container and finished my juice before reaching over and flicking on the coffee machine.

"Why?" Rogan asked.

"Because vamps have advantages I would have thought Dad would want to utilize. Speed, and a natural affinity for the dark, for example."

Rogan shook his head. "Nah, he said he didn't trust anything that didn't age and had no official expiration date."

I burst out laughing, which felt so good I couldn't believe it.

"Yeah, that sounds exactly like him." I laughed again, enjoying the sensation of happiness that had managed to break through the steel covering I'd placed over my grief.

Rogan tapped his fingers on the top of the kitchen counter. "So, since it's a vamp, you can probably wipe out the idea that it's an employee. I'd look at the bounty files, first."

I made myself a coffee and gestured to a second mug. "You want one?"

He nodded. "Yeah, why not. Black, please. Two sugars."

Just the same way as Dad liked it. I made him a mug, my hands shaking a little as I poured.

Strange.

I pushed the drink over the marble countertop toward Rogan. "Here you go. Now tell me more about these bounty files."

He took the mug, drank a little, then sighed happily.

"Thanks heaps. Well, basically, they're client files. We get sent boun-ties to hunt down. Both public and private ones. The files have all the details on the person, their crime, why they need to be picked up and by when, the price for their collar, and any special talents they have in case they turn violent. Which, to be honest, happens in ninety-nine percent of cases. Most of them come down to a scrap. We aren't chasing good guys."

I bit my lip. "Okay. So you think it could be one of the vampires Hunters has arrested and turned in. And what do you mean, private bounties? Is that legal?"

I'd thought bounty hunting was only to bring in people who skipped bail or were wanted by the police.

Rogan grinned. "Now, *that* is a gray area. A line that Jimmy liked to walk, where lots of others didn't."

I leaned forward. "Tell me more about that. If Dad was so strict and straight-down-the-line, then..."

I trailed off. What if my dad had been doing something dodgy? It didn't fit with the guy I knew.

"All legal, for sure," Rogan said, smiling almost nostalgically. "But only just. When someone in the city is looking for someone who has disappeared, you can put out a private bounty for them. There are more rules, of course. Rules against causing injury, and there has to be a valid reason for wanting to locate them. Fraud, or abuse, for example. But we took those private bounties, and they paid well."

I cocked my head. So Hunters didn't just round up bad guys trying to skip town.

"What sort of clients put out private bounties?" I asked, chewing on my lip in thought.

Rogan shook his head. "I don't know those details. You'd have to check over the files."

I had access to everything at Hunters now, so I could. "But, at a guess... do you mean, lawyers, maybe? Husbands looking for runaway wives?"

He shook his head. "No, more like some of the big drug companies, or the big corporations, if they thought someone had snuck off with their designs or shipments."

My mouth dropped open. "And Dad worked with them?"

"Oh, yeah. When I mean drugs, I mean the legit ones. Big Pharma. They have too many employees, too much money, and are majorly paranoid about everything."

Now my brain began to tick even faster. "And they're owned by vamps, aren't they?"

As most successful companies were, nowadays. A vampire's ability to live forever certainly had its advantages.

"Yes." He looked at me thoughtfully, as if guessing where my brain had led.

I picked up my mug and began to plot my afternoon. I had a lot of research to do. Vampires, and Big Pharma.

"I think we have somewhere to start," I said. "I need to go into the workshop, deal with the current order of business, and then we focus on finding my dad's killer."

SADIE

The city streets were busier at lunchtime than I'd expected, but I still didn't regret my choice to walk. I needed to stretch my legs.

Rogan walked beside me. His salty, male, wolf scent tickled my nose, but I wasn't about to complain, even though it was a distraction.

"If you don't mind, I'll drop you at the workshop, then head home to shower and change," he said.

I tried not to ogle as I looked up at him. "Yeah, of course. But why?"

His gaze narrowed, then he lifted his arm up to sniff himself. He grimaced and put his arm down again. "I stink. Can't you smell me?"

I didn't reply.

He frowned as though he was confused. "You *are* part wolf shifter, right?"

"Yeah, a small part," I said slowly. "And yes, I can smell you. But it doesn't bother me."

We kept walking and after another block, he asked, "What do

you mean it doesn't bother you? Because you've got a poor sense of smell, or because…"

We'd almost reached my dad's workshop building, so I stopped on the street and turned to him.

May as well find out if this one is a coward, too.

"No. Because you smell good to me."

I met his gaze squarely, putting both hands on my hips and staring up at him. He had a good four or five inches of height on me, but he wasn't as huge as Fridge, and I didn't feel the least bit intimidated.

"Oh… well, you smell good to me too," he managed, though he didn't smile.

I waited, but he didn't continue. I flicked my hair back over my shoulder.

"You know what that means, I assume?" I asked, pressing the issue. "You grew up with wolf shifter parents?"

He nodded. "Both my parents are half wolf shifter."

"So that means you know what I'm saying."

I wanted him to say it, to acknowledge the link. I still couldn't believe my bad luck in finally finding my fated mate—no, *mates*— and they were both scared of admitting to the sacred bond.

Or that's how it seemed to me.

"Sadie… I don't think…"

I threw my hands up in the air, my voice exploding from me. "Oh, my God. Not you too!"

I twisted around to march off, but he grabbed me and pulled me back.

Damn, his hands were strong.

I didn't try to remove them, wondering if a similar effect would happen to Rogan, my wolf shifter, while he touched me as it had to Fridge, my dragon.

He pulled me in close and stared down at me.

His blue eyes shifted, silver irises around a large pupil. And when he spoke, his voice was dark and gravelly. "I know you're my mate, Sadie, I won't deny that. But we have a murder to solve, a life to build, and a stupid fucking dragon to deal with."

He moved his hands around my body and cupped my ass, drawing me into the cradle of his hips.

I gasped when the hard ridge of his cock pressed into my softness. *Oh... kay.* So, he definitely wasn't pretending the connection didn't exist.

I grabbed for his strong arms to stabilize myself.

He dropped his head and pressed his lips to my ear.

My eyes closed as he whispered, "I won't kiss you here, not with so many people around. I want our first time to be long and thorough, and perfect. Not here. Not now."

I inhaled sharply, my belly tightening with need.

"I can't give you the commitment you need right now, Sadie. But I will promise not to leave your side until this is all said and done, and then you can choose if you still want me. Not because your instincts are telling you that you have no choice, but because you want me as your mate. As the father of your pups."

Did he just say... the father of my pups? I felt like I was about to swoon, especially when his tongue extended and he licked the sensitive whorl of my inner ear. I shuddered, as close to climax without going over as I'd ever been.

And I was on a city street!

I gasped and squeezed my legs together, needing him to touch me more than I wanted to breathe but desperate to try and retain control of myself.

This was most definitely not the right time or place for this.

"Now I'm going to pull back," he said. "Not because I want to. God knows I want to bend you over and sink my hard cock into your wetness right now. Damn... I can smell how hot you are for me."

I bit my lip, stifling the squeal that rose in my throat. If he'd just press a little harder, slide his fingers down...

"Hold on, girl, we haven't even started yet."

He stepped back and away from me, holding on to my arms to prevent me from falling over, which I definitely would have done if he hadn't kept a grip on me.

I felt drugged, drunk. Like there was more alcohol in my veins than oxygen. I could barely open my eyes and my knees were as weak as rubber bands.

Then a loud, booming voice came barreling down the sidewalk at us. "What's happened to her?"

It was Fridge, and before I could stop him, he grabbed my arms, too.

Oh, no...

Oh, yes...

The combined contact with both my mates at the same time pushed me over the edge.

I began to orgasm, my pussy pulsating and spasms erupting right through my belly as liquid fire moved down my legs. I cried out and almost collapsed where I stood, despite their restraining hands.

Only the tightening grip of my mates kept me standing, and as Fridge pulled me closer to give me a firm body to lean on, I heard the distinctive growl of his dragon deep in his chest.

"Let her go," Fridge said to Rogan, his voice booming over us.

Rogan's hands disappeared and I fell fully into Fridge's chest, as waves of ecstasy continued to lap at the shores of my long-starved sexuality.

I closed my eyes and enjoyed the feelings, because Rogan was right. We had a long way to go before we could be together. And that was if we could convince the dragon to be a part of this fated *ménage à trois.*

"Are you okay? What happened?" Fridge asked urgently.

I managed to open my eyes and look up and his nostrils flared as he scented my need.

That was when his self-preservation instincts kicked in and he stepped back, holding me at arm's length.

"You..." He swallowed hard.

I could see the battle with his shifter. The green eyes that flashed to their alternate diamond shape and back again.

He was a purebred dragon. What was he doing in the middle of a city, unable to shift and fly whenever he needed to?

Rogan stepped up and put a hand around my waist. "Sadie needs to get inside, meet the guys, and do some research. Are you up for that, or you gonna run away again like this morning?"

I glanced over to see Rogan and Fridge glaring at each other.

Hmm... interesting dynamic there.

"I..." Fridge lifted his chin. "Where are *you* going?"

"I need a shower and a change of clothes. I'll be back in an hour. *If* I can trust her with you?"

"Of course, you can trust her with me." Fridge snorted, all indignation and fire. "Who do you think you're talking to?"

The question must have been rhetorical because Rogan didn't answer. He simply growled low in his throat like a wolf, and stalked away.

CHAPTER 10
ROGAN

Damn Fridge.

I shuddered as the heat in my blood rapidly cooled, though the message was slow getting through to my cock that we weren't doing anything with Sadie right now.

She had been so ready to mate with me.

I could smell it on her.

Everything in me and all of her wolf shifter genes were ready to hop straight into the sack and make babies.

But until Fridge got his shit together, how was I going to manage this?

The stupid dragon had put up with a lot of crap in his life. He'd had a shitty childhood, and a rougher adult life than most could imagine.

But here she was. The perfect woman, who had connected with *both* of us, and he was running like a pussy.

If I wasn't careful, he was going to screw it up. Not just for him but for me, too. No woman was going to handle being rejected too often by one of her mates.

And I wasn't going to lose her, just because Fridge said he didn't believe in fated mates.

To me, it was brilliant. The perfect solution to my life.

Fate had literally chosen the woman for me, and I was gonna drop down on my knees and say thank you. My nights of loneliness, of picking up random tail, were done.

Hallelujah.

I just had to convince Fridge to forget about his parents' suffering and grab onto Sadie with both hands.

A grin settled on my face as I remembered how hard she'd come with just our touch. She hadn't wanted to, being on the street near her dad's workshop, but she couldn't stop it, not when we both touched her and set off the chain reaction of the fated mate bond.

I could only imagine how much she'd enjoy being with us properly. And how much I'd enjoy being with her.

Naked. Heart to heart.

Soul to soul.

Mate to mate.

SADIE

My head was clearing and my legs were getting stronger.

I stepped away from Fridge and tried not to be embarrassed by what had just happened.

Completely normal. Right?

I glanced around, wondering if anyone else had seen, then cleared my throat. "Would you mind introducing me to the men inside?"

I began to walk past him, but he grabbed my arms, stopping me from moving an inch further. I shivered, fissions of pleasure skating over my already sensitized nervous system.

"What wass... that, Sadie?" he asked, his voice deep and slightly snake-like.

I flicked my gaze up so that I was looking right at him. "Proof that we're fated mates."

I waited a heartbeat for those words to sink in, watching the ripple of unease move over his face. "You ready to go?" he asked.

I tugged my arm out of his grip and walked the last few steps to my father's business ahead of him.

Hunters. Otherwise known as the workshop.

I placed both palms on the front door and pushed hard.

A cacophony of sound hit me all at once. Men everywhere. Talking, training. Moving furniture about.

Fridge was right on my tail.

I turned to him, surprised by the amount of activity. I was sure this level of movement wasn't normal. "What's going on?"

He inhaled sharply, puffing out his already large chest. "Mostly clean-up and checking the infrastructure. I held a meeting early this morning, caught everyone up on what happened last night, and said we couldn't let this happen again. To anyone. The guys are checking the place for bugs, moving things around, and adding more security measures to every door and window in the place."

I was surprised by how organized they already were. "Did you tell them about me?"

He nodded stiffly. "I told them you'd be coming in to speak to them, but that I didn't know what the plans were for the business."

I crossed my arms over my chest. I didn't know enough about the way my dad ran things to guarantee jobs or terms at this point. The enormity of the task ahead suddenly landed heavily on my shoulders.

I glanced around. "Can we go somewhere to chat for a minute?"

He nodded, still tense. "Of course. Your dad's office, maybe?"

"As good a place as any."

Men were beginning to stop work to stare at me, so I lifted my chin and marched up the stairs, making a beeline for my father's office while my skin itched with uncomfortable fire.

I wasn't used to such a testosterone-driven workplace.

My corporate office was at least fifty percent male, but they were all lawyers or administrative staff. Nerds in suits.

Not two-hundred-pound fighting machines, which my dad had clearly trained these guys to be. It was unnerving.

I made my way into my dad's office, waited for Fridge to enter, then shut the door behind him. I didn't want anyone overhearing our conversation.

"Take a seat," I said.

Fridge dropped into the chair nearest the door, but then I didn't know where to sit. My dad's chair seemed wrong, somehow, so I just perched in the second client chair, opposite the desk.

I needed help, and Fridge was the logical place to start. "Okay, how much do you know about how the business side of things runs?"

He cocked his head. "You mean the contracts? The pay? What part do you want to know about?"

I sighed and tugged my hair out of its too-low ponytail, then rearranged it again, higher.

Fridge watched me the whole time. He licked his lips as though hungry.

I didn't ask him if he was okay. I knew he wasn't. He was struggling with my proximity, while I was more comfortable physically than I had been in days. Relaxed, even. My emotions were a whole other story, but hopefully I had them tucked down tight.

"I mean everything," I said. "Shit, maybe I should talk to the accountant."

Fridge sat up straighter. "I can get you that number, but I suppose what all the guys want to know is, do they still have a job?"

I don't know. "That depends on so many factors. How is everyone paid? A daily fee? Only when they bring in a bounty? How does it all work?"

Fridge ran his hand along the arm of the chair. "Most of the guys work as contractors. So, they only get paid when they have a contract and fulfil it. But there's a few of us, Rogan and me included, who work here full-time as salaried staff. We help train the new guys, keep order, help out with whatever Jimmy wanted."

"Okay." It definitely sounded like I needed to speak to whomever Dad had used for financial matters.

I needed to know how the business was doing, and if, without my dad, we could find a way to keep the doors open and employees working.

"Well, I think we should keep everything going exactly as it always has, at least until the end of this month. That'll give me time to talk to the finance people, get through the financials and organize Dad's funeral and everything."

I had to stop and swallow the bile rising in my throat.

Dad's funeral… *fuck me.* I never thought I'd have to deal with that. Part of me had believed he'd live forever.

The stupidly naïve part.

"Well, I'm pretty sure his Will would be stored with his attorney, but he told me once that there's a vault in this room, filled with his personal effects," Fridge said, standing up. He took a painting of a night's sky and full moon down from one of the walls and revealed a small wall safe.

I huffed out a laugh at the small silver door. "Just like in the movies."

He nodded. "I don't know the combination. He never told anyone. But I have the clue, though I have no idea why he gave it to me."

I wondered too, though it was becoming apparent that my father trusted Fridge. Rogan, too. A lot. Which said a hell of a lot about their character.

"What's the clue?" I asked, standing up and walking over to examine the combination lock.

Had my father thought something like this might happen? Was that why he'd made sure Fridge knew where his Will was?

"He said it's the date of the best and worst day of his life."

My chest constricted and my breath caught in my throat. I'd heard that expression once a year, for most of my life.

So, the clue was for me. Somehow, Dad knew Fridge would tell me.

I set my trembling fingers to the dial, thinking about the first number to put in. I was tempted to try my mother's death date, their wedding day, or other dates that I knew were important to him.

But I knew the answer to the riddle.

I moved the numbers around and around until I finished the year, then there was a loud click as the safe cracked open.

"What was it?" Fridge asked, and without even thinking, I told him the answer.

"My birthday."

Fridge stared at me, and didn't ask the obvious question, though I could tell by the way his lips twitched that he wanted to know.

I pushed open the door and found a pile of cash, three thick, leather-bound books, and a small, black jewelry box.

I ignored the cash and grabbed the books. On second thoughts, I took the jewelry box out as well. The velvet slid against my hand, and I shivered. Fridge pushed the safe door shut and spun the dial to close it. I walked back to the desk with my treasure.

This time I sat in Dad's chair.

I placed the books down and stared at the black velvet box. Was it something of my mother's? Something old? Or a new piece he'd bought for a woman in his life?

If it was the latter, I wasn't sure I wanted to know.

"Why was it the worst day of his life?"

Fridge's voice came at me through the clouds fogging up my thinking, and I glanced at him.

I waved my hands. "Sit, sit."

He sat back in one of the chairs and I sighed.

"Seems odd, doesn't it?" I said, because I'd always thought the same thing.

He nodded.

I smiled, remembering all the nights my dad had said those exact words. I licked my dry lips, and began telling the story, strangely relieved to be able to share the precious memory with someone else.

"Every year, on my birthday, he'd sit on my bed and tell me a bed-time story." I took another slow breath and swallowed the emotional lump that rose in my throat. "And at the end of the night he'd say, *'Do you know that the day you were born was the best day of my life, but also my worst?'*"

Fridge's eyebrows shot up and I laughed aloud, recalling the fact that I'd felt the same horror as a child.

I continued. "And I'd say, *'Your worst, Daddy? Why? Was I a bad baby?'*"

Fridge smiled and I fought back tears at the memory. At the deep-seated feelings the story brought up in me.

"He'd say, *'Oh, no. You were the most beautiful girl I've ever seen. That was the problem. I knew that my life had changed forever. That I finally had something to live for. And that was a problem. Up until that day, I'd never feared death. I knew that one day, it would be my time and I would be happy to go. And with my work, being fearless came with the job. But on the day you were born, I knew that I'd finally found something I couldn't bear to be apart from.'*"

I stopped, the tears rolling down my face. I gulped to stem the flow.

"He was..." *The best dad ever.*

But I couldn't say it aloud. My throat had closed up and I could no longer see for the hot tears blurring my vision.

I had been so loved in my life. Even after my mother died, I'd never lacked for anything.

I knew what it was like to be truly blessed, and for that I was grateful. So grateful. But the pain now, as I sat at my father's desk, and the realization that he was gone hit me... the intensity of those feelings was incredible.

Like someone had taken every nerve in my body, and grated them over a hot vent. My heart squeezed tight in my chest as my stomach lurched.

Tears flowed down my face. I pushed my hands into my eyes to try and stop them, but it didn't help.

Fridge stood up, walked around the desk, and picked me up as though I weighed little more than a child. Before I could react, he sat down again and held me in his lap.

I had no chance of pushing back the storm of my grief as it raged overhead.

"Shh... It's going to be okay," he hummed, holding me tightly.

I put my head on Fridge's chest and let the pain overtake me like a tsunami. I was dragged under the wave and I wasn't coming up again.

Heat scorched my face, burned my throat and tore at my heart as I continued to sob.

I'd lost him... I'd really lost him. The only person to truly love me had left me. And I had a massive, gaping hole in my life now.

The thoughts and feelings went on, until finally, *finally* the tears began to dry up.

The tide turned and I began to surface. Through the waves and up, toward the open air.

My face burned like the sun, my eyes stung like I'd been drenched in sea water, and my chest hurt from all the heaving.

But somehow, despite all the pain, I felt better.

Numb in some ways... but more like me.

I pushed up from Fridge's chest where I'd been clinging and stared down at the stain of tears I'd left on his clean shirt. Thank God I hadn't worn any makeup today.

I'd look like a grotesque panda, and he'd have a black puddle ruining his pale blue shirt instead of a clear one.

I put a hand on the wet patch. "I'm sorry. I've made a mess of you."

He glanced down and shrugged. "Shit happens."

And just like that, I wanted to cry again. My chin wobbled and my eyes welled up.

That's exactly what my dad would have said.

I slid off his lap and grabbed for the tissue box on my dad's desk before I could lose control again.

I turned away so he didn't have to watch me. I began blowing my dripping and clogged nose, and mopping up my face. It was totally disgusting and undignified, but hey, I couldn't get much lower than this moment.

Fridge had officially seen me at my worst, so there was only one way to go from here. Up.

By the time I dried my face enough to turn around and speak, Fridge had pulled a bottle of water from a small fridge in the corner of the room and was offering it to me.

I inhaled sharply, my fragile emotions struggling with the show of thoughtfulness.

Get it together.

"Thanks." I cracked the lid, tipped the bottle back and swallowed, my scratchy, dry throat grateful for the kindness.

Time to change the subject and get control of myself.

I indicated to the books still stacked on the desk and tried to plaster a smile on my face. "What are they? Dad's bookkeeping notes, or something else?"

He wouldn't have kept a journal. *Surely.*

Fridge pushed the books across the desk toward me. "I don't know. You check it out." He indicated to the jewelry box. "Is that for you?"

I shrugged. "No idea what's in it."

And part of me was afraid to find out.

"Ah, okay." He pushed the box at me, too, and I was forced to pick it up. I didn't want to look like a coward in front of Fridge after what I'd just put him through.

I was lucky the poor guy was still in the room with me.

I steeled myself for what might be beneath the black velvet. An engagement ring? An expensive watch? Something that would clearly tell me that my father had been in love with someone and I didn't know about it?

I took a deep breath, and opened it.

Worry turned to love as I stared at my mother's small jewelry collection. "These are my mother's things. She didn't have much."

I pulled out the plain gold wedding band and small engagement ring. With the rings was a thin gold chain and her watch. All together. All kept safe.

"Why would it be here?" I asked aloud. "He could have kept this stuff at home."

We had a safe there, too.

Fridge shrugged. "No idea. They're nice pieces, though."

I slid the rings onto my right ring finger and admired them.

My dad didn't have a lot of money when my parents had gotten married, and when he started to earn a good living, Mom had refused to upgrade her rings.

She'd loved the emotions symbolized in the original ones. The love and devotion.

"Thanks." I closed the lid and slid the box onto the desk. I wasn't sure why he'd kept such pieces in his work safe. At the moment, it didn't seem important, but I made a mental note to further explore it. "Now, to the books."

I opened the first one, dated back to when he first began the workshop. There were dates, names and prices.

Almost like a running tally of conquests.

"Looks like an account of every bounty the workshop's ever taken." Fridge pointed to a name halfway down the first page. "Wow… that guy was a legend."

I looked at where he pointed and shrugged. I didn't recognize any of the names.

I glanced at the lists and flicked through the rest of the book. It spanned about a decade or so.

"Here." I passed the journal over to Fridge and picked up the next book. After a few pages, I shrugged. "This is the same."

Losing hope, I opened the third one. There were a few blank pages at the back, but the books were all equally plain and boring.

Fridge looked at me expectantly.

"It's the same," I said with a sigh, handing over the third book. "This isn't as exciting as I expected it to be. Why would Dad keep a list of all the guys the workshop has ever caught? Isn't that just duplicated work? He'd have contracts, computer files..."

Fridge shrugged. "He was an old-fashioned guy in a lot of ways. There may be something we've missed, hidden in the pages. I'll take a look... if you'd like?"

He waited for me to answer but I didn't for a minute, assessing him. If he wasn't my fated mate, would I trust him so much?

He was exceptionally tough-looking. And I didn't know him from a bar of soap up until last night.

So, no, I probably wouldn't be handing all my trust over to a man I didn't know if it were any other day.

But he *was* my fated mate, and I knew that meant he had to be a guy who was loyal, kind, clever, and probably stubborn as hell.

Not to mention the fact that, by all accounts, my dad had trusted him.

"Of course, I trust you," I said. "Please, keep them, look through every page. Tell me if you find anything odd."

He nodded and scooped the three books up off the desk. "You wanna wear your mom's other jewelry or put it back in the safe?"

I glanced at the box, then picked it up. "Back in the safe I think, though I'll keep her rings on. I always kinda wondered what had happened to them. I thought she may have been buried with them."

"Buried?" Fridge repeated as I took the box over to the wall, opened the safe, and slid it safely back inside next to the stacks of money.

God, that's a lot of cash.

"Yeah, why?"

When I turned back around, Fridge was still looking confused. "Was she human? I'd always pictured her as being at least part paranormal, but the only paras that are buried are the..." He trailed off and I suddenly realized my blunder.

All shifters, even half breeds or less, were cremated.

Even the vamps burst into flames when they were staked.

"Yeah, she was human," I hurried, dropping my gaze to avoid him working out that I was a liar.

The only type of paranormals who were buried were the witches. And as far as everyone was concerned, they were extinct.

The vampires had a strong obsession with witch blood, and had killed anyone with a drop of witch in them decades ago.

"So, what do you think I should do next?" I asked him, since he was more familiar with this domain than me.

He laughed. "You were the one who wanted the meeting."

I thought back and then chuckled, too. "Oh, well, that was mostly to find out how this place ran. Does Dad still have a mortgage?"

What sort of finances will we be dealing with if I keep this place going?

Fridge shrugged. "I honestly don't know. I didn't talk money much with your old man. He paid me, and I worked hard. End of story, really."

I couldn't help the temptation to tease him. "So, you never asked for a raise?"

I had to assume that the topic of money came up occasionally. It always did.

He held my gaze. "Never had to. Your dad upped our pay every Christmas without fail."

"Hmm, that was generous. And unusual." I didn't know any other employers who did that. Mine certainly didn't.

Fridge chuckled. "It's sink or swim here. If you work hard, are consistent and loyal, your dad keeps... I mean, *kept* us on. If not... you're let go."

"That's harsh."

Fridge really laughed this time. "That was your old man. Now... can I give you just a little bit of advice?"

"Of course." Whether or not I took the advice was a different story.

"Wash your face. Get rid of the tears, then walk out there with me and tell all the guys things are going to be okay." He shrugged. "At least for the next month."

"Okay. That is good advice. And Dad had his own bathroom?"

Fridge nodded. "Yeah. Through that door."

He pointed behind me.

We always have our own bathrooms.

"Thanks. I won't be long."

I left my dragon shifter in the office while I washed the redness, pain, and tears off my face.

Despite my underlying grief, it was time to show them what Daddy's girl was made of.

CHAPTER 13

SADIE

I stood at the top of the stairs, near my father's office space, staring down at the men milling around, waiting for me to speak.

They were lounging against walls, resting on the stairs or just standing with their arms crossed over their chest.

Rogan had returned from their place, freshly showered and dressed. He stood next to me, at the top of the staircase, while Fridge lingered a step or two away.

"Thank you all for coming in today. I can imagine it was difficult to stay after you learned what happened last night." I swallowed hard, trying to remain calm and imagining it as a courtroom where I was about to present an opening argument.

These men needed to see a strong and united front from me and the two men who stood beside me.

Judging by the numbers, most of the staff members on the books were here today. Seen as a group like this, there were more than I'd expected. All males. All shifters. All rough, rugged guys.

They probably had a whole lot of worry about being led by someone they'd see as young, female and inexperienced.

"I wanted to reassure you that at least for the next month, the workshop will run as it has in the past. All current bounties will be paid, full-time staff will get their wages, and I will be speaking to the accounting firm and legal team to see how I can keep my father's legacy running for as long as possible."

There was a general murmur, though I wasn't sure if the sound was good or not.

Rogan cleared his throat and I glanced his way.

Did he want to say anything? Or was he reminding me to say something about him and Fridge?

"I've asked Rogan and Fridge to take over the daily operations until I get on my feet, or until I find someone to take over permanently, if that's a better option for Hunters. If you have any questions or concerns, you are welcome to approach me, of course, but otherwise, you can direct everything through them. Whatever works best for you at this interim time."

A more positive vibe pulsed through the place now.

I would have liked to say something more inspirational, but I was a twenty-five-year-old female, in a room full of twenty to fifty-year-old men.

I wasn't inspiring anyone. Not with words alone, and not as I was today. Nor with who I would be tomorrow.

I knew how loyalty and love were earned. It was through years of hard-won battles. Showing up every day to do your job better than others had done before you.

Not just being a person who could talk, but being a person of action to back up the words.

I cleared my throat, needing to say at least one more thing. "I realize I don't know any of you, but please be assured that I am my father's daughter through and through. I'll make sure you guys are looked after, and if I can work out a way to keep this business going, I will. He loved working here; he loved everything about his job, and I won't allow what he built up to go down the drain. I promise you that."

This time there were a few small smiles and some of the men shuffled their feet and leaned more easily against the walls.

"So, for now, carry on as always, and come to me, Rogan or Fridge if you have any queries. Thank you." I nodded and waved, then walked back to the office, shivering with adrenaline and excessive nerves.

I made it back into the office before I let out a ragged sigh.

Rogan closed the door and laughed at me. "You did well. They're a tough crowd."

"I know. I know." I began to pace, my arms and legs jittery and anxious.

I needed to exercise. Run. Or something.

There's a clothing place next door. Go grab some workout gear and get moving.

"Is there some gym equipment I can use?"

Fridge crossed his arms over his chest and leaned against the door. "We don't do treadmills and shit like that."

I stopped and stared at him, raising a single eyebrow. "Listen, Fridge, I was throwing knives before I could walk. So, if you've got some throwing mats or a boxing ring, I'll train with you. If you think you're up to it, of course?"

His expression was priceless. His mouth dropped open and his eyes opened so wide he looked like some sort of cartoon character.

"You wanna... *huh*? What?"

I turned to Rogan, who was smirking like a madman. "I need to change into some training gear. I know there's a place next door I can buy some. Can you clear a space downstairs for us, and I'll be back in ten?"

Rogan nodded. "Definitely."

I flicked my hand at Fridge, and he moved out of the way.

I opened the door to the office, jogged down the stairs and out the front door.

This was going to be fun.

Even though I was one hundred percent sure I *couldn't* win a fight against a dragon.

I hadn't trained properly in months, not in hand-to-hand combat. I'd been too busy with work. But what did they say? It was like riding a bike...

I strolled into the business next door, a women's clothing shop. Not my sort of stuff, too feminine and bargain basement. But it looked like they had what I needed.

"Hello, can I help you?" a blonde woman asked as she walked forward and ran her eye over me with a skeptical glance.

I ignored the look and flashed her a smile. "Yes. Hi. I'm Sadie Williams. My dad owned the business next door and I need some workout clothes, if you have any?"

In less than ten minutes, I had tanks, leggings, and a great sports bra in my arms.

The woman rang it all up. I paid with my card, though an image of the cash in my dad's safe flashed into my mind. Was that how he paid his employees? Or was that simply for a rainy day?

"Thanks a bunch."

I left her shop after promising I would visit again, went straight back to Dad's office, and changed in the private bathroom. My heart pumped hard against my ribs and I couldn't believe the amount of excitement thrumming through my system.

It had been too long since I'd had a good fight.

Not to mention the fact that my shifter side couldn't wait to wrap my legs around one of my mates. Even if it was just to take him down.

I almost giggled as I came out of the office. Rogan was waiting for me, leaning against a wall.

I smiled at him. "Hey. Is everything set up?"

"Yeah. But, Sadie, you realize Fridge is a dragon shifter, right?"

My smile turned a little feral. As if that was something I could forget. "Yeah, I do know that."

Rogan took a step closer, concern written all over his handsome face. "If he lets you win or goes easy on you, you'll be fine. But try not to aggravate him, okay? He's strong and won't know how to pull back if his shifter is triggered."

Excitement rippled along my veins. If his shifter was triggered, then I had a chance of hitting the high I got when I trained properly with my dad.

God, I miss that feeling.

"I'm counting on it," I said, heading for the door. "Come on, let's go. Show me where he is."

I raced out the office door before Rogan could try and talk me out of training with Fridge.

I wasn't afraid of a little pain, or a dragon with a temper. I'd fought *my dad.* And he had never gone easy on me.

He'd said, *"If you're in a real fight, they won't take it easy on you, just because you're a girl. So, I'm not going to. You need to know how to get out of tough situations."*

And that training had served me well, if for nothing more than piece of mind when walking the streets alone.

I'd never been attacked or even mugged, and I truly believed that was because something about me exuded a confidence that said, "I dare you." Which was unlike every other woman I knew, who'd had their purses snatched, their boyfriends beaten up. I'd never even been close to it.

As I jogged down the stairs in socks, black compression leggings, and a hot purple tank, I was buzzing.

"Which way?" I asked Rogan as he followed behind me looking drastically underwhelmed.

He pointed to my right. "That way, first door. Says 'Gym'."

I nodded and marched off in that direction.

The smell of sweat and testosterone was high in the air, and I could sense my dragon mate was nearby.

I walked into the room and stopped dead. There were twenty guys standing around, waiting for the show.

Ah... what?

Rogan stepped up beside me and shrugged. "You seriously thought no one would want to see this?"

I shivered.

Why, I wasn't sure. I had spectators in court all the time, though the pressure to perform here seemed higher than in front of any judge I'd ever faced.

The men here would critique me much harsher and more personally than any lawyer. They'd compare me to my father, and I'd always come up lacking.

Although I'd never hold a candle to my dad, this was a chance to prove I was tough and capable—not just a little girl trying to fill her daddy's shoes and finding it impossible.

"Fridge, what are we doing?" I called out to the man-mountain across the room.

He'd taken off his shoes and changed out of his shirt and cargo pants and into some black sweats and a tank that barely covered his nipples.

God, the man was hot. Enough to make my mouth water and my fingers itch to caress every inch of him.

Damn the men standing around. I didn't want to have to struggle to keep my hands to myself, but it looked like I'd have to, now. Couldn't have them thinking I was some weak, lusty woman, or worse—think badly of Fridge for hooking up with the boss's daughter. It wouldn't reflect well on either of us.

I tried to ignore the sexual tension sizzling through the air and walked forward to where Fridge held up boxing gloves.

"Wanna spar in the ring?" he asked.

I sized up his height and weight and realized I'd lose a boxing match pretty fast.

"With someone your size? Not really."

When he looked relieved, I grinned.

"I'd prefer a straight-out sparring match," I said. "We can wear gloves if you'd prefer. But street rules, not ring rules."

His eyebrows rose high on his forehead. "You serious?" He handed the boxing gloves to a man whose name I didn't know and gestured for a different pair.

I chuckled. "I'm a bit rusty, so give me a minute to ease into it, but I'll be fine."

I grabbed the MMA-style gloves he held out and dropped them on the ground. "Anything I need to know?"

A guy behind me called out. "Yeah, you're about to get your ass handed to you."

"Nah... go easy on her, Fridge," another guy said.

I pulled my sloppy pony tail out of its elastic, rearranged the strands, and tied it as high as possible on my head, out of my eyes.

"Yeah, Fridge." I grinned. "Go easy on me." I lowered my voice as I picked up the gloves and pulled them on, wrapping the Velcro straps around my wrists. "After all, you still don't know what my full bloodlines are."

His mouth fell open. "You said your mom was human."

Which, by his calculation, made me three quarters human and no match for a shifter like him.

I turned on my heel and walked off, throwing the challenge over my shoulder. "Maybe I lied."

And I had. My mother had been a powerful witch. A pure blood. The last of her kind. She had instilled in me many gifts, including a spell to increase my speed and strength. Just like she had for my father.

Only my parents knew that, and my secret had died with them.

I reached the edge of the padded mats and turned to face him again.

"Let's go, dragon," I said, smirking as I beckoned him over.

We stood on thick, red workout mats, which would make it harder to move and run, but so much softer if Fridge threw me or I had to take a fall.

Either was possible, I realized, as Fridge pulled on his gloves and bounced toward me.

His eyes gleamed with the challenge and, as I looked closer, his eyes had partially transitioned. Not to fully diamond-shaped pupils, but the iris had changed from green to almost yellow.

Despite his promise of taking it easy, I doubted he would.

He was excited.

"You sure about this, Sadie? I've never thrown a fight before, not even in practice. Maybe you should have asked Rogan." He waggled his eyebrows.

I chuckled. "No. I picked the right guy. Let's go... Travis."

There were some laughs around us.

He narrowed his eyes as though he were angry, but his mouth kicked up at the corners.

Good. We're on.

I put my hands up to protect my face and began bouncing on the spot. With a guy this size I would usually pull out a weapon of some sort, but I didn't know how good he was yet, so I'd wait.

But soon, all bets would be off.

Once we fully engaged, I wasn't backing down.

CHAPTER 14

FRIDGE

I couldn't stop the excited thrill that shivered through me, though part of me didn't want to admit to it.

I was about to fight a girl. Nothing to be proud of there.

And yet, Sadie was no ordinary woman, that was for sure. The very fact that she desired Rogan and me—at the same time—made her exceptional.

If there was nothing else, that would be enough to know that she was someone unique.

But she was also Jimmy's daughter, and that tipped the scales.

He'd taught all of us how to fight.

I was sure he'd taught his only child. What good father wouldn't teach his daughter to take care of herself?

But how was I going to control my shifter, who practically leapt inside me?

My shifter loved a good fight, and he was very quickly falling in lust with the woman before me.

If I shifted during the fight, I could hurt her. Badly.

I shook myself. No. I wouldn't lose control. I hadn't shifted in a very long time. I could pull my punches in this fight and let her hit me as well.

Surely, she couldn't injure me that badly?

CHAPTER 15
SADIE

Fridge wasn't moving. Wasn't bouncing. Wasn't even putting up his hands to guard himself.

Fine. You want me to attack first?

I bounced forward, ducked down, and punched him in the gut with a triple action punch.

One. Two. Three.

I didn't put half my effort into it, as I was still warming up. My muscles were cold, and my technique was sloppy from disuse.

But even so, the impact of his rock-hard abs under the padding of my gloves felt great.

Fridge staggered back and I ducked and weaved away, bouncing on my toes, trying to get my body to behave properly.

The real rush hadn't started yet. Unfortunately, the only way to really engage my skills was to take a few hits. But Fridge wouldn't want to smack me around the way my father had, and he wouldn't know it was what I actually needed to bring out the best in my fighting instincts.

That, or threaten one I loved. And there was no-one left.

The thought had me clenching my teeth against the wave of sadness that buffeted me.

I was like my dad now. Before he'd married Mom. Before they'd had me.

A lone wolf with no one to look after except myself.

Fridge glared at me, like he hadn't expected me to hit him so hard.

I gestured. "Come on. My dad wouldn't take it so easy on me."

His eyebrows flicked up as though he didn't expect me to say such a thing. "Fine."

I threw myself forward, onto one leg, balanced myself, and kicked him in the gut.

Fridge moved so that I only clipped the side of his torso.

He threw a punch that I easily blocked, then I rolled to the ground.

This wasn't working.

I got to my feet and huffed out an angry sound. "Okay. Is there anyone else I can work with? I need someone who's going to actually hit me."

I looked around the room, hoping one of the other men would want to fight. Properly.

But all of them stared down at the ground, like a pack of whipped dogs.

Damn. Looked like Dad didn't have any enemies here. I was protected, simply because of who he had been.

"You want me to hit you?" Fridge asked, his words colored with surprise.

I spun back around. "Well, yeah. Put up an actual fight or don't bother."

"But I could hurt you."

Yes, he could. But only if he was trying to kill me, which I knew he wouldn't. The fated mates link alone wouldn't allow him to do any proper damage.

Fingers crossed.

I laughed at him. "I've only been knocked out twice, and I was pretty young at the time. I have my dad's genetics, so unless you're gonna hit me hard, I can't fight you."

I began to undo my gloves.

He walked forward; his jaw set hard. "Fine. Let's do it."

He hit his gloves together and swung, fast.

I barely got out of the way, the punch missing my jaw by a hair.

Oh, there it is...

The tingle in my veins started to pulse as I ducked and moved out of the way. He danced to the side and attempted to punch me again.

I jumped out of the way, but actually felt the swing as a brush of air caressed my face.

I took the opportunity to step in and swung an upper cut as hard as I could.

He darted out of the way and punched me in the kidneys. *Oh.* That one hurt.

I grunted and staggered sideways.

A growl of irritation welled up nearby from Rogan. I recognized his tone.

Fridge stopped bouncing. Stopped moving.

Nope, can't have that.

I came at him, throwing punches hard and fast. One, two, three at his face. Then an uppercut to his chin.

He blocked every one of my attempted blows with precision and skill. But he was panting now, his body shining with a thin film of sweat.

I stepped back and he swung at me. He clipped my jaw and my eyes shifted.

I was now seeing in black and white, my wolf shifter senses taking over now that my body had decided I was in a real fight.

I growled, a sound I never usually made, but it felt so incredibly natural in this setting.

I pounced on him, hitting him in the gut. As he doubled over, I kneed him in the belly. I put both hands together, lifted them over my head, and slammed them into his back.

He groaned and swung out, grabbing my legs and wrestling me to the floor.

I grunted as my back hit the cushioned mats beneath my feet and I tried to get out from under his weight. I wrapped my legs around his thick waist and bucked at him to try to get him off me.

I could have bitten him, of course, but we weren't in a true battle. It felt wrong to fight as though my life depended on it, when it didn't.

Plus, being in this position already had my belly tightening and my pussy pulsing. If I bit his shoulder and tasted his sweat, who knew what would happen?

When he finally pinned me flat on my back with my arms above my head, he asked, "Give up?"

I couldn't help it. I laughed. Exhilaration pumped through me.

"Yes!" I yelled. "But I want some lessons from you now."

Blood dripped from his lip as he grinned.

My eyes shifted back to human and I could see him in full color. His eyes were green once again I realized and he'd relaxed his grip on me.

"Get up then." He bounced to his feet, put a hand out, and pulled me up with one move.

The atmosphere in the room was electric. The men around the edges of the training mat were grinning and chuckling.

It was obvious they hadn't expected me to win, and part of me was glad I hadn't. They needed to respect Fridge more than me right now. But hopefully they could see from that display that I was no shrinking violet.

I hit Fridge in the arm and he staggered sideways, laughing.

I grinned at him. "You can take a punch. I like that."

He laughed. "Yeah, whatever."

He was rosy-cheeked and glowing like the devil himself. Despite the rejection last night and everything that had gone on, I could feel the connection between us weaving together like piece of rope, blending to become even stronger and tighter. Unified.

Rogan was the only one in the room not smiling. He marched across the mats, a storm cloud on his face. His eyes were hard and his mouth was set in a grim line.

Shit. I needed to back off with my flirtation with Fridge, at least a bit.

How was the jealousy element going to play out with my two mates? Would they be able to share me? Or was this going to be an ongoing problem?

"You okay?" he asked me, as the guys in the room began to dissipate.

I unwrapped the Velcro from my gloves and pulled them off. "Yeah, of course. Why?"

He glanced around to make sure everyone was leaving, then looked back at me, concern clearly written all over his face. "We don't usually get women in here wanting to fight the biggest guy we have. He took it easy on you, but still..."

He handed me a towel he must've grabbed from somewhere in the gym area.

I took it and wiped my sweaty face and palms. "I know he went easy on me, and that's fine for now. I'm out of shape. But I want to be able to take him on properly. One day. Maybe even win."

Fridge crossed his arms over his chest. "The day that happens, retire me."

A ripple of unease crossed my heart. Was that how he truly felt? That if I—a woman—bested him, then he was of no use to anyone?

I didn't like the sound of that. Was he really that arrogant and vain? Or was it simply some sort of misplaced insecurity?

I opened my mouth to ask, but Rogan grabbed my hand. "The

police called for you, about last night. You might want to go take the call."

I pulled my brain back into work mode. Fridge and his insecurities could wait. "Are they on hold?"

"Yeah. In Jimmy's office."

"Thanks." I nodded at both men and ran up the stairs, sweat clinging to the hair at the base of my neck.

It had been a nice reprieve not to think about my dad's death for a short while, but I was already back down into the black hole.

I fell into the executive chair and picked up the phone, pressing the flashing button. "Hello. Sarah Williams speaking."

"Miss Williams, it's Detective O'Connell. We met last night."

Had we? Last night was a blur. Which one was he?

"Hello, Detective. How can I help you?"

"I wanted to let you know that we're looking into possible suspects for last night's attack and are awaiting the coroner's report on cause of death."

My mouth dropped open, then I narrowed my gaze. "You don't know the cause of death? Seriously? What is this, your first case?"

There was a long pause. If I could hazard a guess from the sound of the detective's voice, he was at least fifty.

Definitely not his first case.

"Miss Williams, we never like to assume in cases like this."

"Cases like what? Murder? With an ancient vampire being *literally* the only person able to pull it off?"

The detective cleared his throat. "Now, Miss Williams, we don't like to go jumping to conclusions."

"Jumping to conclusions!" I got to my feet and put my free hand on my hip. "Listen here, Detective. I know that the vampires own half the city, and that they are almost impossible to pin down when they commit murders like this. But if you think I'm going to stand by and let you push off my father's murder as some random death, then you don't understand a thing about me. Or my family."

The detective sighed. "Miss Williams…"

His tone was insufferable. As though he were bored.

I wanted to scream! And tear the guy's hair out. This was a blow-off, I knew it was. And I wasn't having any of it.

"Listen, Detective. My father was smart, strong, and a powerful shifter. A trained and experienced bounty hunter of the highest caliber. The only type of paranormal that could get the drop on him was a vampire, and not a young one, but an older, experienced predator. So, I suggest you start looking at your list of top vampire assassins and start shaking them down. Or I will."

"Miss Williams, that would not be wise. Leave this to the professionals."

My temper exploded. "As I am now in charge of my murdered father's bounty hunting business, I am one of the 'professionals'. So, do your damn job and find this guy!"

I slammed the phone down and groaned in frustration, my hands tightening into fists as I dug my nails into the palms of my hands.

"Fucking. Ignorant. Useless. Prick!"

The door opened and Rogan stuck his head in. "Everything okay in here?"

"No!" I yelled, and managed to knock over my father's massive chair in my haste to get out from behind the desk.

Rogan, instead of running away like any other man who'd seen my temper had done, stepped into the room and shut the door. "What's happened?"

I groaned and paced the area around the desk, an uncontrollable amount of anger pulsing through my veins. "They're giving up on Dad's murder already."

"Who is?"

"The fucking police, that's who! They said it's probably not a vampire. Not a murder. No point jumping to conclusions. You were there last night. Am I jumping to fucking conclusions?"

Rogan held up his hands. "No. You're right. It was murder. And it was a vamp."

"Then why would they call me—today—and tell me that they're keeping an eye on everything, but they really don't know shit?"

Rogan laughed, rocking back on his heels. "Because the police are owned by the vampires. If the guys who pull the strings and pay the purses don't want your dad's murder solved by the cops, it won't be. It'll be put in the too-hard basket. Not enough evidence, whatever."

I felt like screaming. Tears filled my eyes and coursed down my face.

Fridge came bursting into the room like a force of nature, his eyes wide, looking for an attacker. He must have heard my ranting.

"What's going on?" he boomed.

Rogan gave him a quick rundown while I wiped away the wetness on my cheeks.

As fast as my anger flared, it calmed. Somehow it helped to share the burden with two other people. But despite that, the reality of the situation was beginning to settle in.

They're going to get away with this.

"Those fuckers," Fridge cussed, growling. I loved that his response echoed mine.

I chuckled as I looked up at him. "My thoughts exactly."

Fridge crossed his big, meaty arms over his chest and the corners of his lips kicked up into a smirk. "Well, Miss Williams, looks like there's only one thing for us to do, since the police are going to sit on their fat asses, doing nothing."

I walked back around the desk, shaking with adrenaline and fatigue. I righted my father's chair and sat back down. *Fucking police.*

"Oh, yeah?" I said. "What's that?"

Fridge leaned forward and planted his hands on the desk, waggling his eyebrows at me. "We need to catch the prick ourselves."

CHAPTER 16
SADIE

e need to catch the prick ourselves.

Best words I'd ever heard. Because that was exactly my plan.

I'd known, of course, that the police had little to no chance of catching the perpetrator, but to hear them so honestly, so condescendingly, give up before they'd even begun, was terrible.

They were a disgrace to good cops everywhere.

I nodded at Fridge. "Good."

Rogan shrugged and fell into one of the visitor chairs. "This is half the reason we get the private contracts in the city. Most of the time, the victim knows who's committed the crime, but the police refuse to do anything about it."

"Gotcha." My father's business was beginning to make more sense.

He got justice for people who couldn't get it through "proper" channels.

But would that make him a target?

Probably.

Now I was wishing I'd concentrated harder on learning more about the operations of the workshop when I had the chance.

"I really need to get onto sorting out the business side of things," I said. "Do we have time for you to find the contact details for the accountant today, or... what's the time?"

I glanced around the room, looking for a clock.

Rogan pulled his phone out of his hip pocket. "It's past five. They'll have gone home already, but I can email them for you. Ask them to call you first thing tomorrow."

"That'd be great. Thanks."

Rogan nodded and headed out of the office, I assumed to find a computer from which to send an email. He left Fridge and me alone.

I rested against the back of the chair, though my heart ached to reach over to him. Touch him, kiss him... feel those rough, capable hands on me.

But no. Not after last night.

"You sure you're all right after I hit you a few times?" he asked, sitting in the chair opposite me so we were more eye level.

I chuckled. "Yeah, definitely. I heal quickly. And I know you didn't hit me half as hard as you could have. You're fast, especially for such a big guy. Even my dad would have had trouble keeping up with you."

Fridge grinned. I could tell he was enjoying the compliments from the light in his eyes. "Hardly. Your dad was the only one who *could* keep up with me. Even last week, he walloped my ass in a training session."

My eyebrows rose and I crossed my arms over my chest. "I can't imagine that."

My dad was good—better than good—but he was, or had been, almost fifty-five years old. How had he stood up against a thirty-something pure dragon shifter that *he'd* trained?

Fridge nodded. "It's true. He wasn't as fast as me, but he made up for it with brute strength. Once he had you in his grip..." Fridge chuckled. "You were pretty much fucked."

I couldn't help but laugh. "Yeah, he was one tough dude."

Tougher than even I'd given him credit for, it seemed.

Fridge cleared his throat. "I've been thinking about what you said about your birthday and that..."

He trailed off. Emotional conversations were really not Fridge's thing.

"You mean about how it made him feel? The fear thing?" I guessed.

That had to be what he meant. I could easily imagine a man like Fridge having trouble connecting with people for the exact same reason. A fear of getting too close. Of losing them. Or having to leave them.

He nodded. "Yeah. I wonder how he managed it. I mean... feeling that way, but still showing up every day. Fighting. Hunting. He was your only parent, yeah?"

I smiled at the level of consideration he'd given what I'd said. "Yeah, Mom died when I was three."

Under mysterious circumstances that had never been fully explained. Not to me, anyway.

Fridge shook his head and whistled through his teeth. "Whoa... then that would have been doubly hard."

I wasn't sure exactly what Fridge meant by that.

"I guess. I mean... I never really thought about it." I'd taken the compliment of how much my dad loved me for granted.

But thinking about it now, I supposed for a man—a naturally protective man, which a dragon would be—what my dad had done must seem like an insurmountable task.

I shrugged. "Sorry, I can't really help you with that one. I never asked Dad how he overcame it. To be honest, I always assumed he hadn't. That was why he ran the workshop. Got other guys to go out and hunt instead of him."

Fridge laughed. "God, no. Is that what he told you? Your dad always took on the big cases personally. People trusted him the most. So, if you thought he was sitting pretty and safe in an office all day..." Fridge chuckled again. "You really didn't know your dad that well."

My gaze dropped to the carpet at Fridge's feet, the words hitting home much harder than he'd probably intended. *Dad had worked directly on cases himself?*

"I guess so."

It made me feel sick to my stomach, and sad, that I hadn't known my father the way I thought I had.

Or perhaps Fridge had only known that one side of him? The hard-ass wolf shifter feared by so many.

I'd known the sweet, generous, mushy side of my father that no one else had seen. And maybe that was the way it was meant to stay.

Fridge cleared his throat, coughing roughly. "I didn't mean..."

I looked up and waved my hand at the panic flitting across his face. "Oh, don't worry about it. I think I'm just tired."

And I was. May as well use it as an excuse to be emotional.

"Oh, right," he said. "Let me grab a few things, and I'll walk you home."

"That's not necessary," I said. "I can deal with most normal guys. Trust me. Especially if I have access to a knife."

And speaking of which, I need to find that nice little knife that strapped to my calf so easily. Dad put it away somewhere...

I grinned at him and he frowned.

"Rogan and I aren't leaving you alone until we've located the vamp responsible for your dad's murder. Found out why he did it and made sure you're safe. If you can't cope with that..."

I waited, wondering how he was going to finish that sentence.

Finally, he lifted his chin and stared down at me. "Then we're going to have problems."

Now he wanted to be all protective?

I threw up my hands, annoyed that the dragon who had made it perfectly clear he didn't want me in any permanent sense still wanted to do the right thing and stick by me. Quite literally. Well, I wasn't sure I could handle that. Not the way things stood between us.

I narrowed my eyes at him. "Fine. If you want to play bodyguard, I'm not going to stop you, but can't you take turns? It's not like I need both of you."

I threw the words at him, hoping they'd stick, make an impression, and screw with his head a little. His rejection still stung.

He flinched as though I'd struck him. The way his eyes practically crossed at the idea was kind of comical. "You want me to leave you and Rogan alone overnight?"

I stared at him with my eyes wide and as innocent as possible. "Would that be a problem?

It shouldn't be. Rogan was his best friend. And he'd told me he didn't believe in fated mates.

But, as Fridge's eyes flashed from green to yellow, and back again, I wondered how much of a fight his shifter was putting up.

He obviously didn't want to leave me alone with another man—even Rogan—but could he admit that?

I put a hand on my hip and tossed my head back so I could look straight at him. "Fridge? Is that a problem? Is Rogan... untrustworthy? Is there something I should know about him?"

I verbally opened the door for him to slam his friend and waited.

Surely, he'd come up with something?

Fridge opened his mouth to speak, then shut it again.

I waited some more. But nope, his lips were sealed shut.

His loyalty to Rogan, despite his obvious distaste for leaving his friend alone with me, was actually kinda admirable.

Even so, I couldn't help poking the wound a little more. I wanted him to see what was obvious. Fated mates were meant to be together. "So, I'll ask Rogan to come back to my place tonight, and we'll, what? Swap tomorrow night?"

Fridge nodded stiffly, and a strange growl rolled through the room that made me bite my lip, hard, to avoid laughter.

He turned and stomped out of the office. I had to put a hand over my mouth to stop the giggle that bubbled up.

CHAPTER 17
FRIDGE

That little witch was pushing my buttons, and she knew it, too!

Leave her and Rogan alone for two minutes? Nope. Not happening. They'd be all over each other.

Rogan wanted Sadie. That was fucking obvious. And she wanted him. Also obvious.

Who wouldn't, after all? Sadie was hot as hell, and my best friend was a good guy. I should be happy for them. They had found each other and now they could be happy.

Why did I have such a problem with that?

I knew I shouldn't. They were both consenting adults.

I'd had my chance and said no. But I couldn't meet her terms. I just couldn't.

Fuck!

What the hell was I going to do, by myself, at our apartment tonight?

Call someone out of my little black book?

Get drunk and hope to pass out?

Damn my pride.

This is going to be hell.

105

CHAPTER 18
SADIE

amn.

Fridge was clearly so jealous he could barely see straight. But was it because he didn't like the idea of me being with anyone else? Or was it because it was Rogan?

I suppose I'd have to wait and find out.

I glanced around the room, tidied up a little then grabbed the keys to leave.

I didn't know what I was going to do tonight, but I was sure I could distract myself enough.

Hopefully.

I closed my dad's office door and headed down the stairs.

Most of the men had cleared out and there was a strange eeriness to the nearly empty building now, without the hum of talking and action everywhere.

A wave of gratitude for my over-protective shifter men washed over me.

The truth was, I would hate to go home to an empty apartment tonight. To have to see my father's things, the memories and pain of his loss ghosting me at every turn.

I knew I'd have to deal with his death properly sooner or later, but for the moment I was doing okay by mostly avoiding thinking about it.

Mostly, thanks to Rogan and Fridge. They hadn't left me alone since I'd found his body. Not truly alone. I'd been in bed by myself, but they'd been so close by, I could feel their presence.

Luckily, there hadn't been a chance for depression to creep up on me. My grief was shared, understood and empathized.

And thanks to the same men, I wouldn't be alone tonight, either. Not in my apartment, and perhaps not in my bed, if Rogan had his way.

We would have to see...

My wolf shifter genes thought Rogan was attractive, and a perfect mate. He was a wolf, and it felt natural.

But there was also something about Fridge. His strength, his wildness, made my most basic instincts sit up and take notice. No matter that he was a dragon. My genes thought he was just as perfect a mate for me as Rogan.

Footsteps approached from my right, and the two men I had just been thinking about stepped into the foyer.

"Ready to go?" I asked, though neither of them looked happy.

Fridge's arms were crossed over his chest and Rogan's frown could sink battleships.

"What's wrong with you two?"

Rogan's gaze flicked to Fridge and back again to me. "We've... had a disagreement about the sleeping arrangements."

I pressed my lips together in an attempt not to smile. From the scowl the dragon gave me, I don't think I succeeded in hiding my humor at the situation. "Um... what do you mean? Isn't Rogan going to come back and sleep in the spare bedroom again?"

I'd kind of assumed that was the plan. Well, what would be openly admitted to, anyway.

Fridge and Rogan exchanged glances, but neither spoke.

I gestured for them to step outside. "Well, I've gotta lock up. So, you guys sort it out while I check the doors, and I'll see you out front in a moment."

Without a word, they stepped out onto the sidewalk.

I shook my head as I walked around the building, turning off lights, locking the doors and activating alarms.

I'd barely had a proper boyfriend since high school. A few nights here and there, a few men who'd wanted to date, only to find that I had my own mind, could take care of myself, and that my father was... well, my father.

He'd scared off anyone I thought had potential so quickly it had been disappointing to see how little spine they'd actually had.

A wave of sadness passed over me for what Dad was now missing.

I'd found my fated mates. The ones I'd been told existed somewhere, since I was young. But if I were honest, I'd never really thought I *would* find them... and my dad wasn't here to enjoy that fact with me.

Would he have tried to scare these two off, knowing them as he did? Would he have approved of me dating another bounty hunter? Or two?

I chuckled. Two men. *Me!*

Who would have thought it?

When I finally made it to the front door, I checked I had everything I needed, locked up, set the final alarm and stepped outside.

The guys were standing there, scowling at one another.

So much for sorting it out.

I turned to Fridge. "So... should I say goodnight? Or are you coming back to the apartment as well?"

Could he bear to leave me alone with Rogan?

I couldn't wait to find out what he'd do.

Rogan stepped up next to me, his hand sliding possessively

around my waist. "He's heading home. There's no need for both of us to guard you."

"Well, maybe I should take first watch," Fridge said, lifting his chin and jutting it out in a flagrant display of alpha arrogance. "I am the stronger one, after all."

I chuckled and waved my hand at Fridge. "It's all good. I'll see you tomorrow. Thanks for all your help today, and the workout."

I grinned and turned to leave with Rogan. "You ready?"

Rogan nodded and we strode away from the dragon I could feel glowering behind us.

"What's his problem?" I asked Rogan, gesturing over my shoulder with my thumb.

As if I didn't know. *Why do I need Rogan to say it out loud?*

Rogan shrugged, thrusting both hands into his pockets and continuing to walk beside me. "He won't admit to it, but he's jealous. He wants you all to himself."

I frowned. I knew Fridge was jealous, but I assumed it was because he couldn't decide what he wanted and wanted to keep his options open. Not that he actually *did* want me.

I snorted. "He could have fooled me."

Rogan glanced sideways at me and asked gently, "What happened between you two last night?"

I sighed. "He didn't tell you?"

That's disappointing.

I'd hoped Fridge would open up to Rogan, so that I could at least get a straight answer from *someone*.

"No. He won't say a thing."

We crossed a street and kept walking. The night was clear, and the roads were almost empty. It was amazingly peaceful for a time just after most businesses had closed.

Rogan gave me another sideways glance. "You gonna tell me?"

"Well, simply..." How could I explain it? I reached up and rubbed the ache behind my temple. "Ah, shit. Well, his dragon wanted to kiss me, and mate with me... I think. He didn't actually say anything, of course, but he went all shifter-like. His eyes, the growl. Everything. But the moment I mentioned the fated mate bond, he totally recoiled. I don't know why he hated me saying that."

I shrugged. I didn't want it to appear like I was still smarting from Fridge's rejection. But it had hurt, more than it should have, probably.

And after today, the training and the cuddles when I needed them the most, I'd seen more sides to the big dragon, and that had made me want him even more.

CHAPTER 19

ROGAN

I clenched my jaw to stop the expletives that sat on the end of my tongue.

Why did Fridge have to make everything so goddamn hard?

He wanted Sadie, and she wanted him, and I was happy to make us one big family.

So why did the dragon shifter have to fight us every step of the way?

I knew why, of course. His past. His parents.

And as I walked next to the woman I wanted as my mate, I wondered how much I should tell her. How much I should share about Fridge. It was his story, at the end of the day, but if it helped her understand Fridge better, then maybe it was worth it, to tell her.

It had taken me decades to pry the information from Fridge's insane grip.

Sadie squeezed my hand and smiled up at me and my mind was made up.

I was going to tell her everything, because she was going to need every bit of ammunition to make the big man submit to the call of Fate.

CHAPTER 20
SADIE

Rogan frowned at me, his mouth tilting down on both sides. "So, you're saying you wanted to mate with Fridge. But he rejected you?"

My mouth fell open. *I didn't say exactly that, did I?*

I shook my head. "No... I didn't say any such thing. You're both my fated mates. I've been honest and open about that from the beginning. But that isn't a choice."

Rogan grimaced. "Yeah, being a fated mate isn't a choice." He kicked at a raised concrete slab and continued walking. "That's Fridge's problem, I think."

We stopped outside my building and I used my access card to get in. "What do you mean?"

Did Fridge seriously have a problem with the lack of *choice* having a fated mate gave him? Why was that a bad thing? It prevented confusion and unnecessary pain. Divorce. Heartbreak.

Fate literally served up your perfect person—or two—on a silver platter.

We walked into the foyer and Rogan indicated to the stairs. "Let's get inside, set up some dinner, and I'll tell you about the dragon and his history."

I studied him, and then nodded. I had a friend in this man, and I loved that.

Wolf shifters were notoriously pack men, in both hunting traits and the way they formed tight-knit family units. My dad had been the same. Loyal to a fault, and often too honest for his own good.

We walked up the stairs and for a moment there was a flutter of panic in my chest, far too close to my heart. Was this going to be like last night, when we'd come back to find my home had been ransacked?

But this time, when I reached the foyer outside my apartment, the door was still locked. And it looked like no one had been here since we'd left this morning.

I put the key in the door. "Why is it oddly comforting to come home to a door that's actually locked?"

Rogan frowned. "Because those bastards were here last night. But thank God you weren't."

I opened the door, though my heart still pounded way too hard.

I let us both inside, then locked the door again.

Then his words hit me. What if I'd come home early? What if I'd taken the Uber or a taxi rather than walking? What if...

"I hadn't thought about that." If I hadn't planned to go past Dad's place. Hadn't found him...

If I'd come home and been confronted by the vampire, I could be dead, too.

I swallowed hard against the rise of emotions that clogged my throat.

"You might have been here when they came looking for whatever they were looking for," Rogan finished the thought for me aloud. "Oh, don't worry—I've thought about it."

He shuddered, as though horrified by the idea.

I went straight to the kitchen, determined not to play the "what if" game. That never got anyone anything other than depressed, annoyed, or completely devastated.

Nope. Not doing it.

Food. We needed food.

What did we have to eat? Dad kept the kitchen well stocked, but I did most of the cooking.

I opened the fridge and did a quick appraisal. "You want steak, salad and fries?"

Rogan's eyebrows flickered up. "Sure, if you've got everything. We can always order Uber Eats again."

I shook my head. "Nah. I think we both need a good meal. And don't worry, the fridge has enough for ten people."

I turned on the oven, threw fries on a tray, and got the stovetop going to grill the steaks.

"So… tell me about Fridge," I said, as I got the plates ready and seasoned the rib-eyes.

Rogan slid onto one of the bar stools on the other side of the kitchen counter and sighed. "There's a lot to tell."

I gestured to the empty room. "I've got all night."

And I did.

Other than going through some of the files in my dad's office, I had no other plans. And since the bad guys had left behind everything they didn't think was valuable, I wasn't sure how important anything in that room was.

"Well, how much do you know about dragon shifters?" Rogan asked.

I shrugged. "Not a huge amount. I mean… who does? They're so rare."

Rogan nodded. "Especially pure ones."

Definitely.

I leaned forward and rested on my forearms across the kitchen counter. "How is that even possible? I didn't think there were any pure dragons left, let alone two who would breed together."

As a general rule, most shifters believed in mixing up the bloodlines, taking strong characteristics from several different shifter varieties and throwing in a human to make everything look more normal.

There were the occasional shifters who had the Hitler mentality of purity over strength, but they were rare nowadays.

Rogan's face twisted. "I think that's where the trouble started. From what I've gathered, Fridge's parents were forced to mate and had quite a few children for the sake of their bloodline."

Fuck.

I nodded, my chest tightening. "I've heard of such things in the past, but I didn't realize it was still happening."

But it made a strange sort of sense. After all, we did the same thing with animals all the time. When only a few remained of an endangered species, the best conservancies and zoos in the world made sure they got together and started to reproduce.

It was the only way to make sure a bloodline didn't become extinct.

Rogan huffed out a sigh. "Yeah... so anyway, Fridge grew up in a pretty fucked-up environment, I think. An exceptionally strong dad, a submissive mother. Not exactly what you'd call natural parents. Neither of them wanted to be in the relationship at all, let alone produce that many offspring."

"Then why'd they do it?" I asked.

Surely there could have been another way.

He shrugged. "Fridge said something once about them being forced to stay together by the few elders who were left. That wouldn't happen in a wolf pack, of course, but dragon hierarchy can be different."

I nodded. I didn't know enough to comment about dragon laws. When I had time, it was the first thing I was going to research.

"Okay. So, what's that got to do with me?" Although I appreciated knowing more about the man I was probably going to spend my life with, I needed to know what his childhood had to do with him rejecting me.

Rogan ran a hand through his dark, curly hair. "So, Fridge has... issues about being forced into a relationship that isn't of his choosing. He was miserable growing up, and so were his parents. He's always said he'd rather be alone than live with someone who was only with him because she had to be."

I stood up straight, frowning at the logic. "That doesn't make sense."

His parents weren't fated mates. They couldn't have been, or they would have been happy.

For all I knew, they could have been two complete strangers who were forced to marry and have a dozen children.

That would not have worked for ninety percent of the population, especially not two rare shifters who could have had anyone they wanted.

Rogan shrugged. "It makes sense to Fridge."

I opened my mouth to rebut the point, then stopped. There was no sense getting into a fight with Rogan over this. It was Fridge I had to approach to sort things out. But how?

I had to think for a minute, so I went to the oven, checked on the fries, put together two small salads, and decided to start cooking the steaks. I put the frying pan on the flame, sprayed it with some oil and salt, and laid the red steaks down to sizzle.

They didn't take long to prepare, so I got out drinks and cutlery, then served up our dinner at the dining table as soon as it was ready.

"Wow. That looks great, thanks." Rogan's face lit up as I placed a plate in front of him of similar proportions I would have done for my father.

Twice what any normal man would eat.

"No problem."

I sat down with him at the table, and we ate in pleasant silence. Once I'd gotten half the steak into my belly, I looked up, my head clearing as my body started feeling the effects of the fuel I was eating.

"Let me see if I've gotten this straight," I said. "Fridge had a shit childhood."

Something I couldn't really empathize with.

Yes, my mother had died when I was three years old, a trauma most people would count as absolutely life-altering. But I barely remembered her, and my father had done such a good job of raising me, I really couldn't complain.

"So, he... what?" I continued. "Doesn't want a mate? Or is it me in particular he doesn't want?"

I was sure a man like Fridge would want a wife long-term. And children.

So, what was his problem?

Lots of people had crappy parents, shit childhoods. I'd met dozens of them.

But that didn't put them off relationships forever.

Rogan shook his head while he swallowed his food. "Oh, it's not you. Quite the opposite. I know he wants you."

"How?" *Other than the obvious, possessive caveman crap?*

Rogan ate some more steak and grinned. "Well, you're like... everything he's ever wanted in a female. Beautiful, tough, smart."

I resisted the urge to roll my eyes. That sounded like a list from some dating app. "Well, thanks. But that's hardly a reason to want someone."

Rogan shrugged. "He's a simple guy. But he's always wanted to fall in love naturally. Slowly. This situation is his worst nightmare. Lots of adrenaline and danger forcing us all to make stupid decisions. Instant attraction, and then your outright acceptance of a fated mate link." Rogan chuckled. "Fridge's head is, well—"

"Conflicted?" I finished for him.

Rogan laughed. "Fucked. Totally fucked."

Of course, it was. Why couldn't it just be simple?

I got up from my chair at the dining table and walked over to my dad's liquor cabinet, which stood against the wall opposite the kitchen. It was well-stocked, to say the least.

I opened the door and grabbed the vodka. It was time for a drink.

I held out the bottle of un-opened spirits. "Join me? Or if you want bourbon or whatever... Dad had everything."

"Vodka's great. Straight."

I nodded, grabbed some glasses Dad kept on the top shelf of his cabinet, and poured. I gave Rogan his drink straight. Dad had preferred his like that, too.

He tossed back a double shot, and I poured him another.

I gave myself a double, added a splash of orange juice from the fridge, then drank it. Fast.

"Argh..." I winced as the fire-water slid down my throat. More juice in the next one.

I was still standing next to the table with one hand on my hip and the other wrapped around the vodka bottle, staring down at my wolf shifter mate.

He leaned back and stretched out his legs in front of him as though he had all the time in the world.

I set the bottle down. "So, let me get this straight. Because I was honest, and admitted that I felt the fated mate pull, I've probably doomed my relationship with Fridge?"

What a fucked-up way of punishing me for being open with him.

Rogan frowned. "No, not forever. Once all the other stuff settles down, I'm sure he'll be better."

"You mean, all the murder stuff?" I asked, raising an eyebrow.

Was the "my father was murdered" stress ever going to be over? I didn't think so. And even then, it wasn't like a life with two bounty hunters as mates was ever going to be *quiet.*

Rogan threw back his second double shot. "Yeah."

I poured us both another drink and sat down in the chair closest to him.

"Okay, bear with me. Fridge hates the fact that we're fated mates—but we are, there's no question there for me. And although he's being an ass, you think he's into me."

"Yep."

I snorted. "So, if I was a normal girl he'd met at a bar, or in the street, he'd be fine with me."

"As long as you didn't proclaim to be his fated mate, yeah, pretty much."

I growled through clenched teeth, my shifter genetics riling me up. "That is so wrong! His parents weren't fated. Does he even know what it means? It means we are perfect for one another. That we will be miserable if we're *not* together."

I drank my vodka and juice, enjoying the wave of intoxication that was beginning to swell in my bloodstream.

But I wasn't done. "His reasoning is screwed up. Seriously. Doesn't he realize that being fated mates is awesome? We don't have to second-guess anything. We don't have to worry that we'll be faithful, or our love will last. We are *made* for each other."

I shook my head and reached for the vodka bottle. We'd drunk half of it already, and I didn't care.

I'd drink the whole bottle with Rogan tonight if it meant dulling down the ache in my chest. The pain in my head. The anger in my gut.

Bloody dragon.

I poured us both another drink that was way more than a double, sat back in my chair, and stared at my glass.

Why had I told him?

I should have pretended it was just a physical attraction and kept my mouth shut.

"What about me?" Rogan said quietly.

I glanced up. "What about you?"

He rolled the tumbler glass between his hands, from one palm to the other. "Do you believe that about us, too? Or just Fridge?"

I groaned. *Shit.* I hadn't even thought about how Rogan would feel hearing me vent about Fridge.

Mental note. Just because this guy is going to become your best friend in the whole world, does not mean he doesn't want to be treated like he's your reason for existing, just as much as Fridge is.

I stood up, stumbled forward, and sat down on his lap.

The alcohol had definitely gone to my head. My legs were slightly shaky and there was a strange, hot, zing of awareness along my arms and legs.

Perfect.

I finished the rest of my drink, then placed it on the table before I put my arms around Rogan's neck.

"Are you wondering how I feel about you, my wolf?" I asked, smiling up at him.

His hands slid around my waist and his gaze shifted, his gorgeous blue eyes sliding into a silver.

"Of course, I am," he said, shuffling us both as he sat up straighter in his chair. "I know I'm not a dragon shifter, but I still want you. In every way. Fated mate, or not."

I ran my fingers up the back of his neck and tangled them in the hair on the back of his head, cupping his skull.

"You're my fated mate as well, Rogan. I knew it the moment I saw you. Don't you feel it, too?"

His eyes went wide. "I do. But... how is that possible?"

I shrugged. "I don't know. But my dad always joked that it would take more than one man to handle me. I didn't believe him, of course. In fact, as I'm only a quarter wolf, I wasn't sure I'd have a fated mate at all. I was quite settled on the fact that I'd have a normal marriage."

"So, your parents weren't fated mates?" he asked.

I ran my nails through his hair, over and over again, and he arched into my caress.

I tilted my head to the side. "No, I don't think so. My dad never referred to my mom in that way, and I was too young when she died to have heard it from her."

Though, it wasn't impossible. After all, my father had never moved on after she died. Few people had that sort of devotion unless they'd lost their fated mate.

"Then how do you know so much about it?" he asked, then dropped his head, putting his face into my neck and breathing deep.

Desire began to spiral inside my veins, my eyes closing on a wave of lust. "Ah... my mother's family. My dad's uncle. They all talked about it. Explained to me how it would feel."

Rogan lifted his head so that his lips were near my ear. I dug my fingers into his shoulders and clung to his heat, wanting him as close to me as possible.

"How do you feel, Sadie? Tell me."

I shivered, moaning at the intense heat pulsing through my body. He was so close, so kissable. If I just...

"Tell me, beautiful girl. How does the fated mate bond feel to you?"

I tried to open my eyes, but I couldn't. The alcohol was keeping my limbs heavy and my eyes closed.

"Like an addiction," I said, swallowing hard as I fought against the need to give him the full truth. The alcohol, unfortunately, lowered all inhibitions. "Like I need you, want you, crave you. I want you to fight me... fuck me. I want you in every part of my life, and I never want you to leave me."

He groaned in my ear. One hand went down to cup my ass and the other came up to grab my cheek.

He guided my face toward his and our lips finally met. I gasped at the heat of his touch, the perfection of his mouth on mine.

And when he pressed deeper and swept his tongue through my mouth, I melted into a puddle.

The doorbell rang. We sprang apart like a couple of teenagers caught on prom night.

Rogan frowned, glancing toward the sound. "Who..."

There was a loud pounding on the door that could mean only one thing.

The dragon was here.

CHAPTER 21
SADIE

I looked into Rogan's eyes as they changed back from silver to blue, and grinned. "Do you think if we ignore him, he'll go away?"

More banging on the door ensued and Fridge growled. "I can hear you, you know."

I laughed loudly. "Oh, my God. How good is his hearing?"

I really needed to do some research on dragons.

"About as good as it gets," Rogan said.

"So, we can't ignore him. Okay, fine." I staggered out of Rogan's lap and made my way to the front door, which unfortunately was too far away for me at this point in time.

Too much to drink. I giggled when I couldn't walk in a straight line, and I couldn't resist a little teasing.

"Who is it?" I called out, and there was a deep, growled response.

"We don't need any!" I entertained myself by laughing while trying desperately to stay upright.

God, this lightheartedness feels good.

My arms and legs were so loose and tingly, I was pretty sure I had more vodka in my bloodstream than actual blood.

"Sadie! Open this door now, before I kick it in."

"I'd like to see you try!" That door was reinforced with steel. Even a dragon wouldn't get through it.

Fridge went silent and fear tickled along my spine. He wouldn't really try to knock it down, would he?

He'd hurt himself!

"Okay!" I called. "I'm coming. Hold your horses!"

I took three more steps, fell against the door, and somehow managed to unlock each of the locks.

I leaned to the side just as the door burst open.

I peered around the edge of the door to see Fridge, who looked like a Viking on the war path.

His hands were clenched into tight fists. His arm muscles bulged like they'd doubled in size, and his usually green eyes were bright yellow.

Yikes.

"Hey," I said, and he twisted around to stare at me, his gaze skimming me from head to toe and back again.

I knew what he was thinking. That Rogan and I should have started by now.

"What's wrong?" I asked. "Disappointed I'm not naked yet?"

I still wore the clothes I'd had on all day, and although I'd taken my hair out of the ponytail at some point, I didn't look much different than when he'd seen me an hour ago.

He'd been expecting a fight and had prepared for one.

But now he was deflating. Literally.

His bulky muscles were relaxing, his clenched hands were unfurling, and he was shrinking in size before my eyes.

Now that is impressive.

"Can you please come in so I can lock the door again?" I asked, wondering how I was going to make it back to the chair under my own steam.

My legs did not want to keep me upright.

Fridge stepped into the room, still keeping his gaze locked on mine. "Can you?"

I giggled. Tomorrow I'd be mortified at all this giggling. Tonight I couldn't seem to stop. "I'd rather you do it."

Without a word, he shut the door, carefully, and locked it up.

I continued to lean against the wall, enjoying the emptiness of my mind after a truly screwed-up couple of days.

Once he was done locking us in, Fridge looked at me, one eyebrow raised. "What's wrong with you? You smell... different."

I shrugged. I knew he could probably smell my arousal—I mean, with these two in the room, it was impossible for me not to be turned on—but he may not be able to sense the level of it, amidst the steak and booze.

"Vodka. You want some?"

He seemed to relax even more, as though he was glad there was a good reason for my ridiculous behavior.

"I don't drink vodka much."

I pushed myself to my feet and managed to stagger to the liquor cabinet.

"Well, Dad had the best of everything. Whatcha want?" I indicated to the shelf loaded down with bottles. "Tequila? Rum?"

Fridge crept forward slowly. "I'm not sure I should..."

"Pah!" I said, swiping a hand at him and grabbing another shot glass from inside the cabinet. "Join in or piss off, 'cause I'm not stopping. If there was ever an excuse to drink, it's the night after you find your father murdered."

Fridge nodded, as though my point made perfect sense to him. "Okay. Tequila."

"Ha!" I pointed at him and grabbed the bottle of clear liquor. "Here you go." I tossed the shot glass at him, which he luckily caught because it wasn't a good throw, and I managed to get the bottle to him without dropping it.

Then I went back and fell into Rogan's lap, twisting my arms around his neck before looking back at Fridge.

I tried to keep a totally neutral voice when I said, "So, what brings you here this evening?"

Not that I don't already know.

He didn't answer, but instead set the shot glass down, filled it to the brim, and tossed it back like a pro.

Oh, so it's like that, is it?

"Can you make me another drink, Rogan?" I asked my wolf, who nodded, and then leaned forward to mix some more juice and vodka.

"Did you eat dinner?" I asked Fridge. "There's another steak left in the fridge if you can be bothered cooking it. I'm past it now."

Rogan handed me my drink.

"Oh, thank you."

I sipped and watched Fridge down shot, after shot, after shot.

"Hey, where's the fire?" I asked with a grin. "You in a hurry?"

He did two more shots without looking at me. I glanced down at the table and saw that almost half the bottle was gone.

I gaped at him. Even my dad would have been impressed with that tolerance.

Finally, he sat down at the other end of the table, as far away from me and Rogan as he could get in the small space, and stared at both of us.

The intensity in his eyes, in his face, took my breath away. Not the shifter in him, the human side. He looked open, vulnerable, hurt almost.

Wow.

"I don't want to be left out," he finally said.

I glanced over at Rogan who was looking almost as confused as I felt.

"Left out of... what?" I asked.

I knew if I'd been less drunk, I might have been able to interpret him better, but my eyes were heavy, as were all my limbs. And my brain was on a go-slow.

After everything else he'd said and done, I couldn't quite work out why Fridge was here.

He lifted his hands and made a circling motion at us, like we were meant to get that.

I giggled, and drank a little more, pouring another double for Rogan, encouraging him to do the same thing. "Drink up."

Then I glanced at Fridge, who was still drinking tequila at the other end of the table. "Look, bud, you are either gonna have to spell it out, or get to finishing that bottle and hope it loosens your tongue. Me? I'm getting the next one."

Rogan and I had finished the vodka, and there was another in the cupboard below the main liquor bottle area where Dad kept the overflow stash.

I stumbled, dropping to my knees and then figured I might as well stay down. I crawled across the floor.

But before I got to the cupboard, strong arms scooped me up and I was suddenly in Fridge's lap as he sat back down at the table.

This time, he sat in the middle, closer to Rogan.

"I think that's enough for the minute. Yeah?" he asked.

I wasn't sure I agreed with him, but since he was holding me, I didn't complain. Instead, I entwined my arms around his neck, settled into his lap, and let the alcohol already in my system do its job.

I looked up at him, though he wasn't looking at me. He was staring straight ahead as though the answer to life was written on one of the apartment walls.

My belly tightened and lust wove through me as I gazed at him. Damn, he was a fine-looking man.

"So... Fridge," I began, trying not to slur. "What are you doing here? Really. It's not your night."

His jaw muscles bulged as he clenched his teeth and his hands slid around my waist, holding me tight.

"It was a stupid idea to have alternating nights." He growled. "We should both be here with you."

Oh... that's your excuse, huh?

"Really?" I asked as I twirled my fingers in his short blond hair and inhaled his sexy scent. "Why?"

"Because it's safer that way," he said.

I frowned. "I think you need more to drink. You're not relaxed enough. Or honest enough."

I tried to get out of his lap, planting my feet on the ground and pushing up and away from him. I didn't get far.

He held me by the waist so that I barely moved, apparently with very little effort.

"No. Stay," he ground out.

I narrowed my eyes at him. "Tell me why you're here. Now, and quickly. Or you can go home, and Rogan will stay here. With me."

I didn't want to say that I was going to drag Rogan to bed with me, if I could talk the wolf shifter into it. Which, before Fridge had arrived, had been looking quite favorable.

Fridge's hands gripped my waist, moving over my hips and belly in strange, agitated movements. But the way he gripped me also spoke of possession, and that was the main reason I stilled in his lap.

I wanted to be his, but equally, I wanted him to be mine.

"I can't... sit at home, wondering what's going on over here," he admitted.

Well, that's a start.

I stroked his neck and shoulders.

"Why? Because you think we're in trouble?" I cocked my head to the side. "Or because you think we're fucking without you?"

Fridge flinched like I'd hit him and snorted out his nose like a horse.

I rolled my eyes. "Well?"

He shook his head as though he couldn't, or wouldn't answer, and my blood began to boil. In my current state, I didn't have the patience or the time for this level of coyness.

If half a bottle of tequila couldn't loosen his lips, then something had to.

I twisted in his lap and hit both his shoulders with my open palms, then gripped his huge muscles. My head was clearing, and my anger pulsed through me now.

"Listen. You're the one who rejected me! You don't get to tell me who I can and can't be with."

I struggled against his arms and this time he let me go.

But I didn't go to Rogan, who was staying silent and letting me deal with the dragon. Instead, both of us seemed to know I had to face Fridge on my own in this moment.

Despite the alcohol and heat in my blood, I was standing a little better now, bolstered by my fury.

Fridge stood up, slowly, moving with the dangerous grace that only a trained killer possessed. Any other time I would have found it sexy as hell, but now I was just infuriated.

"So, let me repeat my question. What the fuck are you doing here? And what do you want?"

Fridge's eyes burned with a heat I recognized, and it wasn't anger. "I want *you*."

I groaned and threw my hands in the air. Why did it make me want to lose my mind even more to hear those words?

"Actually, you've made it perfectly clear that you *don't* want me. That you reject the idea of us being mates."

Fridge interrupted. "I never said that. I don't believe in fated crap. I don't want to feel forced into this. I don't want you to feel obligated to stay with me if it doesn't work. I just want this to be... natural."

"Natural?" On some level I understood what he was saying. But on another, it didn't make sense to me. What could be *more* natural than fated mates?

With my confidence bolstered by the vodka still running through my veins, I stripped off my black sweater, then threw my purple tank to the floor.

Next was my boring sports bra, my breasts bouncing in the cool air as I discarded the cumbersome thing. "You think this isn't natural? To be aching so much. To have my nipples on fire. To be so wet I'm sliding off the seat just being close to you two! That's what being fated means. There's nothing more natural."

I was panting and growling with the effort it took to speak, and if I thought I could remove my shoes and pants without falling on my head, then I'd be fully naked in an instant.

Rogan's hands came around me from behind, distracting me from my frustration.

His palms slid against the hot skin of my belly, then cupped my breasts, his lips at my neck, breathing hard against me.

I closed my eyes and let my head fall back, enjoying the touch so much more than I expected.

More than I had ever enjoyed anyone touching me before.

Pleasure poured through me as he tweaked my nipples, rolling the aching flesh with his fingers.

"Please..." I whispered.

"Please what?" Rogan asked.

"Take me to bed. Please." I didn't care what he did to me while we were there, as long as he kept touching me.

He didn't move right away, like I expected him to. What other invitation did he need?

I opened my eyes, turned around, and took his hand so that I could pull him down the hallway. Did he need a personal tour?

He didn't move even when I tugged at him.

"What about Fridge?" he asked.

My gaze flicked to the dragon standing stoically a few feet behind us.

Was he waiting for a personal invitation? Because from the bulge in his jeans, it was fucking obvious he wanted to join in.

"Do you want him to join us?" Rogan added.

I bit my lip, not wanting to expose how deeply I craved them both, but also not wanting to lie. Not now.

"Of course, I do." I flicked my gaze at Fridge and directed my words to him. "But I would never force you to do anything you didn't want."

Fridge took several steps forward, his eyes glowing with the yellow of his shifter. "Are you sure you want *me*, and not some illusion you've conjured up?"

I couldn't help the tiny giggle that escaped my throat. If only he knew how accurate that was to my secret bloodline.

"I'm only a quarter shifter—you're a pure blood," I said. "If there's anyone who's going to be most affected by a fated mate bond, it's you. Not me."

I swallowed, the words sinking in hard. Perhaps that was the problem?

How hard was Fridge fighting against the natural need to bond with me?

I stuck my chin in the air. "I'm just brave enough to admit it. Are you?"

He glanced away. "There's something there, I know, but I can't..." He looked back at me. "Don't make me name it yet. Please."

And with those words, and the pleading tone that accompanied them, he stole my heart.

How bad had his parents' partnership really been?

I held out my free hand, encouraging him to join us. "Okay, no labels. For now."

He nodded once and reached for my hand, our pact sealed. As our hands connected, a shiver coursed through my spine, the magic in my veins sealing our connection further.

Damn, this is going to be the death of me.

I swallowed hard.

Now it was time to show them how much I truly needed them. Both of them.

I swallowed hard against the huge lump in my throat. She was right, of course. I could feel something—a need to mate with her so strong that it practically strangled me.

But I couldn't give it the same name she did.

This was lust, desire, obsession.

All things I could control. Things I could feel, without being overwhelmed by them. Without any pressure for the future.

But God... how I wanted her. Enough to share her with Rogan. Enough to want any little bit she'd give me.

Tonight. And maybe tomorrow too...

CHAPTER 23

SADIE

I tugged on both my men's hands toward my bedroom, then let them go so I could saunter down the hallway. Knowing that they were following me.

I wanted them and they wanted me.

I pushed open my door, flicked off my shoes, and began pushing my yoga pants off my hips, but they got stuck. I didn't have the coordination to pull them down.

I almost toppled onto the bed as I staggered forward, wanting to be naked.

"Help!" I called out, then deliberately twisted around and fell onto the bed, on my back, laughing. "I can't get my pants off."

Fridge loomed over me, staring down like I was the only thing left on the plate and he was starving. His eyes were dark pools of desire.

I swallowed hard, my heart pounding faster as I inhaled the scent of him above me. Then, *thank the heavens above*, he began to peel my leather pants down my thighs.

Inch by inch he rolled them, dropping kisses on the skin of my thighs with his hot mouth as he went.

He pushed the pants down to my ankles, then leaned forward and pressed his lips to my belly. I quivered as he kissed the material over my throbbing clit. Finally, he tugged once more, and my pants gave way, sliding off my legs and allowing the cool air to caress my heated flesh.

He stood up, throwing the pants into the corner of the room, and stared down at me.

I groaned aloud.

"Thank you! That feels so much better!" I launched to my feet, my head clearer now. I grabbed Fridge by the shirt and stared up into his gorgeous green eyes. "Why are you still dressed?"

His lips kicked up on either side. "Would you like me to change that?"

"Hell, yes! I want to see you naked."

From practically the first moment I'd set eyes on Fridge, I'd wanted to see what lay beneath his shirt. Then last night, I'd seen him in nothing more than his underwear and I'd wanted to touch him *so badly.*

But I'd been blocked—by Fridge and his insecurities.

Not anymore.

I turned to Rogan who was standing beside the bed, running my gaze up and down the gorgeous shifter. "You, too. Please."

I moved back and sat on the edge of my bed so that I could watch my men—my fated mates—strip down to nothing. Their cargo pants and shirts fell away to reveal the most beautiful bodies I'd ever seen.

Fridge was bigger and broader than Rogan. In every way. Even his cock, which was already lengthened and standing up like a compass needle pointing home, was thicker.

But that didn't detract from the pure wolf-like beauty of Rogan. He was built for speed, stealth. And his cock was beautiful, a deep pink shaft with a blushing red helmet.

"You two are..." I shook my head as I shuffled back on the bed. "Absolutely beautiful."

I didn't know how else to express it.

Rogan prowled toward the bed, knelt on the mattress, and pushed me back so that he could lay down next to me. "You're the one who's beautiful, Sadie."

He slid his hand over my waist, then up to the peak of my breast, cupping the flesh there.

I arched into his touch, wanting to be closer to him.

I reached for his arms and pulled him into me.

"Please kiss—"

His lips were on mine before I'd finished the sentence.

I groaned, wrapping my arms around his neck and pulling him over on top of me. I wanted his weight on me, the heat of his body pressing me down into the mattress.

He pulled back to kiss my throat, my neck, then trailed his wet mouth down to my breasts.

I gasped and arched up when his lips wrapped around the tight peak of my nipple, then I opened my eyes, looking for my dragon and wanting him with us.

Would he still be there? Had he stayed even though Rogan and I had started without him?

He stood by the bed, his cock weeping pearly pre-cum from the slit in its head.

I smiled up at him, happiness flowing through me. "Come here. I want to suck you."

He didn't speak, but he crawled across the bed and knelt next to my head.

I gasped as Rogan continued to love on my breasts. His lips and fingers kneaded my flesh and tweaked the tips, causing arrows of pleasure to shoot through my belly.

Then he slipped his hand into my panties, using his talented fingers to circle my clit and push my arousal higher.

A groan escaped me as I reached for Fridge's cock. I wrapped my hand around the shaft and tugged, bringing him closer.

Fridge fell forward, landing in a push-up position over the top of me, so he could feed his cock into my mouth.

Perfect.

I groaned as Rogan slipped a long finger deep inside me at the same time as my lips wrapped around the head of Fridge's cock.

Oh, my God.

Bliss and sensation buffeted me from every angle. I had Rogan playing my body like an expert musician, while saliva gathered in my mouth at Fridge's delicious taste.

His flavor was pure perfection, salty and male and hot. A hint of caramel, too, somehow.

I moved one hand on his shaft while I sucked and nipped at his flesh.

Rogan removed his talented, tormenting hands from inside my panties, then slid down my body. He pulled my underwear off so that I was soon as naked as they were.

He pulled me down the bed, and I had to let go of Fridge's shaft.

I groaned in enjoyment as I was moved around, loving the fact these guys were strong enough to manhandle me in such a way.

Then Rogan pulled up my thighs, opening me right up, and positioned himself between them.

I moaned loudly as his hot flesh pressed against my slick folds and I felt his cock line up with my opening.

If only he would...

I arched my back, but nothing changed. I was still open, empty, and aching. He was hesitating, but I couldn't wait. Not this time. I wrapped my legs around his waist, tilting up my hips until I felt his cock head slip into the perfect position.

Then I grabbed his ass, grinned up at him, and pulled him into me.

That first entry almost made me pass out. The intensity of pleasure was way too intense for me to feel all at once. Darkness danced on the edges of my vision, threatening to take me.

Magic pulsed through my core, as though every cell I owned claimed Rogan as my mate. My whole body sang with pure happiness.

This was my first true connection with my mate. My wolf. The man who'd never once rejected me. The one who truly understood how much I needed him already.

Lights flashed inside my head as he pulled back and thrust in to the hilt, filling me completely. I gasped, barely able to breathe.

He grabbed my ass with both hands and fell on me, his groan ringing in my ears as he flexed his hips and thrust into me again.

This time I stopped breathing, biting into his shoulder as my whole body swept into an orgasm.

I couldn't stop it.

My pussy rippled around his cock and in response, he began to pound into me, riding the waves of my pleasure over and over until he exploded inside of me.

The pulsations inside me sent me into another round of orgasms, gentler this time, but just as effective at milking him.

His lips found mine in a searing kiss, and I wrapped my arms around his neck, holding him close, pouring all my relief and affection into the kiss.

When he withdrew from me and rolled away, I instantly felt empty, yet hungry again. How was that possible?

I glanced up at the other male in the room, my throat thick. My pussy ached with need.

How was this going to play out now?

"Dragon?" I asked, flicking my gaze up to him, though I wasn't sure what I was asking.

Did he want me too? Would he have me now?

Rogan rolled even further away, then stood up from the mattress as though he were going to leave, but instead hung around. Watching us.

I sat up on the bed, scooted across the mattress, then stood up on shaking legs.

Whoa... I can still feel my orgasm. I can barely stand.

I turned to Fridge. He was intensely aroused, his shaft thick and hard, but his face was conflicted. I didn't know what he was feeling or thinking, and I wasn't sure I wanted to know.

Was this another rejection? After everything he'd said and done tonight to convince me otherwise?

"Sadie... I..." Fridge took a step closer, reaching out a hand to me. I ached to grab for him but I needed to make sure he wanted this. I waited for him to come to me. Then he moved, forward, and my heart lurched with excitement.

From outside the room, the sound of a window being broken and glass flying broke our lusty spell.

I jumped, glancing at the door, then back at Fridge. His face was a myriad of emotions. "That has to be one of the bedrooms," I said. "Everywhere else is hardwood flooring."

The glass would have made a very different sound if it had landed on hardwood.

Fridge and Rogan bolted from the room, still naked.

I couldn't fight in the nude, though.

I hurried to my closet, grabbed a cotton dress, pulled it on over my hot, wet form, and sprinted out the door after them.

Yelling and thumping sounded, and a loud crash.

"Fuck." Those noises were coming from my dad's bedroom.

I ran into the room just in time to see a man with long, dark hair slip through the broken window and disappear. His face had been turned away, and I couldn't make out any of his features.

Fridge was getting up from the floor where he'd obviously been forced and Rogan was panting as he darted up to me from the other side of the room, blood splattered over his face and chest.

"Where'd he go?" he asked.

"Out the window," I said, frowning. "Didn't you see him leave?"

Had the intruder been that fast? Or had my timing been that impeccable?

I tiptoed around the pile of shattered glass, trying not to slice my bare feet, to look out the window. I peered down at the grass fifteen feet below, and the alleyway behind the apartment building.

There wasn't a trace of him, even though we were one level up. Not that the height would be a challenge to a paranormal.

"Sadie, step away from the window," Fridge said.

Probably a good idea. I didn't want to be snatched by some super powerful creature who'd managed to beat both my guys in a fight.

I backed up slowly and Fridge grabbed me into his arms. Before I could say anything, he carried me out of the room.

"We need to get you somewhere safe," he said.

"Safer than here?" I asked, relaxing into his embrace.

In my head, there was nowhere safer than my father's apartment. It was loaded full of weapons, was a layout I knew well, and technically, had a great internal security. Admittedly the security system did seem to be failing lately.

Really gotta get that checked out.

"Ah, yeah," Fridge said, shaking his head as though I were crazy.

I sighed. He was probably right. This was the second time someone had broken into our apartment in two days.

"What do you think he was looking for?" I asked as Fridge set me down on my feet, back in my bedroom.

The guys started to get dressed.

My disappointment was acute as their gorgeous bodies disappeared from view, but we needed to focus on what had just happened.

Not what had been about to happen before the break-in.

I stripped off my dress and grabbed some fresh underwear out of my dresser.

Both men stopped moving to stare at me and I managed a smile while I put on something comfortable. I wasn't sure where we were going, but it was obvious from their attitudes, we weren't staying here.

"It's crap that I don't why this is happening. What he was looking for," I said, frustrated. I looked over at them "*What* was he, anyway?"

He didn't look like a shifter, but if he'd knocked both my guys on their asses, he had to be something pretty powerful.

"A vamp," Rogan said, grimacing as he pulled his shirt back over his arms.

"Do you need a shower or something?" I asked, looking him over and peering at the blood splatter. He didn't seem to be cut anywhere, at least not anymore, anyway.

Shifters had exceptional healing powers, especially if the wounds weren't deep.

He shook his head. "Nah, I'll be fine. We need to get home."

My breath caught in my throat, pain slicing through my heart harder and faster than I'd anticipated.

"Oh, you're leaving?" I asked, trying to sound like I didn't care about the answer.

I failed.

Fridge growled and glared at me. "You're coming with us. Don't think for a second that you're staying here. Those assholes are obviously after something your dad had and they haven't found it yet. We need to get you somewhere safe before they come back again. Which they will."

The tightness in my chest eased. Fridge's feelings for me hadn't changed, despite the fact we hadn't yet mated.

"Great. So where are we going?" I asked.

The guys looked at each other, I assumed silently communicating, then back at me.

Fridge answered. "Our apartment. It's probably safest because no one will think to look for you there. The workshop isn't safe. Neither is this place. Until we find the guys responsible for this, and find out what they want, we need to keep you away from both places."

I nodded. Though I didn't like being told what to do, nor did I like running away, I liked being alive. And these bad guys had proven they were willing to kill.

"Okay. Well, I'll pack a bag, and I suppose we can go right away. Assuming we're done here?"

I indicated to the bed.

Fridge scowled. "We are *so* not done here. Not by a long shot. But for the moment, I hate to say it, we might have to wait."

Relief winged through my heart that, despite his reticence, Fridge would have followed through with our mating.

"Okay," I managed.

Who knows if I would have had the same reaction with Fridge that I'd had with Rogan?

The way Rogan had felt inside me, the orgasm that followed, the connection and love for him that now pulsed through me... I was sure we'd mated tonight.

I looked toward my wolf and smiled at him. I felt more settled, happier, lighter, than I had before. And from the look on Rogan's face, he did, too.

Part of me hurt that Fridge and I hadn't had a chance to complete our mating in the same way.

I began to pack for a week away, grabbing toiletries from the bathroom and clothes from my closet.

When I glanced over at Fridge's grumpy face, I realized that maybe it wasn't such a bad idea to wait to be mated to my dragon.

We hadn't sorted out all our shit yet, and the last thing I'd ever want him to feel was trapped, mated to me against his will.

Perhaps Fate had intervened just in time to stop Fridge and me making a terrible mistake.

CHAPTER 24

ROGAN

I helped Sadie pack her bag and carried her suits and shirts. Though I wasn't sure why she'd need them over the next few days.

My insides were in turmoil, on so many levels.

I'd just mated with my woman. Everything inside me, all of my shifter genes, were dancing with joy. I was settled. I'd made it. I'd found her. I was whole.

But she was in danger, and I had to protect her.

Fridge and I had just gotten our asses handed to us, and if that was the guy who had killed Jimmy, then we were in trouble. He moved so fast I'd barely seen him.

And Fridge... I glanced over at my best friend as he picked up one of Sadie's bags and stared at her with huge, hopeful eyes.

He wanted Sadie as his mate, his lover, his wife, just as much as me.

My big, dumb friend had fallen. Hard.

He just had to come to terms with the fact that our single life was over. And the rest of our lives could begin once he got his act together.

But Fridge had more baggage than anyone I'd ever met, so how long it would take for him to come to the right conclusion was anyone's guess.

Rogan and Fridge lived about fifteen minutes by car out of the city. We took my dad's truck because it was the newest and biggest of all the vehicles available to us.

By the time we got to their place, a large two-bedroom apartment in an older but well-looked-after complex, it was well past midnight and I was exhausted. I could barely put one foot in front of the other.

When we stepped into their unit on the second floor, I dropped my duffel on the ground. Fridge had wanted to carry it, but I'd insisted.

Stupid me.

The apartment was small, but not tiny, with an open living, dining and kitchen area and a hallway that looked like it led to the bedrooms.

The room was clean, but sparse of personal effects.

"Where am I sleeping?" I asked, eyeing the couch as Rogan turned on all the lights.

"With me," he said.

"My bed's bigger," Fridge argued.

If I hadn't been so tired, I would have enjoyed the squabble.

"Can we all sleep together?" I asked, because as far as I was concerned, that was what was going to happen in the future.

Once our mating was complete, I wouldn't want to sleep without either of them.

Fridge and Rogan glared at each other as though they'd never considered such a thing.

I staggered toward the huge, comfortable-looking couch. It was dark brown and the plush cushions were inviting. "Don't worry about it. The couch looks just fine."

Rogan grabbed me up in his arms, stopping my trajectory. "No. You're right. Let's go."

I wrapped my arms around his neck and cuddled into him. He walked us into a huge room with a California king bed, black comforter, and dark, wooden furniture.

"Fridge's room?" I asked, though it was pretty obvious. Part of me expected to see a golden egg somewhere for him to nest over.

Rogan eased me down on the bed. "Yep."

He began to undress, and I slithered off the bed to do the same. I kept my tank top and panties on, then slipped into the middle of the bed beneath the covers.

"I can't believe how tired I am," I said as I closed my eyes and turned onto my side, loving the feel of the firm mattress and fluffy pillows beneath me.

I could definitely get used to sleeping here.

There were sounds of clothes dropping to the floor, lights being turned off, and heavy sighs, before two warm, naked bodies slid under the sheets with me.

I sighed as I nestled into both of them, my ass against Rogan's belly and my hand on Fridge's chest.

"Goodnight," I managed, though a part of me wished for so much more. Especially with Fridge. Unfinished business there.

Then, I fell into sleep like a friend welcoming me home.

~

When I woke, I was alone, and for a moment I had no idea what time it was, nor where I was.

I lifted my head, looking around the room for signs of life or a clock.

When I saw neither, I rolled onto my back and stretched my arms above my head, luxuriating in the feeling of having a well-rested body.

We came back to the boys' apartment last night. And this is Fridge's room... I think.

How long had it been since I'd slept all night without waking?

Years, probably.

I sat up and glanced around. I couldn't hear a thing, then the door opened and Rogan walked in. He was carrying a plate and cup with steam billowing from the top.

He smiled at me with all the love and welcome I'd ever dreamt of from a husband, partner, or mate.

"You're awake," he said. "Perfect timing."

He placed the plate next to me on the bed and the drink on the nightstand.

"What's all this?" I asked.

I hadn't received breakfast in bed since I was a small child. And that was only when I was sick, and we had a full-time nanny.

"Fridge doesn't cook much, but what he does make is a great breakfast." Rogan pushed the plate closer to me.

The smell of greasy, crispy bacon and fluffy scrambled eggs floated up to meet me. There was also a sausage, some hash browns, and even buttered toast.

"I... thank you." I didn't know what to say. The gesture was so thoughtful, I wasn't quite sure what to think.

"How are you doing this morning?" he asked as he sat on the bed next to me.

I could tell he wanted to reach over and touch me, but between the food on my lap and the way I was positioned on the bed, that was difficult.

I considered his question properly before answering. It had been a hell of a few days. "Good, I think. Is it still morning? I can't tell what time it is."

He chuckled. "Yeah, it's not even eight yet. We were thinking of going into the workshop for a bit, then maybe speak to a PI that your dad hires for some of our trickier jobs."

I picked up a piece of bacon and bit into it, my hungry body rolling with pleasure as I began to eat in earnest.

"A private investigator?" I asked. "I would have assumed you guys got all the info you needed when someone hired you."

He shrugged. "This guy is more than a PI. He's a tracker. If we can't find someone, he tracks them down for us, then we make the arrest and get the bounty."

Sounded fascinating.

"What sort of shifter is he?" This guy sounded like a rare breed.

"He's a mix, from what I gather, but no one really knows because he doesn't talk about it. And your dad never told us, if he knew. But with his sense of smell, and the fact that he doesn't want to be a bounty hunter, I assume some wolf, some badger, maybe a little fox. You'll see when you meet him."

I hummed, interested in the new information, but also too interested in my breakfast. It was *awesome*.

I'd inhaled the eggs and the toast and was just starting on the sausage when Fridge stuck his head in through the door.

"Oh... you're awake," he said. "Good."

He didn't attempt to enter the room past the door frame, and I could feel the freeze from where he was standing.

I'd ask Rogan later what that was about.

Instead, I blasted Fridge with a high-wattage smile, trying to melt the ice from where I sat. "Thank you so much for breakfast. This is awesome."

I kept eating and maintaining eye contact with him. He was probably feeling disconnected and a little sexually repressed. That would put anyone in a bad mood.

Eventually he leaned against the door and seemed to relax a little. "Glad you like it."

I swallowed the last of the eggs and picked up the other piece of toast. "Rogan was just saying you guys want to go into the workshop and speak to a PI of some sort?"

Fridge nodded. "Yeah, we need to find out who killed your dad, and more importantly, why."

I cocked my head at him. "The 'why' is more important to you guys?"

I was more interested in the 'who', but that was my need for revenge talking.

"Yeah. Absolutely. If it was just an accidental over-feeding, or they wanted him dead because he posed a threat or something like that, then they would have disappeared without a trace. But they broke into your house, ransacked his office... they're looking for something, and until they find it—or we find them—you're still at risk."

I glanced down at my plate and began to cut up my sausage, heat and love filling my chest.

Fridge was worried about me. That was what this was all about.

He could be grumpy and rough, and not want anything to do with our fated mates link, but he cared about my safety the same way my father had. And that, to me, was love.

I glanced up again, though I was pretty sure my face had gone red from the heat I could feel flooding my cheeks. "Should we just skip the workshop and go straight to the PI? Surely, he has an office or something?"

Rogan laughed and even Fridge grinned.

"What's so funny?" I asked.

"You'll know why that's funny when you meet him, but to answer your question, no, he doesn't have an office. And if he did, we wouldn't take you there," Rogan said.

Was he really that bad?

"And I need to check in on the boys," Fridge said, which reminded me that I'd given them both the reins to the business as far as the other men were concerned.

I glanced from one to the other. "Do I need to do anything in regard to the business and ownership and your roles?"

I had no idea.

Rogan shook his head. "Not today, at least."

Fridge shrugged. "We're not worried about titles or money. But you'll need to talk to your dad's lawyers about all the legal stuff. I'm sure your dad's Will just passed everything down directly to you."

"I hope so." We'd never discussed it. "Not because of money," I reassured them, "but just for ease. I don't want to be fighting anyone in court for my dad's apartment. It's the only thing I really want to keep. It's my home. Everything else is negotiable. Even the business, to be honest."

They nodded as one, and an uncomfortable silence drifted over the room.

Death and money. Fun subjects.

I finished the food on the plate and shuffled off the bed. "Thank you so much for breakfast, but I better have a quick shower if we're going into work soon."

I was sure I still smelled of my time with Rogan. Not to mention anxiety, stress, and sweat.

Fridge reached out and took the plate, then pointed to a door along the hallway. "Bathroom's there. Take your time. We'll leave when you're ready."

"Thanks." I smiled warmly at both of them, grateful for starting the day in such a positive way.

I grabbed up my bag as Fridge left the room and made my way to the bathroom.

CHAPTER 26

FRIDGE

Last night was torture, lying beside Sadie and trying to control my dragon. She needed rest, not me climbing on top of her and fucking her brains out.

My skin was on fire and my heart wouldn't stop hammering in my chest.

I opened the dishwasher and put our plates inside.

I'd hoped breakfast would soothe a few of the wounds I'd created with my words yesterday. I never knew how to say the right things. Rogan was good at that, but I wasn't.

I could fight. I could make breakfast. I was good at actions. Not words.

But I didn't want Sadie hating me.

I wanted her to like me. To want to be with me. Even if I couldn't give her what she wanted in terms of the whole 'fated mates' thing.

Didn't mean I didn't want her, with every cell in my body screaming out for her. Right now.

But how was she going to feel about that, if I couldn't commit to the fated mates idea?

Only time would tell.

SADIE

The bathroom was clean and tidy, just like the rest of their apartment. A little soul-less, but I couldn't be too picky. They were two men living without a woman. But my brain immediately went to small changes I'd make. A little fresh paint, a picture here or there.

I shook my head to clear the thoughts of decorating and hopped in the shower. I didn't waste any time, scrubbing quickly, then jumped out. I was surprised to find I was a little tender after my session with Rogan last night.

It had been hot... too fast, but I supposed that was what matings were for. To fuse the bodies together. To make sure we didn't break apart before the bond was completed.

I wasn't on any sort of birth control, and as I flipped through my phone and checked my cycle, I realized I was a week away from my period and nowhere near my fertile time.

Hopefully.

But with two virile men in my life now, I was going to have to see a doctor about that. The last thing I needed in this mess of my current life was a baby.

Though a little shifter would be cute.

"Stop it!" I warned myself, laughing and shaking my head.

So much had changed in the last few days, I suppose it was natural to want to try and create a family now that I'd lost mine.

But not this fast.

I was high on good food and sex. Obviously, I wasn't being rational.

I opened my duffel bag and pulled on some of the clothes I'd brought with me. A pair of denim jeans and a smart white shirt.

Casual, but fine. The shirt tucked in at my waist and accentuated my breasts nicely without looking like I was trying.

I glanced in the mirror one more time. *Yeah, that'll do.*

I walked out of the bathroom to find both guys waiting by the front door. Fridge had a black bag at his feet and Rogan was scrolling through his phone.

I walked forward. "All ready."

They grinned at me with matching smiles and I couldn't stop the way my hips automatically sashayed toward them.

At this time in my life when I should be curled in a ball, grieving for the man who had raised me, I had an amazing amount of happiness to look forward to in the future. It felt like a gift. Fate had taken something special away, but she had given something special right back.

"So, to the workshop?" I asked, as Fridge bent over to pick up his bag.

I eyed him and joked. "You look like you're taking an overnight bag. Whatcha got in there?"

He unzipped the bag for me to have a look.

I poked my head over the contents and gasped. He had an assortment of ropes, knives in their sheaths, and handcuffs.

Despite the quiver of fear that rippled through me, I was excited. "I do like a prepared man."

He didn't say anything, but the sides of his lips lifted as though he couldn't help but smile.

"Anything else I should know before we go out today?" I asked, surprised at how quiet the men were. Especially Fridge.

Rogan slipped a hand around my waist and grinned. "Just let us know if you feel overwhelmed or need to come home. We're both worried you're gonna crash any moment."

I glanced over to where Fridge was unlocking the front door, and when he turned to me, I saw the same concern mirrored in his expression as I heard in Rogan's voice.

I plastered a smile on my face, loving the fact that they were worried about me, but also not thrilled that they thought me too weak and unfocused to handle this.

I gestured them out the door. "Let's just find my father's killer."

CHAPTER 28

SADIE

The drive to my dad's workshop building was only fifteen minutes, but I used that time to email my boss at work and let him know what was going on.

I'd messaged her yesterday to say there was a family emergency I needed to take care of but hadn't given her any direct details. Just that I needed the day off. But it was way past that now.

Then I emailed my boss's boss, and let him know exactly what had happened and that I would need a month off for bereavement and to sort things out.

I had sick leave and vacation hours stored up if they needed me to use it. I could easily take the time off fully paid, but since money wasn't really a problem, I didn't worry about any of that. I just looked forward to the time off because so much needed to be accomplished.

My corporate career was action-packed and stressful. I could handle sorting out my dad's business, but finding his murderer on top of that added something to the mix I'd never had to deal with, before.

Work may have been a good distraction at the moment, but I

wanted to focus on my father's business and ensure everything was sorted properly before I attempted to transition back to my old life.

If I ever did.

Hopefully, with the help of his lawyers, we could sort this out quickly.

Then I'd deal with the funeral.

I put my phone into my bag and glanced out the window.

The funeral... *heaven help me*. I had no idea what my dad even wanted for a burial.

All shifters were cremated, but my mother's body had been buried in a cemetery. Like all humans and witches.

So, what would my father want me to do for him? I had to assume he'd want to be buried with his wife. But would he want to be in a casket too? Or cremated and in an urn and then his ashes buried with Mom?

Hopefully, he'd detailed it all in his Will.

The car stopped and Fridge turned off the engine. "Let's go."

We stepped out of the car and walked into the workshop. Everything hit me all at once—the sounds of men training, the scent of sweat and leather.

I swayed on my feet, a wave of grief flowing over me. If I walked up those stairs, I should be able to see my father.

This was his place, his men...

A hand squeezed my arm. "You okay?"

It was Rogan's voice.

"Yeah. It's okay." I shook him off. "I think I'll go to the office and make some calls. Can you let me know when the PI gets here?"

Before he responded, I charged up the stairs with my head held high. I could feel the other men around me stop their activity to watch me. I tried to ignore the attention. After all, I'd have to get used to that if I continued to work here.

I reached the top of the stairs and turned around to Rogan, who was still at the bottom, looking up at me. "Oh, and did you locate Dad's lawyer details yesterday?"

He nodded. "Yeah, they're on the desk still, I think."

"Thanks." I gave him a brief smile and headed straight to Dad's office.

There was so much to do. And so little time. Or it felt that way, anyway.

I sat in Dad's chair, ignoring the nostalgic wave of sadness that washed over me. If I was going to take over his business, these moments were going to be part of everyday life.

I shook myself and picked up the phone, dialing the number in front of me.

"Hello? This is Sarah Williams. I'm calling to speak to Raymond Kennedy. He's in charge of my father's estate, I believe."

I was transferred to a man who sounded ancient, but clever, like so many of the good lawyers in town.

Luckily for me, everything seemed to be pretty straightforward in Dad's Will. The apartment and the business were paid off. There was no debt, and I inherited everything.

There was a lot of relief that came with knowing that, but I also wanted to know one more thing.

"Mr. Kennedy…"

"Raymond, please, Sarah."

"Raymond… I appreciate everything you've told me so far. Thank you. I'm very relieved to find out that Dad made things so easy for me."

Raymond chuckled. "Your father loved you very much, and although he didn't expect to leave this earth quite so soon, he didn't want you saddled with debt of any kind. He always hoped that you would want to join him in the business… though I told him that a woman of your intelligence would surely not want to do so."

I cleared my throat. It was easy to assume that a woman wouldn't want to take on a group of fifty bounty hunters.

Even those who had met me, underestimated me. Often.

"Thank you, but there is one other thing I need to ask about. My father's funeral. Did he leave any details about what he wanted done with his body, or the size or location of where he wanted the service conducted?"

I trailed off as emotions closed my throat.

Raymond began to hum and haw. "Well... ah.... No. He didn't say specifically, but I assumed... being a shifter..."

I interrupted him. "I understand. He didn't tell you what he wanted."

"No. I didn't think it needed to be written down. I apologize if that was an oversight on my behalf."

It wasn't. The rules were generally written in stone. Shifters were cremated. Unless Dad had gone out of his way to write down something else, then that was what he wanted. But I would be burying his ashes with my mother.

They'd want to be together.

I leaned back in the chair. "It's fine. Thank you for everything. I'll be in touch next week so we can meet and work out everything."

"Yes. There will be a lot of paperwork, but as a lawyer yourself, I'm sure you understand."

I closed my eyes. Oh, I knew exactly how much paperwork would need to be read and signed. I'd need a drink that day. "I do. Thank you, Raymond."

I hung up and sat for a moment.

I counted my heartbeats and took long breaths.

So, I'd get my dad cremated and buried with my mother.

I had a plan.

In that respect, anyway. Now I just had to find his killer, and with an entire business dedicated to hunting and capturing bad guys, surely we'd be able to find the person responsible.

There was a knock on my door.

"Come in," I called out.

The door opened and Rogan stepped in, clearing his throat. "The private investigator is here. Would you like me to show him in?"

I stared at him, and almost laughed. Was Rogan showing me all this respect and deference for a reason? Who *was* this guy?

"Sure," I said, waving my hand in front of me. "Send him in."

He'd come quickly. That was impressive, and perhaps an indication of how much he respected my father. Or that was what I hoped.

Rogan walked into the room and a man stepped in after him, although stepped, was too strong a word.

His slid in.

His presence made every hair on my body stand on end.

Fridge came in after him and shut the door.

My men stood shoulder to shoulder by the door and this... man walked up to the desk.

I jumped to my feet and swallowed hard, trying not to flinch at the ugliness before me.

He had a hunched back, and when he moved, he had a subtle limp. Somewhat like I always imagined the hunchback of Notre Dame would move.

But he smelled... like a strange, underground shifter.

The guys were right. A wolf, a badger, a... I couldn't tell.

I forced a smile. "Thank you so much for coming so quickly. I'm Sarah Williams. Sadie."

I didn't extend my hand, not wanting to touch his skin. It had a scaly appearance to it that shimmered in the overhead light.

He nodded. "Nice to meet Jimmy's daughter."

I was pleasantly surprised by his voice. It was educated, with an English lilt to his accent.

My gaze rose to Fridge, who didn't meet my eyes. He was standing rigid, as though ready to pounce if necessary.

I gestured toward one of the empty chairs. "Please have a seat, ah... sorry, did I miss your name?"

He shook his head. "Most people call me Shadow."

We sat in our respective chairs and I slid right up to the desk so I could face him properly.

My father had taught me never to judge a book by its cover—I was a great example of that—but this guy was something else.

He pinned me with eyes that were somewhere between blue and violet.

"Can you tell me what sort of shifter you are, Shadow? I've never seen eyes like yours."

He actually smiled, though it was the wobbliest version of a smile I'd ever seen. "I don't think anyone has ever asked me that question so quickly."

"Well, I..."

"Except your father."

That made me chuckle. "Well, they do say the apple doesn't fall far from the tree."

He pinned me with a stare. "I understand your mother was... unusual also. Do you have any of her... traits?"

The air around us shifted in a strange way and I was suddenly more than uncomfortable. "He told you about my mother?"

Shadow inclined his head. "Not exactly. We are distant cousins, you and me."

I sat up straighter. "Really? How so? On Mom's side?"

I didn't know a lot about the distant family. My grandparents had kept in touch over the years, but they lived far away and my aunt had four kids they concentrated on, mostly.

He nodded. "Yes, I believe we share a great-grandmother."

And then the chill in the air was gone. He was part witch too.

Though unlike him, I was almost half witch.

I smiled at him, relaxing. No wonder he was so uncomfortable in society, so strange to the others. The mix of shifter and magical blood didn't always blend well.

"Well, cousin, it is wonderful to make your acquaintance," I said, and I meant it.

Shadow bobbed his head. "Jimmy was kind to me. Gave me a job that suited me, as soon as I moved to town. Made me somewhat of a…"

"Legend?" I finished for him.

He shrugged, now glancing away as though bashful. "Perhaps."

I pushed aside my questions about the other sides of his lineage. He was obviously a mix of many creatures, some of which had damaged his body. Not his brain, though. He appeared to be as quick as a whip.

"So, you'll help me, Shadow?"

He looked me straight in the eye. "To find the people responsible for your father's death?"

I nodded. "Yes. I want to kill the ones responsible, and if they're part of a corporation, take that down too. Are you interested?"

He grinned, with pointed teeth and purple eyes. I'd never felt so repulsed by a person while at the same time, so in tune with them.

"Abso-fucking-lutely."

CHAPTER 29
ROGAN

My mouth dropped open at Shadow's exclamation and I glanced at Fridge, who had a similar dumbfounded expression on his face.

Who knew the guy could talk like this? His accent made him sound like some snotty scholar. Not the underworld PI who got the dirt on the worst of the worst.

Shadow could get in and out of places none of the rest of us could. He had connections everywhere. But he was an enigma. He had no friends. No one understood him. And yet here we were, having a good old chat with the strange shifter.

And he was Sadie's cousin! Who would have guessed that?

At least that meant she was probably safe, because we had been concerned about that.

It hadn't been logical fear, of course. There was no reason for Shadow to hurt Sadie. He'd been loyal to Jimmy, as we all were.

But you just never knew. And it was always better to be safe th

SADIE

I lifted my gaze to Rogan and Fridge, who both were standing by the door. Rogan's jaw had dropped open like he was a cartoon character. Maybe I should walk over and lift it back up again?

Fridge looked equally shocked, his eyes wide and his eyebrows raised high.

"You guys all right?" I asked with a smirk.

Rogan snapped his mouth shut and Fridge nodded.

I looked back at the man who claimed to be my distant cousin. "Do you know what their issue is?"

He leaned forward in his chair and rolled his right shoulder, most likely because he was more comfortable in a flexed position. "I don't usually talk this much."

"And?"

Why was that enough to make my mates look so dumbfounded?

He chuckled, a strange, scratchy noise that made my skin prickle. Normally I'd get an indication of what sort of shifter a person was by the sound of their laugh, but his was quite unusual.

I detected a hint of wolf growly, but there was something else. A fox noise, perhaps?

"You really don't know anything about me, do you?" Shadow asked, the question sounding redundant.

I'd answer it anyway. I shook my head and leaned back in my chair. "No. Rogan and Fridge told me that you could help us track down the guys responsible for killing my dad. That's all I care about."

One side of Shadow's lips lifted into a half smile. "You've got more of your dad in you than you realize, Sadie. He was the best of the best."

I nodded, my throat clogging with emotion. I wasn't sure how long it was going to take me to get used to people saying that, but I was nowhere near comfortable yet.

I swallowed hard so that I didn't make a fool of myself when I tried to speak. "That... is an amazing compliment. Thank you." I cleared my throat again, the thickness making it hard to talk. "Now, what's the plan for getting justice for my dad?"

"Do you mind if I smoke? It helps my nerves," he said, dragging out a pack of hand-rolled cigarettes in a silver case from the inside of his breast jacket pocket.

I opened my mouth to tell him that I *did* in fact care, and that he could wait until after the meeting to smoke. He'd stink up the whole office, and there were no windows in this room.

But Rogan stepped forward and flicked a switch on the side of the desk.

A loud exhaust fan went on above my head and I glanced up. Why hadn't I noticed that before now?

Rogan cleared his throat.

"Jimmy allowed it," he said, and then stepped away.

Well, who was I to break with tradition?

I waved my hand. "Go ahead."

Shadow lit up and began puffing away, the scent much less offensive than expected.

"That doesn't smell too bad," I said, finding it hard not to comment. I generally hated the scent of cigarettes.

He chuckled. "It's a home blend. I wouldn't have asked if I thought it would upset you."

I shrugged. "It's okay. There're lots of new things for me to get used to."

Shadow puffed on his cigarette like one would a cigar and blew out a ring of smoke up toward the fan. Then he leaned back in his chair, his physical appearance visibly relaxing.

How much pain was he in to need constant nicotine? It appeared to be almost like a medication to him.

"How much do you know about this town, Sadie?"

I frowned at him. What did that have to do with anything? "I've lived here all my life."

He sucked in another lungful of smoke and blew it upward. "I know. But how much do you know about the inner workings of politics? The money that moves around the city. The vampires?"

I bit my lip. This conversation had just taken a turn that I hadn't expected.

"I know a bit, I think."

Why was I suddenly feeling stressed and out of my depth? I pushed through the tight feeling in my chest. The one that told me I was inadequate.

Just relax and learn what you can.

"I mean, I work for a large corporation," I continued. "Owned by vampires. I know they run and own practically everything in this town."

He nodded, a patient look passing over his face as though he were talking to a child. "They do. However, do you know anything about the blood system? The way they feed?"

Rogan and Fridge looked nervously at each other. Did they know all of this? Was that why they seemed uncomfortable? Or were they worried about what I was learning?

I focused back on Shadow. "They feed on donors and slaves, their lovers, and..."

Shadow's gaze silenced me. Then he shook his head.

"They... *don't* feed that way?" I said. Why did I feel so slow? So stupid. Why hadn't I ever asked these sorts of questions?

I crossed my arms over my chest and stared at him. "Are you going to tell me the answer, or just leave me hanging?"

He sighed before taking another drag. "This city runs on vampire money and greed. They are immortal and powerful, but they have a significant weakness."

"And what's that?"

I hadn't seen many weaknesses in the vampires I'd met.

"Their hunger. Their need for blood. *Our* blood. It makes them weak."

I shrugged in disagreement. "I don't see why you'd see it that way. It's just their nourishment. And when there's so many people who want to be fed on, women willing to provide it for a price... Why would it be a weakness? That would be like saying I have a weakness for burgers and pizza."

He sighed and again I got that weird feeling in my chest, like I was being led down the garden path. "Have you ever spoken to a vampire, Sadie?"

I nodded. "Of course. My bosses are vampires. I have clients who are vampires."

"Have you ever talked to one of them about their palate? Their particular tastes for blood?"

Their... what? Wasn't blood, just... blood?

I shook my head, trying hard not to shudder.

God, no. Imagine that conversation. I don't want to even think about it.

Shadow continued. "Have they ever stepped too close? Smelled you? Have you ever seen their eyes glisten red?"

Rogan fidgeted by the door, shifting from one foot to another, uncrossing and re-crossing his arms. I knew he wanted to interrupt the conversation. But he didn't.

I shook my head, this time unable to stop the shiver of disgust that ran through me.

Finally, Rogan stepped forward. "Shadow, I'm not sure that Sadie…"

The warning in his words was clear, but his tone was quiet, respectful of the man in front of him.

I lifted my gaze and shook my head. "No. I want to hear it all. If I've been living under a rock, I wanna know the truth."

It would be just like my dad to keep me safe—sheltered—from the world around me.

I looked back at Shadow. "To answer your question, no. I've never seen a vampire's eyes turn red in business. Occasionally at a club when I was younger, maybe, but I've never been approached or harassed by any of them."

He frowned. "That's unusual and I must say, I'm a little surprised they've never even tried."

"Why would you be surprised?" I asked. Surely it was normal for a woman of my age to have gone through her life without a vampire wanting to bite her.

They were civilized creatures, after all.

Shadow stared pointedly at me. "Perhaps we should continue the rest of this conversation alone?"

"No," Fridge said. Loudly.

Shadow looked at me and I understood exactly what he wanted to talk about—my magical blood.

I smiled at my fated mates. "It's okay. I'll talk to Shadow alone."

Fridge shook his head. "Sadie… that's not a good idea."

I rolled my eyes. "He's not going to attack me. Just wait outside the door, okay? I'll call for you if I need help."

There was a lot of huffing and puffing, and stomping of feet, but in the end, my mates obviously decided that I could be left alone with the weird shifter.

Shadow chuckled when the door slammed shut behind them. "Are they both your mates?"

I blinked at him, surprised he read that fact about our connection so easily. So quickly. "How'd you know that?"

He shrugged. "I get a feel for people pretty easily. That and the excessive possessiveness coming from both of them, not just one. They both know me, trust me. I would never hurt a woman, especially not one related to me. So, their need to be in here was... strange."

I smiled at his logic, and the fact that I'd been right. They did trust him. Even if he was odd. "Yes, they're both my fated mates."

He smiled. "You must be a lot of woman to require *two* mates, especially one as strong as a dragon."

I shrugged. "I haven't really thought about it like that."

And I really didn't want to discuss it with a man I'd just met, either.

He laughed. "All right, we won't continue with that conversation. Bit weird anyway, to be honest. Now, let's get back to the topic at hand. You do realize why witches are extinct, or everyone assumes *we're* extinct, don't you?"

"Shh..." I glanced around, as though there could be people listening in the corners of the room.

He lowered his voice. "There are no bugs in this room. Don't worry."

I had no idea how he knew that, but instinct told me I could trust his judgment.

"Okay." I shook myself to focus back on the conversation. "And yes. I do know that the reason witches are basically extinct is because the vampires hunted them until there were none left. I'm not sure why they did that, though."

He nodded, his purple eyes swirling in a way that I recognized as being part warlock. No other paranormal had eyes that color, but men on my mother's side of the family did.

I stared at him, awestruck. "You really are my cousin, aren't you?"

He chuckled. "Yes."

"Then why didn't my father tell me about you?"

Why would he keep a family member from me like that?

Shadow puffed on the last of his cigarette, then pulled out another one from the silver case, lighting the second with the end of the first.

"I think he wanted to keep you separate from this life... until you chose to be a part of it, of course. There are so many elements that are unsavory. Dark. This part, in particular."

I swallowed hard, taking a few, careful breaths to try and slow my thundering heart rate down. "What's *this*, in particular?"

Shadow blew out a ring of smoke and it drifted elegantly to the ceiling.

"The blood ring."

"The... *blood* ring?" I repeated.

It sounded like some sort of weird boxing match.

Shadow shifted in his chair. "Yes. It's an underground blood market for vampires. Where people are forced to breed, then drained of their blood, purely for selling to vampires."

"They... what?" I blinked at him, then threw up my hands, shocked. "Are you telling me there are people locked up somewhere in this city... whose sole purpose is to be bred so that blood can be available for a vampire's appetite?"

Shadow's mouth thinned. "Absolutely. But it gets a lot worse than that."

"Worse? What's worse than babies bred as food for the vamps?"

Nothing, surely, could be worse.

Shadow chuckled. "You really don't get it, do you? The vampires consider us little more than food. Think about the way we see cattle, lambs, chickens. Bred for slaughter. For consumption. The vampires allow us to think we are free in this world, but in reality, they run the whole show."

I shuddered. "Like... cows? Like... steak?"

I swallowed the bile that rose. I'd had such a delicious steak with Rogan last night, just as I had done most nights with my father. Vampires couldn't possibly think of us that way. I couldn't believe it. I worked for some of them!

"But, we're human! We're what they used to be! It's almost like cannibalism."

Shadow nodded. "Yes, I agree with you. But that doesn't change what we are to them or how they see us. Especially the ancient vampires. I've found that once they reach a certain age, two hundred or so, their empathy for the human condition—for anything really— becomes non-existent."

I shivered and ran my hands over my arms. I wasn't actually cold, but the conversation was icing my normally hearty constitution.

"Okay. So, you're saying the vampires run an illegal, and totally immoral, blood ring, to... what? Breed specific bloodlines? Why?"

Shadow shrugged one shoulder and winced. "Why do we, as humans, breed any species? Think about it. Why do we cross certain dog breeds, or cattle?"

I tapped my fingers along the desk, thinking about his point from the perspective he was presenting. "For the strengths of those different breeds. Like designer dogs that look a certain way. Or cattle, for their size and muscle mass." A horrible thought struck me. "Are they breeding us for... traits? Or..."

Were we now designer... donors?

He nodded. "Sort of. What the vampires have deliberately *not* told us over the years of working with us—although it's obvious if you speak to them or live in their world—is that they enjoy certain blood types more than others. Why do you think all witches and warlocks were hunted to extinction?"

Because they were too powerful? The vampires were jealous? That's what I'd always thought.

"I never really looked into it. I guess I just assumed they thought we were a threat to them." I closed my eyes briefly as a wave of nausea passed through me. "Tell me they don't enjoy magical blood more than any other."

He chuckled. "You're quick."

Oh, God.

He sat up straighter, meeting my gaze with his. "They do. They love it. Crave it more than any other bloodline."

He dropped his voice to a whisper. "Why do you think your mother was killed? Or why she would have been encouraged to breed with a shifter like your father?"

I gaped at him. "You think a vampire killed my mother for her blood?" How was that possible? How had my father let that happen?

He nodded. "I know they did."

"You *know*?"

How? How did he know?

Then the other shoe dropped.

"And what do you mean, she was encouraged to breed with my father?" I asked, wincing.

I'd just gotten my head around the idea that my parents could be fated mates, but that was obviously not the case here.

Worry crossed Shadow's face, then he glanced down. "I'm sorry. I shouldn't have said that."

I threw my hands up in the air. "We've come this far, push on. Please. There's no one else alive to tell me anything true."

He sighed and smacked his lips together. "Do you have any water, or..."

"Yes!" I jumped to my feet, happy to do something with all my nervous energy. I grabbed water bottles and Coke cans out of the fridge in the corner of the room.

Luckily, my dad had kept it fully stocked.

I walked back and placed them on the desk. Three of each. "Help yourself."

Shadow took a bottle of water, tipped his head back, and swallowed it the same way a pelican would. All in one long drink.

Impressive.

Then he opened a can of Coke, the crack of the aluminum tab echoing in the room, quickly followed by the effervescent bubbling sound as the soft drink fizzed up.

He took a big gulp and sighed. "Thanks."

I sat down and cracked my can. I needed the sugar. "You're seriously not going to tell me how many different shifters are in your bloodline?"

He chuckled. "I don't tell anyone. But... if you really want to know, I'll tell you, cousin."

I nodded. "Shoot."

He sighed. "I have a base of witch blood, of course. From our great grandmother, but my ancestors, unlike yours, fell in love outside their circle. Quickly, my blood was diluted with wolf shifters, a fox shifter, and a hare."

"A hare?" I repeated. That was a very unusual shifter.

He chuckled. "Yes, unfortunately that did not mix well with my other bloodlines, thus the spinal deformity. However, it gave me extra speed and agility."

"Thank you for telling me," I said, though I was pretty sure he was holding something back. "There's no..." I swallowed hard against the fear that rose. I didn't want him to take this as a rude question, but I was going to ask it anyway. "There's no reptile in there at all?"

His eyes opened wider, then he chuckled. "How'd you guess? No one has before."

I shrugged. "I don't really know. Something about your skin..."

And my intuition that I trusted.

He nodded. "Yes, there is some snake in there, which is probably why the vampires don't bite me."

"Why is that?" I asked, not quite sure what he meant.

"Because they don't like reptiles. They never have. Oh, now it all makes sense."

"What does?" I asked.

He grinned. "I knew they added something to your bloodline to try and keep you safe, but I wasn't sure which shifter. It makes sense that the vampires don't bite you, either. You have some snake in you, too."

My mouth fell open. "Ah, say *what* now?"

CHAPTER 31
SADIE

Shadow smiled. "They never told you, did they?"

They? I assume he meant, my parents. "That my dad had snake in him? No!" I would have been horrified to learn such a thing. Snake shifters were known for being sneaky, underhanded, and savage.

And now that I thought about it, I supposed it was possible.

Shadow laughed. "Okay. I definitely need to tell you some things."

"Like what?"

What else could there possibly be?

How many more secrets did my family, and this city, have to tell?

Shadow took another sip of his Coke, then placed it on the desk in front of him. "Well, first, there's no snake shifter, in either side of your bloodlines. Unlike most shifters who've intermingled for centuries, you dad's line is pretty pure. Human and wolf shifters only."

Well, that was good to know, but did that mean... "And my mother?"

"Pure witch," he whispered. "The last of her kind."

176

"Then how…" He wasn't making any sense. Unless my father wasn't my real father, but I didn't believe that for one second.

Shadow reached forward, grabbed the Coke, and tipped back the last of his can. "It's pretty simple, really. Do you remember the spell your mother cast on you as a child?"

"Ah…" I hated that this stranger knew so much about my life, but I tried to push through the discomfort. "No, I don't *remember* it, but my father told me that she'd conducted a spell to enhance my shifter abilities."

"Like she did for him," he said.

I gaped at him. "How is it you know so much about my family? Honestly, it's…"

"Un-nerving?" he finished with a grin.

I nodded. "Totally."

Worse than that actually, but I didn't have a word for it.

He shrugged. "I listen and have an eidetic memory."

So, he memorized pretty much everything he'd ever been told or read.

I narrowed my gaze at him. Who was keeping secrets now?

"It's more than that," I said. "My father wouldn't have told you all of that information unless he had to." *Shadow has warlock in him, remember?* "Did you put a spell on him? Or…"

The answer came to me in a flash, as though my mother had inserted the piece of information straight into my head.

"You can read minds, can't you? You sneaky bugger."

Shadow cackled with laughter and the door burst open as Fridge charged into the room.

I waved my hand at him. "We're all good in here, Fridge. You can go downstairs and work if you need to. Shadow and I are fine."

Fridge snorted through his nose and I was surprised not to see smoke rings come out his nostrils. Then he took another look around the room and nodded, as though he was satisfied I was telling the truth. He slammed the door behind him when he left.

"You know he is extremely conflicted about the whole fated mates thing, right?" Shadow asked.

I groaned. "Yes, I know. Can you tell me how to fix it?"

He shook his head. "No, that's not really how my gift works. I get flashes of memory, emotions, sometimes words. But its fuzzy, and it has to be at the forefront of someone's mind for me to read it. I can't go digging through their subconscious or anything."

Good to know.

"So how do you know about the spell my mother cast?"

Because that is a secret I never thought Dad would share with anyone.

"I *felt* the memory one day when I was with your father, and I started asking questions. In the end, he told me everything."

Everything. What was everything?

I swallowed hard. Did I really want to know? Yes. Yes, I did.

I had to.

"And what's everything?" I asked, though part of me wasn't sure I could handle any more surprises this week.

Shadow sighed. "The spell your mother cast didn't enhance your wolf shifter powers."

"It didn't?" *That would explain why my sense of smell is so terrible. So, they lied to me?* "Then what did the spell do?"

"It enhanced your speed and skills, but what your mother did was add snake shifter to your mix of blood."

I gasped and jumped to my feet, my heart pounding and my stomach twisting. I felt a little ill.

I pushed the chair back so that I could pace behind the desk. "But why would they *do* that? Why would *she*?"

What a horrible thing for my mother to do!

I tugged on my ponytail, letting my hair spill out. I ran my hands through the strands and rearranged my hair until I wanted to pull it out.

"Stop freaking out, Sadie."

I spun around and glared at Shadow. "Stop freaking out? Are you serious?"

My voice must have risen too much, because the door slammed open and Rogan stood in the entrance, looking ready to fight.

I waved both hands at him, getting annoyed at the interruptions. Shadow was not going to hurt me.

"Seriously, Rogan. I appreciate you standing guard, but I'm fine. Shadow is my cousin and we're in a heated conversation."

Rogan backed out so fast it was funny.

When the door clicked shut, I turned back to my cousin.

"Now, Shadow. Is that the name you prefer, by the way? Or should I call you something else?"

He hesitated, as though he was about to tell me to call him by a different name, then he changed his mind. "Just call me Shadow, like everyone else. It'll be easier."

I nodded. "Fine." I had too much to worry about without trying to convince him to trust me with his real name. "Now tell me, why the hell do I have snake shifter DNA in me?"

"You don't have the DNA, I don't think. It's just a spell."

So, I won't pass it on to my kids.

"To what purpose?" I asked.

I was feeling totally betrayed by the people I'd thought loved me. And I wanted to know why they'd done it.

"To save you."

"Save me? From what?" I demanded, putting a hand on my hip.

Shadow rose and looked me in the eye. We were almost the same height, so it was easy to meet his gaze across the desk.

"Not what. *Who.*"

"Well, then, who?" I snapped, flinging out my arms. But, even as I asked the question, I already knew the answer. "Vampires."

Shadow's lips tilted up at the edge. "You really do have a lot of your father in you."

I grunted, secretly pleased with the compliment. Shadow

nodded. "Yes. They did it to save you from the vampires by disguising your witch blood."

Even though what my parents had done was shocking, especially only finding out now, they had done it to protect me.

I grabbed the chair and sat back down. Shadow flopped down into his chair as well.

My brain was going a million miles an hour, sorting everything into logical categories.

"So, in summary, vampires love witch blood. They killed my mother for hers. And since I'm half witch and that would probably tempt them in a similar way, my mother chose to put snake shifter into my blood via a spell, to disguise my origins?"

Shadow nodded. "Yeah, pretty much. The vamps hate snake shifter blood more than anything. It's the main thing that has saved me from being fed on over the years. And by the sounds of it, it's done the job and saved you also."

I straightened in my chair. "Well, I'm no pushover, and I don't put myself into dangerous situations..."

I liked to think I had a say over what happened to me from day to day.

Shadow chuckled. "Sorry, love, but you are a gorgeous young woman with witch blood. And a high percentage, by modern standards. In fact, you're probably the last true half-blood witch of our time. It wouldn't matter how well you hid yourself, or how well your father trained you, you'd likely be dead by now if your mother hadn't disguised the scent of your blood."

My throat grew thick and I swallowed hard. What a sobering thought.

I wanted to know more. "How does it work, exactly? The snake thing?"

He shrugged. "We're not a hundred percent sure, but something to do with the snake shifter scent. It really puts them off."

"Good to know," I said, nodding.

Of all the things I thought my parents would do to save my life, introducing snake shifter genes—considered the lowest of all shifters—into my blood was *not* one of them.

I took a deep breath and pulled my chair forward so I was closer to the desk. "So... now that I know things about myself that I *never* expected to discover, what are we going to do to find out who killed my father?"

"Well..." Shadow ran a hand through his shaggy hair. "I need to do some digging and investigating."

"How long is that going to take?" I asked.

He shrugged. "Give me a few days. I'll know more by then. Is there anything you need to tell me about his death that I don't already know?"

I laughed. "I don't know what you already know, so how can I answer that?"

His lips quirked up into a strange grin. "True. So, tell me everything."

I sighed and then nestled back in the chair as I filled in how I'd discovered my father's body the night he was murdered, the mess we found when we got home, and then the break-in last night.

He held up a hand as though to say, *stop right there.* "Someone broke into your home twice in two days? Once to trash your father's office and the next time, they broke into your father's bedroom?"

I nodded. "Yes. Though of course I don't know if it was the same person—or people. Fridge and Rogan said it was a vampire both times. But we don't know if it was the same one. We only saw the guy on the second night."

Shadow's nostrils flared. "It seems they are looking for something. Perhaps your father had information they wanted. Which begs the question, was his murder intentional, or a momentary fit of anger when they couldn't find what they wanted?"

"Oh, definitely intentional. I believe so, anyway," I said. "There was no one hanging around afterwards. No drunk, overly fed vampire. And Dad was drained. Like, there were a few drops of blood on his neck near the bite mark, but overall, he was cold as ice and blue as an ocean. They meant to kill him, whoever they were."

Shadow nodded and pressed his lips together, obviously thinking. "Could have been two of them, I suppose. Or three. After all, your dad was a big man."

"Exactly what I thought! But there was only one set of puncture marks on his neck."

Shadow shrugged. "They can feed from any artery. Femoral. Brachial. If there was more than one vamp, they could have taken the blood from several different areas of the body."

I shuddered, trying not to think about it. "He had all his clothes on... but you're right. I didn't check. And with his strength and size, it would have taken a couple of younger vamps, or one very old, very skilled one to take him out. And even then..." I shook my head. "I can't imagine Dad went down without a fight."

"He would have fought," Shadow said. "I know that without question. But why kill him when they obviously hadn't found what they were looking for? That's stupid. And vampires aren't usually stupid."

I played with the rings on my right hand. They looked good there. I was never taking them off.

"So... what, then? They thought they had the information, killed him, then realized it was wrong?"

Shadow grinned. "More like your dad pulled a fast one on them. Hid the real information. That's something I'll keep in mind when I go digging. That they're still looking."

He stood up, and that seemed to be the end of our conversation.

I jumped to my feet and walked around the desk. "Do I need to pay you? How does this all work?"

Shadow shook his head. "No. I'll do this one for free. I liked your dad. I want these vamps caught."

The money didn't matter to me, of course, but the fact he offered his services for free showed how much he'd cared for my father. "I appreciate that. Thank you, Shadow."

We walked to the door together.

I touched his shoulder. "Thank you so much for your help. I look forward to whatever information you can dig up."

He nodded and reached for the door handle.

"What should I be doing in the meantime?" I asked. "I mean... do you have any suggestions?"

His strangely violet eyes glowed beneath the bright fluorescent lights.

"Just look after yourself, and if you can, be careful. Stay alert. It's obvious they still want something, which means they'll be checking this office, your apartment, anywhere your father went regularly. And they'll probably be following you as well."

I swallowed hard. I hated the idea of being watched like that.

"Well, I'm staying with Fridge and Rogan for the moment," I said, trying to sound confident.

He smiled. "Good. Then I'd spend my time sorting out that fated mate bond if I were you, and let me figure out where to go next in the hunt for your dad's killer."

I grinned at him. "Sounds like a plan. Thanks."

Shadow limped out and I closed the door.

The boys had been right. Strangest individual I'd ever met. But also, one that made me suddenly more confident we would find the guy who killed Dad.

CHAPTER 32
SADIE

I'd barely sunk back into Dad's chair before the door opened and my mates hurried back in.

"What happened?"

"Are you all right?"

"What did he say?"

I could barely discern who asked what; they fired their questions so fast.

I waved them in. "Shut the door, and I'll tell you."

Fridge did as I asked, and they both sat opposite me.

I leaned forward and opened the final bottle of water, taking a sip to wet my dry mouth before speaking. "Well, basically, he told me all about how the vampires run the city and have underground breeding programs for specific bloodlines they crave."

Rogan and Fridge looked at each other, a strange guilty expression crossing over their faces.

My mouth dropped open. "Did you guys know about that?"

Rogan cleared his throat. "We've heard rumors, but never seen anything concrete."

Fridge sighed. "That's half the reason I try not to hunt the vamps too often—they love my blood."

He stretched his neck at an odd angle as though remembering times he'd been fed from.

"They do?" I asked, surprised someone as big and strong as Fridge had been attacked by a vampire.

I'd never even been propositioned by a vampire. And now, thanks to my cousin, I knew why.

"I captured one once, part of a bounty, and he was practically gnashing his teeth together over my scent." He shuddered and crossed his arms over his chest. "They like dragon blood, not as much as they used to like witch's or warlock's blood, of course, but they don't have that choice available anymore."

They knew about that... How did I not know?

I nodded, a wave of sadness washing over me as I remembered that part of the conversation. "Yeah, Shadow was telling me that's why witches are extinct. I'd known the vampires hunted them, of course, but I hadn't thought it was for their blood. I thought it was for their magic, or something. You know, being more powerful and therefore a threat that needed to be eliminated."

I'd been stupid not to put it all together.

"The vampires don't go for you?" Fridge asked, as though he was confused.

I shook my head. "No, never."

"Wonder why?" he mused. "Most humans I've spoken to have generally had at least one encounter."

I shrugged evasively. "I've always carried knives. Dad taught me how to defend myself... I don't know."

I used all the old excuses, not wanting to share everything I'd been told today, but they now made no sense. I was pretty sure Fridge and Rogan had always carried knives and been able to take care of themselves. But with everything going on in my head, I couldn't think fast enough to come up with a better reason.

And despite the fact that these men had earned my trust, and that I *should* be able to trust them, especially with the fated mates' connection, the less people who knew about my past, and the threat that my bloodline caused, the better.

"You've been lucky," Fridge said. "Being bitten by a vamp is not fun, despite what they tell you."

I shook myself, not wanting to even think about Fridge being attacked by a thirsty vampire. "The thing is, Shadow didn't know what it had to do with my dad. I told him about the break ins, and he thought it best I not be here at the workshop alone, or go back to Dad's apartment for a while. The guys who killed him are still looking for something."

I agreed with him on that one. I wanted to catch my father's killer, but I wanted to stay alive, too.

Rogan slid forward on his seat, his blue eyes lighting up. "So, you'll stay with us?"

I nodded, happiness winging through my heart to see my mate so excited to spend time with me. "If you'll have me."

Rogan grinned. "Of course."

My gaze slid to Fridge. "Is that okay with you as well?"

Fridge nodded, his face serious and solemn. "Of course. I wouldn't want you anywhere else."

Relief made me huff out a gentle sigh.

"Good. Well... I've spoken to the lawyer. Everything to do with Dad's business and the apartment seems pretty straightforward, which is one thing off my mind. Shadow's going to do some digging and see if he can find out more about Dad's killer, so that's under control as well." I chewed on my lip for a moment, thinking. "What do you guys suggest I do now?"

Fridge shrugged. "I don't know. Do you need to sort out any of the funeral stuff, or do you want a break from all that?"

I sighed. "You're right. That's something I can do."

The men stood up.

Rogan spoke. "We'll get back to work and bring you some lunch in an hour or so. That suit you?"

I smiled, gratefully. "That would be great."

Food was one thing I'd forgotten about.

They headed out and I turned on my dad's computer, researching local crematoriums and funeral services I could use.

I'd never been to a funeral. Well, not since my mother's, and being three years old at the time, I really didn't remember much. I had no idea what the protocol was, or even where to start.

I sighed as the minutes ticked by and I didn't find anything I liked. Not that I knew what I was looking for. How was I going to organize a suitable funeral for the most complex, intense, fantastic man on the planet?

Rogan cracked open the door and stuck his head in. "Chinese for lunch okay?"

"Yeah. Fried rice for me please. And chicken and corn soup," I said.

He nodded and headed off again.

I picked up the phone to call the first funeral home on my meager list, then realized I didn't even know when my father's body would be released for cremation. That was probably something I'd need to know if I wanted to organize his funeral.

Then Shadow's words swirled in my head. Would the autopsy reveal multiple puncture marks?

I'd need to make a different sort of phone call to have those questions answered.

I glanced through the notes I'd made on the pad of paper on my desk and flipped through my cell. Where was that phone number I needed?

I found it on my received calls list. *Detective Lazy,* who'd phoned yesterday to say that everything was fine, and that they really weren't investigating much.

I dialed the number on the workshop landline so I could check emails on my phone at the same time. My work had signed off my leave quickly and without fuss.

"Hello, this is Detective O'Connell."

"Detective, it's Sarah Williams here."

"Hello, Sarah. What can I do for you today?"

Other than your job, you mean?

I forced a smile to my lips, which I knew helped keep my tone more pleasant. "I was calling for a couple of things, but mostly to find out how the investigation was going."

"We're investigating leads and security footage in the area to see if we can identify anyone who looks suspicious, since you said they left through the back door when you arrived on the scene."

I pressed my lips together. No self-respecting vampire would be slow enough to be caught on any sort of security footage, but *okay.*

"Great. Next question is, when will my father's body be released so that I can organize cremation and a funeral? I don't know the normal timeframe for these things."

I had to assume that it would take at least a week for an autopsy and the other things that would need to be done with a suspected murder.

"I received an email this morning that your father's ashes can be picked up as soon as you'd like. Or they can be sent onto your chosen funeral home."

My mouth dropped open. "My father's... *what?*"

He hadn't just said what I thought he had. Had he?

"Your father's ashes. He was a wolf shifter and, by state law, he was cremated yesterday."

"I'm sorry... state law... what? Since when?"

Since when did they cremate people without the family's consent? That was ludicrous.

"All shifters are cremated now. Wasn't that his wish?"

He was also half human! And they liked to be buried. Since when did the paranormal element trump all others?

And as far as I knew, yes, he did want to be cremated, but that really wasn't the point.

"Shouldn't you have checked with me first?" I asked, trying not to sound as irritated as I felt. "He was, after all, half human. Plus, I didn't even get to see the body once after you took him away. Where's the closure in that?"

"You wouldn't have wanted to see your father like that, Sarah."

I snorted, clenching my teeth together. *How condescending.*

"Well, I have a few questions about his body."

Specifically, if they thought one vampire had drained him. Or two.

"Sarah—"

I jumped in, not wanting to hear him lecture me about my place in all this, like I was some simple-minded female who couldn't conduct a conversation. "When do you get the coroner's report on his autopsy? I assume he signed the death certificate and listed the cause of death, if Dad has already been cremated?"

I didn't know how they'd gotten his autopsy done in a single day, but maybe it was a slow month for murders.

"Well, unfortunately, there was a bit of a mix-up with communication at the morgue."

"I'm sorry. What?"

I waited for him to continue, my stomach tightening as each moment ticked by. *A mix-up?*

"Well…" He coughed once, then twice.

"A mix-up in communication?" I repeated, in case he needed a reminder of what we were talking about.

"Yes. I was informed, unfortunately, that the coroner believed your father was a heart attack victim, and simply cremated him without an autopsy."

"*He. Fucking. What?*" I screamed into the phone.

"Miss Williams! Lower your voice."

"I will *not* lower my fucking voice," I hissed, then took a breath and grabbed hold of my control, so I was at least intelligible. "Are you telling me that the coroner, or whoever put my father's body in the furnace, did *not* determine cause of death before they did so?"

There was a long pause, and part of me thought the detective may have hung up on me.

"Yes," he said finally.

I closed my eyes, angry magic pulsing through me at the speed of light.

I didn't usually feel my mother's magic inside of me. It had never been trained and I wasn't focused on it, but by God… if the man on the phone had been standing in front of me in the flesh, I may have blasted him to dust.

"So," I growled into the phone, then inhaled through my nose to bring back my humanity. "You're telling me that they destroyed all evidence of my father's murder?"

"*No!* No, Miss Williams. We have your testimony, everything found at the scene. We still have a case."

I leaned back in the chair, the composure of a well-trained lawyer passing over me at his tone. I'd take them for every penny they had.

"Really?" I asked, struggling to be calm enough to communicate, but using years of corporate training to speak correctly. "What case? How many puncture wounds were on his body? What was the cause of death?"

"We're investigating possibilities."

"Such as?" I asked, tapping my fingernails on the desk in front of me.

"Well, as the coroner has ruled it a heart attack, we are no longer following murder protocol."

"You're no longer…" *Oh, wow.*

This imbecile couldn't be this stupid, could he?

"Well, ah…"

I slid my hand over the cool wood of the desktop. "So, tell me, Detective. Are you on the take, like half the city and probably half the police force? Or are you just covering for the coroner who was paid to destroy the evidence so it would be impossible to catch my father's murderer?"

There was a gasp and a sharp growl on the other end of the line. "If you're accusing me—"

I lifted my hand up and slammed my palm down on the desk. "I *am* accusing you of being a filthy, no-good sack of shit. My father did not deserve to die, and I will make sure his killer is brought to justice, so you'd better stay out of my way."

"Miss Williams, vigilantes are not looked upon favorably by the state."

"I am not a vigilante," I corrected him. "I am putting out a private bounty on my father's killer, with a million-dollar price tag. I wonder how many people will be interested in my father's murder with that?"

"Miss Williams—"

I slammed the phone down so hard my hand vibrated with the force and I let out a growl.

Fridge opened the door, holding containers of steaming hot Chinese.

His smile and greeting froze on his lips, then his eyebrows lowered as he frowned. "What's wrong?"

I let out a frustrated growl, tearing at the air as I paced back and forth behind the desk. "Can you believe it! The fucking... stupid... pigs!"

I wanted to smash something. I wanted to punch that detective in the face. I wanted to cry and knife him, straight through his over-sized beer belly.

Those motherfuckers! I'd make them pay.

Fridge came forward, put our lunch down on the desk, and straightened up, puffing his chest out as though he were readying himself for a fight.

"What's happened?" he asked. "Tell me."

"They... they..." The tears begun. "Fuck! No."

I wiped at the wetness on my face. I would not cry over what the corrupt cops and the coroner had done to my father. I would get even. There was no better revenge than that.

"The coroner... the police... They cremated my dad's body yesterday. *Without* an autopsy. They're ruling it a heart attack, not murder."

The growl that rolled through the room was menacing and would have scared me if I didn't know the dragon was on my side.

"They... what?" he roared. "How the hell are they going to catch a killer if they can't... Oh, those pieces of shit! They're covering it all up."

"Yes," I practically yelled, pointing at him. "This is a total cover-up. Which means the vampires who killed him were important!"

That would make sense.

He nodded. "Or at least the vampires who hired the killer are important. Otherwise, why would they bother to go to such lengths to cover it up?"

I placed both of my palms down on the desk, leaned over the wood, and stared at my dragon. "I don't know who did this, Fridge, but I'm going to get them."

Lunch was delicious once I finally got down to eating it. I'd have to find out where they ordered from, so I could make it a regular lunch for myself.

Fridge and I talked strategies while we ate, mostly about the best way to kill vampires, then he went back to work.

It turned out, a stake to the heart was still the only sure way to destroy a blood sucker. Silver slowed them down, but even a silver bullet to the heart wouldn't kill them. But a wooden stake did. No idea why.

No one knew. But it was with that in mind that I spent the afternoon researching silver bullets and the best way to carry a stake on your person.

Happily, when I asked Fridge about the possibility of getting some vampire weaponry later on in the day, he said my father had a stash in the armory.

I gaped at him, sitting on the desk while I gazed at my big dragon. It was sometimes hard to focus on a conversation when he was in my view. He was too yummy. "The armory?"

"Yeah. You haven't seen it?"

I shook my head.

He grinned. "Then you are in for a treat."

He led me out of the office and down the stairs. We turned to the right, going around the large staircase, almost doing a full one-eighty.

Fridge pointed to a plain-looking door beneath the stairs.

"Is that it?" I asked, surprised he was so excited at such a small thing.

He nodded. "Yep."

"Wow." I'd walked past that door a million times and always assumed it was a cleaning supplies closet.

Apparently not.

"How..." My gaze slid from one side of the enclosed room beneath the stairs to the other.

The room had obviously been built into the warehouse. It was boxed in and looked quite unobtrusive at first glance. Though now that I studied it, I wondered how on earth I hadn't noticed it earlier.

I shivered. That room would have no windows inside and I wasn't sure I'd like that. I wouldn't say I was claustrophobic, but I liked to see through a window, at the very least.

I tilted my head and looked up. A security camera was aimed at the doorway.

Fridge opened the plain, wooden door, revealing a metal door behind it, with a fingerprint scanner as a lock.

"Whoa," I said, glancing at Fridge.

That was unexpected.

He grinned. "Yeah."

"Who has access?" I asked. The scanner looked like some pretty high-tech stuff.

I could imagine that what lay within was expensive.

"Your dad, of course. Rogan, me and Terry."

"Terry?"

Have I met him yet?

Fridge nodded. "Yeah, he's one of the older guys. Doesn't come in much anymore, but he's been working here practically since the inception of this place."

"Terry… oh, you mean Uncle T!" I grinned. He was my dad's oldest and most loyal friend.

He was a wolf shifter as well and had been muscular in his day. He had a well-rounded pot belly now but was as loveable as ever.

A thought struck me. If my father put Rogan and Fridge in the same level of trust category that he did Uncle T, then Fate had blessed me with two remarkable mates.

"I really need to call Uncle T," I said. "Do you know if he knows about Dad?"

Fridge shrugged. "I don't, sorry. I can find out for you, though."

He turned toward the door and pressed his thumb to the panel.

The metal door clicked, then popped open.

Very cool.

Fridge opened the heavy door fully and flicked on a light switch inside the room. "Welcome to bounty hunter heaven."

He revealed the contents with a flourish of his hand.

My mouth dropped open. "Now that is some serious hardware."

If they'd told me the police or the army had outfitted the room, I wouldn't have been surprised. It was stocked!

Fridge tilted his head. "Go on in. I'll shut the door behind you for security reasons, and you just open it back up when you've got what you need."

I nodded, trusting Fridge and whatever process he thought was best. This was way above my pay grade.

I walked forward, into the brightly lit room. Fluorescent globes bounced light off the bright, white walls and multitude of silver weapons.

The door shut behind me and I jumped. It was like being locked in a jail, with no sunlight and limited air.

I took a deep breath to steady myself. This was *intense!*

I ambled along the first aisle, staring in amazement at the number of weapons my father had accumulated over time.

The walls were lined with every gun I could imagine. Shotguns, semi-automatics. Long guns and handguns.

Then there were the knives.

A smile curled my lips and my pulse began to pound a little bit faster as I examined the handles and blades.

I'd definitely inherited my father's love of sharp knives.

I strolled around the room, which was about the size of a large bedroom, inspecting everything carefully.

There were so many nice knives I'd love to take home and play with, but what I really *needed* was something to harm, maim, or kill a vampire.

I lifted my hand and ran my fingers along the handles of some impressive swords and long knives, then came across a section that looked like it was designed just for vampire hunting.

"Here we go." I squatted down to rifle though a large chest of wooden stakes, finding one that was perfect for me. It had a long, thin shaft, with a smaller handle that was easy to grip. And just to make it more perfect, it was stored inside a sheath with a strap for my ankle or wrist. Or if I got a strap extension, I could probably wear it around my waist.

I picked it up and tied it around my wrist, the wood warm against my forearm.

I admired my new addition with a happy chuckle and a grin. "What else have you got, Dad?"

I found a handgun that fit my palm perfectly, a box of silver bullets, and a box of wooden ones.

I wasn't sure if a wooden bullet would kill a vamp—but I'd ask one of the guys outside and find out.

I did a few more rounds of the armory, tempted to grab a few more toys, but in the end, I didn't. I could always come back later. After all, the place was mine now.

What a strange thought.

I'd have to arrange to get my fingerprint added to the locking system.

I headed back to the door and opened it up.

Fridge was still there, arms crossed, standing guard.

"You're waiting for me?" I asked.

He grinned. "Yes, but to be honest, I'd have to supervise anyone who went in there. Every item taken is always catalogued, logged, and returned. If we didn't do that, there would always be hell to pay from Jimmy."

"How come?" I asked, running my hands over the new, shiny silver gun I held.

"Those weapons equate to about a million dollars in assets," he said. "Not to mention the safety and risk aspects if they ended up in the wrong hands."

I glanced back at the room, and then tugged the door shut. "A million. Wow."

"Yes."

Rogan walked up with a towel around his neck, his face covered in sweat, and a grin on his lips. "What are you two up to? Oh... got some new toys, Sadie?"

I laughed and nodded. I was glad he felt the same way I did about these weapons. "Yeah. I've been researching some vampire killing techniques and wanted something I could carry on me. You know, just in case. How long have we got before we knock off?"

Rogan glanced at the watch on his wrist. "About an hour, a bit more."

"Cool. I'll see you guys then. Thanks, Fridge."

I knew others in the building were watching us, and although I was showing Fridge and Rogan extra attention, I didn't think it was too obvious how much I wanted them both.

Not yet, anyway.

We wouldn't be able to keep our relationship a secret for too much longer.

I headed back up the stairs and got on my dad's computer once again. This time, I did some fun research—on dragon shifters, mostly to try and understand more about Fridge and his motivation to ignore our bond.

From what I gathered, dragon shifters were notoriously difficult to bond with, in any way.

They loved to create families, but rarely stuck around. The men especially, but even the females tended to expect their babies to fly early and not rely on parental care at all.

"No wonder the species is dying out."

Any other shifter in our community—wolves, bears, and even foxes—valued commitment to their offspring. And anyone with human genetics mixed into their bloodline, which was practically one hundred percent of the population of our city, wanted a father to stick around for his kids.

I continued reading.

Vampires love their blood...

"Yeah, Fridge mentioned that."

And the research went on.

Super-strong.

Super-fast.

Hard to tame.

Damn it.

I pushed the computer keyboard away with a disgusted grunt, talking to myself. "Yeah, so he's a catch and a half, if I want a strong baby the vampires want to bite, but with major commitment issues. I get it."

I leaned back in my chair and pulled my hair out of the elastic containing it.

Why would Fate have sent me someone who wouldn't accept our bond? It made no sense at all.

The simple answer was, Fate wouldn't do such a thing. So, how did I overcome Fridge's issues and garner his trust and love?

Time, probably.

I caught up on some emails and soon enough, Rogan was knocking on my door, telling me that most of the guys had gone home and that it was our turn to leave.

I smiled at him as I started to shut down all the tabs open on my screen. "Great. Give me five minutes and I'll meet you both downstairs."

I took my time shutting Dad's computer and packing everything to go home. I still had my new stake strapped to my wrist and my new gun packed nicely away in my shoulder bag.

But now it was time to deal with my mates.

And damn, it had been hard to keep my hands off them today.

Rogan was always smiling, and so strong and capable. Perfect for loving, kissing, and living with.

Fridge was so possessive and huge. When I thought about mating with him, I imagined him taking me standing or up against a wall. Sex with the dragon would not be slow, and it would not be gentle and loving.

But damn, it was going to be satisfying. I could tell already.

So much so that just thinking about it made me ache in all the right places.

I locked everything up, did a quick sweep of the building and then marched to the front door.

When I walked out the front, I pulled the door shut, a sigh leaving me. I hadn't realized I was carrying so much tension.

My two mates were waiting for me outside.

"You okay?" Rogan questioned as he took my hand. He walked me over to Dad's car.

"Yeah. I'm okay," I said as I hopped in the passenger side front seat.

Fridge got in the driver's seat and Rogan jumped in the back.

We took off, into the tail end of peak hour traffic.

Rogan's hand slid over my shoulder, squeezing it for a moment. "You don't sound okay. I know it's been a big day, what with Shadow and then that cop. Fridge told me about that. I'm so sorry, Sadie."

I patted his hand so he could let go of my shoulder and release another sigh. "It's not that. Thought it has been a big day—huge when you look at it with that list. Finding my cousin, the stuff he told me about our city and the vamps. Then that cop and what they're doing to cover up my dad's murder."

I growled. Obviously, my dad was onto something big, or the people responsible for his murder had more money than God. How much did it take to bribe a city coroner?

"Well, if it's not all that shit, what's wrong?" Fridge asked.

"I don't know exactly. I suppose I can't believe I've managed to get through two days of my life without my dad." My throat stuck, and I had to grab a bottle of water from one of the cup holders in the car and swallow some down.

The boys didn't interrupt, so I kept talking.

"I mean, he used to joke about me working with him. About all the skills he taught me, and how they were a waste in a corporate setting."

Rogan chuckled from the back seat. "Yeah, I can't imagine you'd have too many chances to practice your knife fighting skills with your lawyer clients."

I laughed. "Exactly. But now, working with you guys... I like it. I like being at the workshop. The smell, the noise. I know I haven't gotten into the nitty-gritty yet—payroll and bounties and all that—but I suppose I'm just regretting not doing more with Dad... before he died."

And that was at the heart of my feelings.

I regretted so much.

The time I'd wasted with friends, instead of him.

Choosing law when I could have done business management and helped Dad out.

"If I'd known..." I stopped, and had to swallow down the pain, trying not to cry *again* in front of these men.

If I'd known I was going to lose him so early, I would never have left his side.

Fridge cleared his throat, loudly, and slid a hand onto my denim-covered thigh, squeezing lightly. "You didn't know, and even if you did, your dad wouldn't have changed anything."

"How do you know?" I asked.

He laughed. "Because he did nothing but brag about you. How smart you were. How successful. He left out the bits about how beautiful you were, but I can understand why."

I laughed and relaxed back into my seat. "Thanks."

We passed by my apartment building and kept driving, all the way to Fridge and Rogan's apartment complex.

I hoped they were right that Dad went to his grave with no regrets, because although it was true that I could not have loved my dad more in this lifetime, I did wish I'd made a few different choices.

But, hopefully, it wasn't too late to right some wrongs.

CHAPTER 34
SADIE

Dinner was thrown together by Rogan—pasta and meatballs—and a salad I managed to scrounge up from the few ingredients they kept in their fridge.

"I may need to do a bit of shopping if I'm gonna stay here for a few days," I said, chopping up tomatoes that were just about past their use-by date.

Rogan stirred the pasta sauce and gathered bowls out of the cabinet for us. I glanced over and almost laughed. The bowls were the size of serving dishes.

"A few days?" Rogan repeated, his tone incredulous. "It's gonna take longer than that to solve this case. So, if you need anything, just let us know. We can buy anything you need, or... you know, whatever suits you."

"Thanks," I said. "I'll get a few things tomorrow though."

Yogurt, juice, fruit, and vegetables.

These guys seemed to live on carbs and protein. And very little else.

Not that I had a problem with steak and pasta. But a girl needed a salad on occasion, or I'd blow up like a balloon.

We ate dinner with the TV on and chatted while sitting on the couch. It was casual, and fun, and so different from anything I'd ever experienced with any previous boyfriends.

The fact that I didn't have to worry about ever losing Rogan was already a great help in making me feel secure.

If not yet loved, I was needed. Wanted. Desired. At least, it felt that way.

Only one way to find out for sure.

I lifted my hand to cover my mouth, yawning loudly.

The sun had gone down, but it was still early.

I was exhausted, but not too exhausted for a bit of fun. "Do you guys mind if I have a quick shower before bed?"

"Go for it," Rogan said with a grin.

"I'll get you a towel." Fridge got up and came with me, showing me where the linen closet was and pulling out an oversized bath sheet.

I took it and held it to my chest. "Thanks. Are we… all sleeping in your bed again tonight?"

His mouth hardened and that muscle in his jaw ticked. He looked angry, but as I could only imagine the type of frustration he would be feeling, I didn't take offense.

Finally, he nodded. "Yeah, I think that's best."

"Okay. Thanks. Won't be long." I jumped into the bathroom and shut the door before my excited squeal popped out.

I stepped into the shower and scrubbed myself from head to toe.

Normally, I loved long, hot showers, but when I had two shifters waiting to take me to bed, well… I wasn't going to dilly-dally.

I wrapped myself in the massive bath sheet that fell almost to the floor and picked up my dirty clothes. I'd make it a few more days with what I had in my bag but would definitely need to go back to my apartment for another change of clothes—or ten—if I was staying here semi-permanently.

Both men were in the kitchen cleaning up when I walked past.

They looked up and saw me wrapped in only a towel, my face flushed from the heat of the shower and my hair wet.

"Should I, ah, get dressed for a movie or something?" I asked. "Or are we going to bed soon?"

"Maybe." Rogan glanced at Fridge. "Maybe put on what you were wearing to sleep last night, just so we can talk for a sec, before bed."

My stomach dropped. That sounded ominous.

"Okay. No problem." I hurried to the bedroom to grab my black tank and a clean pair of black cotton undies. Exactly what Rogan had asked for.

CHAPTER 35
ROGAN

Damn it. I hated to see the disappointment on Sadie's face. And I hated even more asking her to put clothes on.

What sort of idiots were we? Requesting she get dressed so we could talk, rather than have sex? Because it was obvious that was what she had in mind.

She was wet, and clean, and sparkling with expectation, and my stupid best friend was about to drop a bomb on her.

I wanted to stop him, of course. What he needed to tell her had the power to ruin everything.

Hopefully it didn't, of course. But I knew Fridge, and this situation, and the topic of fated mates. It all had the potential to blow sky-high.

But there was no way around it.

If we were going to be together forever, and I certainly never had any intentions of leaving my mate, then we needed to get this right.

Lay everything on that table. Be totally transparent.

I had no problem with that. I was happy. Content.

But Fridge was a concern, and I had no control over him. None whatsoever.

CHAPTER 36

SADIE

I considered pulling on some sweats to cover myself up even more, but as I checked myself in the mirror, I figured I exposed more at the beach, and besides, they wouldn't give me bad news while I was only half-dressed. Would they?

I lifted my chin high and walked back into the living room, my breasts bouncing a lot more than normal due to the lack of a bra. I swung my hips for fun.

"So, what do you guys wanna talk about?" I asked.

Fridge whistled from his spot on the kitchen counter stool, his gaze scanning my body from head to toe and back again.

Rogan grinned as he leaned over the kitchen counter, giving my boobs a good look before he got back to my face.

"You look fantastic, Sadie," Rogan said. "Wow."

I put one hand on my hip and flicked my drying hair back over my shoulder. "You told me to put on what I wore to bed last night."

"Yeah, but..." Rogan grinned. "I forgot how sexy you were in it."

I shrugged and crossed my arms over my chest, suddenly a little self-conscious. "So, should I sit down, or...?"

"Yeah, grab a chair. Hopefully, this will be quick, and we can get to bed."

I pulled out a dining chair and sat down, waiting with my heart in my throat for them to tell me what was wrong.

Was this about my dad's death? Or was it about Fridge's inability to commit? Or something else?

Maybe the sex last night going unfinished with one of them was causing a problem.

Damn, there were a lot of things this could be about.

"Come on, don't leave me in suspense," I said. "You're freaking me out."

Rogan frowned. "Sorry. That wasn't the intention. I'll be quick then. So, basically, I wanted to check with you... last night, did we officially mate, you and me?"

I opened my mouth to answer his question and he jumped in over me.

"Like, I know we had sex, and you've said you think we're both your fated mates, but is there a ceremony, or is that it? What does it mean, exactly?"

I relaxed in the chair. I could handle this sort of conversation. With Rogan, anyway.

"Well... I'm new to this too, so I'd have to double check with my aunts or something, to give you a perfect answer, but yes... if you're asking me, I think we've mated already."

Fridge's eyebrows shot up as he sat straighter on the stool and glanced at Rogan.

I shifted to the edge of my chair. "Not that I meant for it to happen like that, or anything. You know I spotted our connection from the beginning, but that doesn't mean I thought mating would be easy. I thought it would need certain words, or a ceremony, or something."

I took a breath, trying to slow down the pace at which I was talking. "But as soon as you were inside me, Rogan, I could feel the change. The bond clamping down on both of us. I didn't think it would happen like that, or so quickly. But I suppose because you were so accepting of it, the bond just took over. I don't know. Why? Is that how you feel too?"

He gazed at me, his eyes shifting from blue to silver, then back to blue again.

Then he nodded. "Yeah, it is. I feel... settled. Happier, somehow. And I can't imagine being apart from you, ever again. And I don't feel trapped by that, in any way." He glanced pointedly at Fridge and back to me again. "I feel relieved, like I've found a missing piece of myself."

I couldn't stop the smile that spread across my face. Happiness unlike anything I'd ever known radiated up inside of me.

"That's great. I mean, we barely know each other, but I feel the same way. So settled and happy, knowing that I'm done looking for the one—or the *ones*. I've found you."

Fridge got up so suddenly he pushed the stool over, the metal piece of furniture clanging to the ground.

"Hey, what's wrong?" I asked, also standing up.

I felt too small and too weak sitting on a chair while Fridge was towering over me with all his muscle bulk and height.

He hissed and growled in a strange way as he began to pace the room. Which was difficult, because his legs were long, and the room wasn't that big.

"Fridge. Hey... what's..." I looked over at Rogan and raised my eyebrows in question. "A little help?"

Rogan rounded the counter and sidled over to me, sighing loudly. "This isn't good. I know those noises, and if he can't get himself under control, we're gonna need to get him outside. Real quick."

"Outside? Why?"

Fridge turned to me, his eyes shifting to full yellow, his pupils the shape of a diamond.

"You... mated with him. But not... me," he hissed.

I put my hands up. "But I *want* to mate with you! You only need to tell me you want me too and we can go to bed right now. In fact, to hell with the bed, take me here."

Fridge's hands tightened into fists at his sides and he vibrated with some kind of emotion I couldn't read.

"No... I don't... want to..." he hissed at me.

I turned to Rogan, my heart squeezing painfully. "What does he mean, he doesn't want to? He doesn't want me, at all?"

Rogan grabbed my hand. "He doesn't mean it like that. He was afraid that if he had sex with you, he'd unwittingly bond with you for life. And he didn't want to do that. Not without discussing it first. Without deciding on the rules of the relationship. Hey!" He yelled at Fridge. "Get a hold of yourself. There's no danger here!"

When I looked back at my second fated mate, he was beginning to change in a totally different way. His head was changing shape. His tongue, when it snaked out, was forked.

Fear shivered up my spine. "What's happening?"

"He's shifting. We need to get him outside. Now."

Rogan ran to the window connected to the fire escape and threw it open.

"Fridge!" he yelled in the direction of the kitchen where the dragon was still shaking. "Quick! Before it's too late."

Fridge looked at me, and all I could see was blazing emotion in his gaze, before he sprinted to the window.

Once there, he looked back at me again, and the conflict was obvious in his eyes. The hurt and the pain and confusion.

I needed to say something... but what?

"Please come back," I managed to choke out. "Even if you don't want me as a mate, I still need *you*."

It took every bit of my courage to admit that to the man before me. A man, who by all accounts was rejecting me. Again.

"Stay. Here," Fridge hissed before he jumped onto the fire escape and began stripping off his clothing.

Rogan grabbed the clothes and stepped back and I ran up to him, wanting to watch this shift more than anything in the world.

I'd never seen a dragon shift. Few people had.

Fridge's massive, muscled, human body began to contort as his skin scaled and blackened. His arms shrank as his back sprouted wings the color of sapphires.

I put my hand over my mouth to cover the gasp of awe that escaped me.

Fridge kept transforming, kept getting bigger, until he was in danger of hurting himself on the fire escape where he stood.

He leaned forward and launched himself off the metal grate, his wings flapping almost soundlessly on the breeze as he flew high into the air.

I ran to the window and looked up, watching him fly farther away. Into the sky. Into the distance, above the city and beyond.

I watched until he was out of sight, until I was straining out the window to see.

"Come back in. You'll get cold," Rogan said, pulling me back with his strong, warm hands. He shut the window.

"Aren't you going to leave it open for him?" I asked. I didn't want Fridge locked out of his own apartment.

"He'll be gone most of the night. But I won't lock the window, don't worry. If he wants to come back in, he will." Rogan walked back to the kitchen and grabbed a bottle of water from the fridge. "Time for bed?"

I wandered after him, feeling dazed. "Ah, yeah. But I have questions."

He nodded and tilted his head in the direction of the bedrooms. "I expected that. We may as well go sleep in Fridge's bed again, in case he comes back before sunrise."

I thought that was a good idea too. The last thing we wanted was the big, insecure, jealous jerk thinking we were freezing him out of the relationship. Even if it had been his choice to leave us.

Rogan walked into the large, dark bedroom where we'd slept last night. "Jump in. We can just chat, unless you want to…"

I shook my head. "I don't think I can after that."

While sex with my wolf mate was something I'd looked forward to all day, my heart was now shivering with anxiety. Fridge was gone, and he'd made it clear that the last thing he wanted was to be mated to me.

If I wasn't about to be cuddled up with Rogan, my heart was on the brink of being totally broken.

I crawled into the middle of the bed and climbed beneath the covers.

Rogan slid into the bed and lay on his back beside me. "Come here. Don't worry. I won't bite."

He reached for me and I went to him willingly, putting my head on his chest.

"What the hell happened just now?" I said.

Rogan sighed and ran his fingers through my hair and down my back. "I know it sounds trite to say it's not you, but it's *really* not you."

"Does he do that often?" I asked.

"You mean shift?"

"Yeah."

He chuckled. "No. Hardly ever. I've seen it maybe a dozen times in twenty years. It only happens when there's a pretty massive emotional turmoil going on inside of him."

I lifted my head and arranged my arm so I could look down at Rogan. Was he serious? "I caused some sort of… emotional turmoil?"

Rogan stroked his finger over my cheek. "Unfortunately, we both did. I felt so different today, I thought I'd warn him that having sex with you, our fated mate, would bond him, since I know how afraid he is of forced commitment. I just thought having the knowledge might help." Rogan sighed. "I'm sorry if I made it worse."

I shook my head and sniffed. The tears brimmed in my eyes, but this time I wasn't stopping them.

"I don't blame you. I was surprised how intense last night was. I actually don't think that if Fridge and I had sex, our shifters would mate so quickly. We're different, for one thing, unlike you and I who are both wolves. He's also so resistant. I think the fated mates magic only worked last night because we were both open to it." I sighed and snuggled into him. "At least one of you wants me. I can't be upset about that."

But I was. Part of me was heartbroken. My dragon, one of my fated mates, was in such turmoil over loving me. I never wanted to be the cause of such pain for Fridge.

Rogan kissed the top of my head and sighed, holding me tight. "Sweetheart, he wants you so much he can't see straight. But unfortunately, getting him to see that, and agree to bonding for life, is going to be a lot harder than either of us thought it would be."

I nodded, unable to say any more, and rolled onto my side so that Rogan could spoon me.

It was time for sleep.

For healing and dreaming about a world where everything was right.

A world where I didn't have a murder to solve and a mate to tame.

What a mess my life has become.

But even at that terrible thought, Rogan slipped his hand around my waist and held me tight. I knew there was one thing right with my world—I was mated to my wolf.

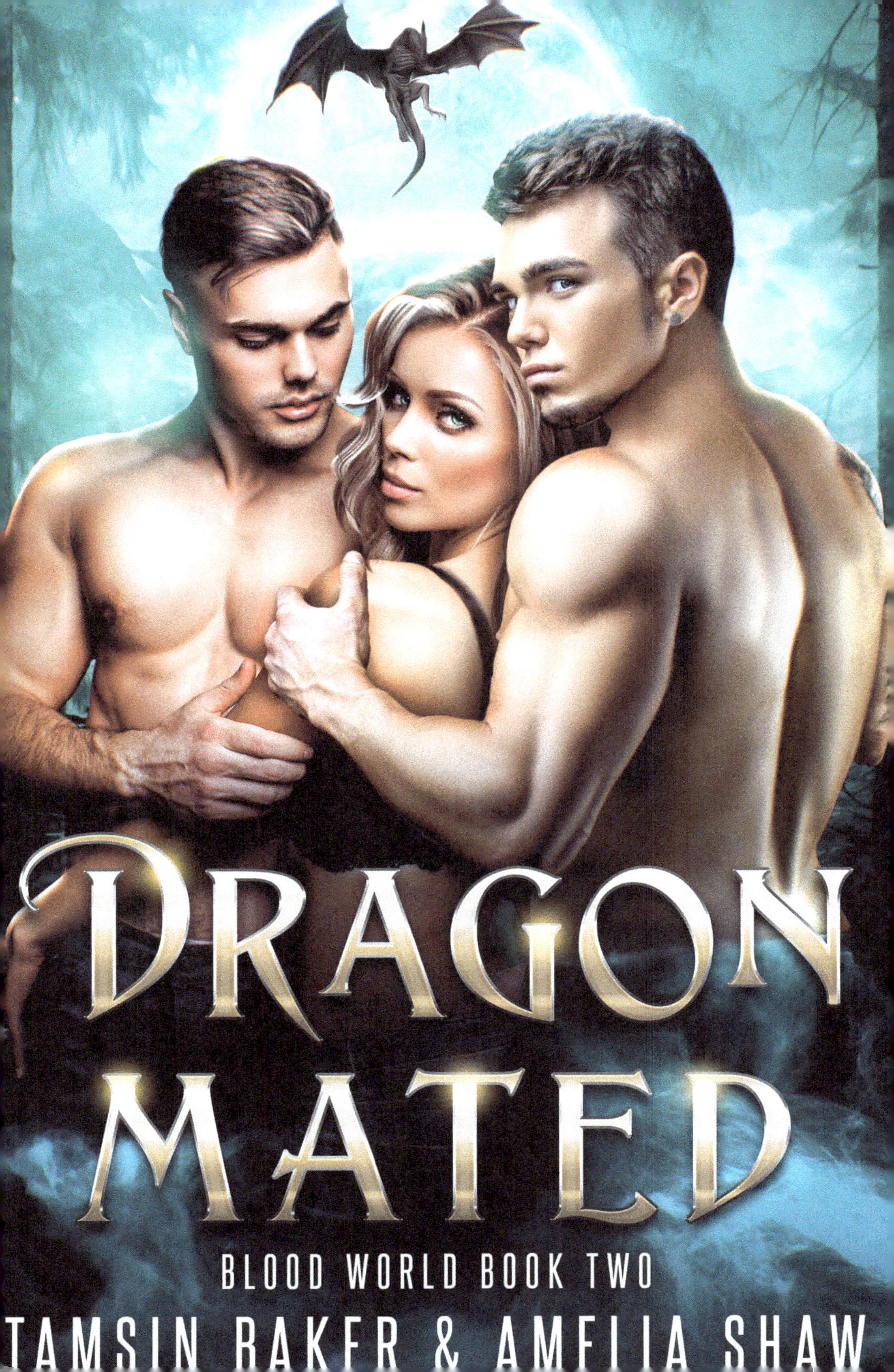

DRAGON MATED
BLOOD WORLD BOOK TWO
TAMSIN BAKER & AMELIA SHAW

DRAGON MATED

THE PARANORMALS BLOOD WORLD BOOK 2

CHAPTER 1

SADIE

Swimming up from a dream about my dad and into the light of day was both devastatingly sad and beautiful at the same time.

I never wanted to forget a single thing about him. The way he laughed. The way he joked. The loyalty he showed his friends, and the strength he'd displayed in everything he did, from the way he handled my mother's death and raising me, to running a business of fifty strong men on his own.

There was also his kindness. The way he'd held me when I cried, read me bedtime stories and made me feel safe. Always. Even when a boy would break my heart in high school, or I'd miss my mom so much my chest would feel like it was going to crack open.

He had been there for me. Always.

I smiled as I arched my body, connecting with hot flesh and firm limbs. Hopefully my mates would show our children the same things my father had taught me. There was a time to be strong, a time to be kind. A time to be smart with your head, and a time to use your heart. But there was always time for family.

Speaking of which...

Rogan's hand slid over my thigh, caressing my flesh before moving north and stroking across my belly.

Tingles of awareness and arousal curled inside me.

"Good morning," I said as my eyelids fluttered open.

I lay on my side, facing the spot where Fridge normally slept. Rogan pressed against my back, the heat of his body radiating over me, making me want to snuggle in even closer.

"Good morning, beautiful," Rogan replied, kissing my neck. Then he sighed, sounding happy, and his breath caressed my skin like a hot wave.

Stretching out a hand in front of me to the empty side of the huge bed, I curled my fingers into the sheets.

I frowned. The space was cold. Then I realized there was no indent in Fridge's pillow and sadness hit me all at once.

I swallowed down the emotions that clogged my throat. "He didn't come home last night."

Rogan sighed, this time with a touch of resignation. "He must be bad."

I rolled onto my back and looked up at my beautiful wolf shifter who was half propped up against the headboard now. Damn, he was gorgeous. His dark blond hair was tousled, and I wanted to reach up and play with the strands. So, I did, combing my hand through his hair and stroking my fingers along his cheek.

He stared down at me, the intensity of his gaze warming the sad, cold parts of my heart.

"What do you mean?" I asked. "About Fridge being bad?"

Rogan turned his head, kissing the palm of my hand that I had cupped around his face, then looked at me again. "He would normally be home, that's all. He's had enough time to cool off. I would have thought he'd have flown back by now."

I gazed at the open bedroom door. "Do you think he came back, and maybe slept somewhere else in the apartment?"

I could imagine Fridge on the couch, all huffy and mad at us, but at least he would be here and we could start to sort out everything.

Rogan shrugged. "Only one way to find out."

He dropped a sweet, gentle kiss on my lips, then jumped up out of bed.

Damn, he's fine.

Unable to stop myself from following his every move, I loved the way his ass cheeks flexed with each step he took, and admired the breadth of his back and the incredible strength in his arms.

He was shredded, strong, and gorgeous.

"Hey, Fridge!" Rogan called out, still wearing his boxer briefs from last night. "You around?"

I hadn't been up for any sort of intimacy with Rogan after Fridge left. The last thing I'd wanted was for Fridge to come home and feel like we'd deliberately excluded him, especially when the reason he'd left was mostly due to his insecurities and jealousy. Which seemed a little ridiculous to me, knowing how I felt about him, but obviously those feelings were very real to him.

We'd slept in Fridge's bed. And I was pretty much still fully clothed, so that if and when Fridge did turn up, he wouldn't have a reason to be even more resentful. Or, that had been the plan, anyway.

Rogan walked through the bedroom door and disappeared from view, then within a few minutes sauntered back into the room again, shrugging.

"Doesn't look like he came home at all." He ran a hand through his hair. "I kinda assumed I'd wake up and he'd be here cooking breakfast and pretending like last night never happened."

I sat up, remembering the breakfast he'd made for me yesterday. "Yeah, me too."

I wrapped my arms around my knees and sighed. What should we do?

Rogan walked over to the bed, knelt on the mattress, and crawled over to me. "Come here, beautiful."

He flipped over and lay down on his back on top of the covers. Then he pulled me down so that I lay with my head on his chest, his heart steadily beating beneath my ear.

He stroked my hair. "This is not your fault, Sadie. And it's not mine, either. We've just gotta wait for the big idiot to get his shit together and come back."

I nodded against his chest but didn't speak. My eyes were hot and my throat was clogged again.

I was *never* this emotional. It must have been everything that had happened this week. My father's murder, finding my mates, and then meeting my cousin, who I hadn't even known existed.

There was only so much a person could take. Even one who didn't normally cry.

I cleared my throat, wanting to change the subject, because thinking about Fridge and the hurt he was obviously carrying was just too much at the moment.

He was my Fated Mate but he had serious issues about that term. All I knew was that he was a sexy guy and I desired him an incredible amount. Clearly, he wanted me in return. And yet, he was fighting our connection because he didn't want to be "forced" into a mating that hadn't been of his choosing. As if any Fated Mate had a say in who they could choose or not. Fate was the one who chose, in that instance.

"So, what's the plan for today?" I asked, pushing myself up and sliding out of bed, ripples of annoyance at Fridge moving along my clenched jaw.

Channeling annoyance rather than worry toward Fridge was actually a good way of pushing forward. It beat feeling melancholy and rejected.

At least I still had one mate who wanted me!

Rogan sat up in bed and leaned back on his hands. His skin

glowed in the morning light and a curl of desire moved through my belly.

Yum...

"Well, we need to go into work, I suppose," he said. "And Fridge could be there. He barely leaves the place. That suit you?"

I grinned. "Yeah, of course. It's my business now, I suppose. So, I'll have to get used to being there every day."

He nodded as though agreeing with me, but his expressio was thoughtful.

I opened my mouth to ask what he was thinking about, something my father had always said *not* to do with a man.

We're not women, Sadie. Half the time we're not thinking about anything other than what needs to get done at that moment. And the other half... you probably don't want to know about anyway.

Rogan jumped up and grinned at me, distracting me from my question. "I'm gonna hop in the shower and get dressed. Wanna join me?"

He waggled his eyebrows in a suggestive fashion, and I dropped my gaze to the floor. I didn't want to say no to him, especially as he was my mate, but I wasn't able to control the guilt that came flooding in.

"I'd love to, but..."

"But you're concerned about Fridge's feelings if he finds us in there together."

I glanced up, meeting Rogan's gaze. "I know I shouldn't be worried about him. I wasn't the other night, when we had sex in front of him. That was pretty hot actually. And he's the one who ran away last night; rejected me. I shouldn't worry. And yet..."

Rogan chuckled softly. "But you *do* worry about his feelings, and that's totally okay. We've got the rest of our lives to enjoy love-making and showers together, don't we?"

I didn't like the slight question in those last two words. Was Rogan doubting us? Doubting me?

I nodded quickly. "Yes! We do!" We were mated, or at least, our wolf shifter sides were. I was pretty sure that meant the human side automatically followed suit. It was a done deal. Breaking that fated mate bond would probably kill us both.

"Great. Well, I'm gonna grab some clothes. You wanna shower first?"

Not really. But I should.

"Yeah, thanks. I'll be quick."

I scrubbed myself from head to toe, then jumped out of the shower the moment Rogan stepped into the bathroom.

We were both showered and dressed and driving to work within the hour, drive-through coffees in hand.

"Muffin?" I asked him, opening the bag of food I'd bought at the coffee place. "Chocolate or raspberry?"

"Not fussy," he said, so I gave him the double chocolate one.

He bit into it, crumbs falling to his lap.

I smiled as I ate my raspberry and white chocolate muffin, the strange normalcy and complete relaxation between us at odds with the short amount of time we'd known each other.

We parked a street over from my father's bounty hunter business, otherwise known as the Workshop, and walked up to the building in pleasant silence.

Rogan pulled out a set of keys from his pocket and opened the door for me. "I'll go switch on all the lights and set up a few things."

I nodded, amazed at how quiet the large converted warehouse was without all the men who worked there. "Doesn't anyone else have keys to open up if we're late?"

Rogan shook his head. "Nope. Just Fridge and me. And now you." He stopped and grinned. "The guys won't be long, though. They know we're pretty reliable on opening time."

I smiled at Rogan, then glanced at the staircase that led up to the second floor. "I'm gonna head up to the office."

He nodded. "I'll see if Fridge is here, hiding out somewhere, and let you know if I find him."

My chest tightened. "Thanks."

I ran up the stairs, part of me expecting Fridge to pop out of the shadows.

But he didn't.

When I entered my empty office, my stomach dropped.

He's not here.

Fridge was a fiery one, in more ways than one.

Every time I looked at him, I could feel the chemistry between us. There was so much potential for us, if we accepted the mate bond. We would ignite like dragon's breath, if—no, when, I corrected myself—we came together. Our mating would be hot and all-consuming, and part of me knew that was exactly what Fridge was afraid of.

The power of our connection. The potential for our love.

I sat down in my father's large executive chair behind his imposing desk, and sighed into the empty room.

I desperately wanted my dad back. But that was never going to happen.

Physically shaking myself, I wished my melancholy away. The only way to push through depression, in my limited experience, was to stay busy. Accomplish something useful.

And what was on my list for today?

I glanced down at the handwritten to-do list I'd scribbled yesterday that lay next to the computer on my desk.

Pick up Dad's ashes.

My heart twisted with pain in my chest.

I can't believe he's gone.

I got to my feet, angry at myself for being so weak. For allowing myself to be pulled closer to the quagmire of grief that I knew would kill me if I let it tug me down into its depths.

One step at a time. Get things done.

Grabbing the remainder of my muffin and coffee that I'd dropped onto the desk, I slung my bag over my shoulder.

I didn't want to go and collect my father's ashes, though I wouldn't mind kicking the ass of the coroner who had deliberately sabotaged my father's remains. That man's actions would make Dad's murder so much harder to solve.

Not that it wasn't already an almost impossible task to prove who'd killed him, since a vampire was the murderer, and they were notoriously difficult to pin down.

But still...

I left my dad's office. Even in that short time the place had transformed. Instead of silence, the warehouse was now bustling with the sounds of my father's staff. The men were training and getting ready for the day.

Smiling, I headed down the stairs and met Rogan, who appeared to be on his way up.

He grinned as our gazes met. "I was just coming to tell you that Fridge hasn't gotten here yet, which I can tell you has never happened before."

Rogan shook his head like he was disappointed in our mate.

I wasn't surprised, unfortunately. Even though I'd hoped to be wrong, I had the feeling this issue around fated mates ran very deep for Fridge.

"He's probably perched on a rocky mountain somewhere, blowing fire rings," I said, as flippantly as possible to hide my concern.

Apprehension for my reluctant mate weighed heavily on me. My stomach twisted every time I thought about him. But I couldn't do anything to help him at the moment, so I was using that nervous, worried energy for something else. Namely, heading out to pick up what was left of my father.

I forced a smile to my lips. "I'm off to the coroner to pick up Dad's ashes. Let me know if Fridge turns up, okay? I have my cell."

Rogan frowned, concern written all over his face. "You want me to come with you?"

I shook my head. Rogan had already seen me in every state imaginable in the few days since we'd met. Grief-stricken, lustful, fighting and crying. He didn't need to see any more, and I had no idea what was going to happen to me today and if I could control my emotions.

"I'll be fine. But thank you for offering. I'll take Dad's car if you'll hand over the keys." I grinned, holding out my hand.

Rogan tossed them to me and nodded. "You just call if you need me. I can be there in a few minutes."

I swallowed hard at the solemn expression on his face. I was pretty sure he was offering to shift into wolf form and run the length of the city to get to me if I needed him.

We had laws against shifting in public in the city, but it seemed my mate didn't care about such things.

"I'll be okay." I gave him one last, lingering smile before heading out the door.

Out of all the darkness of this past week, Rogan was a true star in my inky sky, giving me hope and guiding me home.

But as I headed out the door and into the sunshine, a shadow cast across my path. I was about to pick up the remnants of my father's body. A task I'd never dreamed I'd have to do.

CHAPTER 2

SADIE

The drive to the coroner's office was slow due to heavy traffic, and each block only pushed my temper higher.

My father had been murdered, for God only knew what reason. And those in power, namely the coroner and the police in this instance, were covering it up. I'd bet my life on it.

By the time I arrived at the drab, old gray building, my hands were clenched into fists and my jaw was tight and painful.

I parked, jumped out of the car, and stormed in through the front door.

"Can I help you?" an anemic-looking male clerk asked as I strode up to the desk.

"Yes. My name is Sarah Williams, and I'm here to pick up my father's ashes."

The man pushed a form at me, attached to a black clipboard. "Fill this out."

I glared at him. "While I do this, can you go get the coroner? I want to speak to him."

The clerk's eyes widened. "He's, uh, working."

I narrowed my eyes. "I don't care. Tell him I'm here and I want to see him. Now."

I scribbled out the details of my father's death and identification, then pushed the clipboard over the desk.

When the clerk didn't move, I practically growled at him. "Go!"

The man jumped and ran out the back door of his office and into the inner sanctum of the morgue.

I inhaled and exhaled sharply, trying to get a feel for what type of shifter the clerk was. He was some sort of weird mix, but it was difficult to tell with all the strange chemicals in this place. The walls were painted a sterile, hospital white. The floors were a drab, pale linoleum.

I inhaled again and grimaced. A person would probably be able to eat off any surface in the place as far as cleanliness went, if their gut could handle the toxic level of disinfectant.

The door behind the reception area opened and the man scurried back in.

"Miss... here you go." He pushed a plain silver urn at me.

I frowned. Was that it? They simply gave me a jar and expected me to be on my way?

"Where's the coroner?"

You know, the man who didn't even bother doing an autopsy on my dad before he incinerated him?

The clerk's eyes darted down and left, then right. He was an odd little man. Creepy.

"He's busy," he said, then flicked his gaze up to me. "I'm sorry, but if you would like to speak to him at a later date, we can schedule an appointment."

My fingers itched to go for the knife I had strapped to my ankle, but it wouldn't do any good to threaten him.

I glanced toward the exit. No, leaving didn't feel right either.

Forcing myself to calm down, I attempted to smile in a relaxed way, so as not to put the weird shifter on alert.

I picked up my dad's ashes and nestled the urn into my elbow, holding it close to my body.

"I'll wait," I said calmly. "Can you go back there again please, and tell the coroner I'll wait here until he is free, and ask him when that is likely to be?"

The man's eyes darted from me, to the counter, then back to me.

Walking over to the ugly waiting chairs pushed up against the wall, I sat down. I crossed my legs, settled in, and gripped my father's ashes, all the while forcing myself to remain as calm as possible.

Panic flashed across the clerk's face.

I pulled my cell phone out of my bag and began flipping through the contents, checking emails and making a big show of the fact that I was quite happy to be there all day if needed. The weird little shifter wouldn't want that, I was sure.

"I'll, uh, go speak to him again," he said, and hurried out the door behind hisdesk.

As soon as he was gone, I jumped up and charged for the swinging doors that would lead me into the inner recesses of the coroner's world.

Pushing through the double doors, I walked along sterile, white corridors, listening for any signs of life.

Then I heard what I'd been listening for. Quick footsteps on the linoleum floor and hurried whispers to my right.

I pushed through a door into another sterile room, my heart hammering in my chest.

Where was that traitor? That sell-out.

The voices were getting louder and more heated.

I followed the sounds, moving with deliberate intent, looking left and right, ready to defend myself against an attack.

Maybe I should have brought Rogan with me.

I shook off the thought as I plowed through another set of double doors and came face to face with the coroner.

His mouth dropped open as I approached. "What are you doing in here?"

He was a vampire, though he didn't seem to be a particularly strong or dangerous one. His skin was as pale as moonlight and he was as thin as a whippet.

I lifted my chin. "I want to speak to you about my father's death."

There was a dead body on the table in front of him. The coroner had obviously been examining the body before I'd walked in. His hands were gloved and he still held a scalpel.

I glanced down, trying not to absorb the sight of the man on the table. He'd been beaten to death, by the looks of his mangled face and upper body.

My stomach lurched and my empathetic heart cried out against the injustice of such a death.

My spine straightened as I strengthened my resolve. "Are you going to burn this man's body before you do a proper autopsy as well?"

The coroner's eyebrows flew up, then he frowned. "I don't know who you think you are, young lady, but—"

"I'm Sadie Williams. My father was Jack Williams. He owned the business, 'Hunters'. Remember now? You destroyed his body before even doing a proper report on his death."

The coroner's mouth flapped up and down. "There was no autopsy ordered from the police or the judge. It was an open-and-shut case."

"Open-and-shut case?" I repeated, anger boiling up inside my belly. "It was murder! How could you have destroyed the only evidence we had to find the killer?"

My hands tightened into fists and every instinct I had was on high alert. Every noise was magnified. Every beat of my heart sounded like a war drum in my ears.

The coroner stuck his nose in the air. "There was no evidence of the killer, young lady."

I laughed, though what he said wasn't funny. "He was killed by a vampire. Don't tell me there was no evidence. Or that a professional like yourself couldn't give the police any evidence pointing to a suspect."

The coroner smiled, though there was no humor in his expression. I could see the tips of his fangs. "Miss Williams, you have no case here. I suggest you take your father's ashes, perform whatever ceremony you mortals do to say goodbye, and move on with your life."

I clenched my teeth as my temper snapped. I wanted to snatch the knife from my calf and threaten him with it. Who the hell did he think he was?

But something stopped me from doing what I craved. Whether it was the knowledge that he was a vampire and could probably fly out of here the moment he saw my weapon, or the fact that he was dirty.

Dirty as hell.

He had connections, and he'd been bought. Making it obvious that I was after him and his owners wasn't smart. It would only put a target on my back, if there wasn't one already.

"You're right," I said, dropping my head but secretly seething on the inside. "I'll go."

I left the sterile room and the horribly depressing building with my tail between my legs. Or that was how I wanted it to appear.

But I wasn't giving up. Nowhere near it.

They thought they'd gotten rid of the threat my father posed, but I was coming for them. Whoever *they* were.

I WAS numb on the drive back to the Workshop. I'd buckled my dad's ashes into the passenger seat so they didn't spill anywhere, but I couldn't stop looking over at the urn.

How was that urn my dad? How was it possible that the only thing left in this world of his strong presence was ashes in a jar?

It was so... wrong.

I shook myself as I got closer to work. I didn't want anyone there seeing how badly affected I was by this turn of events.

Should I set up some sort of memorial service? Tomorrow, maybe? Or wait until the killer had been brought to justice?

There wasn't any rush, after all. Dad wasn't going anywhere.

I parked across the road from the Workshop, grabbed my bag, and my dad, and ran to the entrance of Hunters. Should I give my cousin Shadow a call and see what he'd found, if anything? Or did he prefer to contact me? I would have to ask Rogan what normal procedure was.

As soon as I opened the doors, I knew something was wrong.

For one thing, there was no one around.

"Where is everyone?" I called out, wondering if anyone was available to answer.

There were strange noises coming from the back of the building. A grunt, then a pained groan. I listened harder. I could head the crack of punches landing in the unmistakable sounds of a fist fight. And it didn't sound like a normal training session.

Every part of my intuition knew who was fighting: *my two mates.*

I ran to the training room, where everyone was standing around watching Rogan and Fridge go at it.

I pushed past two of the men, gripping my father's urn securely in one arm. I assessed the situation in a second. Fridge was winning, that was for damn sure. Rogan's shirt was ripped off his body, blood splattering his chest and arms and the training mat from his nose and cuts on his head, whereas Fridge looked mad as hell, but untouched.

"What the hell is going on?" I yelled, using all the command and force that my father had bred into me.

Fridge and Rogan stopped fighting and turned to look at me, while the spectators glanced at the ground. Why? Because they hadn't stepped in to aid the wolf shifter? Or because they knew the root of the issue was me?

Fridge was panting, his huge shoulders and chest heaving as he breathed roughly in and out. He was dressed in jeans and a t-shirt, drenched with sweat.

I stood there staring at them, and as the seconds ticked on, I relaxed. It appeared I didn't need to intervene physically.

Both of them glanced at the urn in the crook of my arm, and to their credit, each looked slightly sheepish.

I turned my attention to the crowd of spectators. "All of you, back to work. Now!"

Then I stepped over the mat to my mates, one of whom was more injured than I'd originally assessed. Rogan's shoulder looked dislocated, his arm hanging at a weird angle.

I steeled myself against the pain twisting in my chest. "Rogan. Fridge. My office."

Turning my back to them, I walked away, calling on my "boss" personality to save face. Mine and theirs.

A large part of me wanted to go to Rogan, though. I wanted to help him, check his wounds. But he wouldn't thank me for highlighting any signs of weakness—his or mine—so I marched up the stairs and walked into my father's office, placing his ashes safely on the desk.

I shook out my hands, my palms sweaty and my stomach clenched with worry.

Where could I secure Dad's urn until I worked out where I was living long term? Perhaps the wall safe.

The door opened and Fridge stormed in, his sweaty body radiating the most incredible pheromones.

My knees actually shook as I breathed Fridge in. His battle heat.

His anger. His jealousy. It was all there in the notes of his scent. I didn't need to be a full shifter to appreciate them.

Rogan limped in after Fridge, dragging his leg and holding his shoulder.

Happily, though, the arm that had been at an odd angle downstairs now seemed to have righted itself.

"Shut the door, Fridge," I said, sitting down in my executive chair and casting my gaze over to Rogan as Fridge turned away to slam the door.

You okay? I mouthed at Rogan.

He nodded and fell into one of the chairs opposite me, barely stifling a groan.

Fridge stalked over to us and stood behind the other visitor's chair. I didn't ask him to sit. He would have refused.

Instead, I laced my fingers together over my chest and leaned back in the chair as though I were as cool and calm as could be. "So... what the fuck happened?"

Fridge growled, a strange and threatening sound.

I stood up, placing my knuckles on the desk, and leaned forward. "Don't you fucking *dare* growl at me like that. You hear me? I won't stand for it, and frankly, I don't deserve it. Rogan doesn't, either. You're the one who abandoned us last night, so if I were you, Fridge, I'd start apologizing. Hell, I'd be on my *fucking knees,* begging for forgiveness."

I stared him down with all the strength of my genetics. Half witch, part shifter, mad as fucking hell.

Fridge dropped his gaze and finally sat down in the chair opposite me.

My heart hammered in my chest and I could feel the magic in the air, the stir of change around us. It was time for this stupid dragon to get his head on straight.

"Do you wanna try that again?" I demanded, remaining in position despite the fact my arms were beginning to shake from the strain.

Fridge didn't lift his head, and I glanced over at Rogan.

His lips were turned down and his forehead was lined with stress.

What the hell was going on in Fridge's mind?

CHAPTER 3

FRIDGE

She was right. God knew she was right.

She'd just walked in holding her dead father's ashes, for Christ's sake. I *should* be on my fucking knees, begging for forgiveness. For leaving them. For making Sadie feel like I didn't want her. Then for injuring Rogan.

He was my best friend and I'd snapped his fucking arm.

I swallowed, hard. My throat constricted and my heart felt heavy in my chest. "I'm sorry."

And I was.

"Keep going," Sadie said. This time, she sounded calmer.

Bet she's regretting having me as a mate... not that she had any choice about it.

Guilt swam up and swallowed me whole. That was the problem with the Fated Mates trap. You were stuck with the person that Fate supposedly chose for you. How could I be a good match for Sadie? For this... triple. Threesome. Whatever the hell it was called.

"I..."

"Look at me, Fridge," she said, her voice soft.

I forced myself to do as she asked, knowing there would be a shimmer of a tear in my eye. I didn't cry. Hadn't in a very long time. But I could feel the heat behind my eyeballs, the clog of emotion in my throat.

I was broken. Couldn't they see that?

They shouldn't want me. Not now. Not ever.

Sadie walked around the desk and perched on the edge, looking down at me. Worse than anything before, there was now pity in her gaze.

I dropped my eyes to the ground, disgusted with myself.

"Don't look at me like that," I said.

"Like what?" she asked.

"Like you feel sorry for me. I know I'm a fuck-up. I know that you got the raw deal here." A thought occurred to me and I glanced up at her again. "Maybe I can move to another city? That would help, wouldn't it? You two would be happy and you wouldn't need to worry about me."

I glanced over to Rogan, who was healing quickly. His chest and face were still stained with dried blood, but the cuts were closing. His posture was straighter as the bones knitted back together, too.

Rogan and Sadie exchanged a look.

I wasn't sure what to read from their faces. They didn't seem relieved at my suggestion. Their eyebrows were high, their eyes wide open.

There was no reason I couldn't find another place to live, to work. Somehow...

Sitting up straighter in the chair, I cleared my throat. "I'll do anything to make this up to you both."

"And you think leaving us will make it better?" Sadie asked, her voice barely a whisper.

The look on her face made me pause, because beneath all the anger, the insecurity, the jealousy... I knew that leaving her—them— would probably kill me.

I chose my words carefully, a part of me realizing that this moment was one of those defining times of one's life. A single word, or choice, could change my path forever.

"I don't want to. But I'm willing to do anything to make up for last night. For... today." I looked over at Rogan. "I'm sorry I hurt you, man. I didn't... Well, I'm so sorry my temper got the better of me."

To my surprise, Rogan grinned and wiped his mouth with the back of his hand. "I get it. I always knew you had a wicked temper and that I shouldn't get on the wrong side of you."

I nodded, humbled by the compassion Rogan was showing me. Forgiving anyone who did to me what I'd just done to Rogan seemed outside the realm of my experience.

"What happened exactly?" Sadie asked suddenly.

Rogan grunted. "Nothing specific."

Sadie rolled her eyes. "Well, then, what happened non-specifically?"

I cleared my throat. "I came in looking for a fight. And Rogan was here. So..."

I shrugged.

That was pretty much the whole story.

I'd still been mad as hell about last night, and Rogan was bouncing around, looking happy and healthy. I'd lost it.

Sadie stared at me. "So, leaving us last night and not coming back wasn't punishment enough?"

I cocked my head. "For who?"

"For us!" she said, her voice full of anger. "You punished us by abandoning us. Me! For what? And why?"

She threw her hands around as she spoke, like a crazy person.

"I told you why." How many times did I have to admit to being weak? Selfish?

She narrowed her eyes at me. "You mean you were jealous of Rogan and me? But you don't want to mate with me, either." She stopped to rub her forehead with her fingers like she had a headache.

"Have you figured out what you want yet... or are you just here today because it's your day job?"

She crossed her arms over her chest and glared down at me.

I swallowed hard and shrugged. "I... don't know. I'm sorry. I don't."

I'd gone over it a thousand times and still couldn't see my way out of the maze.

I didn't believe in Fated Mates, but Sadie did. And she believed we were destined to be together and had no choice in the matter.

That sat badly with me. My parents had been forced to live together—breed together—for the sake of the dragon shifter bloodline. It had been hell on earth for us kids growing up in *that* home.

I'd sworn I would never be trapped by such an agreement. Not for anyone.

Sadie rolled her eyes as she slid off the desk, walking back around to the executive chair and plonking herself down.

Rogan stood up, groaning as he rolled his shoulders. "I need to get changed. Probably need a quick shower too."

Sadie looked at him. "You wanna head home and come back?"

Rogan nodded. "Good idea. I won't be long."

He shot a glance at me and I stood up too, offering my hand to him.

"I'm sorry. Forgive me?"

Rogan nodded once and shook my hand, though the handshake was short and terse. "You owe me, though."

I clenched my teeth, imagining what sort of favor he might ask of me one day. Then I swallowed my pride and agreed to it. "Anything, man."

Rogan gave me a half smile, one side of his lips tilting up. "See you in an hour."

He left the office and I turned to Sadie, who was now sitting up straight in her dad's chair, a grim look on her face.

"So..." she said.

"So?" I repeated, sitting back down so that I wasn't towering over her. "I suppose I need a shower too. But I'll wait."

I was drenched in sweat, and it had begun to dry so the t-shirt I wore was molded to my body, the cotton dirty and stiff.

"You do, but... I wanna talk to you. Without Rogan."

I leaned forward, resting my elbows on my knees. "Shoot."

Sadie could say anything she wanted. I could handle it. I would sit here and take it, because it was the right thing to do.

"Where did you go last night?"

My eyebrows flicked up. That wasn't what I'd expected her to say.

"I flew up to the Easter Mountains and perched in a cave for the night."

"In dragon form?"

I nodded. "Yep. Didn't shift back until this morning."

That was what happened when I couldn't cope with what was going on in my human world. My shifter came out, swooped down, and took me away somewhere safe. Somewhere solitary.

Sadie continued. "Then you came in here and beat up on your best friend, all because you don't like the hand that Fate has dealt you? Dealt all of us."

My jaw dropped open. She was serious.

My stomach twisted with worry about the next thing that had to come out of my mouth, but I refused to hurt her any more than I already had.

I wouldn't lie about my readiness to commit to this strange relationship.

"I'm not..." I stopped, not sure exactly how to approach the topic. "I... don't want you to feel that you have no choice but to be with me, Sadie. I want you—no, I *need* you—to make that choice when you're ready. But I want it to be a conscious choice."

She frowned at me. "Fridge, I don't know how to make this any clearer to you. I want you. Fate, no Fate, I don't give a shit. If you don't want me, then that's a different story. I'm done chasing you. I. Want. You. But it's up to you now."

She stopped talking and stared at me, the silence in the room stretching between us like an ocean.

I cleared my throat, shifting on the chair. "I don't want to lie to you Sadie, or give you false hope. I want you, more than I've ever wanted anyone, but whether or not I can commit to mating with you and taking on Rogan forever as well—I really don't know if I can do that."

I exhaled in a rush. There, I'd said it all.

Heaven help me.

Sadie nodded, her gaze shifting away to stare at something on her desk, then slowly she moved her attention back to me. "All right. Then I think I need to make some decisions, for my own mental health, as well as yours."

A chill crept over my body, making the skin on my neck tingle and the hairs stand on end.

"What sort of decisions?" I asked, my stomach dropping as I waited to hear what she was going to say.

How strong was my conviction to stay away from them?

If she wanted to walk away from me, could I let her?

"Well," Sadie began, pulling her chair in closer to the desk, looking professional and serious.

"Well, what?" I prompted.

She straightened, folding her hands together and placing them on the desk. "Last night was horrible for me. I put myself out there, told you how much I needed you, and you rejected me. In the worst possible way. You literally flew away. I couldn't be happy after that. I hurt Rogan because, after you left, I was miserable. Every thought I had was about you. How you'd feel if you came home and found us together. So I wouldn't let him *be* with me. Not like that, without you. We slept in your bed. We waited for you. And you never came."

Sadie's declaration hit me right in the chest. Had they really worried about me that much?

I'd assumed that they'd taken advantage of my absence and fucked the night away.

"I... I'm sorry."

She shook her head. "You say you're sorry, that you'll do anything to make it up to us, but the only thing we actually want is for you to get your head around the fact we're meant to be together." She sighed heavily. "And it looks like that's the only thing you can't do."

I clenched my jaw, nearly cracking my teeth.. "I could try. But I..."

She shook her head. "No. I don't want you to try. Being together should be as easy as breathing. And if it's not like that for you? Well, then, I'll focus on Rogan and hope we can find a way to be happy without you."

"Without you" rang in the air, and jealous anger pulsed in my blood. My heart raced and my dragon roared in my head.

"So how do you want to do that?" I asked. They'd said they didn't want me to leave the city, but I didn't know how we were going to accomplish this.

"Well, I think I need to sleep somewhere else..." she began.

"Where?" I demanded. "You dad's place isn't safe."

Despite my worries about my ability to commit, her safety was still my number-one priority.

"I agree. Until we get to the bottom of my dad's murder, or at least find out what they were looking for when they came to kill him, I think I need to stay at a hotel. I have money, so I'll just choose somewhere close to work."

I swallowed the lump in my throat. The idea that money wasn't an obstacle in life was a new concept to me. But Sadie had inherited her father's estate, not to mention the fact she was a corporate lawyer and likely had money of her own.

"Okay," I said.

What else could I say?

"So," Sadie said, biting her lip, "I think the best thing to do is to leave your apartment to you and I'll move out for a while."

My stomach lurched and I tasted acid in the back of my throat. If she was leaving the apartment I shared with my best friend for me to sleep in, that meant...

"And Rogan?" I asked, though I knew what the answer was going to be. Why would he stay in our apartment with me?

She shrugged. "We're mated. He'll want to be with me."

So do I.

But I couldn't admit that to her. Not unless I wanted to take that final step and declare that I would mate with her also. So, I swallowed the words down and forced myself to be calm, diplomatic.

"Okay." I nodded. "Sounds like a good plan. For the short term. You'll be safe, and we can work together during the day—assuming you still want my help catching your dad's killer?"

It took all my energy and strength not to reveal the extent of my feelings at this point in time. They were bubbling like a brook in my bloodstream.

Rogan and Sadie would be together... alone. Mating without me. My dragon roared his frustration inside my mind. My fingers tightened into fists and my heart began to pound.

If it wasn't so far to the front door of the building—to safety— my dragon shifter would be ripping through me to deal with the pain.

The white-hot jealousy.

The red, pulsing anger.

The self-loathing for being the one to put us all in this position.

Sadie smiled serenely at me. "I'd love your help, of course. Thank you for offering."

That was when I knew I was losing this battle to stay aloof from her.

This woman would be the death of me.

Or she would be the beginning of a brand-new life.

Both alternatives were equally terrifying, and yet, I couldn't walk away.

SADIE

Pushing Fridge away for his own good, and for mine and Rogan's, was one of the most difficult things I'd ever done. Especially when I read the misery on his face.

But, calling on years of training, specifically in my career as a lawyer, I put on my poker face and laid out the plan.

A plan I knew he would hate. It would drive a wedge between us and no doubt cause us both a whole lot of heartache. But it was a necessary evil, at least for a short amount of time, to make the bull-headed, stubborn-ass dragon come to terms with the fact that I was his mate.

I forced a smile to my face. "Great. Well, if you want, I suppose you can go home and get showered and changed, too."

I twisted in my chair to turn on my computer, dismissing him with the action. After a moment, he stood.

My heart ached in ways I never thought possible.

But I kept smiling as I flicked my gaze up to his and raised my eyebrows in question as he continued to stare down at me.

"Is there anything else?" I asked.

He shook his head. "Uh, no. I keep extra clothes here in my locker downstairs, so I'll shower here instead, and go change now."

"Great," I said, pretending to be chipper despite the tension in the room. The tightness and pain I could see in Fridge's face was obvious, both in the set of his jaw and in the tension squaring his shoulders. "Well, I've gotta organize a few things, so I'll see you later."

Fridge nodded and headed out the door, quietly shutting the door behind him.

I collapsed back against the head rest and groaned, my gaze moving to my dad's silver urn. "Seriously, Dad. Did you have this much trouble with Mom when you first met?"

I shook my head as I stood, opened the safe using my birthdate as the passcode, and placed what was left of my father inside.

Nothing looked like it had been touched in the safe. The money was still there, along with the leather books and my mother's jewelry.

I glanced down at my hands. I was still wearing her rings.

I considered taking them off and placing them back in the safe along with the rest of her things, but after the night and day I'd had, I couldn't bring myself to do it. I wanted something to remind me of the family I'd once had. Of the love I'd been surrounded by my whole life.

If I included Rogan in those thoughts, then the love I was still surrounded by, too.

Rogan was beautiful. A thoughtful, hardworking mate. But even as I thought about him and the comfort he gave me, a part of my heart ached for the missing element.

Fridge.

"I hope that pain goes away," I muttered to myself as I went back to the desk and sat down.

If Fridge refused to mate with me, to join our triple, then where would that leave Rogan and me? It was becoming obvious that I would continue to feel lost, helpless and empty, even with my beautiful wolf shifter by my side.

I sighed and opened my father's company email inbox. "Whoa."

There were literally hundreds of unopened emails, all received in the last few days.

I pushed thoughts of my mates aside and got to work. I couldn't have my father's business going belly up because I ignored it. There were new bounties coming in, new clients enquiring about the Workshop's services.

I was going to need an assistant at this rate, but since it was only me at the moment, I immersed myself in my father's sent items and got familiar with the prices and language he used, and the way he dealt with his customers.

Luckily, Rogan came back within the hour and helped me go through the emails and deal with the phone calls I received throughout the day.

My father's business was more complex than I had first realized, but thanks to Rogan's assistance, I was beginning to see the light at the end of the tunnel by the end of the day.

As the sun began to go down and the building quietened, Rogan walked back into my office with a questioning stare.

"What's up?" I asked as I began to pack away my cell phone and shut down the computer. I was mentally exhausted, but at least I'd begun the huge process of converting my brain from corporate lawyer to owner of a bounty hunter business.

"Fridge said you wanted to sleep somewhere else tonight?"

"Shit! I didn't book the hotel! I was thinking of the Marriott just around the corner." I glanced up at him as I grabbed my cell off the desk and googled the phone number for the place. "I hope you want to come with me? Or would you prefer to go back to your apartment with Fridge?"

Rogan stared at me with wide open eyes. Shocked, maybe? I wasn't sure.

"Rogan?" I asked, my thumb poised over the call button.

"Of course, I wanna stay with you. I'm never leaving you again. But Fridge…"

"Fridge and I had a discussion earlier, and he made his choice," I said, making the call and putting the receiver to my ear. "And I'm not spending another night waiting to see if he'll come home, or flip out or…"

"Marriott Hotel, King Street," came a voice on the other end of the line. "How can I help you today?"

"Hello, yes. I'd like to book a room for the next five nights please." I grinned at Rogan as I began to make the reservation.

The clerk listed the options and the exorbitant prices, and I pushed any worries about money away. I hadn't had a vacation in years. Literally, years. This would be several days of luxury. And room service. And hopefully, sex. Because I couldn't keep denying myself, or Rogan, just because Fridge refused to join us.

"The suite will be fine," I said. "Thank you." I took out my credit card, recited the numbers and hung up with a smile. "All done."

Rogan frowned. "Five days?"

"What's wrong?" I asked, picking up my bag and throwing it over my shoulder. "Not long enough? I'm sure we can extend it if we want to."

He shook his head as I approached him. My stomach automatically tightened and my lower belly melted as I inhaled his delicious scent.

I wanted to leave the stress of today behind me and fall into the arms of my mate. Somewhere safe. Somewhere we could be alone.

"I'm worried about this, Sadie," Rogan said, though his hand slipped into mine, interlacing our fingers and holding me tightly. "Pushing Fridge away may have dire consequences."

I rolled my eyes. *Oh ye of little faith.* "Please. Why do you think I booked the biggest space they have, except for the penthouse? Fridge couldn't even let us have dinner alone the other night. I'm hoping he'll come to his senses and join us sooner rather than later."

"So you're doing this to try and force him to choose?"

Put that way, it didn't sound very nice, but I suppose it was true. "Rogan, to be honest, I'm struggling to handle everything that's being thrown at me at the moment. Discovering I have two mates, my father's murder, taking over his business, finding out about a blood ring in the city, and secrets surfacing about my mother. And to top it off, a dragon mate who doesn't want me, simply because I admitted to feeling the pull of a fated mate instead of saying that I chose him of my own accord. It's been tough."

His expression was serious as he studied me. "Yeah, I get that. But you are tough, Sadie, and you're handling it all far better than most."

"Maybe." I shrugged. Didn't feel like it to me. I felt like I was on the edge of breaking down all the time. "But now that I have you, at least, why can't we share a night together, Rogan? Or five? Don't you want to?"

He shot me a lascivious grin and used his free hand to grip my ass and pull me into him. "Of course, I do, but last night—"

"Last night I was in your apartment—Fridge's bed—and I was terrified for him. But now... he's a big boy. I can't be more honest about what I need from him, so now its up to him to choose. Commit, or not. It's not like there's a time limit. He can decide tonight, next week, or next year. I'm not going anywhere." I sighed and ran my hands up Rogan's arms, focusing on him, on his scent. "In the meantime, I want to make love to my wolf."

"Oh, do you now?" Rogan said, then dropped his head and kissed my lips gently.

A hesitant knock on the door interrupted us. I turned, breaking the kiss.

Fridge was standing there, blocking most of the door, his face splashed with redness and his gaze on the floor.

He'd obviously heard what I said about wanting to make love to Rogan, and as I lifted my chin defiantly, I decided not to care. I would say the same thing to him if he made the decision to jump into the Fated Mate bond with both feet, just like Rogan and I had.

Fridge cleared his throat. "Just wanted to say good night and check if you needed anything."

"We're all good, I think. Thanks, Fridge," I said.

"I'll walk you out," he said, and without waiting for a reply, turned and trotted down the stairs.

"Okay then," I said, sharing a wry smile with Rogan, though the look in his eyes told me he was more worried than amused. "Stop stressing," I whispered. "I'm going with my gut on this, and my gut says he'll come round."

I prayed I was right. Because the alternative—a life without Fridge in it—wasn't one I wanted to consider.

I left Rogan to close up the training area. I went around turning off some of the lights, then met my men at the main entrance.

I tossed my dad's car keys to Fridge. "I've booked a suite at the Marriott, so we can walk. It's just around the corner. You wanna take the car?"w

Fridge nodded, his lips turned downward in a frown.

"You okay?" I asked, grabbing Rogan's hand and arranging the strap of my bag on my shoulder.

Fridge took a deep breath and smiled, though it was forced. I admired him for trying to put on a brave face.

"Yeah, fine. You guys gonna be all right for clothes or...?"

I glanced at Rogan. I hadn't even thought about that. "Well..."

"I can bring you some in the morning, if you want?" Fridge offered quickly.

I glanced at him and smiled. "That would be great. My bag at your place is pretty much still packed."

He nodded, heading onto the street. "No problem. I'll swing by the hotel in the morning."

He waved at us and jogged across the road to where my dad's car was parked.

I didn't want to watch him leave, so I tugged on Rogan's hand. "Let's go. A night of room service and a long bath awaits us."

"A long bath?" Rogan repeated as we walked down the street and away from the Workshop.

"Definitely," I said as I grinned at him. What a dream it would be to slip into a warm bath, surrounded by my hot man. "I'm sure you can think of something to do with me once I'm all nice and clean."

Rogan growled and his eyes flared with a heat that made me melt. I couldn't stop the excited chuckle that rose in my throat.

The best part about the Fated Mate bond for me was knowing that my mate truly wanted me. Desired me. Lusted after me. He would, by all accounts, never leave me. Just as I would never leave him.

After a lifetime of wanting the same sort of love my parents had shared—that all-consuming, totally committed sort of love—I finally felt like I'd found it. At least with Rogan.

I just had to wait for Fridge to come around to the idea and want to join us.

And he would.

Until then, I was taking my wolf to a luxury hotel suite so we could ravage each other the way I'd dreamt about.

And for the first time, I wasn't going to be looking over my shoulder to check if the dragon was okay.

Hopefully, anyway. He did, after all, know where the hotel was.

CHAPTER 5

ROGAN

I hated that Sadie had paid for the hotel suite, when traditionally I knew that to be my role. But considering her father's company—now Sadie's company—paid my salary, I was going to have wrap my head around the financial side of our relationship. My money *was* her money. Quite literally.

Instead of being macho and stupid about it, I decided to be smooth. I took her hand as she grabbed the hotel room key and guided her upstairs to have my way with her.

If she could relax in a place like this, then so could I, even though the polished marble and swanky staff everywhere made me feel extremely uncomfortable. The opulent, thirty-floor building wasn't my usual comfort zone. I couldn't imagine being that high off the ground.

The elevator made its way to the third floor and the door opened.

"Not too high," I said with relief. I hated being too far up in the sky.

She laughed as we stepped out of the elevator and stood in the small foyer area. "I know what you mean. I like being closer to the ground, too. Must be a wolf thing."

253

I pulled her into my body and kissed her, tasting her sweet lips and loving the way she melted under my hands.

Her fingers gripped my shirt, tugging at me, her apparent desperation to get closer to me escalating. I groaned beneath the onslaught of her passion, her taste. The scent she was giving off told me how much she wanted me.

I dragged my mouth away from hers as my blood pulsed south, throbbing in my groin. I needed her more than I liked to admit. Last night had been torturous. Lying next to her, feeling her warm, soft body next to mine, and not being able to make love to her how I wanted, had kept me awake for most of the night.

I'd respected her feelings, of course, understanding her insecurities and fears for Fridge. Now that she was ready to become mine once again, I wasn't sure I could wait until after we'd had a bath. More foreplay and waiting would kill me.

"Quick. Which room?" I asked, dragging her down the brightly lit, plushly-carpeted hallway.

She laughed as I caveman-hauled her along.

"Room 306," she said.

304... 305... I stopped in front of the door she'd indicated and stepped back so she could open it for us. My pulse thrummed away like a guitar string vibrating in my veins. Damn, I couldn't wait to see her naked again. Feel her pussy wrap around my cock and squeeze tight.

Sadie swiped the card and the moment the light on the door handle turned green, I swept her up into my arms, her hands grabbing onto my shirt as she squealed in fright and excitement.

I twisted so I could protect her body as I pushed open the door with my back, swinging her around once we'd entered so that I could march through the room with my new mate.

Sadie was grinning and laughing as I strode through the living area of the suite, briefly noticing how fancy everything was. There was only one thing in my mind, and that was to get her naked as soon as possible.

I turned right and headed into the bedroom, charging straight over to the massive bed and tossing her on it.

She bounced on the mattress with a giggle, then slid up and lay down on the pillows so that she was on her back and staring up at me.

She licked her lips, making them glisten with invitation. "You wanna have a shower first, or…"

"No," I said, pulling my shirt over my head and tossing it across the room. "I need you. Now."

She jumped up onto her knees and attacked the rest of my clothing while I pulled off hers. There was no time for preliminaries. I could smell the heat in her body, the wetness of her sex as she threw her nakedness against me and kissed my lips.

I grabbed her around the waist and lifted her off the bed, her legs wrapping around my hips.

My cock was already hard and pulsing, crying out to be fulfilled, to sink within her. To make my mate feel as amazing as she did the same for me.

When she pressed her soft breasts against my chest and kissed me deeper, I grabbed her hips and positioned the head of my cock at the entrance to her body.

She gasped against my lips, trying to push down with her hips to take more of me.

I grinned and held her hostage, loving the way she wriggled and struggled against me, trying to impale herself.

"Rogan!" she whined, pouting.

I chuckled. "What do you need, beautiful girl?"

"I need you inside me. Please."

The words were everything I'd ever wanted to hear from my mate. Such perfection. I couldn't withhold from her a minute longer.

I shifted my hands, grabbed her firm thighs, and pulled her straight down onto me in one fast movement.

Her cry rang out through the room, mingling with my own satisfied groan. Damn, she felt good.

Better than good. *Heavenly.*

She threw back her head and arched her back, clinging to my shoulders as she began to ride me.

Our moans filled the room as I pulled her up and down my cock. Her perfect pussy tightened around me, squeezing me, pushing me toward orgasm.

It was fast and hot, and unbelievably sexy to feel Sadie on me. Around me. Without reservation. Without looking over her shoulder and wondering how Fridge was feeling.

She was in the moment and loving it.

Her pussy began to tighten. She gasped louder as she slowed her movements, unable to maintain the same rhythm. I took over, grabbing her hips and pumping into her, forcing her toward orgasm as I was dragged toward my own finish.

She began to pant and moan louder, the sounds exquisite to my ears. There was nothing better than watching her find pleasure in my arms.

Her pussy squeezed tightly, then began to convulse and ripple around me. I thrust into her one more time, burying myself deep in her core, the heat of my own desire and orgasm rushing up and over my back, exploding over my skin.

My balls pulsed in time with her pussy as it milked me, swallowing every drop of my seed as I finished within her.

I growled loudly, the strength leaving my legs. I staggered to the safety of the bed so I didn't tumble to the floor.

Whoa.

I fell sideways onto the mattress, cradling Sadie.

She unwrapped her legs from around me and we rolled apart, untangling our limbs, then coming back together with our heads on the pillows and the blankets pulled up over our sweaty bodies.

She lay her head on my chest. I was sure she could hear the thundering of my heart and my ragged breathing. I'd never been so sated, so satisfied in my life.

"That was... incredible," I managed.

Sadie giggled and ran her fingers up and down my arm, finally letting her splayed hand come to rest on my chest. "It was. I needed to feel you like that, so badly. Thank you."

I chuckled and kissed the top of her head. "It was entirely my pleasure, I assure you."

She laughed. "Not *entirely*. I guarantee it."

I brought my arms up and wrapped them around her, wishing this intimate moment could last forever.

"Thank you for asking me to come and stay here with you," I said, wanting her to know how much I valued her choices. And her.

She looked up at me, meeting my gaze. "I never want to be apart from you, Rogan. We're mated. My wolf would kill me."

I smiled. "And the other half of you?"

She looked down. "All of me is committed to you, I promise."

I'd hit a nerve there, and I wasn't even sure how.

"Hey," I said, reaching for her chin and lifting it so that our gazes were locked. "I didn't mean anything by that. I'm sorry."

She nodded, though I could see the tears in her eyes. What was that about?

"What's wrong?"

"My mother wasn't human. She was a witch," Sadie whispered, closing her eyes as she spoke.

My breath lodged in my throat.

Her eyes sprung open and she stared at me. "You're shocked."

She moved away and I let her, feeling her mental withdrawal as well as her physical.

When she sat up, clinging to the covers, I slid up against the headboard and reached for her hand. "Don't move too far away. I want to talk about this."

"What's there to talk about?" she asked, looking down at the blankets.

This was not the Sadie I knew. The toughness was gone. There was a vulnerability in her expression, in the taut way she held herself, that I hadn't expected.

"Hey, come here." I dragged her closer.

She didn't cuddle into me, but she did come closer, for which I was grateful.

I sighed. "I'm not rejecting you or anything, Sadie. I'm just shocked. There hasn't been a witch born in, well, decades. Everyone thought they were completely extinct."

She shrugged. "Yeah, that's why my dad never told anyone. Why I don't say anything. It's dangerous."

I nodded, understanding dawning. This was a huge step for her. A sign of true intimacy. The sharing of secrets. "And yet you told me."

She shrugged. "I feel like I have to. You need to know who I am. *What* I am."

I smiled and reached out to cup her cheek. She finally looked up at me.

I stroked her cheek, loving the feel of her soft skin beneath my fingers. "Sweetheart, all it means is that I'll make sure no vampire gets within a hundred feet of you. Your blood is way too tasty to them." Then my heart dropped into a cold vat of fear. "Oh, fucking hell. Is that why they killed your dad? For information on your mother?"

She shrugged, her shoulders sagging even further. "I honestly don't know. Mom died twenty years ago, so most of her legacy and magic died with her. But thanks to Shadow, I now know that my mother cast a spell to include some weird shifter blood into mine so that the vampires can't smell the witch in me."

"Was your mother a quarter witch? Less?" I asked. The less the better, as far as Sadie's scent went. I certainly couldn't smell any magic on her, not that I'd know what that smelled like.

She shook her head. "No. She was pure witch."

I hissed out a gasp. "That's impossible. All full bloods died out hundreds of years ago."

Sadie shook her head. "Nope. Ask Shadow. Anyway... I just wanted you to know."

"Wow," I said, stupefied. "That would make you half witch, half wolf shifter... and one of the rarest blood types in the world. I knew you were unique—special—but I thought I was being biased because you're my mate. But, wow, Sadie."

A tear slipped down her cheek and horror struck me across the chest.

"Hey, hey, hey. What's all this?" I asked.

She began to cry harder and I gathered her up and held her in my lap while she sobbed. I wrapped her tighter in my arms, reinforcing the warmth with the thickness of the blankets on the bed.

I rocked her gently as I held her, wishing away her pain, but grateful that I'd met her just in time to help her through this part of her life. I hated to think how she would have managed without me. Without *us*.

"I'm sorry," she said when the sobs finally subsided.

I pulled her chin up and kissed her full, pouty lips. "You do not need to be sorry. Quite the opposite. *I'm* sorry. I obviously didn't handle that very well."

She broke out of my arms to grab some tissues from beside the bed and blew her nose before wiping the tears from her face.

"I've been holding it in for so long, I suppose I just wanted someone to know who I really am. Who my mother was."

"Can you perform any magic?" I asked. "Because that would be cool."

She huffed out a laugh, then sighed as she relaxed her shoulders.

"No. Mom never taught me any, and unfortunately, I don't have much to do with her family."

"We could change that, you know," I said with a grin. "I'm sure, between all of our contacts, we could find someone who could turn you into a truly badass hybrid."

I didn't know any witches, and if there were any around, they were in hiding. But surely someone would know how to train her.

She lifted her gaze to mine. "You're not upset?"

"Upset?" I repeated. "Why on earth would I be upset?"

She shrugged and I realized that this, in her mind, was a burden.

I kissed her quickly and rolled up and out of the bed. "Listen, Sadie, nothing you could tell me will ever make me turn away from you. Nothing. The only thing this changes for me is that I'm going to worry about you being around vamps, but if you're telling me your mom covered that for you, then I'll try not to overreact when they sniff you."

She giggled and wiped at her still red and wet face. "As I told you guys, no vamp has even *tried* to bite me. Mom made it so that I smell bad to them."

I didn't really want to know which shifter they added in her blood to put off vamps because I didn't care.

"All I care about is your safety, oh beautiful mate of mine." I grinned. "And your happiness. So how about I go run that bath for you and we both get warm and clean, before I get you dirty again?"

She sat up straighter on the bed, grinning like the Cheshire cat. "That would be awesome."

I nodded before heading into the luxurious en-suite bathroom and turning on the tap in the huge bath.

"This is incredible!" I called out to her. "We could easily fit all three of us in here, even with Fridge's bulk."

Sadie giggled from the other room. "Then let's hope Fridge gets his shit together and joins us before we have to leave. *Hey*... what the hell are you... It's *you!*"

Sadie's outraged voice turned into a scream. I tripped over the bathmat as I darted back into the bedroom.

"Sadie! What the…"

She wasn't on the bed. Neither was one of the sheets.

My gaze flew to the window just in time to see a vampire jump from the third story window, with Sadie draped over his shoulder.

I bolted to the open window, my wolf growling inside my chest and my heart pounding.

I stuck my head out to see the vampire land safely, cradling Sadie in his arms. My mate was still wrapped in the bed sheet. He took off down the street at an impossible speed.

My wolf began to howl silently inside of me.

I would never catch him now.

CHAPTER 6

SADIE

The vampire who'd snatched me out of the hotel room looked just like the one who'd broken into my dad's apartment. I was pretty sure it was him. And yet, right now, he held me in his arms as carefully as a baby.

After I'd screamed for Rogan, the vampire had managed to swipe the sheet off the bed and wrap me up like a swaddled newborn, before lunging for the window and jumping from the three-story building. The landing barely jostled me.

He clung tight to me as he ran through the city streets like his life depended on it. And if he knew what was good for him, he'd keep on running.

When I finally got my breath back and the world stopped moving at such an un-natural pace, I was going to give him a piece of my mind. That was, if Rogan and Fridge didn't kill him first.

He obviously didn't want to kill me, or he would have done it already, but who the hell did he think he was kidnapping me? While I was naked!

I closed my eyes and forced myself to relax in his arms, saving my strength for the fight to come. As I turned my head into his chest, his scent wove around me, into my nose and through my senses, waking me up in a familiar and yet totally new and tantalizing way.

My eyes popped open and I groaned out loud as the realization flooded over me.

No. No. No.

I'd sensed something special about him. I'd ignored it the first time I saw him, but now... the goddamn fated mate thing.

What the hell was I going to do?

"Hold on," the vampire murmured, though it was literally impossible for me to do so. My arms were trapped within the sheet on either side of my body like a wrapped fish. I was completely helpless, which was why, up until this point, my heart had hammered like it was ready to explode.

But now, it thundered for a whole new reason.

Fridge is definitely gonna kill me for this. Rogan might, too.

The vampire leaped up and I couldn't help the shriek that erupted from my throat as he landed on a balcony of some sort, pushed open a door and walked into a heated room.

I shivered. "Thank God for that."

He lay me down on my back and stepped away. I immediately looked around to assess my surroundings. I was lying on a large leather couch, in an apartment living room.

The room itself was sparse and clean, and... lovely.

I swung my legs off the couch and sat up, struggling with the sheet to get my arms up and out.

"Who the hell are you?" I demanded, glaring at the man before me.

No. Not a man... a *vampire*.

He was so beautiful, with thick, dark hair, high cheekbones, and blood-red lips.

I narrowed my gaze as I took in his features. "Oh, my God. You *are* the vampire who broke into my dad's apartment! I thought so."

He was the one who'd disturbed us the night Rogan and I mated.

He'd laid out Rogan and Fridge that night, so even though he looked like a normal-sized man, it was obvious he had the skills, speed, and strength of an ancient vampire.

"Did you kill him? My dad?" I demanded, though I hoped to God he hadn't.

The idea that this man—my third and hopefully final mate—had killed my beloved father made my knees shake and my stomach heave. I would never be able to forgive him if he had.

"No!" The word practically exploded from him. "Of course not."

His voice held a slight English accent, as though he'd spent some of his life overseas, but had been in America a longer period of time.

"Then what the hell did you kidnap me for?"

I wriggled some more, tugging and pulling at the twisted sheet, desperate to come out of my cocoon.

"Let me help you." He stepped forward with an elegant hand outstretched.

"No," I said, jumping to my feet and trying to step away, only to trip on the sheet.

The vampire grabbed me, righted me on my feet, then stepped away once again.

That was when the sheet decided to untangle, and the whole thing fell off me to the floor in a spectacularly embarrassing *whoosh*.

Cool air brushed over all my warm skin, my nipples going tight and tingly.

"Shit!" I scooped the sheet back up and tried to re-wrap myself, but not before I saw the way the vampire's eyes devoured every inch of my exposed flesh. "I need something to wear."

He walked away, into a nearby room, and returned with an armful of hangers holding clothes.

"I grabbed a few things for you, in case you needed them."

He dropped the clothes on the couch, and there were some ridiculous price tags still attached to designer jeans, a black dress, and knit sweater.

"Expected to kidnap me naked, did you?" I asked, the accusation in my tone clear.

His handsome face flushed a pale pink as his nose went up in the air. "I did not. However, I was planning on keeping you here for a day to talk and thought you may be more comfortable in clean clothes."

He backed away and I grabbed for the jeans and the sweater, noticing he'd bought underwear for me as well. Not the sort of stuff I usually wore, though. These were ruby red and lacy as all get out.

I glared at him. "You expect me to wear those?"

He grimaced, his lips pulling to either side. "I'm afraid I left the choices of both the clothes and underwear up to the sales assistant."

I grabbed for the bra and panty set, gasping at the price. "And she rang up the most expensive thing in the store?"

He shrugged. "Money is of no importance."

It never was to a vampire.

"Don't go anywhere," I ground out as I clumsily grabbed the clothes I wanted and shuffled to the bedroom. *As if he would.* But my annoyance levels were high and I was scrabbling to get back some sort of control of the situation. "We need to talk."

He may have kidnapped me, but I had a lot of my own questions to ask.

He chuckled, the sound soft and a little rusty, as if he didn't laugh often. "I'm not going anywhere, Sadie. This is my apartment. And *I* brought *you* here, remember?"

Smart ass.

I slammed the bedroom door and dropped the sheet. "Asshole."

As I pulled on the surprisingly comfortable underwear and beautiful clothing he'd bought, a strange hysteria took me over. I began to smile then giggle at the absurdity of the situation.

Three mates? How the hell could one woman have three fated mates?
Truly ridiculous.

I took a quick look around the room, not seeing anything of note except for the fact that it was a bedroom. Could have been from any hotel for all the personal touches there were—namely, none. Glancing in the large mirror that hung on the wall, I took a deep breath and then headed back into the living area.

Time to work out who this guy is and what we're going to do about the situation.

When I opened the door, the vampire was still standing where I'd left him, surprisingly still.

When his gaze met mine, his eyes burned with a depth and passion I hadn't expected. It had an immediate effect on my body—an effect so strong it embarrassed me. Despite the strange kind-of-hostage situation, my nipples tightened in their new bra and my belly heated. I had to glance away.

I forced myself to walk forward on legs that were no longer steady and collapsed onto the large, comfortable couch.

"Okay. Tell me what this all about," I said.

He smiled. "Introductions first. I am Vincent Harlow. And you are Sarah Williams, known to your father and friends, as Sadie."

I nodded, crossing my right leg over my left and nestling into the couch to make it look like I was a lot more comfortable than I actually was. "How do you know so much about me?"

"I've been following you."

I blinked. "Did you just admit that out loud?"

He smiled. "Shouldn't your next question be, *why are you following me, Vincent?*"

This time I didn't even try to look friendly. I crossed my arms over my chest, glaring at him. "Fine, Vincent. Why?"

The name suited him. He appeared calm and regal. Probably had something to do with his age.

"And how old are you?" I added.

He moved to the edge of the couch and sat down on the armrest. "I'm almost three hundred years old."

Three hundred? Talk about a cradle snatcher.

I shook myself. "Okay, and the answer to the question of why you've been following me?"

He sighed. "It's a complex answer, so please hear me out."

I nodded and relaxed my arms a fraction.

He sighed again. "I work for some very powerful vampires. Or rather, I did. They've had your father on their watch list for over twenty years and recently decided to take him out."

My breath hissed in my throat as I stifled a gasp, but I kept my mouth firmly shut and gestured for him to continue.

A good lawyer knew to let her client talk. To get them to provide *all* the information before interrupting. It was a skill I'd never quite mastered. But right now I was giving it a red-hot go.

He continued. "I was the one who was tasked with watching him, finding a weak moment, and ending his life."

"But you said you didn't kill him." My voice came out in a squeak.

"I wouldn't be standing before you if I had," Vincent said, his voice deeper. "I saw him one night, in his apartment, with you."

"And that... stopped you?" I asked.

He nodded. "Yes. I knew as soon as I saw you that you were my..."

He halted, as if unable to finish the sentence.

"You feel it too?" I asked, my voice barely a whisper.

"Too?" he asked, but his expression gave nothing away.

I dropped my arms back down and ran my hands along my denim-covered thighs. "You're my soul mate as well, aren't you? My Fated Mate. Whatever special word you use for this." I gestured between us.

He nodded, his dark eyes going even darker—almost black. "I don't know how it's the case."

"*You* don't?" I asked with a laugh. "How did I end up with a wolf shifter, a dragon shifter, and now a vampire?" I shook my head, unable to even fathom how this was all going to work. "I mean, talk about natural enemies, right?" Tears gathered in my eyes and I wiped them away. "Enough," I muttered to myself.

Before my father had been murdered, I never cried. Dad didn't like it, and I was tough. Always had been.

No more tears.

I stood up, unable to stay lounging on the couch while Vincent propped nearby as though he could fly away at any moment.

Energy sizzled along my veins, making it impossible to stay idle. I paced the living room, the carpet surprisingly soft beneath my still bare feet.

I needed to make sure I understood this correctly. "Okay, so you were asked to kill my dad, you saw me, worked out we were... you know, and then you refused to kill him?"

He nodded. "Yes. And I tried to stop the hit on your father, too. I went to my boss's boss. To the top of our family tree. But there was no stopping it. I'm sorry."

I shivered at the intensity of his words, and regret plowed through me. If he'd come to me, this might not have happened.

I would have tried to...

I shook myself. What was done was done. I would return to the blame game, or what I could have done to save my father, later.

"Let's leave that aside for the moment," I said. "There's too much to unpack here without talking about what might have, could have, or should have, been."

He nodded. "Agreed."

I clapped my hands together to distract myself and kept moving. "Okay, so why did you take me tonight? I don't think you got to that part yet."

I'd jumped in as usual and stopped him from finishing the story.

He smiled, his eyes gentle. "I needed to speak to you. About your father. About... the blood ring. But mostly, I wanted to get you away from those two shifters for a few minutes and see if what I was feeling was real. Part of me believed I may be hallucinating, or something like it."

I frowned. "Why would you be hallucinating? What do you mean?"

Sadness overtook his beautiful dark eyes. "I'm almost three hundred years old, Sadie. I've been waiting for you for a very long time."

My heart broke and remade itself all in that one moment. To know that he'd been waiting for me, to find his true love... for all that time.

It was the stuff true romances were made of.

I returned his tentative smile and opened my mouth to say something hopeful, something life-altering.

The glass doors that led in from the balcony smashed to smithereens.

Vincent leapt over to me, covering my body with his.

But there was no need to protect me. It was Vincent that needed protecting.

Because my dragon shifter was here.

CHAPTER 7
FRIDGE

When I got my hands on the guy who'd taken my mate...

"Fridge, shift back," Rogan demanded as he slid off my back and onto the carpet of the apartment we'd crashed through.

After Rogan had called to tell me what happened, I'd picked him up in my shifter form and followed Sadie's scent through the city. I had narrowed it down to this building. This apartment.

And I'd been right. There she was.

Only, she didn't look like she was in danger. She didn't look unhappy at all.

I narrowed my eyes, inhaling deeply. I wished I had better control of my fire breath. Because if I did, I would barbecue the vampire that stood before me.

He deserved it for kidnapping my mate.

"Fridge. Shift back," Rogan repeated, his tone firm and commanding.

I shook myself. Shifting twice in a week was unheard of for me and I was struggling to control the changes. I was going to have to spend more time to sharpen my skills in this form if I was going to shift every time something happened to Sadie.

Our lives with her would never be boring, of that I was sure. I needed control of my dragon side as much as my human side. More, actually, given the potential for untold damage if I lost control of my dragon.

I walked back through the broken doors, the glass crunching beneath my heavy, purple-scaled dragon claws. I closed my eyes, focusing on bringing back my humanity.

Letting go of the anger, the strength and the wings, so that I could once again become a man.

My body contorted, shrinking, my bones reconfiguring and snapping back into place.

It was more uncomfortable than painful, and I felt vulnerable in the weirdest way as the people around me watched. But Rogan was there if I needed his protection, and that gave me some comfort. If the vampire attacked, we would at least stand a chance.

No one moved, and finally I was back in human form. I was naked, but hey, it wasn't like Sadie hadn't seen me in that state before.

A pair of black sweatpants were thrown at me from someone—was it the vamp?—and I grabbed them without thinking.

I glared at the vampire who had indeed tossed the clothing, but didn't say anything as I tugged them on. They were a little tight, but they'd do.

Sadie rushed around the vampire, her face a mixture of shock and annoyance. *She* was annoyed? *Why?* We'd come to rescue her!

"Are you guys okay? What are you doing here?"

My hands tightened into fists as rage poured over me like a hot shower.

"What are *we* doing here?" I repeated, growling in my attempt not to yell. "You were kidnapped! What did you expect us to do? Let the vamp just take you and go about our evening business as if nothing happened? What do you take us for?"

Sadie crossed her arms over her chest and lifted her chin. "Oh, there's an *us* again, is there?"

I growled again, a noise I was becoming increasingly comfortable with. "You fucking know there is. Now—what the hell happened?"

Rogan walked forward and cupped Sadie's face. "Are *you* okay?"

I rolled my eyes. Trust him to take the soft approach.

She relaxed as she looked into Rogan's face. "Yeah. Vincent never meant to hurt me."

"Vincent?" I repeated. *What the fuck?* She was on first name terms with her kidnapper now?

The vampire glided up, his strength and speed masked in his lithe, small body. Well, smaller than me, but most everyone was. He was larger than a normal human. Despite our relative size difference, I wasn't underestimating him. He was a vampire. Those who underestimated vamps, usually ended up dead.

His heels clicked together as he straightened to his full height, then he gave a small, mock bow. "Vincent Harlow, at your service."

I knew this guy from somewhere. How did I know his face?

"Hang on a minute. You're the asshole who broke into Jack's apartment," I said as I narrowed my eyes.

The vampire nodded and turned to address Rogan. "I apologize for injuring you at the time. I only meant to see if the information the elders wanted was at the apartment."

Rogan shrugged off the apology. "You didn't hurt me."

Sadie turned to the vampire. "What do you mean, you were looking for information at Dad's place?"

I stared at her and raised my eyebrows. "Oh? You didn't get to that part of the conversation with your *kidnapper* yet?"

Vincent gestured to the inside of the apartment, which I assumed was his. "Please. Come. Sit. I'll explain everything."

Rogan and I shared a look. Could we trust this guy?

Sadie stepped closer, her face pleading. "Please. Can we hear him out? I really want to know everything I can about my dad's killer."

Rogan sighed. "Okay. We can stay and talk."

He took Sadie's hand and led her to the couch, sitting down and pulling her onto his lap. Sadie was such an independent person, but such was the strength of the mate bond that she seemed content to stay on Rogan's lap, within the circle of his arms.

I didn't want to do this; walk into a vampire's home and listen to whatever lies he had to spew. But I wasn't abandoning my mate and my best friend to leave them with this stranger.

I took a few steps forward, into the vampire's den, then stopped, not wanting to go any further. Every instinct within me told me to stay close to the balcony, to the sky. I didn't trust this prick. He'd already proven that he was faster and stronger than Rogan and me when he fought us at Jack's place.

I didn't want to admit it, but if he wanted to kill us today, he might possibly succeed. The only thing that would save us would be my dragon, and I couldn't shift inside the apartment. It was too small. I needed the balcony, only a few feet away. So I hovered near the broken glass doors, glowering with rage and wishing we were anywhere but here.

"Explain," I demanded, then crossed my arms over my chest.

Sadie sat up straighter in Rogan's lap. "Yes. I want to know too. You hadn't gotten to this part during our conversation."

Really? What had they been doing for the hour or two since he'd taken her?

Vincent perched on the armrest of the massive leather couch and sighed. "All right. But get comfortable. It's a long story. First, I've already told Sadie this part, but in short, the Fathers asked me to kill Jack Williams."

My breath whistled in my throat. "And... you did?"

Surely, we weren't all standing around with Jack's killer shooting the breeze, when we should be exacting revenge?

Vincent shook his head. "Oh, no. Of course not. I refused."

His gaze slid to Sadie, but he didn't continue. There was something there they weren't telling us.

Vincent coughed to clear his throat. "But, anyway. What I wanted to tell Sadie, and you two also since you're on the trail of his killer, is the information I have on hand. I don't know everything, but what I do know will either make you stop looking, or…"

"Or?" Sadie asked.

Vincent frowned. "Or it will make you even more determined to find out who's responsible."

Sadie huffed out a laugh. "I can't imagine anything that would stop me from wanting to catch my dad's killer."

Vincent sighed. "Even if it means putting your own life in danger?"

She nodded. "Of course."

"And that of your mates?" Vincent asked.

Sadie didn't jump straight into a yes for that one. Instead, her gaze slid to me, then Rogan, and I could sense her hesitation.

I lifted my chin and focused on Vincent.

"Keep talking, vampire," I said. "We're with Sadie on this investigation. To the end."

Jack wouldn't have expected anything less. and we weren't letting him or our mate down.

Vincent straightened up on the sofa, his face turning hard. "Twenty years ago, a woman was captured by the blood ring. I assume you know what I mean by that?"

We all nodded.

"Yes," I said. "We know that vampires have been kidnapping people and draining them for their blood in an underground market."

Vincent grimaced. "It's a lot worse than that. Twenty years ago, anyone with witch blood was hunted down, kidnapped, and forced underground to be…"

He trailed off, his gaze averting.

"To be what?" Sadie prompted.

"Well, to start with, they were hooked up to machines and their blood drained slowly, over weeks. Sometimes they lasted months, if they were strong."

I glanced over at Sadie, who was growing paler by the minute.

Vincent continued. "But as the population of witches dwindled, the blood ring decided on another method of keeping their blood supply replenishing."

"What?" Sadie asked. "Draining them slower?"

He nodded. "Yes, that. And…" He took a deep breath as though preparing to tell us something terrible. "They began breeding the witches and other women with desirable bloodlines."

There was a stunned silence that echoed through the room.

They fucking what?

"What do you mean?" Rogan asked.

Vincent shuddered. "The vampire elders brought in an old warlock they'd found and forced him to impregnate the women so that there was a new and constant supply of blood with a heavy magic content."

Sadie's sudden sob was audible to the whole room, though she swallowed and tried to stifle the sound by covering her mouth with her hand.

This was becoming strangely personal to Sadie, and I couldn't figure out why.

"Sadie, is there something I'm missing?"

She stood up from her place on the couch, her legs seeming to shake as she faced me. She turned toward Vincent. "You know, don't you?"

Vincent nodded. "Yes."

"But how?" she demanded of the vampire, but he didn't respond.

I didn't like the feeling of being so out of the loop. Again.

I walked forward, into the den that I'd promised myself I wouldn't enter. Away from the balcony. "What is it, Sadie?"

She turned to me, lifting her chin to look me in the eye. "My mother wasn't human. She was a witch."

My mouth dropped open before I slammed it shut again. "Um, what do you mean she was a witch? What sort of percentage?"

We'd been told that almost all witches were gone, extinct due to the vampires hunting them down. But I supposed an eighth or sixteenth could be possible.

"One hundred percent."

Wait. "What?" I blinked, sure I hadn't heard correctly.

"My mother was a pureblood."

I gaped at her. "Impossible."

She laughed, though it was strained. "No, not impossible at all. So, I'm actually half witch, quarter human, and quarter wolf shifter."

I stared at her, then at the vampire, then back at her. "But you said that no vampire has even shown interest in your blood, let alone fed off you."

"I've been wondering about that part myself," Vincent said softly.

She nodded, crossing her arms over her breasts. "My mother cast a spell that disguised my scent. Though I don't know why she didn't do it for herself."

I reeled back.

Vincent stood up, capturing our attention. "I think she did. That's making more sense now."

He seemed to be talking to himself.

"What do you mean, vampire?" I asked, frustration growing in my gut. I hated everything about this situation. One, that the vampire seemed to know more about Sadie than I did. And two, that we'd had to rescue her from a man, who by all appearances, she didn't want to be rescued from.

What the hell was happening today?

"Well," Vincent began, his eyes lighting up with excitement, "I wasn't there, so this is hearsay, and most of the vampires on watch that night died. So again, I'm only reporting what I've been told."

I growled. "Just spit it out."

"Sadie's mother was taken from the streets where she'd been shopping, I believe. The vampire who grabbed her said he sensed some witch in her, but not a lot. Back then, any sort of witch blood was considered a find, especially if the woman was young and could be bred with a warlock to increase the population."

Sadie jumped to her feet. "Are you telling me my mother was raped so they could steal her baby and drain it?"

I shuddered, the very thought of what she was saying truly repulsive. I'd always thought vampires were harsh, heartless, soulless creatures.

But this?

The whole concept was horrific.

Vincent shook his head. "No. I'm saying they completely underestimated her powers. I'm sure they never thought she was a full witch, or she would have been taken to the Fathers for feeding."

"So, what happened?" Sadie asked.

Vincent chuckled, then ran his hand through his hair. "Your mom blew the whole place up."

CHAPTER 8
SADIE

I stared at Vincent, a portion of my brain refusing to believe what it was being told. I gaped at him, but when the other two remained silent, I found that I simply had to ask, "Say what?"

Vincent began to pace as though he was only now putting everything together. "Right, okay. Twenty years ago, your mother was taken, but no one knew she was a pureblood witch. If they'd known that... God, the elders themselves would have rushed down to taste her."

He shook his head incredulously. "Instead, she was put in a cell like all of the other women, and within a single night she'd managed to get free, release most of the prisoners and some of their babies. Which really upset the elders, I can tell you." He stopped pacing and smiled suddenly. "People always wondered how she managed it. But if she was that strong a witch, of course she managed to free everyone!"

My heart squeezed tight with a mixture of pride and pain for my mother. Vincent spoke as though he admired her, but I only wanted to know one thing. "What happened to her?"

His gaze turned sympathetic, so I knew whatever I was about to hear would be difficult. "They say she managed to get most of the witches out, but when some of them got caught trying to escape, she blew up the tunnels to give everyone a chance to run. I'm sorry to say, Sadie, that she died in the explosion. But it is my understanding she took several vampires with her."

My heart stuttered and my legs gave out.

I staggered sideways and fell back onto the couch. For a moment there—for just one single, sweet moment—I'd thought she may be alive. Just... maybe.

"Thank you for telling me," I forced out.

The men went strangely silent around me, then Vincent slid onto the couch next to me and took my hand in his. "I'm sorry, Sadie. I wish I had different news. Sometimes I forget that death for mortal species is, well..."

I pulled my gaze up to the man beside me and read dark pain behind his gaze.

"It's not your fault," I managed.

"I'm sorry," he repeated. "I've been a vampire too long."

I nodded, understanding what he meant. He'd lost his empathy for the human condition. For the finality of death to us mere mortals.

"It's okay." I practically choked on the words. It wasn't okay. Not at all. I swallowed hard. "So, she died saving other witches and she destroyed some of the enemy, too. That was noble of her, wasn't it?" My voice sounded wooden and far away.

Noble, yes. But she'd still died. And I was devastated by that fact all over again.

"I think it's time to take you home," Fridge said. He reached for me, tugging me up off the couch and pulling me out of the strange stupor I suddenly found myself in.

"No," I said, struggling against him, not wanting to leave yet.

He dropped his hands away from me, which I appreciated, though his wounded look confirmed he was offended.

"I don't want to leave," I said. "Not unless we bring Vincent with us."

The room went deathly quiet and if I wasn't so shocked, so numb to sensation due to the emotional bombs that had been dropped on me today, I may have felt bad for Rogan and Fridge who sported matching shocked expressions.

But I didn't. I might regret this decision later, but for now I was acting on instinct. Vincent needed to come with us.

"Why? Because he knows about your mom?" Rogan asked quietly.

I shook my head. "No."

How was I going to tell them that Vincent was my soul mate, too? Who on earth in this world was lucky enough to get *three* fated mates?

Vincent stepped forward, effectively cutting off anything else I might say. "I can help you. If you still want to catch Jack's killer, I can find out who it was. Track him down. Feed you the information you need. We can work together on this, if you let me in."

I stepped to the side to include Vincent in the conversation circle.

"Now there's so much more than finding Dad's killer," I said. "The blood ring needs to be shut down. I can't believe it's still running if they believe all witches are extinct."

"That's what we were told," Rogan said.

"That's what they want everyone to believe," Vincent said. "And although the bloodlines are diluted, there are still women with magic in their veins being drained for their blood. I've heard one of the vampire Fathers boasting of it."

I gestured to Vincent's grim expression. "See. We can't let it stand. We have to do something."

A sudden thought struck, making it even more imperative we close down the ring. Those poor captive women could be related to me.

Rogan picked up my hand and squeezed it. "You can't go after the blood ring, Sadie. Given your heritage. They'll kill you."

Like they did my mom.

"Well, I can't sit back and knowingly let them keep women trapped in some kind of dungeon as their own personal breeding blood bank."

I shuddered just saying the words. What repulsive, disgusting creatures.

Cattle were treated better than that. Although, that was probably how the vampires saw humans. As little more than animals that provided a source of food.

"Then we need more than a plan," Rogan said. "We're gonna need a miracle."

I shrugged. I didn't care at the moment how impossible destroying the blood ring seemed. I needed to do something. For all I knew, some of my mother's family—*my* family—could be locked up down there as witch hostages.

"I'm getting used to miracles at the moment, so I'm up for it," I said, and took a step toward Vincent.

"What do you mean?" Rogan asked, his gaze sliding from me to Vincent, then back again. He could sense there was more to the story, I was sure. And suddenly, I wanted no more secrets or lies between me and my mates. I wasn't going to lie about this.

Vincent reached out to me, touching me ever so lightly on the arm. "Sadie, I don't think you should—"

"I disagree. I should."

I turned to face Rogan, looking him directly in the eye. "Vincent is my fated mate as well. I suspected something the night he broke into my dad's apartment, but I knew what it was for sure when he grabbed me tonight."

I forced myself to turn and meet Fridge's gaze, trying to harden my heart and my stare when I did.

"So, Fridge, you'll have to decide if you still want me, when you have to share me with not one, but *two* other men."

Fridge's mouth, which had dropped open, snapped shut and his gaze blazed with sudden fire. "But he's not a man! He's a vampire."

I threw my hands in the air. "Well, tell that to Fate, or whoever the hell organizes this shit. Because this is it. This is me. This is obviously how we're meant to live. A witch, a wolf, a dragon and a vampire. And since you're the one who's had issues about our family unit from the start, it's up to you now, to choose."

Fridge's nostrils flared and a strange growl rolled up from his throat. "There's no choice here. You know that."

My heart sank. *He didn't want us?* To cover my upset, I put my hands on my hips and glared at him. "Then leave. If you don't want to stay here, go!" I flung my arm out and pointed to the window, my temper flaring as my hurt rose. "Fly away and never look back. That's what you want, isn't it?"

I bit my lip, trying to hold back sudden tears. *I will not cry. I will* not.

Fridge began to shift, his skin changing color to an electric purplish-black, as tendrils of smoke began to come out his nostrils. He was becoming a beast right in front of my eyes.

Vincent grabbed me and rushed to the back of the room with vampire speed, pushing me behind him.

"No," I said, shoving at him. "I want to talk to him!"

Fridge's fists were clenched into tight balls, and he wasn't moving. Shivers wracked his body. His eyes were closed, and his muscles trembled as he fought against the shifter wanting to take over his body.

I walked around Vincent and hurried back over to where Rogan was trying to coax Fridge outside so he had the space to shift properly and fly away.

I crossed my arms over my chest. "I think he should stay and give me an answer." I spoke more calmly this time, aiming for reason to keep his shifter side from emerging too fast. "Fridge? Give us all an answer. Please."

Fridge's eyes popped open, revealing irises that had shifted to a diamond shape. He was panting like he'd run a mile, but slowly, he began to gain control.

His huge body stopped trembling so hard and his eyes switched back to human.

He exhaled sharply, locked gazes with me, and then marched over to where I stood waiting.

I craned my neck to maintain eye contact as he came close, then gasped as his hands slid around my hips, grabbed my ass, and hauled me against him. Instant heat pooled between my legs.

He leaned down and whispered in my ear, "You listen, little lady, and you listen good. I'm not leaving you ever again. I said there was no choice to make, because I've already decided. You're *mine*. You hear that? Mine."

I shivered as his whisper turned sibilant as his dragon poked his head up one more time.

Fridge continued, "And when I sink my cock into you, Sadie, you're gonna *know* you're mine. I don't care if there's two others, as long as you choose me, too."

Oh my God. I moaned with the pleasure his words evoked in me. The intense and hungry way he'd shown me his choice—his commitment, his passion—inflamed my desire.

I grabbed his head and pulled his lips to mine, pressing myself against him as though I wanted to join with him as one right this minute. Because I did. I craved that, desperately. My breasts squashed against his bare chest and our tongues danced in a deeply erotic kiss.

I wanted him, in every way there was. I wanted Fridge to mark me as his. To fill me with his cock. His seed. His child.

Oh, crap.

I pulled away, the reminder of everything surrounding us coming back with that single thought.

My mother. Those children. The witches.

It was all too horrible to even fathom. It made me sick to my stomach and my heart ache.

As if he could sense the change in my energy, Fridge immediately let me go, though the still had a bulge in his pants. His naked chest was hot and sweaty and so sexy my core pulsed with wanting him.

"I'm sorry. I have to..." I waved my hand around as I struggled to breathe. Struggled to find words.

"It's okay," he said, stepping quickly away.

I extended my hand to hold him in place, needing to touch him. To reassure him that I wanted him. *So much.*

"It's not okay," I said. "I've dealt with too much today. All the shit about my mother. The witches. The blood ring. Please don't think I'm rejecting you, Fridge. I'm not. I want you more than ever."

I meant every word, especially now that he'd decided he was going to commit to our relationship. Our bond. Finally, he wasn't fighting anymore against the path that Fate had chosen for us.

I glanced around the room, at Rogan and Vincent who had remained back while my interaction with Fridge played out. "So, everyone can cope with this?" I indicated our circle in a sweeping arm motion. "The four of us being together?"

The men looked at each other and I held my breath, waiting to see who would break the tension.

Vincent smiled. "Well, as long as the shifters don't expect me to do anything for them in bed. A lot of vampires swing both ways, but I haven't had the pleasure."

"Oh, no. No. No!" Both Fridge and Rogan yelled at once, shaking their heads and backing away.

I laughed at the wide grin on Vincent's lips.

"So, the vampire has a sense of humor," I said, pleased.

He smiled back. "But, of course." He winked, then slid his gaze to Fridge. "Not that they aren't fine specimens. I just don't usually..."

I held up a hand. "It's all good. I don't know how I'd feel—" I stopped mid-sentence. If each of them had to watch me have sex with the others, I certainly should be comfortable with any or all of them being close. "Actually... if any of you want to..."

Fridge groaned. "No!"

I laughed again. "It could be hot, you know."

Fridge put both hands over his eyes and Rogan ran a hand through his hair.

"Okay. I'll stop teasing," I said, but damn, they did look cute when they were feeling awkward. "So, everyone's okay with this?"

I looked at Vincent, who inclined his head with a regal nod.

Rogan shrugged. "You know we're already mated. I'm never leaving you. No matter what."

That only left Fridge to make the final declaration. In front of everyone.

"And the dragon?" I asked, and although he'd already said as much into my ear moments before, my breath still hitched, and my stomach still twisted.

Fridge clenched his jaw, a muscle popping in his cheek. Then he nodded. "Yep," he said firmly. "I'm in."

CHAPTER 9

FRIDGE

As I stared at my mate—little, feisty Sadie—my heart all but expanded to fill my whole chest.

Was I still afraid of sharing her? Hell yes.

I was terrified about what that would do to me, to my shifter. Would the jealousy consume me?

I was also afraid of being tied down, and the sense of impending disaster that came with the knowledge that I had a mate counting on me. A mate, who at some time in the future, might begrudge the fact that she was forced to be with me.

Just like my parents. That festering resentment had destroyed their lives, and it had definitely had a detrimental effect on their children. On me.

Sadie was not just any plain, old mate, either. She was a Fated Mate—the woman who had been designed for me, by Fate. The one *I'd* been created for, destined to love with the intensity of a soul-connection. That, in itself, scared the ever-loving shit out of me.

But topping all of that, was the terror of losing her. I could not live, without my mate Sadie in my life.

It had been difficult enough when I'd told her I wasn't sure about us. Then I'd had to climb into Jack's car after work and drive home without Sadie or Rogan. With depression swirling in my head and heart, I'd been lucky not to kill myself in traffic.

When Rogan had called to say a vampire had snatched her straight out of the hotel suite, I'd shifted so quickly my head had spun like a top.

I'd flown immediately to the hotel where Sadie had taken Rogan, had him climb on my back, and we'd flown out in search of our mate. I'd never had anyone ride me before. It had been debasing, and yet somehow also liberating to know I could do it.

I'd also never been so scared in all my life, thinking about the atrocious things a vampire could be doing to Sadie while we searched.

My heart had pounded at the imagined scenarios that raced through my head. Images of him torturing her, draining her, killing her slowly. I imagined her screaming for me and Rogan, and us not finding her until it was too late.

The very idea that the last thing she would remember of me was that I'd rejected her because of some childhood crap about intended mates being a death sentence for joy had all been put into perspective.

I had been a dickhead.

If I lost Sadie, I would die myself. Why would I want to live in this world without the one person who completed me?

That was the moment I'd accepted Fated Mates as a strange sort of cursed blessing.

I needn't look any further. I had the perfect woman. And she had me.

And she also had Rogan... and now a fucking *vampire*.

I could deal. Somehow. I had no choice.

Because I wanted Sadie in my life. And that meant accepting all of her—including Rogan and Vincent.

"Hey, Fridge, you okay?" Sadie asked, pulling me back into my body and reminding me of where we were.

I glanced around. Everyone was staring at me.

"Yeah. All good."

Sadie smiled at me and I reached out to her. "Come here. Please."

She stepped toward me, and instead of pulling her hard against my needy body as I wanted to, I took her hand and led her to the couch to sit down.

I was trying to give her space, though a large part of me rebelled at that thought. I wanted her in my lap, as close to me as possible.

"So, what's the next step then?" I asked.

I didn't want to hunt the blood ring. Anyone who went after them seemed to die or simply vanish. There was too much money in providing immortal vampires with the tastes they craved, and too much power behind those same vamps.

And now that Sadie had revealed her witch heritage, the danger was magnified a thousand-fold.

But with Vincent on our side, was it possible we could stand a chance?

Maybe.

Sadie grimaced. "I need to keep pursuing this. I'm sorry. I know you guys would rather I didn't, but I have to know who ordered this and why." She turned to Vincent. "You still haven't told me the motive behind my father's murder. Only that my mother did something pretty incredible twenty years ago."

Vincent frowned. "They didn't tell me, but my theory is that they believed your father had information on more witches and their locations, because they were definitely looking for something tangible when he was killed."

Was that possible? That Jack knew more witches?

"And they killed him looking for that information?" I asked, glancing at Rogan, who seemed just as clueless as me. "Because as far we all knew, witches were completely extinct."

Rogan nodded. "Yep. That's what I thought, too."

Vincent shrugged. "If we're going after the blood ring, that's something we'll have to investigate. What they killed him for, and if they've managed to acquire it or not. Though instinct tells me they haven't found what they were looking for. Yet."

Sadie sat up straighter on the couch, her eyes searching as she glanced from one of us to the next. "So, you all want to help me solve my father's murder? You'd do that for me?"

"Hell, yes," I said. "We told you that from the very first night."

Jack had been more of a father to me than my own parent. I owed the man everything, and finding his killer meant almost as much to me as it did for Sadie.

Even if that meant taking on the blood ring.

Rogan and Vincent both agreed as well, but Sadie continued to look at me, and move closer, until our bodies were pressed tightly together. The heat from her skin against mine was delicious torture.

I reached out and clasped her hand. When our palms met Sadie gasped as her gaze flew to mine.

There was another tingle, a much harder, faster one, moving through me. I needed to bond with my mate. Urgently.

But where? How?

"Can we go back to the hotel?" I asked, changing the subject abruptly. "Is there room for me?"

I wasn't sure what she and Rogan had already been up to, and I didn't care. It was my turn to be with Sadie.

Her eyes flicked up to meet mine, and she nodded. "Definitely. I made sure we had a suite because I was hoping you'd come round."

Part of me remembered that the room had seemed large, but I'd been in such a hurry to grab Rogan and go on the hunt for our mate that I hadn't paid the hotel suite much heed.

Vincent stood up. "May I accompany you?"

I frowned. I didn't really want the vampire anywhere near us, but that was something I was going to have to get over.

Sadie wanted him, and he would be an asset in the battle we were facing. Could I stand by and watch him have sex with Sadie?

Only time would tell. But I was damn sure I needed to mate with Sadie first. I couldn't wait much longer.

Her gaze flicked over my face as though reading every one of my thoughts.

She turned back to Vincent. "Could you and Rogan follow in an hour or so? I need some time alone with Fridge."

She squeezed my hand and I struggled to keep the triumphant grin off my face.

"Do you wanna fly?" I asked, imagining how it would feel to have Sadie on my back, her thighs clinging vice-like on my back.

She laughed nervously. "I'd love to but... maybe another day?"

I nodded. Probably a good idea. I hadn't even thought about the ramifications of someone seeing me flying over the city. Pure dragons were rare as hens' teeth, and the last thing we needed was more people hunting us.

Not to mention the laws about shifting in the city. But I could deal with the police. It was the other hunters I worried about.

I pulled Sadie into my side. "Cab ride, it is."

Rogan and Vincent studied Sadie, then me. Neither of them looked angry, but simply a little shell-shocked. Maybe none of them had expected me to about-turn, tonight?

Then Vincent grinned. "Wanna borrow a shirt, man? You might look a little conspicuous catching a cab like that."

I glanced down at my bare chest and the too-tight black pants. Might be a good idea. "Yeah. Thanks."

Vincent disappeared into the bedroom and I took the time to look down into Sadie's eyes, loving the way she stared back at me. There was hunger, and promise, in her gaze.

When the vampire returned, he threw me a stretchy white shirt that I could already tell would barely fit me.

I grimaced as I extricated Sadie from my side and tugged on the shirt. "Thanks, but if we're gonna spend more time at your place, I really should pack a bag of clothes that fit."

Vincent chuckled. "You're a lot bigger than I first thought."

I wasn't quite sure how to take that. Even though the vampire said he wasn't bisexual, something about his interest in my body told me otherwise.

Not that it worried me.

"Thanks, anyway."

Sadie rose to her feet, tugging me in the direction of the door. "Do we just go down the elevator, Vincent?"

Vincent nodded and zipped ahead to open the door to the hallway. "Yes. I'm only on the third floor, so go down in the elevator and outside you'll find Main Street. We'll meet you at the hotel in an hour or so?"

He glanced at Rogan, who shrugged. His eyes burned with a hint of jealousy, but also understanding. "I can hang here, I suppose."

I looked at the window I'd smashed. Should I offer to pay for that?

"Sorry about the glass."

Vincent shrugged and flicked a hand. "I'll get it cleaned up. I... admire the way you fought for Sadie, Fridge. I have a feeling we're all going to be needed to protect her now that we know who she is, and *what* she is."

I pointed a finger at the vampire. "Speaking of which... Sadie's blood is—"

"No." I had been about to say off-limits, but Vincent cut in. "I have no interest in Sadie's blood. At my age, my appetite for blood is minimal and I survive quite easily from donors. Do not worry about me. The mate bond does not stem from that."

I narrowed my eyes. I was still pretty sure the fact that she had the most sought-after blood in the city would tempt him, but for now, I had to trust that his mating attraction to Sadie would overwhelm that primal urge.

"All right," I said, impatience rising in me. "We'll see you both later."

Sadie and I barely spoke on our way back to the hotel, but it was a pleasant quiet. A bonding time. Just being in her presence put me at ease, and I couldn't believe I had nearly given up this woman.

Never again.

Tonight, I would finally commit myself to her for life.

My Fated Mate.

Sadie

My hands shook as I requested an extra key from the front desk since I didn't have one on me when we re-entered the hotel complex. I was nervous and surprised at how much my body quivered.

As we rode up in the elevator and walked the few feet to the suite, my heart pounded against my ribcage. Nervousness skittered through my body like firecrackers. Every move Fridge made, every sound, was so delicious. And nerve-wracking.

I wanted him desperately. I had done since I'd first seen him in my father's apartment, half-naked and getting ready to sleep on the couch.

I glanced up at his gorgeous face, and when he grinned at me, heat flooded my cheeks.

Damn, I want to get my hands on that sexy-as-sin body.

I slid the card into the electronic mechanism and the door clicked open.

Fridge swung me up into his arms and I couldn't help the squeal that rose from the surprise of being lifted off my feet so easily.

He kicked the door open and carried me over the threshold like it was our wedding night. It was similar to when Rogan had carried me in, but there was something different with how Fridge held me high against his chest. Proud. Possessive.

I clung to his neck and smiled up into his serious, handsome face. Every cell in my body pulsed with how much I needed him.

He set me down on my feet, closed the door, then turned to me with heat blazing in his eyes.

I jumped at him, not wanting to let the furnace die down for even a moment.

He caught me, grabbed me around the waist, and hauled me up so that I could wrap my legs around his body. His hands gripped my ass as his lips captured mine in a fierce kiss that consumed me.

I wanted him as close as I could possibly get him. Wrapping my arms around his neck, I gave myself completely to the kiss. I closed my eyes and pressed my lips against his, sucking on his tongue as he swept in to taste my mouth.

Heat poured through me, igniting me from the inside out.

My hands trembled as I tore at his clothes, pushing the ugly borrowed shirt out of the way so I could touch his chest. On his hot, slick skin.

He lifted me up and away, encouraging me to untangle myself from him so we could remove our remaining clothing.

I didn't want to lose contact and cried out at being torn away. But I knew why he'd done it. There was no way of getting out of my jeans while I was still wrapped around him.

He set me on my feet, and I yanked down my jeans and tore off the beautiful black sweater I'd been wearing.

Tossing the clothes to the floor, I paused, aware I was now standing in only my underwear, my breasts encased in the sexy lace. Would Fridge like this fancy stuff?

His eyes flickered with the yellow diamond of his shifter as he voiced a reptilian hiss.

"Take those off. Slowly."

He stood there watching me, his chest heaving as he panted for breath. Seemed like he did like lace.

I'd managed to get his shirt off with my frantic fumbling, but his pants were still in place.

"You, too," I said, pointing at his legs. "Take those pants off. Quickly."

He grinned at my demanding tone and, as I stared at him with my mouth watering, he grabbed the waistband of his black sweat-pants and dropped them to the floor.

Standing upright once more he presented for me. My mouth dropped open at the sight of a naked Fridge.

Fuck, he is magnificent.

His body was hard and huge, and so amazingly fit. But his cock... damn, it was beautiful.

He growled at me. "Your turn, Sadie. Strip."

I almost laughed at the roughness of his tone. Had he changed his mind about me doing it slowly?

I hadn't.

Though my panties were wet from arousal and the waiting was killing me, I decided to draw out the moment.

Reaching behind me and unclipping the bra, I allowed the lacy confection to slowly slide down my arms, one inch at a time, until I dropped the bra onto the carpet, exposing my breasts fully to his gaze.

My nipples were hard and aching with a strength I'd never felt before.

Fridge pointed to my panties and growled that strange hissing sound. "Off."

I nodded, shivering as I grabbed the edges of the waistband and bent to slide them down my legs, taking my time to step out of them one leg at a time, and then slowly standing up again.

But Fridge was no longer standing in front of me.

He'd moved fast, almost silent, while I was bent, and he now stood behind me, radiating heat and with the scent of his desire rising up to engulf me.

CHAPTER 10

FRIDGE

Controlling my dragon shifter was getting harder by the second. He was rising up inside me with the ferocity of a tornado, restless to claim his mate.

Our mate.

I grabbed her by her rounded hips, loving the feel of her naked flesh beneath my fingers. Finally, no more clothing or any other kind of barrier between us.

"Damn, you're sexy," I hissed, though whether she could understand me with my sibilant shifter voice in play, I didn't know.

Sadie shivered as she turned her head to look at me over her shoulder and I pulled her hard against my body. She didn't try to stand up fully or turn around to kiss me. Perhaps she wanted me in the same way I wanted her. Hard and fast and frantic.

She gasped as I pressed my aching cock against the soft flesh of her naked buttocks, every instinct in my body demanding I take her.

Right here and right now.

But how could I do that when this was our first time?

"Fridge," she said, opening her legs in invitation. "Please."

Oh, fucking hell. How was a man supposed to ignore an invitation like that?

"Touch your toes," I said.

Sadie obediently bent forward and lay her hands on the carpet, her fingers splayed and her beautiful hair tumbling down.

The position allowed me to see her pussy properly, exposing her opening in all its glistening glory.

I couldn't stop myself. I dropped to my knees, grabbed her thighs, and licked her pussy lips like a starving man in search of water.

"Fridge!" Sadie cried out, her hands scrabbling on the ground for a better anchor, her knees wobbling. "Oh, my God…"

She squealed as I ran my mouth over all her swollen, juicy pink bits.

I couldn't contain the groan of pleasure that rolled over my tongue as I learned her taste. Perfection.

Her swollen clit pulsed as my lips circled the bud, and when I stuck my tongue deep into her pussy, the resulting moan from Sadie made me almost come on the spot.

The sound held delight and pleasure, and the cream that coated my tongue made my cock scream for release. I couldn't stand it any longer.

I jumped to my feet, lined my cock head up with Sadie's pink channel entrance, and steadied her hips with both hands.

"Are you ready for this?" I panted, wanting to hear her assent.

"Yes!" she practically yelled. "Please."

Excitement raced up my spine as I dipped into her body. Just the tip of my cock to start with, giving her the head to squeeze.

Oh, hell.

Her body was pure heaven. Made for me.

I held still, wanting to enjoy every moment of this coupling, but she didn't seem to feel the same way about the slow pace.

She pushed back, hard, encasing more of me.

I gasped at her demand for possession as my dragon shifter took over to ride my needs. I growled as I grabbed her tight and thrust hard, joining us completely in one long move.

Sadie cried out as my cock became fully seated inside her, but now I couldn't stop. I couldn't be gentle or slow. I could feel the mating link there, tenuous and thin.

There was only one way to strengthen it, to lock us together for all time. For the first time in my life, I wanted that commitment. That bond. I wanted Sadie to need me, and I wanted to need her in return.

The sounds of our slapping flesh filled the air as I fucked her hard and fast. I gripped her hips, and her spine arched up as her hands went to mine, holding me in place.

She cried out over and over again as I filled her up. Every thrust was met with an even more excited gasp.

Then, with a groan, she began to come. Her pussy gripped me so hard I almost withdrew to stop myself from toppling over with her, then realized that was exactly what was meant to happen.

So, instead of fighting the intensity of my feelings, I let them in.

I let the heat flood over my back, down my legs, and through my belly. Sadie's thighs shook and her scream echoed in my ears as I fell over the edge into climax. My orgasm roared through me.

There was no muffling my cry of completion as I sunk my cock balls-deep inside my mate and released my seed inside her.

Heat pulsed out of my body and into hers, setting off another round of orgasms for us both as her pussy milked my cock, squeezing it with delicious, perfect ripples.

Sadie sagged against me and I somehow managed to gather her up into my arms and stagger to the bed, getting us under the covers before collapsing against the mountain of pillows.

I was covered in sweat and Sadie was passed out on my chest. Against all odds, I joined her in sleep moments later.

WE WERE WOKEN BY KNOCKING.

"Shit. I think that's the other two," Sadie said, popping her head up from beneath the covers and looking toward the door. Her eyebrows were high, and her mouth had dropped open. Then she giggled and covered her mouth with a hand. "Oops."

I laughed and climbed out of bed. "I'll get it."

"Like that?" she asked.

I glanced down at my naked form and inhaled deeply through my nose. The scent of our sex was still heavy in the air.

I shrugged and sauntered to the door, proud as a peacock. "I'm pretty sure these two need to get used to seeing my naked ass."

If we had to live together forever, they definitely needed to get used to me.

I glanced through the peephole, and after confirming it was Rogan and Vincent on the other side, I threw open the door. "Come in."

As they entered and the door fell shut, I sauntered back through the living space and into the bedroom. Sadie had disappeared.

"Just having a quick shower," she called out from the ensuite bathroom.

I frowned in her direction. Was she trying to wash off my scent? That wasn't going to work. A wolf shifter and a vampire would be able to smell me from a hundred feet away.

I turned around to Vincent and Rogan, who stood apart from each other, just inside the bedroom doorway, arms crossed over their chests. They glanced up and down and to the side. Basically, they looked anywhere except at me.

Rolling my eyes at their bashfulness, I grabbed the sheet from the bed and wrapped it around my waist. "I really need to get some clothes."

Rogan chuckled. "Yeah, you were supposed to bring me some from home too."

I nodded. I was, but when the call came in that Sadie was in trouble, I'd shifted and flown out the window so fast I hadn't thought of anything but saving her.

Vincent piped up. "I could go get some things for you both."

I turned to him, surprised by the offer. "Well, I did leave everything out on the sofa, but... you know where we live?"

He nodded. "Yes. If you give me a key, I'll return in a few moments. Vampire speed, you know." He shot us a quick grin. "Then you can get some sleep. Assuming that's the plan for tonight?"

His gaze slid to the bathroom door and he froze.

I turned to see what he was looking at.

Sadie, otherwise known as my Fated Mate, was standing in the doorway with only a small towel wrapped around her gorgeous body. A cloud of steam surrounded her. As she walked forward, it was like watching a nymph emerge from a forest.

I couldn't stop staring. My gaze moved over the curve of her breasts only just covered by the towel, and down her long legs.

She bit her lip and looked at Vincent. "I probably need to get some sleep soon," she said. "It's past midnight, I think."

Glancing at the clock in the room, I realized she was correct.

Leaving to go get clothes now wasn't an option. I couldn't leave my mate. Everything in me told me to stay with her.

I forced myself to look back at Vincent. "Okay. Well, thanks. That would be great."

Rogan took his keys out of his jeans pocket and tossed them to Vincent. "You sure you're all right to find everything?"

Vincent nodded. "Yes. I won't be long."

The inference a minute ago that he possessed extraordinary quickness suddenly sunk in. I hadn't yet seen him move with vampire speed, but Rogan had told me that he was pretty powerful. That could definitely be an advantage to have him on our side.

"Thank you." I stretched my back, audible pops and cracks releasing a whole lot of tension. "I could probably use some sleep, too."

Vincent nodded in that strange, formal way he had and left the room.

Rogan looked at me with one eyebrow raised. "You gonna shower, or...?"

I grinned at him. "Why? Do I smell like sex? Or Sadie?"

"Both. And unless you want me taking Sadie as well tonight, I suggest you go wash her scent off you. It's getting my wolf all rowdy."

Sadie held her towel tightly to her breasts. "I'd love to but..."

Rogan laughed. "I was joking. I know you're tired. But Fridge, go get cleaned up."

I pulled my mate into me for a kiss, then walked past her. "Yeah, yeah, yeah."

I made my way into the huge shower and turned on the hot water, scrubbing myself quickly so I could get back to my mate as soon as possible.

When I returned to the room still naked because I had nothing to wear, Sadie had changed into a bathrobe and I assumed she wore nothing underneath. She was sitting on the bed chatting with Rogan, the atmosphere in the room relaxed and happy.

Sadie turned to me and her face lit up in the same way I'd seen her look at Rogan in the last few days. That expression called to me and I couldn't stop myself from walking over to the bed and sitting down beside her.

"No regrets?" I asked, hoping she would know what I meant.

She shook her head. "About mating with you? Hardly."

I ran my hand over her thigh, moving beneath the robe to find the heat of her skin. "So, you can feel the change, too?"

Because I certainly could.

For the first time in my life, I felt... settled. My dragon lay slumbering inside my mind. There was no urgent desire to run, to fight, to chase, to fly. Those were the feelings I had lived with on a daily basis for as long as I could remember. A need to escape my world.

But not now that I had Sadie. A reason to stay anchored to the earth. A reason to live.

The thought made me flinch.

I was happy now, but what would happen in five years? In ten? In twenty? Would Sadie come to despise Rogan and me? And us her? She would be unable to part from us due to the mating that we had all agreed to this day.

"Yes, I can feel it," she said, smiling. "There's such a strange duality to it. To feel so happy, so complete, because of you two. But then knowing I should be upset and enraged because of what has happened to my parents. Oh, speaking of which, the coroner this morning basically did everything to avoid talking to me."

"So, you didn't get anything out of him?" I asked.

She shook her head, then lifted her hand to cover her mouth while she yawned. "No. And part of me realized that if I pushed harder, it would come back to bite me in the ass, so I decided not to push. It was time to walk away and fight another day."

She smiled softly, her eyes half closing.

"I think it's time for bed," Rogan said. "Up you get so I can arrange the blankets."

I grabbed my mate and pulled her off the mattress, holding her in my arms and kissing the top of her head.

She leaned into me, putting her trust and her weight in my hands. "I'm so glad you decided you wanted to be a part of this relationship, Fridge. I don't know what I would have done if you'd walked away."

I glanced up at Rogan, who stared at me intensely. Had she really been that worried?

I tilted her chin up so that she was looking at me. "You had Rogan. You would have been fine."

Her eyes shimmered and she blinked. "You don't understand. I need both of you to feel complete. I wish it wasn't like that. But it is. I'm sorry."

She tried to drop her head and look away from my gaze, but this was too important to ignore.

"What do you mean?" I asked, narrowing my eyes. "You wish it was only you and Rogan?"

Surely, she couldn't mean that. Not after what had happened tonight between us.

She laughed softly, "No, of course not. I just wish you felt like you had more of a choice in this. Surely, you understand that? You speak of our relationship like... I don't know. Like you have to be with me, but you wouldn't choose it."

Grabbing her up in a fierce hug, I held her tiny body against mine and closed my eyes. I didn't want her to ever feel like I didn't want to be with her. That was just so wrong.

I kissed her hair and spoke into her ear. "Sadie, I adore you. I want to be with you. Nothing will ever tear me away from you."

"Then why..." she started to ask, then stopped.

I sighed and kissed her hair again. "Because I want to be all you need and want, and my stupid ego is going to have to get out of the way and realize that you need more than just me. I'm learning, beautiful. And I'll get there. I promise. You're worth it."

She pulled back and stared at me but didn't say anything for a minute. Then she cupped my cheek, and the look in her eyes said she was pleased with what I'd said.

I'd only spoken the truth. She did more than me, and it was up to me to work on my own feelings of inadequacy and jealousy.

After all, envy was one of the seven deadly sins.

CHAPTER 11
VINCENT

I bolted through the city, running through the shadows and streets, hiding from the people who wanted me dead.

When I'd refused to kill Sadie's father, as far as the Fathers were concerned, that made me a traitor.

I had betrayed my blood family, the ones who'd turned me centuries ago. They proclaimed me an outcast. Unfortunately, that meant anyone was welcome to take me out.

I had no regret for my choice, of course. Not for a moment.

For years I'd ignored the blood ring, not wanting to think about my brethren who treated humans in such a terrible way. But once I'd seen Sadie that fateful night, everything had changed. I'd been desiring my mate, craving my mate... for so long. To finally find her was a gift, even if she was a mix of creatures, both human and not. Adding further complication was the fact I would have to share her with two others. None of those factors mattered though, because she was the right one for me. I had complete faith in our bond.

I managed to get through the city without being accosted and located the apartment Fridge and Rogan shared. They didn't ask how I knew where they lived, and I was kind of glad. I didn't want to admit to the level of research I'd done on them when I'd found out their link to my mate.

The whole place smelled like Sadie, which made my fangs descend and my groin tighten with desire.

When she'd walked out of that bathroom earlier, still smelling like sex, it had taken every ounce of my control not to race across the room and lift her into my arms.

Damn, I want her.

But tonight had not been the right time for Sadie and me. Tonight had been for Fridge, and I would need to wait for the moment she was ready for *me.*

After all, I could turn her in a few years if she so chose, and we could live together, forever. If she wanted.

And those shifters too. *Maybe.*

I shook my head. We had to get through the next day, the next week. I shouldn't be worrying about the forever immortal life. No just yet, anyway.

Especially not now that I knew Sadie was part witch. I shuddered. Damn, it was going to be an enormous problem if any other vampires found out about her. Fridge, Rogan, and I would have a full-time job simply keeping her alive, let alone away from the blood ring.

The daughter of a full witch. It was just unheard of in this day and age.

I grabbed the clothes that the dragon shifter had laid out on the couch, and stuffed them into two bags lying nearby. I had to assume they were to be taken as well, since they were all clustered together.

Then I made my way back to the hotel room where my new family had taken up residence and knocked on the door.

Rogan opened it, his eyebrows fluttering up. "Damn, you are fast."

Shrugging, I walked inside the room. "I told you I'd be back as soon as possible."

I wasn't being boastful. I *was* fast, even for a vampire.

Sadie jumped up and headed for the bags and clothes I laid on the bed. "Thank you so much for getting these, Vincent."

She took one of the bags, so I guessed it must be hers, and moved across the room, opening the zipper and taking out a pair of underwear and a tank top.

She pushed the bathrobe off her shoulders and it dropped to the carpet.

My fangs elongated and dug into my bottom lip. *Damn...*

Her ass was luscious and round and firm. Her legs were long and strong, and her back was beautiful.

I wanted to run my hands down the indent of her spine, press my lips to her neck and explore every nook and crevice of her beautiful body.

The dragon cleared his throat and broke the spell.

I glanced around, seeing the other two men staring at Sadie in the same way I had. With lust. But more than that, with adoration.

When I looked back at her, she'd pulled on her panties and soon the tank covered most of her top half. She turned around and her face was flushed, as though she knew we'd all been staring at her.

"Do you need to sleep, Vincent?" she asked, her tone curious and completely naïve.

I smiled. "You don't know much about vampires then?"

She shook her head. "No, my father didn't like them much."

The dragon snorted. "Much? That's an understatement."

I tried not to be offended by the slight. I hadn't known Sadie's father, and he had never met me.

"I can imagine," I said. "There aren't a lot of shifters who like vampires."

"Can you blame us?" Fridge asked, puffing up like I'd offended him.

I narrowed my gaze. "I believe you were casting aspersions on my species. I wasn't insulting yours."

Fridge crossed his arms over his massive chest. He'd managed to pull on some sweatpants while I'd been ogling Sadie, but he was still a very impressive-looking man.

"You didn't answer the question," Fridge pointed out. "Do you blame us for feeling that way?"

"That way" hadn't been clearly defined, but I ignored that part of the question. I took a breath, trying to remove myself from the equation. He didn't know me.

"No, I don't," I said, shaking my head. "The vampires in this city have done terrible things to shifters and humans. But that's not me. I don't attack shifters. I don't bite humans unless they beg me to. I have kept as much of my humanity as possible, considering the long years I have spent waiting to find my soul mate."

Surprise rippled across Fridge's expression and his arms relaxed. The dragon didn't say anything else but the cogs turning inside his mind were obvious. Fridge and I were going to have some issues, that was clear. As clear as the scars from vampire bites that I could see on his skin. He'd been attacked, and more than once from the looks of things.

"As a bounty hunter, I'm sure you've fought every species known to man," I told him.

He nodded sharply. "I have."

"So please don't judge me too harshly, dragon shifter."

Sadie stepped up next to me and slid her hand in mine, capturing my attention.

"You didn't answer my question," she reminded me.

Which was? Oh, yes. "No, I don't sleep."

Her eyes widened. "You *never* rest?"

"Well." How much to tell them? It could put them all in danger. "We don't usually tell people this, of course, but..."

My gaze slid to the wolf and dragon shifter who both stood in the room, staring at me.

"Go on," Sadie urged. "You can trust Rogan and Fridge. They're part of our family now."

She said it with such an endearing, worried smile that I found myself relaxing.

"I suppose so." And they were. I'd committed to Sadie, and so had they. And that meant we would all be together until the end.

I took a deep breath and swallowed hard, preparing to expose vampire secrets that were centuries old. "Well, it's the day walking."

"Yes?" she asked while Rogan and Fridge found a place to sit and listen as though I was giving a lecture. "What about it?"

"It takes a lot out of us to day-walk."

"What do you mean?" Sadie asked with a frown.

I exhaled against the pain in my chest, fighting the panic that set in. A shallow laugh huffed from my chest. "I have to tell you all that there are rules within the vampire population about not exposing these truths to anyone outside our world. Punishable by death."

"Well, we won't say anything," Sadie said.

Rogan shook his head. "No way."

Fridge nodded. "I won't say anything. Swear."

Somehow, I believed them. I had to. There was no way I could be with my Fated Mate if I could not trust the others in the relationship as well. We had to be in this together.

Hopefully, they were in agreement. It was up to me to put the trust out there, to expose a vulnerability.

"Okay. Well, most of the humans and shifters have been told that we have mastered the art of day walking. And since we don't need to sleep and live forever, it makes us seem invincible in so many ways."

Fridge rolled his eyes. "Yep."

Sadie nodded. "Well, the vampires pretty much own everything in the city. Every business. Every restaurant, or the majority, anyway."

"Well...." I took a deep breath. "We have a weakness. A big one. Day walking consumes a vast amount of energy. So those who work a normal job and spend most of the time in the sun need to sleep at night. They become weak, human-like."

Fridge got to his feet. "So, you're telling me that those vamps who try to live a human life end up having human weaknesses."

I nodded. "Yes. And there's nothing we can do to change it. I avoid day walking as much as possible, so that I don't need to sleep through the night."

It also kept my speed intact, and made me stronger than most other vampires. Many of them sacrificed a lot of paranormal advantages to spend time in the sun.

Sadie stared at me. "So, if you lived with us and formed the same habits as us, you would need to rest, to sleep through the night. You could be almost human?"

The thought hadn't occurred to me before. "I suppose so, yes."

"Well, you may need to be out with us during the day occasionally, so it's nice to know that I'd get to sleep next to you as well during the night." Sadie yawned loudly and I glanced at the time.

Almost one a.m.

"Speaking of which," she said as she staggered toward the bed. "I really need to get some sleep. Especially if we're going to work in the morning."

"Looks like a late start is in the cards for tomorrow," Rogan said. "I'll set an alarm for eight and we'll just roll out of bed and walk to work."

"No need," I told him as he started playing with his cell phone, likely to set an alarm. "I'll be here, and awake. I'll wake you."

Rogan tugged off his shirt, revealing a well-built chest. "Thanks, but an alarm is fine."

Sadie crawled into the middle of the massive bed and slid beneath the sheets. "You're not going to just stand there and watch us sleep, are you, Vincent?"

She seemed disturbed by the idea, so I made up my mind to run an errand I'd been indecisive about. "No. I need to see someone, actually."

"Who?" Sadie asked as she settled against the pillows and her two Fated Mates got into the bed on either side of her.

It was an erotic thing to watch as they nestled close, two sets of possessive hands moving over her from either side of the mattress.

"Shadow."

Sadie's eyes popped open. "My cousin?"

"Your *what*?"

Her hand covered her mouth. "I don't think I was meant to tell anyone about that."

"Oh, that makes sense now." I nodded to myself. "Shadow's been asking a lot of questions about the blood ring. Your dad... I hadn't put it all together yet and he's very good at staying off the radar."

"Please don't tell anyone," Sadie said, then bit her lip.

I waved my hand through the air. "Your secret is safe. Don't worry."

Sadie nodded and settled back against the pillows, her eyes closing. "Well, make sure you take a key card to get back in, and let us know in the morning what he said."

I nodded. "Sure thing."

I backed away from the large bed, feeling strangely excluded from the group as the other three began to fall asleep, nestled in their cocoon of warmth and human flesh.

With their mate. *My* mate.

Was that what I needed to feel close to Sadie? Would I need to adopt a more human existence? To stay up during the day, and sleep all night?

If I were honest, I didn't want that. The cost was too high. It would feel un-natural and make me weak. But if I didn't, was I destined to always be on the outside, looking in as Rogan and Fridge lay with my mate?

"See you all in the morning," I called out as I exited the room, hoping I didn't sound as envious as I was.

Despite the fact that Sadie felt our connection, it was obvious I was going to have to wait for her to want to mate with me as well as the other two.

For now, I had a plan. A date. I headed out into the dark with a smile on my face. This was my playground, when night was at its darkest.

I'd agreed to meet Shadow at an underground bar, though at the time I had been unsure of that decision. The underground was full of vampires, and it was still unknown if anyone was pursuing me.

But things had changed. I had a real reason to meet Shadow now. I would give him the information he wanted and ascertain if he needed it for himself or for Sadie.

If he was digging for dirt on Sadie's behalf, then my main objective was to let him know that we were now on the same team.

Because if we weren't... things could get ugly.

CHAPTER 12

VINCENT

The place in which Shadow had suggested we meet was underground, quite literally. A meeting place for all para-normals, shifters, and low lives.

One had to enter a sewer, go down another level, then come up under a prolific law firm that employed some of the oldest and most powerful vampires in the city.

It was where you went if you didn't want anyone to know your business.

I snuck into the bar and kept my head down. No one wanted me killed, technically. Not that I knew of, anyway. But I had no vampire family anymore, no protection should anyone decide to take me out.

The place was almost empty, Wednesday nights being slow. It was smoky and dark, and lit with only a few old candelabras.

A nod to the old world. An era before electricity.

Several lifetimes ago for most humans, but a time most of us vampires had lived through.

I ordered a B-positive and headed for a booth in the back. My drink was delivered in a shot glass and just as the sexy little vampire waitress backed away, Shadow snuck into the booth, sliding onto the seat almost silently.

"I wasn't sure you'd come, Vincent."

"Neither was I, but here I am." Nodding at him, I lifted my glass and inhaled the aroma of the deep, red liquid.

Fresh. Female. Maybe thirty years old. Very nice.

My fangs descended and part of me paused, relishing the moment. I wanted to drink the blood slowly. Truly enjoy the warmth and taste. But I also didn't want to wallow in my vampire instincts. Not in this company, especially.

Shadow was sitting there with his odd eyes staring at me, watching me, assessing me. Same as he did to everyone. So, I tipped back the sustenance that kept me alive and swallowed hastily.

Slamming the glass back down on the table, I forbade myself from ordering any more, even though the craving was strong. That one shot was enough blood for a week or so. I was getting good at surviving on less and less.

"So, Shadow. How can I help you?" I asked.

No one knew much about his lineage, but it was clear he was a real mix of breeds. Obviously, being Sadie's cousin, he had some warlock in him but I wouldn't have known that before Sadie had let the fact slip.

Shadow walked with a limp and, in the past, I'd been certain I saw a magical purple swirl in his dark eyes.

Not that I could say anything about that. Hinting that he was even part warlock would be a death sentence for the man. He certainly didn't smell of anything good. Quite the opposite, in fact. There was a shifter in the mix that was very unpleasant to my vampire nostrils.

A rodent, or perhaps a reptile. I couldn't tell.

He was Sadie's cousin, though. That meant he wielded at least some level of magic.

"Word is that you're on the outs with many of the high-end vamps, Vincent," Shadow said, lifting one eyebrow.

I couldn't help but laugh. "You don't beat around the bush, do you?"

Shadow inhaled sharply, his eyes going wide and round. "Why do I sense... a dragon shifter on you?"

"Anything else you smell?" I teased, leaning forward, before dropping my voice to a whisper, though there was no one close by to hear. "Your cousin, perhaps?"

Shadow's mouth dropped open. "No way."

I laughed, finding the casual words tumbling out of the powerful shifter's mouth quite funny.

Shadow maintained a strong position in the underground world. He was mysterious. He was untouchable. But I was now seeing a totally different side to him.

I had shocked him. And I liked that.

He leaned forward, all pretense of power games gone. "You can't be," he said, inhaling even deeper. "I can't smell her on you yet, but you're... She can't possibly have three Fated Mates, surely? That would be extremely rare."

I chuckled, but squashed the sound when the waitress looked my way with interest. "It is rare. I would have said that it is closer to impossible, but yes, Sadie is my soul mate."

"But she already has Rogan and Fridge," Shadow said, as if more for his own benefit than mine.

"Yeah, I've met them," I said, enjoying his turmoil a little too much. "Sadie sends her regards. So, tell me, why did you contact me?"

I'd received the message sometime yesterday that Shadow was looking for me. That would usually mean someone powerful wanted me. But when he'd suggested this bar, I had reconsidered my conclusion.

He'd needed something different from the norm. Something more unobtrusive.

Shadow sat back in his chair, calmer and more composed now. "For Sadie. She's investigating her father's death and we know it was a vampire. And I know that you're currently on the outs with the Fathers."

"You were hoping I could provide some information for her?" I said, filling in the blanks.

Shadow nodded.

I shrugged. "Sorry to disappoint, but I've already told Sadie everything I know. And, not that you asked, but I'm on the outs because I refused to kill Jack Williams when they asked me to."

Shadow's eyes flashed that strange purple at the mention of the man that I assumed was his uncle. At least through marriage.

Shadow stood suddenly, his strange, sloped shoulders catching my gaze.

"Then I'll be going," he said. "Thanks for meeting me, Vincent."

He turned to leave, and I got to my feet.

"I'll walk you out."

I did, though I could tell the shifter was uncomfortable by the way he kept his body rigid and remained a decent distance away from me.

But even so, he didn't try to put further distance between us as we entered the sewers. We walked back through the sludgy pipe together and up to the road.

It was pitch dark, and yet I could hear the movement of night vamps trawling the city.

"What else did you tell Sadie?" Shadow asked, his gaze shooting left and right as he continued to watch his back.

"I... told her a little more about her mother's death that she didn't know," I admitted.

Shadow nodded slowly. "So, you know?"

"About her bloodline? Yes. And it makes her mother's escape from the underground so much easier to understand."

Shadow continued to nod, though I couldn't tell if that piece of information was new to him or not.

"Do you know where they keep them?" Shadow asked cryptically.

I stared at him for a minute.

"No. I've never had any interest in the blood ring," I admitted. "I thought most of it was shut down."

Shadow shook his head. "No. They simply moved. The demand is too high, and unfortunately, Sadie's mother's display of power put the vampires on a mission to find more like her."

I sighed. That sounded accurate. "So why haven't they gone after Sadie then?"

He shrugged. "I honestly can't answer that. She doesn't smell appealing to a vampire, I've heard."

He looked at me for clarification.

I nodded. "That's true. Not for blood purposes, anyway." I thought about teasing him a little, and saying, *just like you*. But the guy was wound quite tight so in the end I kept my mouth shut.

Shadow stretched his shoulders, a strangely pained grimace moving through his features. "They discovered what her mother was, so I have to assume there's another reason they've left her alone. Let us hope that it doesn't come back to bite her in the ass now."

I clenched my jaw. "We'll be ready if they do."

Shadow turned to walk away.

I grabbed for him. "Hey..."

He evaded my touch so quickly I barely saw him move.

"Yes?" Shadow asked, pulling his features into a semblance of calm.

I frowned but decided not to ask why he'd reacted in such a way.

Instead, I asked, "What are you going to do next?"

He began backing away, his gaze going to my right, where there were some noises in the night. "She's going to want to find them. I need to know where they're being kept."

"That'll be dangerous," I said. "For all of us."

Shadow shrugged. "She won't stop until she gets closure on this, so you're either with us or against us."

He turned and bolted before I could yell out, *I'm with you.* With Sadie as my mate, I would follow her into the depths of Hell. Or in this case, into the depths of the blood ring, and back again.

"Hey, Vincent. Long time no see..."

The familiar female voice had me turning toward the alley to my right.

Celeste, an old donor of mine, staggered out onto the road, the single streetlight casting a soft light over her emaciated body.

I cringed. I hated seeing what happened to those humans who became addicted to a vampire's bite. It was very similar to any other drug. When used occasionally, a vampire drinking from a vein could be pleasurable, but when abused, the body wasted away while the occupant sought out more and more.

"Celeste. What are you doing here?" I asked, taking in the thread-bare clothes and fresh feeding marks on her neck. "Who were you with?"

Two vampires slunk out behind her and stepped into the light, wiping at their mouths in dramatic fashion.

I frowned. *Stephen and Tank.* Two bottom feeders.

"Well, well, well," Stephen said as he walked toward me with a smirk on his face. "I heard you were still around, though I don't know why. Isn't it time you moved on?" he asked, as they both began to circle me.

My muscles trembled as I readied to fight or possibly flee. I could take these guys on, of course. They were barely fifty years old, and currently drunk on blood.

I was faster, stronger, and had a much clearer head.

But dead vampires raised too many questions from the Fathers, so I decided to try to talk my way out of this, or run. But if they threw the first punch…

"Move on?" I repeated. "This is my home. I'm not going anywhere."

"But you have no family. No friends. It would really be better for everyone if you just found somewhere else to live," Stephen said, moving behind me.

The hairs on my neck prickled. I twisted around just in time to duck the fist swinging at me.

I didn't hesitate. I shifted on the balls of my feet and swung an upper cut hard and fast at Stephen's jaw.

The loud crack sounded in the quiet of the night. Celeste screamed as the vampire flew backwards, landing like a pile of excrement on the sidewalk.

I turned to take on Tank. His fangs were exposed and he lunged for me, grabbing at my arm, his mouth wide.

That was a low blow, and a suicidal one at that. One vampire biting another would be poison for both.

Instead of twisting his head off like he deserved, I jumped behind him, wrapped my arm around his neck and squeezed.

"Who hired you?" I demanded. No self-respecting vampire would try to die that way. There were much better ways. "Who?"

"The Father… Samuel," Tank wheezed between breaths.

Samuel? What the hell? Samuel was an ancient and powerful vampire. I was surprised I would even be on his radar, despite my perceived crime.

"What does Samuel want with me?" I asked, keeping an eye on Celeste, where she was staggering over to Stephen, who lay comatose on the sidewalk.

Tank tried to pull at my arms, twisting in an attempt an escape my grasp.

I tightened my arm until I heard a vertebra in his neck make a soft pop.

"I can kill you, you know." I breathed into Tank's ear.

"Okay, okay," Tank said. "I can't... speak. Like. This."

I eased up a little with my arm. "Talk. Now. You have three seconds."

"He didn't tell me exactly, but it has something to do with a girl. Some chick you're hanging around. A bounty hunter."

My breath caught in my throat, my chest tightening. *Bollocks. They know about Sadie.*

Stephen was starting to stir. Celeste had propped his head up in her lap where she sat next to him and was stroking his hair.

My time was up. I needed to go.

"What do you know about the blood ring? Where do they keep the girls they drain?" I asked Tank.

He huffed out a strange laugh. "You think they'd tell me that?"

"I think you have a vague idea where they might be," I bluffed. I wasn't sure if he did or not.

I squeezed tightly, waited, then let him go and pushed him forward. He stumbled a few steps before finding his balance and turning to face me.

I began to back away, ready to make a run for it.

Tank called out, "You know what? I will tell you what I know, because if you go after them, you'll be dead faster than the sun can rise."

Stopping, I stared at him. "Tell me. I dare you."

"I don't know for sure..." he began.

Of course, you don't. You're a bottom feeder.

"Yes?"

"But there's a section of the underground, under the morgue. We can't go down there. The sewers are blocked off. I'm sure you'd find something if you went looking there."

Stephen staggered to his feet and wiped blood from his mouth with the back of his hand, his gaze narrowed on me.

I wasn't in the mood to kill either of them. I had a lead, and needed to get home and share it with my new family.

Saluting the two vampires and ignoring the glare from Celeste, I took off at my greatest speed to make sure no one would catch me.

CHAPTER 13
ROGAN

My alarm blared with an unpleasant sound and vibrations shot me straight out of the warm dream I was in.

"Shit." I rolled away from Sadie's soft, sweet body and grabbed my phone from the bedside table, poking at the screen to stop the noise.

I groaned, rolling onto my back and stretching my arms above my head as my temples pounded with a headache. I needed more sleep and some water. Maybe some Advil.

"Told you an alarm was the wrong way to go," came a male voice from the other side of the room.

I sat bolt upright. Vincent stood in the doorway beside a room service cart that held several serving plates.

He indicated to the food. "I didn't know what you all liked, so I ordered some of everything."

He lifted the silver plate warmers and the smell of bacon and eggs and coffee wafted toward me.

There were groans beside me as Sadie and Fridge stretched and sat up.

"Do I smell coffee?" Sadie asked, a smile breaking over her face

"Yes. How do you take it?" Vincent asked.

Sadie threw back the covers and crawled across the mattress between us, toward the food.

I glanced over at Fridge and he had the same confused, annoyed expression on his face as I was sure was still on mine.

So that's how it was, huh? Abandoned for caffeine.

"Rogan?" Vincent asked, offering me a mug of coffee.

"Damn it," I said, throwing my legs off the mattress and heading to the headache salvation. "Thanks."

I took the mug from him and added a dash of cream from a little pot that sat on the silver trolley.

"What happened last night?" Sadie asked, shoving a croissant in her mouth. She chewed and swallowed before adding, "Did you see Shadow?"

Fridge ambled up like a big bear, grabbed one of the plates, and piled on some of the delicious-smelling bacon and eggs.

Vincent stepped away to give us room, not eating anything. I'd never asked, but from what I'd gleaned over the years, I was pretty sure human food was deadly to a vampire.

"Well, I found out that Shadow had asked to speak to me because he thought I'd be able to tell him where the blood ring operates from, and where the girls are kept."

I stared at him, surprised. "Why is *he* looking for them?"

"Because he believes Sadie wants to know. So, he's finding them for her," Vincent replied.

Sadie frowned. "I didn't ask him to do that."

I glanced at Sadie with a grin. "That's impressive. He reads minds, too."

My attention turned back to Vincent, the vampire. Sadie's third mate. My head still hadn't wrapped around that part.

Leaning forward, I sniffed him. "Why do I smell something weird on you then? Is that blood?"

I blinked at him. Had he been out feeding? I suppose I couldn't blame him. He needed sustenance from somewhere and so long as he didn't get it from Sadie, I shouldn't complain.

Vincent lifted his arm and sniffed, and that's when the bloodstains on his shirt got my attention.

His gaze followed my pointed look, and he shrugged. "I had a run-in with some other vampires," he said. "Got one in a head lock and he'd been feeding on a donor before that."

He dropped his arm, not seeming phased by the blood smears. What would it take to rattle a vampire?

"Hey, how old are you?" I asked.

Vincent rolled his eyes. "Why do humans always want to know that?"

Now I was human? I ignored his question. "A hundred?"

His way of speaking, his choice of clothes, all indicated he wasn't born in this century. Maybe not even the one before.

"Closer to three hundred," he said.

"Whoa." I slid my gaze over to Sadie. Was she okay with that?

She ignored me and turned to Vincent. "Did you find out anything else?"

"Yes. But I probably should do some research before revealing everything. Find out if the tip is valid."

I grinned and glanced over at Fridge. He was going to try and keep something from Sadie; from us?

"Hey..." I began, but Sadie jumped in.

"If you know something about the blood ring, Vincent, you need to tell us. You're not alone. You have us. We're a team. And you know if you don't tell me, I'll just go looking for things in the wrong places..."

She trailed off and I couldn't help rolling my eyes. Did she seriously think that was going to scare a three-hundred-year-old vamp?

But when I glanced back at Vincent, he seemed rattled.

"Sadie," Vincent began, "you need to be careful. You're too precious to all of us, and despite your unappealing blood aroma, if any vampire were to actually bite you and find out what you are…" He shuddered. "You wouldn't escape death. And I couldn't live with myself if that happened."

My gaze flicked to Fridge, who was watching the interaction between Vincent and Sadie with as much interest as me.

They didn't touch each other, and from what I'd gathered, nothing physical had happened between them. But there was a connection, that was for sure. Sadie gazed at him with longing, and the way he looked at her… well, my wolf didn't like it.

Vincent looked like he wanted to tuck Sadie up in his arms, rush off somewhere and hide her. It was a hard thing to watch, and yet, I wanted Sadie to be happy. To have what her heart longed for.

The struggle inside me was intense.

Sadie set down her empty cup of coffee on the room service cart. "Do you know where the women are being kept?"

I wasn't sure if Sadie was most concerned about the women being tapped for their blood, or for the babies bred for their witch heritage. Both were equally evil as far as I was concerned.

Vincent took a deep breath, not looking away from Sadie's intense face. "I have a lead."

"What is it?" I asked, grabbing for some buttered toast. "Is it reliable?"

Vincent finally looked away from Sadie and directed his attention at me. "That's debatable. Which is why I'd rather look into it myself."

"No," Sadie said. "They'll kill you without a second thought."

Vincent smiled slowly. "I'm not that easy to kill, Sadie."

Fridge finally interjected, groaning. "Just tell us, and we'll decide if we wanna step in or not."

I nodded. "Yeah. Out with it."

Vincent sighed. "You guys know that the sewers are used for many of the paranormals—mostly vamps, I know—as an underground village of sorts?"

I nodded. "Yeah. I've heard there are houses down there. Dens, bars... everything."

I hadn't actually ventured down there, but that's what I'd been told. Most shifters wouldn't venture into the sewers, especially not wolves or dragons like Fridge and me. We liked the open air too much. Being able to see the sky and feel the breeze on our faces.

Fridge shuddered. "I couldn't think of anything worse."

Neither could I, but I kept that to myself rather than openly insulting the vampire in the room.

Vincent went on like he hadn't heard Fridge. "Well, the rumors are mostly true. Not many vampires live down there, but there are establishments to frequent. I met Shadow at a bar down there last night."

"And you think these sewers are where they've set up their... blood ring?" Sadie asked.

Vincent nodded. "Yes. I always assumed they had to be down there, somewhere. Where else would vampires be able to work, day and night, in safety, away from prying eyes? Unless it was out of the city."

"The city's huge," I said. "And the underground is multi-leveled. Did your source give you a more specific location than 'somewhere under the city'?"

I hoped so, because I wasn't trolling through endless layers of filth in search of the vamps who were committing such crimes.

"Yes. He did."

Oh, my God. Could he drag it out any more?

Sadie leaned forward. "And?"

Vincent sighed, a defeated sound. "Tank said it's all set up under the city morgue."

My mouth dropped open. But that would mean...

Sadie stumbled backwards and landed on the bed, staring at us with huge, shocked eyes.

Then her gaze sharpened and an angry glint lit her features. "That means the coroner and all his cronies are in on it. I fucking knew it!"

Which meant Jack's death was linked to everything we'd learned so far, and there was more than one city official who had been bought by the vampires in charge.

But what did that mean for us and our mate?

SADIE

I knew it! I freaking knew it!

I jumped to my feet. "Those bastards! I knew they had something to do with my dad's death. But to know they're in on the blood ring too? Holy shit."

My instincts had told me there was something dodgy going on with the coroner and the way they'd handled Dad's death, but there was more to it than even I'd realized.

"We need to go in and get them out. Help the women escape..." I was rambling but I couldn't help it.

"Do you have any powers?" Vincent asked suddenly.

Staring at him, the realization that I didn't have any real clothes on hit. A tank top and a pair of panties did not an outfit make.

"What do you mean?" I asked, charging across to my duffle bag and pulling out a pair of jeans and a bra.

"Well, your mother didn't survive rescuing the women last time, and from what you've said and what I've been told, she was very powerful. So, I'm asking, do you have powers too?"

Oh. Magical powers, he meant.

I tugged on my jeans, then slid my feet into some black flats. I'd seen some clothes in my father's vault room that had looked like they were made of Kevlar. If they could prevent a vampire from biting me, it may be worth investing the time to go get them and put them on.

"Ah, no. I don't," I admitted. "My mother died well before I could take lessons, and I don't know any of her family." I often felt the presence of my magic simmering just beneath the surface of my skin. In my awareness of the people around me and what was going on, but actual powers? Nope. Nothing. "But I've got you guys, right?" I grinned at my trio of amazing men. A vampire, a dragon, and a wolf. "Surely, with all four of us on the job, we can get in and out without anyone getting hurt."

Fridge began to laugh. Like, really laugh.

I glanced over at him. "What's so funny?"

"The fact you think we could get in and out of a business undiscovered or unhurt, that by all accounts makes the vampires millions of dollars, is funny. We'll be lucky to get out *alive,* Sadie."

That was a sobering thought. "Oh."

I needed to put on my bra and that meant taking off the black tank.

I considered making a quick trip to the bathroom or turning my back as I had last night. But seeing as I was standing in a room with my mates, I decided to face my fears and not be shy.

"We have an entire workshop full of bounty hunters, too," I reminded him. "I would never risk you unnecessarily. And if you don't want to come with me, I would totally understand. But as I said last night, this is something I have to do."

The desire to see this to the end, to right this wrong, was riding me hard. And I wasn't fighting it. With Shadow's help, and the killers my father had trained for thirty years by my side, I was sure we could set the blood ring on its ear.

I pulled off my tank top, the coolness in the room making my nipples tighten as all three men's eyes went straight to them.

Heat flooded my face as the atmosphere in the room changed

dramatically. I could hear their breathing turn heavy, as pheromones clogged the air.

I grabbed my bra and pulled it on as casually as possible, just like any other relationship where couples get dressed for work in front of one another.

"Could you grab my black shirt, Vincent?" I asked, swallowing hard as lust poured through my belly. The way the three of them were looking at me, I would never have to worry about their desire for me waning. "The one behind you."

Vincent took the hanger that he'd put in the closet and soundlessly glided toward me, like a predator stalking its prey.

His fangs protruded over his bottom lip. He didn't speak; likely because he couldn't. His vampirism made my stomach quiver with unease and—I hated to admit it—excitement, too.

I'd heard from a friend once that the bite of a vampire was orgasmic, or could be, if they didn't kill you.

Perhaps one day Vincent would let me experience it with him. Without killing me, hopefully.

The thought made my lips quirk up and the tension faded a little from the room. "Thanks," I said, taking the shirt and slipping it on. "Shall we get going?"

Vincent nodded and stepped away from me to wait near the door.

Fridge and Rogan stiffly moved about the room, getting dressed themselves, though I could see the bulges in their pants that showed how much my little "reverse strip show" still affected them.

My body tightened and pulsed with need for them, but we didn't have time for a lovemaking session this morning.

I had to get to work. We all did.

Besides, I hadn't yet worked out how Vincent would fit in with us in that regard.

There was so much to figure out, and sex could wait until later. Especially since I'd already had a sensational session with Fridge last night. Damn, it had been so much hotter than I'd expected. To be taken like that, in the middle of the room, without even a piece of furniture to cling to.

So animalistic, so... desperate. I had anticipated having sex with Fridge would be passionate, but it had surpassed my expectations. Not to mention the fact that now we were mated, sex with Fridge would probably become even better.

I grabbed my bag and headed to the door. "We gonna walk, or...?"

"Do you mind if I stay here for a few hours?" Vincent asked. "I tend not to go out in the daylight if I can help it."

I opened the door, Fridge and Rogan joining me. "Sure. How can I contact you if we need you?"

Vincent opened his mouth, then stopped.

"You don't have a cell phone?" I asked. It would be strange if he didn't. Everyone had one, these days.

He shrugged. "I was born before the invention of the telephone. It's not something I think of."

I bit my lip, the idea of him not being in easy contact not appealing to me. "If I got you one, would you carry it?"

Vincent was ancient and wise, strong and extremely fast. Surely it would be important to be able to reach him if I needed to.

He nodded. "Of course."

I smiled, my gaze falling to his full lips. I'd yet to kiss Vincent, but he had fully accepted me as his mate, even without the physical confirmation. Such a different courtship from the one I'd had with Rogan and Fridge. And yet, equally as exciting in many ways.

"Great. I'll grab one at lunchtime today," I said, thinking of the little electronics store around the corner from the Workshop. They'd have cell phones. "Will you come into the Workshop at all, or will you be here when we get back after work?"

I didn't like the idea of leaving Vincent, but I didn't want to make him venture out into the daylight with us if he was convinced it would weaken him.

Needing to sleep at night hardly seemed like a weakness. It would make him more human. More in sync with the three of us and our lives, and what we did every day and night. But it would be selfish of me to ask him to do such a thing—become more 'human-like'—so I kept the thought to myself.

"I'll find you. Don't worry about me," he said.

I clenched my jaw against the need to ask. I wanted to know more, especially about what he was going to do during the day while we were working. Would he go looking for leads at the coroner's office without us?

I kept my mouth shut. He was an ancient vampire and clearly able to look after himself. Who was I to monitor him?

"Okay. See you later then."

I was tempted to kiss him goodbye, but Rogan grabbed my arm and pulled me out into the hallway.

Disappointment swamped me. I wanted a physical connection with Vincent as well, but the opportunity hadn't yet risen. And my first kiss with him shouldn't be a random, perfunctory nothing-kiss.

It should be something special.

"Let's go," Rogan said, leading me down the hallway and into the elevator.

I smirked at the men who were rushing me away.

"You that excited about getting to work today?" I asked them.

"I've got a few things to get on top of," Fridge answered. "There's a lot that's slipped through the cracks this week."

I frowned. "You mean since my dad died?"

Fridge cringed. "Yeah. I had no idea how much work he did behind the scenes."

I reached out and grabbed his arm. "Thank you for taking over while I dealt with all the other... crap." I sighed. "I still need to organize some sort of memorial."

I had Dad's ashes hidden away in his vault so at least he was safe, but he deserved more than that. He deserved a true tribute to the man he'd been, from those who had loved him.

"Once we find his killer, then we can celebrate," Fridge growled out as the elevator doors dinged open.

I glanced up at him as we walked out the door. Damn, he was a good-looking man. With his bright eyes and strong jaw, it made me want to kiss every ridged contour of his face.

"You feeling okay about last night?" I asked Fridge, wanting the reassurance from someone to whom I'd committed my life.

Fridge grinned down at me. "Of course. Why?"

I shrugged. "Just wondering."

How did I explain to him the guilt I felt about his comments last night? That he was struggling with the fact that he alone wasn't enough for me.

I wished it were different, but at the same time, I couldn't. I didn't want to lose any of them, especially not Fridge and Rogan, since they were the two I'd mated with and therefore felt closest to.

But I also wished I could give them peace of mind. To know that they were wanted, needed. So deeply.

Fridge must have felt my sudden sadness because his hand went down to grab my ass as we walked.

"Hey!" I said, swatting him away.

We were only a block away from Dad's workshop. I didn't want anyone seeing.

Fridge grinned. "I would have liked to strengthen the bond again this morning, but you know, workers gotta work."

Rogan grabbed my ass from the other side and I jumped again. "Hey!"

They both laughed.

"Yeah. Me, too," Rogan said.

I bit my lip, though it was on the tip of my tongue that they'd both had me last night. They couldn't be that hungry for me again, surely?

As I looked at them, with the thoughts in my mind, I realized they would answer quite differently.

"Okay, let's talk work," I said, trying to get my head into the right space.

"Before we do," Rogan began, "what do you think about what Vincent said? That the blood ring runs their operation under the city morgue?"

"I don't see why they couldn't," I said. "Why not? Though you'd think a hospital would be a more likely spot to grab blood and people who were at death's door. Not a morgue."

The vampires had rules about who they could feed from and under what circumstances, and murder was still murder if they killed someone. Though it was always harder to prove who'd committed the crime with a lack of physical evidence being left behind.

"Yeah," Rogan said, frowning.

We crossed the road and walked the last hundred feet to the workshop.

Fridge opened the door. "Milady."

I couldn't stop myself from reaching up and cupping his jaw. "My mate."

His eyes opened wide and there was a brilliant flash of sweet vulnerability before he covered it up with a smirk.

"You better be careful today," he said, "or I'll come in and take you on your desk during lunch break."

I only just muffled my squeal as I rushed past him, my stomach in knots at the sheer exhilaration of what could happen today.

Walking up a couple of steps of the staircase in the entrance hall, I turned around to face Fridge and Rogan. "I'll see you guys later, but if Shadow or Vincent come in, can you send them straight up to my office?"

"Yeah, of course."

"Thanks." I flashed them a grin and headed upstairs to my dad's office to do some more investigating.

Among many other things, I wanted to research more about vampires. For information on how to take them out, so I could avenge my father's killer. But also, I wanted to know more about my new mate. Because, despite the fact that the vampires were now our number-one enemy, Vincent was now family.

Unfortunately, I knew next to nothing about him.

CHAPTER 14
FRIDGE

I set myself up a computer in a corner of the training room. There were a large number of emails and business-related tasks I needed to stay on top of because Sadie wasn't able to at the moment.

Was she capable of running a business this large and complex? Absolutely. But was she obsessed with Jack's murder and tracking down the killer? Yes.

That wouldn't make her a good boss. Not this week, anyway.

"Hey, Fridge," Jason called out to me, walking up to the makeshift desk that I'd set up in a corner of the main training room. Jase was a wolf shifter like Rogan, lean and fast.

"Hey, Jase. Did you get the file I shot over to you this morning?" We had a new client who wanted a woman found. A female cougar shifter. Rare.

Jase nodded. "I did. And I'm on it. But I was just wondering about pay. Will it go out like normal tomorrow? Or should I try to sort something out? It's just cos rent's due and... err..." He trailed off as if embarrassed to have brought up the matter.

"Oh, yeah," I said, swallowing hard. Money was the last thing on my mind, and I guessed that might be the same for Sadie. "I'll make sure Sadie takes care of that today. Not an issue. And if it gets to tomorrow and you don't have it in your account, come back to me. I can always get cash out if need be."

I now had access to Jack's stash in the vault, and if the men needed to be paid, they needed to be paid. We couldn't lose any of them, especially if Sadie was intent on taking on some old and powerful vamps.

"Great. Thanks," Jase said, his face lighting up.

He turned away then stopped, before twisting back around slowly to look at me again.

He didn't say anything, but I could sense his concern.

"Yeah?" I asked. "Something else?"

"Sadie... do you think she's gonna stick around like she said she would?"

"Freaking hope so."

Jase laughed. "Why? You want her? Because you know Rogan's already..."

I lowered my head and growled at him. He had no right to talk about my mate—and his boss—in that way.

Jase stared at me. "Both of you?" he asked, his expression bordering on horrified. "Isn't that a bit... gross?"

Anger brewed in my gut. Who did this wolf shifter think he was?

"Jase. How 'bout you keep your private life private, and I will too."

"But you're a dragon shifter! You can't share! Rogan, maybe. Wolf shifters are pack animals. But you can't!"

"Back off," I hissed at him, my voice coming out with my shifter's tone.

Jase scurried away and I was left with clenched fists and anger radiating down my spine.

Rising to my feet, I was unable to stay seated while so angry. Was this how people were going to judge us? As some sort of freaky, unbalanced...

"Hey, Fridge. You okay?" Rogan asked, his eyebrows drawn into slashes as he walked up to me.

I tried to shrug it off, but the worry settled in the pit of my stomach. "Ah, yeah. Think I just need a good training session."

"You look like you need a good fight, actually." Rogan laughed.

"You're right," I said, sitting down and getting back on my computer. I'd seen the perfect bounty for me come in this morning. Scrolling through the files and emails, I located the one I wanted. "I'm going to sort this one out today. Myself."

Grinning at Rogan, I punched in the details for a contract and sent it whizzing through email.

"I was joking," Rogan said.

"I'm not!" I said, elation filling my chest. "There's a bounty out on the human wife of a vampire. She's reported to be staying with some shifters downtown for protection. Maybe I can get some information for Sadie and get into a brawl at the same time." I waggled my eyebrows at Rogan and grabbed my cell phone from the desk. "You okay to hold the fort if I leave for a few hours?"

As I walked to the front door, Rogan followed me. "Yeah, of course I can. But I'd rather come with you for back-up."

"Don't need it," I told him. Not with the frustration of the past week pulsing in my veins. I could take down an army of shifters if necessary.

Punching in the code to the weapons room, I hurried inside and loaded up with two handguns and some silver wolf bullets.

"Won't be long!" I called, and walked out the front door.

Jack was always one to use his emotions in his work. And today was the day for me to do exactly the same thing.

～

SADIE

I rubbed my stomach, trying to quieten it down. It ignored me and grumbled hungrily for the second time.

"It can't be that late," I said, glancing at the clock. Two p.m. "Oh, yeah, I guess it can."

Standing and arching to stretch my lower back, it occurred to me I hadn't moved from my chair in five hours. Definitely not good for my posture staying hunched over a computer for that long.

And where were the guys? It was unusual for them to leave me alone at all, much less for this long.

I hope nothing's wrong.

Leaving the office, glad to be out and about once again, I trotted down the stairs.

Where were they?

The place was quiet today, but I suppose that shouldn't be a surprise. Fridge had said that most of the men who worked here were contractors, so they probably only came in when they absolutely had to. Otherwise, they would be out chasing down bad guys.

"Hey, beautiful girl," Rogan said as he glided up to me with a massive grin.

"Hey." I smiled at him, struggling to squash the impulse to throw my arms around his neck and squeeze him tightly. I ached to kiss his lips and moan at the heat that would flood my belly. It always did.

"We gonna do lunch?" I asked.

Rogan nodded, grinning as though he knew my secret urges. "Sure. I was trying to wait until Fridge got back to come up and get you, cos I can't really leave the place open and unattended."

"Fridge left? Why?"

As though my words had called forth the man I spoke of, the front doors opened and my big, strong dragon shifter all but fell into the Workshop.

He was bleeding.

"Fridge!" I ran for my mate, getting beneath one of his arms as he stumbled forward.

Rogan called out for help and I groaned as Fridge's weight partially dropped on me. Damn, he was heavy. Carrying him wasn't possible, but I wasn't letting go. He wasn't going to hit the floor. I planted my feet and braced my back, my thighs burning with the struggle.

Then his weight was suddenly eased up as Rogan and two other huge men lifted Fridge and carried him down a passageway to the right of the stairs.

Following them, I wiped the sweat from my brow and found myself standing inside a mini-medical room. I hadn't seen this room before.

"We have a first aid room?" I asked, rather stupidly, as Fridge groaned and rolled around on the examination table in obvious pain.

Rogan was barking out orders and ripping Fridge's clothes from his body.

"What happened to him?" I asked, feeling numb with shock and somewhat helpless.

"He's been bitten," Rogan snapped back, grabbing some sort of bottle full of silver fluid from the first aid shelves and pouring it over Fridge's neck, shoulders and upper body.

My mouth fell open as Fridge flailed around under Rogan's ministrations.

"Bitten? By what?"

Or who?

And what the hell was that silver stuff?

My heart pounded hard as panic pulsed through me. Fridge couldn't die on me. Not now. Not when we had our whole lives ahead of us.

I jumped as Vincent charged into the room, moved me out of the way, and headed straight for Rogan.

"What happened?" he demanded.

Rogan gestured to Fridge. "He went out for a bounty and came back like this. I think he's been bitten by a vampire, but I can't tell. He said he was going to the home of a wolf shifter."

Vincent gestured to the two men who were holding Fridge down. "Get back. Let him go."

The men glanced at Rogan with worried looks on their faces.

Rogan nodded. "Let him go."

They stepped away from the table. Vincent stepped forward and worked his way from one end of Fridge's body to the other, smelling him, touching him, moving so fast he was practically a blur in front of my eyes.

Then he grabbed the bottle Rogan held. "Did you pour this on his wounds?"

Rogan nodded. "Yeah. I thought it would help."

Vincent grimaced. "It wasn't a bad call, but there's too much venom pumping around his system. I'm going to have to suck some out or he's going to die."

I darted to stand next to Rogan, gripping his arm in my anxiety. "Is that dangerous?"

Vincent nodded. "More for me than him, I'm afraid, now. That silver is toxic."

"What!" I gaped at him. "For you?"

Vincent ignored my question and sighed heavily. "This is going to hurt."

Then he lay a hand on Fridge who continued to groan and arch on the table. Vincent opened his mouth, and there was flash of white before he bent and sank his fangs into Fridge's neck.

Fridge cried out and flailed, trying to grab for Vincent, but the vampire didn't stop, nor defend himself against Fridge's punches and grasping hands. He simply kept sucking.

I squeezed Rogan's arm tight, my heart aching in my chest. If Fridge died... If Vincent died...

I felt so helpless, watching, waiting.

Finally, Vincent fell away, dropping to his knees and vomiting up blood and silver onto the concrete floor.

I dug my fingers into Rogan's arm, terror ripping through me. Was that a good sign or a bad one?

Vincent looked up, his dark gaze growing hazy and unfocused. "Get me out of the sun. Soon. Okay?"

Rogan grunted assent, just before Vincent fell to the ground with a thump and a splatter, his face smooshed in the blood he'd just regurgitated onto the floor.

"Vincent!"

I hurried over to him and rolled his body out of the blood and silver mess, while Rogan checked on Fridge.

I held Vincent in my arms and tried to feel for a pulse, but there was none.

Of course, there isn't, you idiot. He's a vampire.

"Is Fridge okay?" I asked and Rogan turned to me with a mystified smile.

"Yeah. I think he's going to be all right." He frowned, his forehead creasing. "Is Vincent all right?"

I gripped the cold vampire in my arms. "I don't know. I hope so."

I didn't know enough about vampires to ascertain his state of health.

"Who's the vamp?" one of the men in the room asked Rogan.

"He's a friend," Rogan said, and offered nothing more.

Worry struck me to my core. "What on earth happened?"

There was a loud groan on the table as Fridge began to sit up.

"Help him!" I called out and gestured to the men still standing about and staring at me cradling the vampire.

Fridge was as pale as Vincent, but at least he was finally sitting up with his eyes open.

"What happened?" I asked him.

Fridge ran a hand over his bloodstained chest and up to his neck, wincing each time he came across a fresh wound. "I found the bounty, and then things got out of control."

He rolled his neck and groaned.

"You could have died!" I yelled at him, tears clogging my throat.

Fucking, selfish, asshole.

Fridge nodded as he ran a hand over his wounds that were now closing up naturally, healing quickly. "I know. Why didn't I?"

I gestured down at the comatose vampire in my arms. "Why do you think? Vincent saved you. But..."

I couldn't finish. Instead, a sob caught in my throat as I clung to Vincent's body.

Please don't die on me, vampire mate.

FRIDGE

Sadie demanded we take Vincent home to get him out of the sun, and *home* at present was the swanky hotel she had booked for the week. Luckily for us, it had room service, a huge bathroom, and blackout curtains that made the space almost completely dark.

Rogan had carried him, mumbling something about the least he could do after what Vincent had done. The vampire had woken briefly from what seemed to be an unconscious state, and spoken in a half-whisper. "Bed. I just need rest."

So, we'd placed him into the huge master bed, and he'd promptly closed his eyes.

"Still can't believe he did that for you," Rogan said from his chair at the dining table, glancing at the doorway to the bedroom where Vincent lay.

"Yeah," I said, because what else could I say? I barely remembered anything after I'd made it back to the Workshop, other than the excruciating pain, which had intensified when Vincent had been sucking the toxins out of me.

Sadie finished her club sandwich and dusted off her hands. We'd ordered room service as soon as we realized Vincent was going to be okay, and had spent the last half hour devouring everything.

"You should have seen it, Fridge," Sadie said. "It was… amazing, really. He took all that silver into his body, knowing it might kill him, to save you."

I stared at her. *Seriously? Why?* "But he doesn't even know me."

"Yeah, but you're my mate. I assume that's why he did it. We're all a family now." Sadie smiled softly.

The words hit me with incredible force. Was that why he'd done it? We were… family?

"I'll thank him when he wakes up," I said. "And I've got stuff to tell you all about what I found out this morning."

Sadie's eyebrows lowered as she glared at me. "I hope it was worth you almost dying."

I rolled my eyes. "It wasn't that bad."

Rogan choked on the water he was drinking, then bashed himself on the chest with his fist to clear it.

"What?" I asked. Why were they both looking at me like *I* was the crazy one?

Rogan stared at me. "Fridge. You know that I've seen you come back from a lot. Hell, last year you almost died after the run-in with that feral dragon shifter."

I whistled. "Yeah, that one hurt."

Rogan leveled me with his stare. "This was worse."

"Really?" I shook my head. That couldn't be.

Sadie stretched out a hand and squeezed my forearm. "Don't you remember?"

I shrugged. "Not really."

The bedroom door opened and an even paler-than-usual vampire staggered out. "Hey, guys. I'm gonna need some blood pretty soon so I better get to a vampire bar."

Rogan jumped to his feet. "I'll go. How much do you need and what type do you like?"

Vincent's surprise rivaled mine.

I stared at Rogan. "Since when do you know how and where to get blood?"

My best friend hated vampires almost as much as I did. Why was he rushing out to help Vincent? Even if he was one of Sadie's mates?

Rogan ignored me but motioned with his thumb in my direction while he stared at Vincent. "I owe you for saving this pain in the ass," he said. "So, whatever I can do…"

I swallowed hard as my throat tightened. Had I really almost died today? Did I owe my life to a three-hundred-year-old vampire?

Vincent tried to smile, but I could see how much effort it took by the pain in his eyes.

"If you're able to find it, I need at least a quart. Any type is fine, of course, but I do have a preference for B-positive."

Sadie froze, her gaze flicking up at the vampire, then back to me.

I narrowed my gaze at her. "What's wrong? Squeamish?"

She shook her head. "No… it's just… that's my blood type." Her throat worked as she swallowed hard and heat flushed her cheeks in a healthy blush. "Would you like me to…"

Hell, no!

I opened my mouth to tell her there was no way she could feed this vamp, but Vincent beat me to it.

"No. But thank you, Sadie. I think I need to lie down again."

Rogan grabbed his cell phone and keys from his jean pockets. "I'll be back in fifteen. Don't start the de-brief without me."

He left the apartment and Vincent staggered back to the bedroom.

I glanced at Sadie. "Do you want to talk about this morning, or…?"

"We'll wait for Rogan to return," she said, then raised an eyebrow. "Though if you want a suggestion, you need a shower."

I glanced down at the old sweatshirt I'd pulled on at the Workshop. I didn't see why I needed to rush, but it was a good way to waste fifteen minutes.

"Will do."

Rising to my feet, I bent to kiss her. She lifted her lips to me, but there was no passion, no happiness in the action.

I pulled back and frowned down at her. "You mad at me?"

"Yeah, I kind of am," she said with a nod. "You went off and almost died, totally unnecessarily. And you didn't even think about me, or how it would affect us. Our family."

Irritation hit me. "I was doing my job."

She crossed her arms over her chest. "You knew it was dangerous, didn't you? And you still chose to go. By yourself. No back-up."

I opened my mouth to rebut the statement, but she stared me down. Besides, she was right and we both knew it. I kept my mouth shut.

"Exactly," she said. "Go take a shower. Hopefully what you learned this morning was worth endangering yourself."

Oh, it was.

I went to the massive bathroom and enjoyed a long, solo shower.

Sadie was right. I did stink. Of shifters and blood, and that silver shit that Rogan had poured all over me.

My injuries were healing, but damn, I had been torn up. I could still feel the itchy pain where the skin was knitting together, the torn muscle tissue aching with a deep throb that was hard to ignore.

By the time I'd cleaned up and gotten dressed again, Rogan was back and delivering the blood to Vincent, who was still lying in bed.

There was strange slurping, then moaning sound, as Vincent drank.

My stomach churned, so I walked out of the dark bedroom and into the living area.

Staring at the wall, I tried to contain myself. I'd spent decades loathing vampires, and not only did I have to share my mate with one, but I was now in his debt.

Leaning against the wall, I turned to face the men as they walked back into the room.

Vincent finally had some color in his cheeks, looking almost back to normal, and Rogan hovered over him like a mother hen.

What the hell was happening here?

"Many thanks for procuring that for me," Vincent said to Rogan as Sadie led him to the dining area and he sat down in one of the chairs.

Vincent lifted his gaze to mine. "So? What did you learn?"

Sadie settled into the couch and Rogan joined her.

All three of them turned toward me as the sole focus of their attention.

I sighed. May as well start at the beginning. "Okay, so the bounty that came in was for the human wife of a vampire. It said she'd run away to a pack of wolf shifters and was hiding from her vampire husband."

Vincent frowned, but didn't say anything.

I agreed with his look. It had sounded suspicious from the beginning, and I should have known it.

"I located the house where the client reported his wife had last been seen, and it was the den of a pack of wolf shifters. But they hadn't captured the vampire bride to ransom her, or mate with her like the file had suggested."

"What were they doing with her?" Sadie asked.

"They were torturing her, slowly. For information."

It had been a pretty disgusting scene. The woman was human and had been cut, bruised and bleeding from every limb by the time I got there.

Why her vampire hadn't gone after her himself, I had no idea.

Sadie gasped and Rogan leaned forward in his chair. "You mean, the sort of information we're after?"

I nodded. "Yeah. Found that out later. I managed to fight off most of the shifters around the house." I'd taken a bit of a beating from one of them and had a nasty bite on my leg from another, but that was healing fine. "I freed the woman from the basement where she was being held."

I stopped and shuddered, remembering the way she'd felt in my arms. How frail and tiny. As if she were barely clinging to life.

"What happened next?" Rogan asked, his tone eager.

"I carried her up and out of the basement, and then a group of vampires attacked me."

Vincent sat up from where he rested on a chair. "Did they come to protect the girl? Or were they there to kill her?"

"How'd you come to that conclusion?" I asked.

Vincent sighed. "There's been talk for a while about the integrity of the blood ring system. Information's been getting out that it isn't safe. Too much money's been lost when people have escaped. Blood has been stolen. Humans and vampires both killed. I wondered if it was possible there was a leak."

I nodded. "I didn't realize what was happening right away. I thought they'd come for her, to take her home. Avenge her, maybe. The vampires had been the ones who hired me to rescue her, after all. But as soon as the girl saw them, she started screaming for help, for me to protect her from them." I sighed, remembering the pain as they bit me. "They attacked. Four of them. I barely got out of there with her."

Sadie stared at me, her eyes wide with shock. "How did you?"

"I shifted," I admitted. "Something I'd normally never do, but there was no other choice. I grabbed the woman and flew out of there then dropped her at our old apartment for safekeeping and so I could grab some clothes."

"Did she tell you anything?" Sadie asked, the atmosphere in the room tense and silent, except for the pounding of my own heart.

I ran a hand through my hair. "She did. It's all pretty foggy now, but I got what I could from her, then ran for the Workshop. I knew I needed medical attention, but I barely remember much past the first block or two."

The pain had been incredible. Vampire bites were often poisonous for shifters, and all four of the bastards had latched on to me at the same time.

I shuddered, remembering the feeling of them ripping into my flesh and the agony as their venom entered my bloodstream.

"Well, you made it to the Workshop. Practically fell in the front door," Sadie said. "What do you remember about what she told you?"

I swallowed hard. Catching Jack's killer was important, but the closer we got to finding those responsible, the closer we came to putting Sadie in very real danger. Now that I knew that her mother was a pureblood witch, I wasn't sure I wanted to find the culprits. Especially since they were almost certainly vampires.

"Ah..."

"Come on, Fridge. Tell us," Rogan said.

Inhaling deeply, I crossed my arms over my chest. "She told me the blood ring wants more exotic bloodlines. Their forced breeding programs haven't worked well and, without an influx of fresh witch or warlock blood, those who spend a lot of money for their product will stop buying from them."

"So their preference is still witch blood?" Sadie asked, as though she needed the clarification.

Vincent nodded, jumping in. "I'm afraid so. And even though it was always the most sought after, now that it's nearly impossible to obtain, the older vampires seem to crave it even more."

That made perfect sense. Things that were rare always had a higher value. Supply and demand.

"Did she say anything else?" Sadie asked, glancing at me.

I nodded, feeling the suck of the proverbial rabbit hole. The inevitable pull of Fate. This next step would take us along a path from which there would be no turning back.

"Yes. She confirmed what Vincent told us this morning."

"Which was?" Vincent asked.

I sighed. "That the blood ring runs from rooms in the underground, set up beneath the city morgue."

Sadie's eyes lit up in that way only she had when she was excited or determined about something.

A grin pulled at both sides of her mouth. "Let's go, then!"

CHAPTER 15
SADIE

I jumped up off the chair, filled with excitement and adrenaline. We knew where the victims of the blood ring were holed up! Now we could do something about it.

"Come on," I said to Rogan as he sat back in his chair looking shocked. "Let's go."

He frowned at me. "Go where? Into the lion's den? Without careful planning first? You've gotta be joking."

I put my hands on my hips and glared at him. "What are you talking about? This is the piece of information we've been waiting for."

Rogan shot to his feet and pointed across the room. "Fridge is barely alive after his run-in with a pack of vampires this morning. Vincent needs more time and more blood to heal. Or are you suggesting just the two of us go? Or worse, drag Fridge and Vincent into the underground to fight and die? Because that's what you're asking of us, Sadie."

My mouth dropped open at the vehemence in Rogan's voice. The way he described it made me sound like the worst sort of person. I would never endanger them. Not on purpose.

"You're saying that like it's my fault that my dad died. That the vampires are torturing people."

I blinked rapidly to make sure the tears didn't gather, nor drop onto my cheeks. This was not the time for stupid emotional weakness.

Rogan groaned. "That's not what I said. But you need to be a little more patient, or someone's going to get killed."

I staggered away from Rogan's anger, hurt and confused. "Why are you so mad at me? I want to *stop* others dying, not deliberately lead the men I love to their deaths."

Rogan's hesitance didn't make sense. Didn't he want to go rescue those poor witches?

Rogan ran a hand through his hair. "I want it stopped too, Sadie. But I need to be the responsible one here. Because I'm the only one of your three mates still standing. I need to protect the other two, who will obviously throw themselves into harm's way for you without a thought. And I need to protect *you*. If you want to keep all three of us alive, then we need to formulate a plan before we go charging into the underground."

I began to pace up and down the room, adrenaline shooting along my veins but common sense taking over my brain. "You're right. You're right."

I was stupid to even think we could do such a thing. Especially now.

My gaze moved to Fridge, who was leaning heavily against the wall, then to Vincent. They were both still pale and obviously weak.

"I'm so sorry to make it sound like I wanted to rush into the blood ring without thought." I stopped pacing. "Okay. We need a plan."

Rogan snorted. "Yes. And you need to decide which aspect we're focusing on. The blood ring or Jack's killer."

I frowned at him. "What do you mean? Aren't they one and the same?"

That was how I saw it, and how Shadow had seemed to assess things, too. If they weren't exactly the same, then the two things were inextricably interwoven.

Rogan shook his head and met my gaze with his own powerful one. "No. One path leads to the underground. To the center of the vampires' financial power, and probably to a place where dozens of people are trapped and being tortured."

I nodded. "The blood ring."

It sounded like hell on earth. No wonder my mother had sacrificed herself to save those kidnapped and tortured.

Rogan put a hand on his hip. "Yes. I'm not sure we can get in and out alive, let alone what will happen to us if the vampires find out we messed with their blood supply."

My stomach tightened as I asked my next question. "And my dad's killer?"

I wasn't sure I wanted to hear the truth about which path Rogan hoped we would take. What if it didn't match what I wanted?

Rogan sighed heavily. "There are only two ways to find out who killed Jack. The first way would be to find the right vampire and somehow get him to confess, which would be unlikely. The second way would be to attack one of the oldest and most powerful vampire families in the city and demand they tell us who ordered the kill." His gaze slid to my vampire mate, then back to me. "Vincent could no doubt help us down that road, but it won't lead to the underground and the blood ring. That path of action would take us to an assassin, or several. To a vampire fast enough and strong enough to take down your dad in his own business. I'm not sure you really want to take that path, do you?"

He was right. Even though the last thing I wanted was any of my mates coming to harm, I just *knew* that my father's murder and the blood ring were interlinked somehow.

When I didn't say anything, Rogan continued. "Which is more important to you, Sadie? We need to start there."

I inhaled sharply. Having to choose was unpleasant. But, if I had to, the choice was easy. My dad was already gone. Vengeance wouldn't bring him back. But doing something to help the people imprisoned in the underground would change people's lives.

"Let's save the people in the blood ring. It's what Dad—and my mom—would have wanted."

Rogan exhaled sharply, and nodded. "I agree. I think that's the right way to go, but we need a plan. We can't just jump into the sewers and start poking around."

Vincent stood up, joining the conversation. "I know the underground well. We could do some surveillance, some reconnaissance first. It wouldn't be too risky. And as long as I'm with you, you'll have a good cover story if we're caught."

I looked at his pale face and bit my lip, worry pulsing through me. "But when will you be healthy enough to go? You still don't look well."

If I thought I could help him, I would offer my own blood. But my fear was that if I did, he would drain and kill me. Once he tasted the witch blood my mother had handed down to me, would he be able to control himself?

Or had her spell that imbedded snake shifter genetics into my scent worked to make my blood unpalatable to him as well?

Only one way to tell and I wasn't sure I wanted to test that theory. Not yet, anyway.

Vincent smiled, his lips pale. "Give me one day and I'll be fully restored."

Tomorrow...

I glanced over at Fridge. "And how are *you* doing? You almost died today."

Fridge flexed his shoulders, the muscles rippling beneath his skin. "Thanks to our resident vampire, I'm good as new. Though, I may need to wear some of that vampire Kevlar when we go in to fight them."

I raised an eyebrow. "You weren't wearing any this time?"

He shrugged with a slightly sheepish air. "I thought the vampires were the money men, not the guys I went to fight. So, no, I wasn't prepared properly, but next time I will be."

I sighed, love flooding my body in waves of heat and tingling pleasure. Rogan was right. These men cared enough about me to put themselves in mortal danger.

Vincent and Fridge had both been hurt today, and yet they were willing to jump straight back into the fray—for me.

"Thank you, both of you. I can't really believe you want to help me."

"Of course, we do," Fridge said, pushing himself off the wall and staggering toward me.

I laughed as I grabbed a hold of him. "Good as new, huh?"

He grinned and maneuvered us to the couch. "Maybe I need a day or so, too."

Vincent and Rogan came closer, sitting one each side of Fridge and me.

"So, reconnaissance tomorrow, then?" I asked.

Rogan looked at the other men, then answered. "Yes, I think Vincent's right. We need to do some recon before we even consider getting anyone else involved. We go into the underground as a group, using Vincent's vampire status if we need to, and we go check it out. We don't even know if our sources are correct. The blood ring might not even be under the morgue like we expect."

I nodded. "Okay. So we just go for a little look-see. Not to do anything, just to check out what's down there? Look for any chinks in the armor. Any flaws that might give us some idea of what action to take next."

The trio of men all nodded.

I couldn't help the zing of excitement in my blood, nor the way my heart pounded. In that moment, my reasons for wanting to become a lawyer became clear.

I wanted to right the wrongs of the world. Fight the bad guys. Release those who had been wrongly imprisoned.

But up until now, I'd gone about it a different way to my dad. The legal way.

My dad had known there was a better way, but he'd gotten it wrong as well. He'd helped a lot of bad guys get good people off the streets, too. I was sure of it.

Now, though, combining the strength of my father's convictions and my brain, I was sure I would be able to change the world and help a few good people—if not a whole city.

My gaze slid to the men, desire pulsing through me in recognition of their connection to me. And mine to them.

But they were exhausted. The last thing I should be thinking about right now was instigating a session of lovemaking.

Especially since I hadn't even kissed Vincent yet.

"Tell me about the underground, Vincent," I said, trying to distract myself from thoughts of ravishing his mouth. "Are there easily accessible exits in case we get into trouble?"

Vincent chuckled and shook his head. "No, not at all. That's one of the reasons the vampires use the underground. There are clear entries, but they're sparse, and well-planned. Once you're in, you're in... until you can find another entry point."

I swallowed hard, glancing at Rogan, who was frowning darkly.

"Keep going. Tell us everything," I said. If we were going to put ourselves in danger for people we didn't even know, then we had to have as much information as possible.

Vincent settled back into the couch cushions and started talking. "The underground is at least two stories below the ground level. They use the sewers and tunnels to enter the underground, but then you drop down another level or two beneath the sewers, using ladders. It's pitch dark except for some strategic lighting here and there, so unless you're a vampire, you will struggle to see in that sort of darkness."

"We can see in the dark in our shifter forms, but not in human form," Rogan said.

"But we have night vision goggles at the workshop," Fridge added.

Vincent smiled. "Good. You will definitely need them."

I shivered, then hugged my body as a premonition crept over my skin. So, we could get in, but would struggle to get back out? Great. Bad things lurked beneath the surface of this city. I could already feel the dread.

"Tell us more," I said.

Vincent spent the rest of the night explaining everything he knew about the underground. How it was built, how it was used, and where the entries were that he knew of.

We talked through dinner, supplied by room service, and almost until midnight.

Then it was time to sleep.

The shifters and I curled up in the huge bed in a pile of hot flesh, while Vincent rested nearby on an armchair, his eyes burning with desire as he stared at me through the darkness of the room.

Even with danger on our doorstep and a perilous adventure in our near future, I went to sleep knowing I was surrounded by love. I was happy.

Though not quite complete.

CHAPTER 16
VINCENT

I slept through the night, something I hadn't done in decades. Whether it was due to my ingesting that silver cure-all for shifters, or due to a connection to my new mates, I didn't know.

I woke up hungry, and the scent of the three people in the room made my jaw ache. My fangs descended and cut into my lower lip.

Swallowing hard, I tried not to breathe through my nose. Sadie smelled especially good to me, closely followed by Fridge.

I got up slowly out of my chair. It was still dark, but I needed to feed. The blood Rogan had gotten me from the bar yesterday was gone, and my activities with Fridge had caused a need for more sustenance than usual.

I shook my head while creeping toward the door. Trust Sadie to be B-positive. Truly my favorite taste.

"Hey. Where you going?" Fridge grumbled from the bed.

I turned to him and whispered, "The silver took a lot out of me. I need to feed again. I'll be back in an hour or so."

"Hey, wait," Fridge said, before rolling out of bed and creeping over to me, naked.

Not that I went that way, but after centuries of existence, I could admire the body Fridge had. He was strong, fit, and gorgeous.

"Yes?" I asked, trying and failing to retract my fangs.

"I... wanted to thank you for yesterday. I don't think I have properly."

I tried not to smile at his discomfort. He was looking anywhere but into my eyes.

It was kinder to just be gracious, rather than point out how cute he was running a hand through his hair while gazing at my feet. I doubted a dragon shifter would appreciate being called cute.

"You're welcome. I hope there will come a time when you can truthfully say you'd do the same for me."

Fridge's gaze shot up at to mine then, his eyes wide and searching as he stared at me.

I let the words marinate with him, then when he didn't say anything more, I stepped toward the door. "I have to go. I won't be long."

Fridge nodded and muttered, "Thanks again."

He hurried back to the bed and our mate. I envied the ease with which he and Rogan cuddled and touched Sadie. I ached to do the same with her, but it never seemed to be the right moment.

I went to a blood bank and purchased another full bag. Normally I would never drink so much in such a short space of time. In fact, I had been stretching myself between feeds lately, wanting to have as little "need" for blood as possible.

With Sadie determined to search out the blood ring's location, I had to be ready. On guard and strong. And that meant more frequent feeds for me.

Upon returning to the hotel, I ordered them breakfast from the front desk and headed up to the suite.

Sadie was in the shower, Rogan was dressed, and Fridge was still lounging in bed when I arrived.

The scene was so normal, so relaxed, it was almost unnerving how comfortable everything was.

But the tension ratcheted up the moment I entered the room, and disappointment pulsed through me.

"It's okay. I'm not going to bite anyone," I said, and the men jumped as though I'd threatened them. I sighed. "Sorry, that was uncalled for. I just... You don't have to be nervous around me. I'm well past the age of letting my hunger rule me."

Fridge relaxed back against the headboard. "Then what's with the attitude?"

I gestured to them as a whole. "You two are very... comfortable with one another. And with Sadie. You're already bonded with her. I feel like a third wheel. Or in this case, a fourth. I walk in, and everyone here is suddenly on edge."

I'd tried to ignore it, to push past the feeling, to just be grateful that I'd finally found my soul mate. But their connection—coupled with my lack of it—was beginning to weigh on me.

"Well, hey," Rogan said, getting my attention. "I've known Fridge since school. We were best friends and roommates for a decade before we even met Sadie. And even we had problems with each other when we found out we had to share her."

Fridge snorted and glanced away. "Damn right."

The bathroom door opened and Sadie walked back into the room dressed in her underwear.

I couldn't help but stare at how beautiful she was, curved in all the right places, and strong in all the others. My whole body ached to swoop across the carpeted floor and take her in my arms. I didn't. Of course. But I couldn't help the slight groan as I said, "God, you're spectacular," I said.

Sadie grinned and walked over to me, her breasts bouncing in her black lace bra. "Good morning to you, too."

She didn't stop, and I saw intent in her face as she stepped up and put her hands out to run them up my arms and around my neck.

She was going to kiss me. *Finally.*

Not hesitating, I reached out for her tiny waist and pulled her hard into me. She lifted her chin and presented her face.

I dropped my head and pressed my lips against hers, the warmth of her creeping in to steal away my coldness. I moaned as her flavor seeped through the kiss, making my head spin like I was imbibing the most intoxicating bouquet of wine.

Need filled me and my cock hardened. She gasped, grinding her hips into me, pressing closer as she opened her lips so that I could slip my tongue into her mouth and taste her properly.

As visions of what I wanted to do to her moved through my mind, I gently pulled back, lest I begin to ravage her right there on the spot.

I simply couldn't wait to taste her pussy and sink my cock deep inside her.

Clearing my throat with a rough cough, I stepped away but kept one hand on her waist. Sadie stumbled forward, into my chest, her eyes still shut and her body trembling. I braced her from toppling over with my arms.

When her eyes finally opened, her pupils were dilated and she looked dazed.

I smiled as a mixture of desire and happiness radiated through me. I loved that I could affect her in such a way. "Are you okay?"

She nodded, one of her hands lifting to her lips, pressing into them with her fingers as though she wanted to imprint my kiss on her mouth forever.

"Yes. That was..."

My smile widened. "Yes. It was."

I lifted my gaze to where Fridge and Rogan were keeping themselves busy getting dressed and doing a poor job of trying to ignore what we were doing.

I grinned as amusement filled me. Now they knew how I'd felt, watching them.

I was in the game. At least a little. Finally.

"So, when would you like to leave for our expedition?" I asked Sadie.

Her eyes lit up as she walked over to where her clothes lay on a nearby couch. "What time do you suggest?"

I pressed my lips together, thinking. "I would say that the best time to go would be during the day. Less guards around."

At least, that was what I thought, but couldn't be sure.

Rogan walked over to us. "Even with the pitch dark of the underground, vampires would still keep nighttime hours?"

I nodded. "Yes, I think so. We are naturally nocturnal and any other timeline feels... odd." And physically painful at times to be up and active during the day, even out of the sunlight. "Though I'm only guessing."

Fridge joined us, his massive size making it necessary for me to step back to accommodate him in the circle.

Fridge said, "Sounds like as good a plan as any. We'll need to go past the Workshop, check on the guys and pick up some equipment, but we could go today."

"What do I wear?" Sadie asked.

We all turned to look at her still standing in her beautiful underwear, her lips slightly swollen and red from my kisses.

"Jeans? A sweater? Workout gear?" she prompted.

I grinned and shared a look with the two other men. Only a woman would wonder what to wear on an adventure down into the sewers that very well could lead to all our deaths.

"Ah, Fridge?" I gestured to the dragon shifter. "How heavy is the vampire Kevlar?"

"Oh, yeah," he said, shaking his head. "Wear something dark, lightweight, and comfortable. The Kevlar is heavy, and you'll need to wear it pretty much over all of your body. So maybe some layers to protect your skin, too?"

Good advice.

Sadie set about pulling out more clothes from her duffle, sorting through them with a thoughtful air.

A knock came at the door.

"That'll be your breakfast," I said. "I'll get it."

I headed off and let the hotel waiter into the room.

Today was the day that I helped my mate and her two shifter mates take the first steps toward destroying the blood ring.

Heaven help us all.

Fridge

We went straight to the Workshop from the hotel and found the doors locked, just as they should be. No one had keys except Rogan, Sadie, and me. But since Jack had died, I'd been paranoid about the security.

"I'm gonna email all the guys and tell them they have two hours to use the Workshop, then we're closing up again," I told Rogan as I unlocked the front door and headed for my computer to send out a group message.

"I'll get on the equipment," Rogan called out after me and headed to the weapons room.

I checked emails, sent out messages and made sure Jack's business stayed on its feet.

When I returned to the foyer, Sadie was already there, looking through the weapons Rogan had accumulated.

I glanced over at Vincent. "Do you want to carry anything? Just in case?"

"Like what?" Vincent asked, cocking his head at me.

I chuckled. "Come this way."

Ushering the vampire into the inner sanctum, Jack's favorite place, I tried not to shudder at what felt like a betrayal to the man I'd loved like a father.

But Vincent was the mate of Jack's daughter, and he would have accepted it, somehow. I was sure of that.

"Take whatever you need," I said, gesturing to the rows and rows of guns, stakes, and knives. "If you need help, let me know."

I went straight for my favorite corner, grabbing silver bullets, handguns, and two knives, strapping them to my ankles, around my waist, and on my upper arms.

When I found Vincent again, he was standing in the large knife section.

"You want one?" I asked.

He nodded. "Yes. But the silver will burn me. Do you have any with a handle I can hold? Or something covered?"

I could have slapped myself in the head. Here I was thinking I was doing the vampire a huge favor, and all I'd done was show off weapons he couldn't use.

"Ah, crap. Sorry, I forgot about that. There is one, but it's in the safe upstairs. Let me get it for you."

I gestured for Vincent to come out of the weapons vault and locked it up after him.

"I'm gonna grab the large silver knife that would actually suit Vincent's needs from the office upstairs," I said to Rogan.

His eyes bulged. "You're giving him Jack's knife?"

Vincent's gaze went straight to my face and heat spread up my neck. I tried to play it cool, but Rogan and I knew how big a deal this was, even if the other two didn't.

No one touched Jack's weapons. They were sacred. They were special.

But Vincent was here to avenge Jack's death, and more importantly, he was probably the most capable of saving Sadie's life if it came down to a fight between us and them. Which was highly likely.

The vampire needed a weapon. If the weapon was Jack's, and Vincent used it to protect Sadie, then there was poetic justice to the full circle of revenge.

Then a thought struck me and I shot a glance at Sadie, figuring I should check with her first. She shrugged and nodded. "Okay by me," she said, so I turned for the stairs.

"Be right back." I jogged up to the office that Sadie had taken over, and opened the safe As soon as I did, I saw the pile of cash. "Oh, shit."

I'd totally forgotten to ask Sadie about the men's pay.

I grabbed the cash and the large hunting knife, and headed down the stairs.

Sadie's eyes bulged as she saw what I held. "You think we're gonna need to buy our way in?"

I chuckled. "No. I forgot to remind you to put in the men's payments yesterday. You didn't happen to remember, did you?"

Sadie paled and shook her head. "Oh my God. No. I'm sorry."

I grinned. "No issue. That's why Jack kept cash around. For the bounties to be paid at any time, if necessary. I'll just need an hour or so to get it all worked out and let the guys know they can come pick it up. You okay with waiting?"

Sadie nodded. "Yeah. Of course. It was my fault. Thanks for saving my ass."

I chuckled and winked at her. "Anytime." I handed Vincent the knife. "Here you go. Nicely sheathed to keep you safe."

Vincent took the leather belt from me. "Thanks."

I pointed to where the knife hung from the belt, the huge black handle and covered sheath making it look like a miniature sword. "It's covered, like you need. Leather and plastic handle. Silver blade."

No wood or anything to hurt the vampire.

"This is great. Thank you again," Vincent said, situating the belt around his waist and pulling the buckle tight.

I swallowed. It was hard to see the weapon of a true master—my mentor—hanging from the waist of another person.

I sighed. "Well, welcome to the family, as Jack would say. I won't be long."

My heart pounded with too many emotions. I walked away to my computer to divvy up the money for the men who worked with me.

It felt strange performing such a mundane task while we had an extraordinary one waiting just ahead of us.

Two hours later the men had been paid, we were equipped with everything we needed, and the Workshop was locked up once more.

"I can't believe how nervous I am," Sadie said, laying a hand on her stomach, her voice alight with excitement.

She sounded as if we were heading off on a vacation rather than delving into the darkest depths of the city to look for killers.

I rolled my eyes and met Rogan's gaze, which was dark with worry.

Sadie was young and beautiful, and despite how tough she liked to think she was, she'd been protected by a large, fierce father. She really had no idea what this city was capable of doing to a person, nor how truly evil a bad vampire could be.

I turned to my small group. "Just remember that we're only down there looking for a bar to hang out in. For Vincent to find some blood."

We'd come up with that cover story last night.

Vincent nodded. "Yes. If anyone finds us in a place we don't belong, then we plead that we're lost. Nothing else."

Sadie nodded. "Okay. We're lost. We're there for Vincent. Gotcha."

She was decked out in protective gear, multiple knives, and a large stake strapped to her back. Not that anyone could see it beneath her layers of clothing.

She must be uncomfortable, but the protection was necessary. She was a lot safer this way.

"Follow me," Vincent said, who looked cool and calm. Too cool, in my view. But that was exactly how a three-hundred-year-old vampire should be.

We followed him down the street and along the road for the next two blocks. My heart pounded with every step I took, adrenaline coursing through my muscles and veins.

I had to admit, there was a large part of me that was afraid. Afraid of heading so deep below the earth. Away from the sky. Away from freedom.

That part, of course, was my dragon shifter.

If we got into trouble, I would never be able to shift and get us out of there. I would probably kill everyone around me if I even attempted it.

But I refused to let that part of me dominate. I was a trained bounty hunter and fighter in my human form. Since when did I even think about my shifter's comfort?

Since meeting Sadie.

Eventually, we arrived at a large sewer grate outside one of the largest vampire bars in town.

Vincent gestured to the metal bars of the grate. "This is the closest entry point."

I glanced up at his face, then down to the entry—the dark hole that we were supposed to happily jump into.

"Makes sense why the red center was set up here," I said, gesturing to the bar behind us.

Vincent grinned. "You'll find prominent vampire bars at every entry point." He glanced around at our group. "You guys ready?"

I glanced at Rogan and Sadie. They both nodded.

"Let's go," I said.

Sadie put both hands out as though to stop us. "Please, wait. I... want to thank you all for helping me. I wouldn't be able to do this without you. And I know Dad would be grateful and proud to know I have such wonderful mates by my side."

. . .

I GRINNED AT HER. "Yeah, and don't you ever forget you need us, because I can tell you that we don't forget how much we need you."

Sadie swallowed hard, her mouth pulling to the side as her throat worked, and for the first time, true fear resonated in her eyes. "What if one of you gets hurt?"

I chuckled. "Sweetheart, I almost died yesterday just doing my job. Danger is part of life."

Her gaze slid to the other two men, and in answer, Vincent lifted the grate up and opened the left half like a door on hinges.

"Rogan, you wanna go first?" he asked.

Rogan nodded, though I saw trepidation flicker in his gaze. He hid it well, but I knew the guy. "Definitely. I've always wanted to know what the underground looked like."

With that, Rogan took the ladder down into the hole, giving Sadie the answer she needed.

"After you, beautiful," I told Sadie, and she took the same ladder down.

I glanced at Vincent, who was still holding open the grate door with apparent ease.

"This going to be okay?" I asked him.

His face didn't change but something in his eyes worried me.

"What?" I asked him.

"This is only the first step," he said. "If we succeed in locating the blood ring, not only will we need to decide what to do with the people we find, but how to survive the wrath of the vampire Fathers. They will rain hellfire down on us for this. If we survive at all."

I clenched my jaw and tightened my fists. "We'll survive, Vincent. For the first time in my life, I have something worth fighting for. Worth living for."

I moved over to the ladder and began the descent into the dark.

But my ears pricked up at the whispered words from the vampire above.

"You and me both... my friend."

CHAPTER 17

SADIE

My dad had taught me to be strong and fearless. But as we stood in the dark, smelly underground of the city, my heart raced like a thundering horse. My legs and arms trembled with the need to climb back up that ladder and into the light.

Back to safety.

I'd been excited for this adventure, for the chance to save people in a place where no one dared tread. But as I shivered in the dark, I had to admit to myself, I was fucking terrified.

"Hang on, I'll just turn on the light," Rogan said.

I shivered again, trying not to breathe through my nose. It smelled like shit and dirt and blood. Like a battleground.

Yuck.

Suddenly I was blinded, the bright, white light of Rogan's flashlight blasting into the darkness.

My hands came up to shield my eyes, a gasp in my throat.

"Sorry! Sorry," Rogan said, and the blinding light was gone.

Holy moly.

I blinked my eyes open and shut until they returned to normal and I could now look at our surroundings.

I was somewhat disappointed when I did. I'd been expecting... more.

It was just a tunnel, with murky water at the bottom, and multiple directions to choose.

There were noises behind me and above. I squinted in the dark, trying to make out the shapes and faces of those around me.

Fridge sidled up next to me and clicked his light on, too.

"Whoa." I couldn't stop myself from gasping as he blasted the wall in front of him with light. "Damn, those things are bright."

Fridge glanced at Rogan. "The night vision goggles might be better."

"They'd be less conspicuous," Vincent agreed.

Rogan opened the duffle bag that he carried and handed me a pair of goggles. "Sorry for almost blinding you."

I laughed. "No problem."

I grabbed the goggles and pulled them over my head, blinking into them. "I can't see anything."

It was as dark in the goggles as it was before they turned on the lights.

"Hang on, we'll just turn the lights off." Fridge clicked something on the side of the goggles, and I could see.

"Wow." My vision was like being in an army video game. "This is very cool."

I looked left and right, up and down, loving the ability to see all sorts of details, including...

"Gah!" I jumped to the side and clung to Fridge's arm.

"What's wrong?" he asked glancing around.

I swallowed down the scream that stuck in my throat. "Just... a rat."

There was a round of masculine chuckles around me and I swallowed against the heat that rose in my cheeks. I didn't respond to their taunting. They were right. It was pathetic of me to be scared by a scurrying little furball.

"There will be much scarier things than rats down here, beautiful," Fridge said.

"I know," I whispered, reaching up to play with a few of the focus settings until I could see everything clearly, including the three men around me. Fridge and Rogan sported matching goggles, but Vincent obviously had no need of them.

"This way," Vincent said, gesturing for us to follow him.

Fridge indicated I should go next, and I did as I was told. They were in charge down here.

We crept along the sewer, taking a right turn, then going left again.

Vincent stopped and we walked up to him. My hands shook and my heart still raced.

"Why did we stop?" I asked.

He lifted another strange door.

"Because we have to go down," he said. "This is just the sewer. The underground is another level lower."

Both of my shifters flinched. We had to go even further down into the ground.

I shuddered visibly. "I think I want to go back."

The men chuckled, and I pursed my lips.

"Yeah, right. Only to tell us tomorrow you want to come back again," Fridge said.

I marveled at how well they knew me.

"Yeah... but..."

"Come on Sadie," Vincent said. "This is the way to the whole system."

I inhaled sharply, though I shouldn't have, as the putrid odors of the sewer swept up my nose. I gagged. "Okay. Okay."

I moved past Vincent, who grinned at me.

"It's not funny," I said.

He laughed, harder this time. The sound was beautiful and soothing. I liked the idea of hearing that sound every day for the rest of my life, and hopefully that would be many, many years to come.

I grabbed onto my courage, willing my father's spirit into my fingers as I climbed down the new ladder.

I counted every rung and got to twenty-two before my feet hit solid ground. Damn, we were deep into the earth now.

I got out of the way of the men coming down after me and looked around the underground. On this level there was a real paved street, with dimly lit lights, and I could see a bar up ahead.

"This is like a real city," I said, mostly to myself.

Rogan stepped up next to me. "Whoa."

"Yeah."

Fridge was next, staring at the world we'd just discovered.

When Vincent stepped up next to us, I was sure we all looked ridiculous, our mouths hanging wide open.

"This way," he said. "We're about half a block from the city morgue now."

We turned right and went in the opposite direction of the bar, though I saw a few sets of eyes watch us as we walked off.

"What sort of place is that?" I asked Vincent.

"The bar? That was where I met Shadow the other night," Vincent said.

"Is it safe?" I asked.

He chuckled. "For whom? You? Definitely not."

That made me walk just a little bit faster, fear shooting along my veins. Would the vampires bite me even though I smelled bad to them?

I wasn't sure I wanted to find out.

We walked in a single file, like an army troop. Or maybe a line of ants. I wasn't sure which image I liked better.

My hands kept wandering to the weapons that were closest to

me. The knife strapped to my thigh. The gun I had in a holster at my waist.

Everything in me just knew that this was going to turn into a fight, but part of me was also hoping that, because we were so well prepared, it wouldn't happen at all.

We kept walking down the strange paved street, then we turned right and found ourselves facing a brick wall.

"Huh?" I said. "What's a brick wall doing down here?"

It just looked so out of place. Also, it was a dead end. Which meant, we'd probably taken a wrong turn somewhere.

Vincent put a hand to the bricks as though testing them for their strength. "This is a recent build."

Maybe we hadn't taken a wrong turn then.

I met his gaze. "So, they're trying to keep people out? Where-abouts are we right now?"

He pointed up. "We're directly beneath the city morgue."

This was it.

"So, if the blood ring is set up behind this wall, there has to be another way in, yeah?" I asked, swallowing hard against the lump building in my throat.

I was uncomfortably hot. Between the pounding of my heart and the weight of the Kevlar, I was sweating from my neck to my ass crack.

Vincent frowned as he stared at the wall. "I don't know of any other way to access this part of the underground, unless they've created their own doorway."

I glanced back at my shifter mates, an involuntary grin forming on my lips as I stared at them wearing their night vision goggles.

They looked like strange beetles. No doubt I looked the same.

"What do you guys think? Should we keep looking or head back?"

Fridge rolled his shoulders as though readying himself for a fight.

"We're already down here, so let's give it one more shot." He indicated to Vincent. "Lead the way."

Vincent nodded and headed back the way we'd come, turning down the next tunnel. "It's possible there's another entry."

We kept walking, and then rounded a bend, and then suddenly there was a black door blocking us from going any further. It was studded with metal like a vault door and enormous in size. Beside the door stood a large guard. He was as tall and wide as Fridge, with shoulder-length black hair and a thick mustache.

"What are you doing here?" he demanded, glaring at us.

I froze. What were we going to say?

Vincent stepped up. "Just showing my friends the underground," he said, putting on an English accent. "I arrived here a few months ago and was told of your hospitality."

The guy narrowed his eyes and crossed his arms over his chest. "Piss off."

Vincent chuckled. "So perhaps the hospitality isn't as welcoming as they claimed." He lifted his chin. "What's behind the door, old chap? An exclusive club? Because I have money if there's a fee."

He opened his jacket and made out that he was pulling out a wallet.

The guard charged forward and picked him up by the front of his jacket. "Go back the way you came. Now."

Without warning, he threw Vincent at Fridge and Rogan.

I gasped and my hand flew to my knife. Was he going to attack us? What should I do? It was a hell of a long way back to the surface if we had to run.

The guys caught Vincent and set him on his feet, Rogan bared his teeth and growled loudly at the guard.

The guard opened his mouth, exposing long, pointed fangs. "Put your dog back on his leash."

My back straightened at the insult, but I shuffled back toward the group. Fridge's fists were clenching and unclenching, but Vincent seemed calm considering he'd just been tossed like a bag of potatoes.

"Seems like money can't buy everything," Vincent said with a chuckle, as he tugged on his jacket and straightened himself up. "Looks like we've gotten a bit lost."

"You *are* lost," the guard hissed at us, his eyes glowing red. "Move along."

"Sorry. Sorry," Vincent said, backing away and tugging on my arm. "Let's go get a drink at that bar we saw a while back."

Then Vincent's hand drifted from my arm, and he moved so quickly I didn't even see him leave. Wow. He'd left fast. I started walking the way he'd directed,.

Groans and gasps sounded behind me.

Rogan and Fridge darted in that direction. I twisted around and there was Vincent, one of his arms wrapped around the guard's neck.

I stood there and gaped at his speed, his strength. He'd gotten behind the guard and held him in a death headlock and I hadn't even realized he'd moved in that direction.

The guard grappled and pulled at Vincent's arms, his eyes rolling back in his head. Then he swung his body around, throwing himself this way and that, trying to dislodge Vincent's grip.

"He's not going down. Stake him, Rogan," Vincent commanded.

Rogan pulled a stake out of a holder on his back and lunged for the vampire.

The huge guard jumped out of the way, even with Vincent on his back.

"Fridge. Quick. Hold him," Vincent called out.

Fridge wrestled the big guy to the ground, holding his legs while Vincent gripped his upper body.

The guard screamed out as Rogan used all his force to thrust the wooden stake straight through the guy's back, piercing his heart.

It all happened so fast, I didn't have time to react or help.

"Jump back," Vincent said.

They did, and seconds later the vampire exploded, leaving nothing but a pile of black dust on the ground.

My heart hammered in my chest, but I couldn't look away. "Whoa."

I'd never seen anyone killed before. Not even a vampire.

"Are you okay?" Vincent asked, coming up to me and grabbing my hand.

I swallowed and nodded, berating myself for not going to his aid. "I'm sorry I wasn't any help."

He smiled. "I'm sorry you even had to see that."

I shivered.

"So, you changed your mind about walking away?" I asked, rather rhetorically.

He held up his hand, and in his palm was a large key. "Since we made it this far, I think we should see what's behind the door."

"You snagged the key?" Fridge asked, then nodded slowly. "Impressive."

Rogan dusted off his hands and walked over to us. "Damn, you're fast, Vincent."

Vincent shrugged as though it wasn't a big deal, but somehow, I knew there was another story behind his skill level. I would ask him about that later.

"So?" I asked. "We're really going in?"

Vincent nodded. "Yes. But I don't know what's behind these doors. If we encounter an army of guards, we run."

I nodded, indicating to what was left of the doorman. "Especially if they're like that one."

Fridge huffed. "Damn, he was strong."

"Makes sense to have someone like that on the door," I said. "They're presumably hiding something pretty damn horrible."

Vincent held up the key. "Let's see, shall we?"

He sauntered over to the large black door, running his hand over the metal studs as though searching for something.

The keyhole, perhaps? I couldn't see one.

His hand stopped and he pushed open a flap, then inserted the key and turned it.

There was whirring and clicking, and Vincent began to pull at the door, but nothing moved.

He then looked over his shoulder and called to us. "Fridge. Rogan. A little help opening it."

Fridge and Rogan went over and together, inch by inch, they opened the door. It must have been enormously heavy if it took all three of them to open it.

"This can't be the main entrance," I said. "Wouldn't it be almost impossible to get people in and out?"

Vincent grunted as he pushed the door open the last few inches. "Yep. But that's probably the point. The only ones coming in and out would be vampires transporting blood or women. But I think you're right. There has to be an easier way in."

I looked into the room behind the door, and it was badly lit. "No lights in there either?"

"Stay behind me and be ready to fight—or run," Vincent said.

I nodded and we moved single file, stepping into the lair one by one. Vincent was at the head of the line, and Rogan and I were in the middle. The huge dragon shifter brought up our rear.

Time to find out if all the legends, the fairytales, and the disgusting stories of vampires were true.

CHAPTER 18

SADIE

Sweat dotted my forehead and my heart thumped so hard in my chest I struggled to hear anything above the beating sound in my head, but I kept walking. As quietly as possible, we took measured steps along the strange tunnel, then Vincent stopped.

I halted right behind him.

Rogan and Fridge bumped into me, and I stumbled into Vincent.

He twisted around and caught me. "Shh..."

I stared as he pointed ahead of us.

"Oh my God." I put my hands over my mouth to stop the scream that rose in my throat. The tunnel we were walking along opened into a large room with women attached to blood siphoning machines.

Some of the women were laying on beds, others were sitting in chairs.

They all looked half dead, emaciated, and drugged. Their eyes were closed, their breathing labored.

Then my gaze fell on one woman in a chair as she stretched out her back. She was pregnant. Very pregnant. As she moved her hand over her swollen belly, I let out a loud sob.

Gut-wrenching horror rose up like a wave and slapped me in the face.

The sound of my sob attracted her attention. "Who are you?" the woman asked, her eyes coming to focus on us. "Are you here to help us?"

The other women around her stirred, a swell of noise rising in the room as they began to open their eyes, look around and notice us.

"Hey!" one of them called out to me.

"Please. Help me!" another one cried.

My heart broke as my eyes filled with tears. They were alive. And conscious, and... dying.

"This isn't good," Vincent said.

"We have to help them," I cried, grabbing onto his shirt.

I lunged forward, though I wasn't sure how I was going to get any of them out of here. How did I even take those IVs out of their arm?

Vincent grabbed my arm, holding me back.

"Vincent. Please! You have to let me get them." I punched at Vincent's chest, feeling hysterical. My eyes burned with tears and I could barely see behind the night vision goggles.

"Someone's coming," Fridge said, but I couldn't hear anything above the drumming of my heart in my ears.

Vincent cocked his head. "That's more than a few vampires. We have to run. Now."

He grabbed my hand and pulled me.

"No. Vincent."

"Fridge. Now," Vincent said, as though they'd pre-organized a move.

Before I could react, my big dragon shifter threw me over his shoulder and started running.

I cried out in pain and shock, but didn't fight him as we bolted through the tunnel and back through the door we'd entered from.

"Help me close this," Vincent commanded.

Fridge dropped me to the ground, but I managed to stay on my feet. My knees wobbled and I staggered sideways.

The three men used all their strength to push shut the door, loud sounds and screams coming from inside the tunnel.

Inside the blood ring.

"We left them," I said, staring at the door as Vincent locked it with the key and pocketed it once more.

"Sadie," he said, his voice firm but full of concern. "If you want any chance to save those women, we need to run. Now. Before they find us."

I wanted to argue with him, to tell him he was wrong. To demand we go back right now. He was right, though. We might have been able to take down one guard, but not a whole swarm of them. This had been a recon attempt, not a rescue. We were not prepared to save those women—yet.

I nodded, lifted my night vision goggles, and wiped my eyes. "Okay."

"Let's go. Quickly," Rogan said, gesturing for me to follow.

We ran without speaking, all the way back to the bar we'd first seen when we came in.

I stopped, looking at the entrance to the bar. Maybe we should see if there was a way into the blood ring through there.

Vincent appeared at my side, pressing into me. It was as if he could read my mind. "No, Sadie. We need to leave. Now."

I opened my mouth to ask why the rush now that the black door was shut—none of the vampires beyond the door had actually seen us—when two large vampires sauntered up to us.

"There you are, Vincent," one of them said with a chuckle, his eyes blazing in his dark-skinned face. He looked lethal, with his leather pants and black tank top revealing bulging muscles. "The Fathers have been looking for you."

"Tell them I'll contact them," Vincent snapped, stepping in front of me so that his body blocked most of me from their sight.

"Who have you got there?" the other vampire asked, sliding around Vincent and coming toward me.

I grabbed for the knife strapped to my thigh, but Fridge knocked him away.

"Get back," Fridge said, pulling out one of his guns from a holster at his waist and pointing it at the smiling vampire.

The two vampires both laughed, and my three mates circled me, their backs against me, using their bodies like shields.

"They're hunters," Vincent hissed.

They were what? I hadn't heard the term before, but it couldn't be good.

Vincent addressed the two hunting vampires. "We've got no issue with you. If you let us leave, we won't attack."

The two vampires laughed again, the sound menacing and evil. "The Fathers mentioned you have a new pet, Vincent. A bounty hunter, they said. But she doesn't look like much."

The other vampire whipped around us, grabbed Rogan, and moved to throw him aside. In a blur of motion, Vincent snapped the vampire hunter's neck. He fell to the ground like a sack of potatoes.

I gaped, staring at the fallen creature.

The one remaining standing hissed loudly, but before Fridge could shoot, the vampire was gone.

"Coward," Fridge spat.

Rogan adjusted his shirt, and then grabbed my arm. "Let's go."

"Definitely," I said, as we jogged back toward the entrance. "What was that all about, Vincent? Care to clue us in a little?"

Vincent sighed as he hurried along beside me. "The vampire Fathers have put a hit out on me. I assume it's partly because of my new connection to you, but mostly I would say, it isbecause I refused the hit on your father."

I groaned. Something else to worry about now.

When we reached the ladder, a sense of relief flooded through my body. We'd gotten in and out of the underground, and we now knew where the entrance to the blood ring operation was.

Even worse, we knew the stories were true.

We climbed the first ladder, then the second, stepping up and out into the sunlight once more.

Suddenly I was blinded by the sun coming through the night vision goggles.

I pulled them off my face and wiped the sweat and remnants of tears out of my eyes. "Fucking hell, that was horrible. I can't believe we were right about everything."

My heart was broken in places, but in other ways, I felt angry. Determined. I had a real goal now. A purpose. I would get those women out. Somehow.

Rogan and Fridge were packing away their goggles in the bag and I handed mine over too.

"Should we head over to the Workshop or home?" I asked.

"The hotel I think would be best," Vincent said quietly, blinking rapidly in the bright daylight.

I looked at the other two. "That okay with you guys?"

They stared at me like they were surprised I asked their opinion, but it was time that I ceded some level of control. I needed their help and their cooperation in every way.

"Of course," Rogan said.

Fridge nodded. "Yeah, let's go. Work can wait until tomorrow. I need a shower after that hell hole."

He shuddered dramatically and we all laughed, though the sound was brittle.

"Agreed," I said. I felt dirty as sin, and not the good kind. "Let's go."

We made our way back to the hotel, to be met on the way by a shifter who shared some of my own DNA.

I smiled at my cousin as he crossed the road to greet me, his limp more noticeable today than the last time I'd seen him.

"Shadow! We're just heading back to the hotel. Wanna come with us? Or is running into you not a coincidence?"

Shadow smiled, the purple swirl of magic obvious in his eyes in such bright sunlight. "No... no coincidence. Lead the way. I need to talk to you."

I frowned but decided against asking him to explain yet. As a group of five, we made our way back to the large suite I'd rented.

Thank goodness I'd splurged and chosen a room with both a bedroom and a living space, because there was no way I would have been able to take Shadow back with us otherwise.

As we entered the room, Vincent went straight for the curtains the housekeeping staff had left open. The table and kitchenette had been wiped down, and the bed was made.

Darkness fell as he closed the curtains, then Fridge flicked on the lights.

Fridge groaned. "I need a shower."

"Me, too," I said, but waved at him. "You first. I'll talk to Shadow."

"You could join me," Fridge said with a lascivious grin as he pulled his black shirt off over his head.

His huge, muscular body was drenched with sweat, every ripple of muscle gleaming, even in the artificial light.

I smiled at him and tilted my head. "You go."

Vincent sat on the couch, while Shadow groaned as he lowered himself into a chair, pain flickering over his face.

"You okay?" I asked, worry coursing through me. Was he hurt, or was this part of his twisted spine issues?

He nodded. "Yes. I can wait," he said with a crooked smile. "It's probably best if you're all around to hear what I have to say."

"Do you wanna order some room service for all of us?" I asked, inching toward the bedroom door. "Get whatever you want."

"Oh, yeah, I'm starving," Rogan said, pushing the phone at Shadow and walking toward me with a glint in his eye that made a bubble of excitement rise in my chest.

"You want a shower too?" I asked.

He chuckled as he ran in my direction. I bolted into the bathroom with a squeal. I doubted we would just be showering if all three of us got naked at the same time.

Today I had seen pure torture, evil. And for this moment, I was going to celebrate life. And love. Then tomorrow, we'd deal with what came our way.

I stripped off my clothes in a hurry and jumped beneath the shower as Fridge's hands moved over me in a possessive caress.

CHAPTER 19

VINCENT

I knew Sadie and the two other men were trying to be quiet in the shower. They were behind two closed doors, but I could still hear the soft moans and sighs coming from the bathroom. I tried my best not to stare at the closed bedroom door and wished I'd been invited in.

Instead, I concentrated on ordering food and trying not to imagine what was going on in the shower with my mate.

"How are you feeling about that?" Shadow asked me, indicating the bedroom.

I shrugged and smiled blandly. "Which part?"

He shrugged. "All of it. The fact you have to share her is the one that springs to mind first and foremost, though."

I chuckled. "It's not an unusual thing in the vampire world. Many families are made up of triad, quads, even larger couplings. Having an immortal life tends to make you... flexible about your time with your soul mate, or mates."

"But?" Shadow led me to continue.

"I wish I wasn't so far behind. Her connection to the shifters is cemented and very strong."

Shadow tapped his fingers on the table. "It won't take long, once you spend some time together. Plus, look at the bright side, you'll probably outlive them both."

I opened my mouth to ask him if he meant purely because I was a vampire, or if he had "seen" such a thing with his premonition abilities. But there was a knock at the door, and I went to answer it.

It was our food, delivered on a tray by housekeeping.

By the time I pulled the tray inside and arranged the food on the table, the other three were back in the room.

Sadie's face was pink and shining with good health, and the men now looked relaxed and happy, despite the danger they'd endured today.

There should always be celebrations after escaping death.

Sadie met my gaze and her smile fell, guilt tugging her lips down.

I forced a smile to my face, though envy ate at my gut.

"Your food arrived," I said, though the statement was clearly rhetorical.

"Thanks," she said and the men rushed forward to eat.

Sadie hung back and I stepped toward her, taking her in my arms and kissing her gently on the lips.

She tasted clean and fresh and she wrapped her arms around my neck and held me tight. The feeling of being alone evaporated, replaced with a sense of acceptance and hope.

"So, what's this about, Shadow?" Rogan asked from behind us.

I pulled away, but held onto Sadie, keeping a hand on her waist as we turned toward her cousin.

"I have news about the blood ring and Sadie's mom," he said.

Sadie shivered in my grasp, so I led her to the couch and encouraged her to sit next to me as we waited for Shadow to explain. She pressed right up against me, her hand on my thigh and her focus on her cousin.

I lapped up the affection and the attention, knowing that my turn with Sadie would be coming very soon.

"Tell us," Sadie encouraged.

Shadow nodded, leaning forward on his chair. "Vincent has explained to me what he told you, though I was sure there was more to the story. So I dug deeper. Spoke to more of my vampire contacts, bribed some people, got into a fight. Or two."

He winced as he moved a shoulder and flicked his wrist and hand.

I narrowed my eyes, looking for the injuries he so obviously carried. There was nothing obvious to the eye, but shifters healed quickly, and with Shadow's already twisted frame, it was hard to distinguish between new and old ailments.

"What did you learn?" I asked.

"And thank you for following your leads," Sadie jumped in. "I'm so sorry you got hurt."

Shadow smiled at Sadie then, a true smile of affection, one I'd never seen Shadow bestow on anyone.

"Just part of the job," he said.

I met Rogan's gaze, and he rolled his eyes.

I wasn't certain what the look meant, but I could almost hear Rogan's voice saying, "See, everyone who meets her, falls in love with her."

Shadow continued. "The information the vampire Fathers wanted from Jack was about Sadie's mother."

"My mother? Why? She died twenty years ago."

One side of Shadow's mouth kicked up in a smiley sort of grimace. "Yes. And unfortunately, she was the last strong witch that they know of."

Sadie sat up straighter, sliding to the edge of the couch. "What about the babies they've been breeding with the warlock?"

She shuddered suddenly and I knew she was thinking of the pregnant woman we'd seen in the blood ring dungeon. That had been truly horrible to see.

He shrugged. "I don't know how successful that has been. Because if it had been, they wouldn't be looking for new witches."

"New witches?" Rogan asked. "What do you mean?"

Shadow continued. "That's what they came to Jack for. Information on his wife and her family. They're looking for a strong witch bloodline, and as she blew up their last blood ring premises with her magic, they know she was strong."

Sadie stood up and began to pace. "What about me? Do they know about me? What I am?"

Shadow nodded and Sadie bit her lip.

Shadow put out a hand to calm her. "They know that you're her daughter, and they've sent vampires after you multiple times."

"Well, why haven't they taken me then?" Sadie asked.

I wanted to know the same thing.

Shadow leaned back in his chair. "They've tried, but either your dad got to them first, or they reported back to the Fathers that you simply couldn't be a witch and they refused to bite you."

"How come?" Sadie asked.

Shadow grinned. "Because you smelled too goddamn bad to them."

He laughed, and it was a strange, strangled sort of sound.

I grabbed Sadie's hand and tugged her back to the couch.

Her eyes were wide, her mouth open. "Mom's magic worked. She totally disguised my scent."

"What do you mean?" I asked. "You smell damn fine to me."

Sadie met my gaze. "Damn fine as in, you want to bite me?"

I shook my head. "No…"

"Exactly," she said proudly. "Mom cast a spell that disguised my witch scent by injecting snake genetics into me, or something like that. I don't know enough about magic to understand how she did it."

"That's what that scent is!" I turned to Shadow. "And you have it also."

He nodded, though from the way his mouth twisted, it wasn't news he wanted spread around the city.

"So, what do we do?" Sadie asked Shadow.

"Depends what you want to do," Shadow answered. "If your plan is to break up the blood ring, free the women trapped underground, you're gonna have a hell of a time."

"We know where the entrance is," Sadie proclaimed and Shadow's shocked gaze met mine.

I nodded. "We do."

"Then you know more than most," Shadow said, licking his lips. "But you need to understand that for every woman you free, they will simply replace her with another."

"Not if they want specific, exotic bloodlines," Sadie corrected him.

I frowned. "They need blood no matter what, although you are correct. They don't want the same blood you can get at any bar, or blood bank. They want something very specific."

Something like my mate's blood.

*S*ADIE

My head spun with the new information Shadow was giving us, but there were so many questions that were still unanswered.

"Do you think my dad had information on Mom's family?" I asked.

Shadow frowned. "I hope not, because that would lead the vampire Fathers to take half of our family prisoner."

My ribs squeezed tightly around my chest, making my heart hurt.

Shadow got to his feet. "Please make sure that no matter what, nobody knows we're related. Unlike you, I know where some of your family is. As I told you, there aren't many full witches like your mother left, but they're half or a quarter magical, and that would be enough for the blood ring. They'd be strung up and drained within hours of capture."

I shuddered at the imagery and nodded. "Of course. Is there anything else you want to tell me?"

"Just that you need to go through your father's things and delete anything that looks remotely like a list or contact details of anyone that isn't a client or work-related. Its possible Jack had a book of family details around, but the vampire who killed him didn't find it."

I swallowed hard. *Speaking of which...* "Do you know who killed him yet?"

Shadow shook his head. "No, I'm sorry. No one seems to know."

Disappointment dropped into the pit of my stomach like a stone. "Thank you for trying."

Shadow moved toward the door. "I have to go, but if you need anything, Fridge knows how to reach me."

"Thanks," I said, and walked my cousin to the door. "For everything."

He opened the door, smiled at me once more, and left.

I walked back into the room and collapsed on the couch, untouched by anyone for a brief moment.

"So, Dad had information worth dying for," I said.

Vincent slid closer to me on the couch. "If he had the locations of full blood or even half-blood witches, then yes, he had information that people would kill for."

I bit my lip. "And my father died to protect it."

Vincent nodded and I sighed, reaching for his hand and holding it tight.

"So, what's our next move?" I asked, as Fridge and Rogan huddled in.

"What do you want to do?" Vincent asked me. "Do you want to pursue this still?"

I nodded, though I felt guilty thinking about the danger I was putting my men in. "I do. And I'm sorry that I do. I know it'll put you all in harm's way. I know that stopping one blood ring operation probably won't change everything, but I need to do something. I can't sit back and just... get on with my life, while those women— maybe even some of my own flesh and blood—rot away down there beneath the earth. Slaves to the vampires."

I would never get those images out of my head. Of the pregnant woman's body being drained of blood. The women's cries, reaching out their desperate hands to me for help.

I shuddered again and wrapped my arms around my body. We had to do something. I wasn't stopping now.

"Then we don't stop," Vincent said, squeezing my hand.

Rogan nodded. "We're with you, Sadie."

"Till death do us part," Fridge said, and grinned at me.

I couldn't help but smile at the men around me, but especially at my dragon shifter. A man who'd overcome so many of his fears and his demons to mate with me.

And now I was not only wolf mated, but I was officially dragon mated, too.

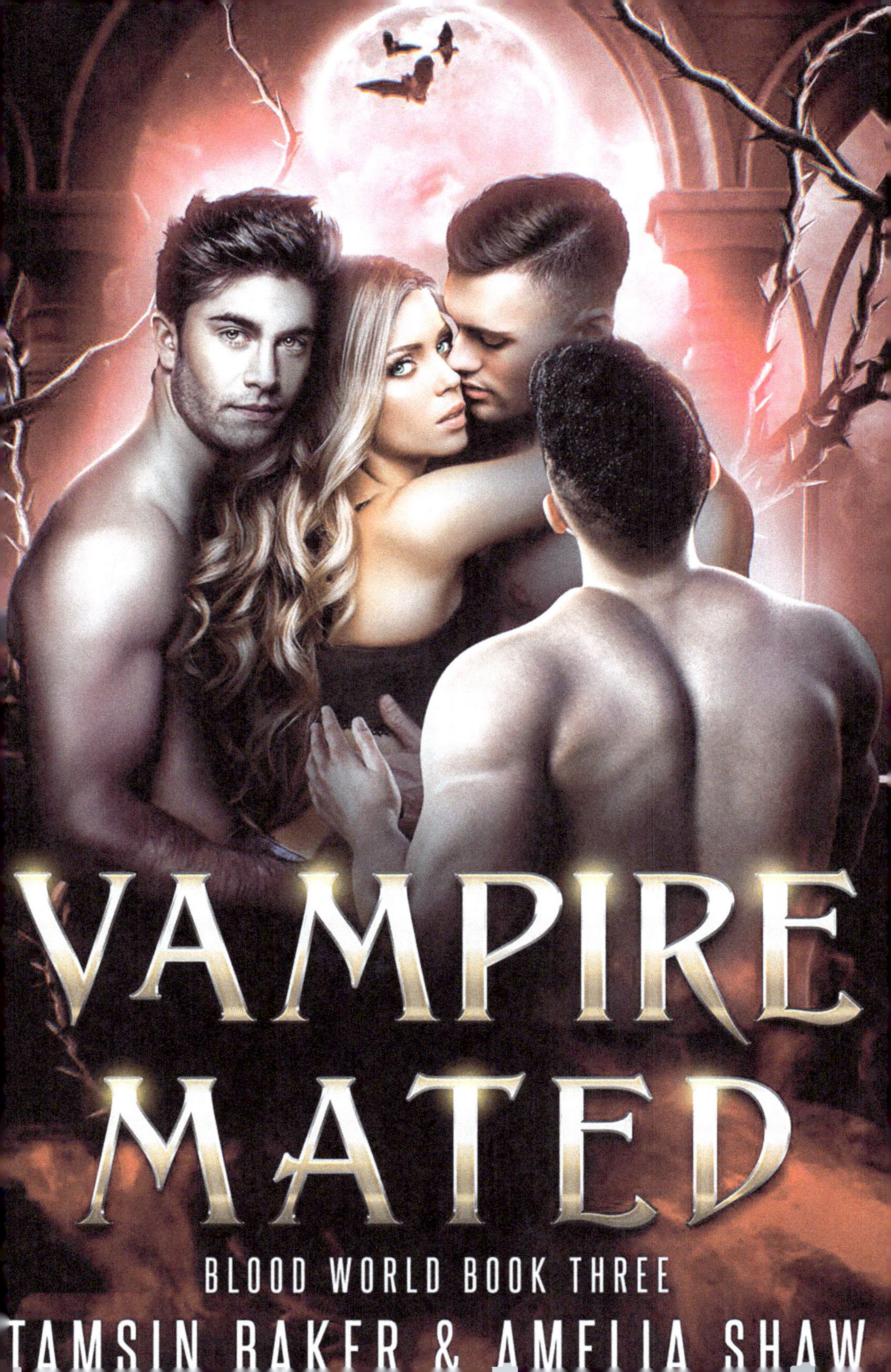

VAMPIRE
MATED
BLOOD WORLD BOOK THREE
TAMSIN BAKER & AMELIA SHAW

VAMPIRE MATED

THE PARANORMALS BLOOD WORLD BOOK 3

CHAPTER 1
SADIE

I never thought I'd be here. Standing in a little room, at what is officially my father's funeral.

I stared out at the sea of people that filled the too-small space. All were dressed as somberly as me. It was an ocean of black and gray with the occasional flash of silver from a mostly-hidden blade or gun, sparkling eyes and muscled arms.

I took a deep breath and began. "Thank you all for coming today. I know my dad would have been glad that you did."

My throat clogged up, as though a hand had wrapped around my windpipe. I coughed to clear the knot. This was something I wanted to do. Something I *had* to do. "Ah... Dad was not a formal sort of guy and he wouldn't have wanted his funeral to be that way, either. I've asked you all here today to say a few words about my father, then we can remember him over a glass of whiskey and the food that will be served right after the service."

There was a smile or two among the crowd as I began my speech about Dad's life. Where he'd grown up, what he'd accomplished. His short marriage to my mother and, of course, his business. His pride and joy.

Most of the men in the room had either worked for Dad, or were his clients. They were a tough, rough lot. As I glanced up from my speech on occasion, I saw a swarm of tattoos and gnarly expressions.

Dad's people.

When I finished what I needed to say, Dad's oldest friend Terry stepped up out of the crowd and my heart squeezed tightly to see his beloved face. "Uncle Terry! You came."

"Of course, I did." Terry said, then turned to address the crowd of men. "I think Jack would have wanted us all to have a drink and spend the afternoon reminiscing about him. So, let's all relax in the lounge. Sadie and some of the boys have set it up like a bar so everyone should be comfortable as heck."

The men in the room all turned with a smile and left the parlor where we'd held the official ceremony. Dad's urn was in the center of the room on a dais, and photos of him were displaying in a slow slide show on a large projection screen.

I glanced at the wall to my right. A photo of my parents on their wedding day hung there in pride of place. My father was so very large, my mother, so small. Both were grinning like they'd won the lottery. And in the love stakes, they had.

Speaking of love...

"You okay?" Rogan asked quietly as he stepped up next to me and slid a possessive hand around my waist.

I sighed and rested my head on my wolf-mate's shoulder. I was glad the official part was over. Now I could relax and truly celebrate the man my father had been. "Yeah, all good."

Fridge stepped up in front of me, his hands thrust into the front pockets of his trousers. His huge chest and arms looked like they were about to burst out of the black shirt he wore. My dragon-mate was such a primitive-looking man, with his size and unsettled aura.

I smiled up at him, seeing the tension in his face that I figured must be reflected in my own.

A muscle ticked in his jaw and his nostrils flared. Fridge was angry we hadn't found Dad's killer yet, and so was I.

But right now, it was time for the funeral and to celebrate the memories of Dad. He had been in a lot of battles throughout his life. He'd fought hard and long. And it was time for him to rest in peace.

Resuming the hunt for my father's murderer could wait a few hours.

"Are you going to bury him with your mom?" Fridge asked, lifting his head and gesturing toward the urn where my father's ashes stood.

In our town, humans were usually buried, shifters were cremated, and vampires turned to dust. My mother had been buried, as everyone who knew her had assumed she was human. But she wasn't. Not in the true sense. She was a full-blood witch, not that anyone had known. No one except my cousin Shadow and my mates.

I nodded in answer to Fridge's question. "Yeah. I think so. They would have wanted to be together. But, with Dad being a shifter... do you think that's okay?"

Fridge snorted. "Of course, it is. Screw shifter law. Jack definitely would have wanted to be with his wife."

Hot tears trembled in my eyes at hearing the vehemence in Fridge's tone.

"There was never anyone else for Dad, was there?" I asked Rogan and Fridge, then glanced at my dad's oldest friend, Terry, as he moved over to join our circle.

"No, never," Terry answered, a sad smile tugging at his lips. "Your mom was his sun and moon." Then he opened his arms to me. "Come here, sweetheart."

I flew into his embrace, sobbing against his chest for a moment in sweet relief. Terry had been like a second father to me. Closer than any other family.

He wrapped his arms tightly around me and kissed the top of my head. "Your father would have been proud of you today, kiddo. You did good."

I sighed against his huge chest and when I felt strong enough to do so, stepped away, toward my mates.

Fridge's hand found mine and he tugged me back to him.

Terry's eyebrows fluttered up momentarily as his keen gaze took in both Fridge and Rogan's protective stances over me. Terry was a full wolf shifter and would understand their body language better than most.

I was mated to both of them, and they were making that fact pretty obvious to anyone who observed us.

When his old, gray eyes came to rest on my face, part of me wanted to say, *"I've got a vampire lover at home as well."*

And although it was partly true, it wasn't necessary to rub my love life in Terry's face. Especially as he'd known me since I was a child and would probably have trouble reconciling that image of me with the one I currently offered. Not one, not two, but *three* lovers.

I coughed to clear my throat and focused on Terry's face. "We've been trying to find out who killed Dad, Terry. Have you heard anything in the pipeline about possible leads?"

Terry's eye twitched for a second then he blinked rapidly, forcing the tic away.

I frowned. Nervous tic? Or did that signify he knew something? "Terry?"

"Um... you know I've been out of the game for a few years, Sadie."

I crossed my arms over my chest and stared up at him. "That didn't answer my question."

A little smirk tugged at his lips. "No. It didn't. You always were a sharp little tack."

"What do you know, Uncle Terry?" I demanded, putting as much heat into my stare as possible.

He sighed and glanced at the ground near our feet, clearly

avoiding my gaze. "Nothing you can use, sweetheart. Seeking revenge would be suicide."

I stepped closer and dropped my voice, pitching it only for Terry's ears. "I know about the blood ring. About Mom. I know that the vampires want my dad's contact lists."

Terry's head came up and his gaze snapped sharply into focus. "You know too much, little girl."

That sounded strangely like a threat, but I pushed the thought aside. This man wasn't an enemy.

"I don't know who ordered my dad's hit. And I don't know which assassin pulled the trigger... so to speak. But I want to know. I deserve to know. And I'm not going to stop until my father is avenged."

Terry hesitated, then opened his mouth to answer. But suddenly, a large hand clapped onto Terry's shoulder and the man I'd known since I was a child, shut up.

I glared at the newcomer. "Excuse me, we're in a private conversation."

The man slid up next to Terry and stared at me.

My breath caught in my throat. This was no man. It was an ancient vampire. One of the oldest in the city. A "father", as Vincent would call him.

He had long, silver hair, a high brow, and long, flowy black robes, which made him look like some sort of priest.

"I hope you will allow me to convey my condolences," he said, his voice thin but somehow strong.

I relaxed a little, though my spine shivered with unease. Where was Vincent when we needed him? I wanted to know who this was, and where he sat in the hierarchy. By the power exuding off him, I'd guess pretty high up.

"Of course," I managed. "Did you know my father?"

The vampire smiled and his fangs protruded over his lip.

I inhaled against the fear that pushed through my heart. Was he here to feed on us? Or was that normal for a vampire of his age?

He must have noticed my shock because he gestured to his teeth. "I apologize. Once you reach a thousand years old, they do not retract as they do in the young."

He was how old? Holy shit!

I swallowed hard and glanced at Terry, who had turned uncharacteristically pale.

"Thank you for explaining that... ah... I'm sorry, I didn't get your name."

"I am Bartholomew," the vampire father said, and held out a wrinkled hand.

I took it, and shuddered at the coldness of his grip. I didn't know what I was expecting, but an icicle wasn't it.

"I'm Sadie Williams." I said, probably unnecessarily. "And this is Fridge and Rogan. Two of the men who worked for my dad." I gestured to my men, whose edges seemed to have sharpened since the vampire walked in.

"Charmed," Bartholomew said, inclining his head.

He didn't say anything else, but I had to assume he was here for a reason. I took a step closer and made eye contact with the paranormal who could be the one responsible for my father's death. My stomach clenched at the thought and my mouth ran dry.

Was he here to gloat?

"I'm sorry," I started, though I wasn't sorry at all. "I don't think you had time to answer my first question. Did you know my father at all?"

Bartholomew nodded and smiled again, flashing his gnarly fangs and making me shudder. How many people had he sunk those things into over the centuries?

Probably too many to count.

"I did. I was a client of your father's business for many years.

Terry was one of the men who worked my bounties, did you not... Terry?"

My uncle nodded stiffly and then met my gaze with an expression that spoke of true fear.

And Terry wasn't afraid of anyone. Or, at least he hadn't been, back in the day.

Since when did my father work with vampires?

"Yes," he squeaked, then cleared his throat loudly. "Yes, I was."

I put up a hand, my heartbeat quickening with my impatience. "I'm sorry. But why do I get the feeling you're here to deliver a message, Bart?"

The old vampire's mouth twitched. He didn't like the shortening of his name, obviously, but I didn't take it back.

He wouldn't dare attack me here, in broad daylight, surely? We had so many laws in this city about vampire feedings, and there were too many witnesses to buy off.

But suddenly his face cleared and he began to laugh.

I glanced at Rogan, then Fridge. They both looked as worried and surprised as I felt.

When I turned back to the vampire, he was grinning and chortling still.

"What's so funny?" I asked him.

"You're so much like your father," he said, shaking his head. Then the laughing stopped and he met my gaze. "He never knew when to back down, Sadie, and I hope you'll learn the lesson that he should have."

Fridge's rumbling growl rolled out beside me and I put a hand on his arm, stopping my mate from launching at the vampire in front of me.

Fridge may have been huge and powerful, but he was a thirty-year-old shifter with only moderate control over his dragon. He was no match for a truly ancient vampire.

Instead, I steeled myself to go toe-to-toe with the creep. "Are you threatening me?"

He grinned and inclined his head regally.

That was a yes?

I wanted to vomit. Here he was, literally telling me that he was the one who'd killed my father and he expected me to back off?

Another growl sounded, and this time it was from my left side. The wolf was enraged, and that was the last thing I needed. Rogan would never survive a clash with this vampire.

And in that moment, I saw with such clarity how important it was to keep my mates alive. Out of danger.

I wanted revenge for my father's murder, but not at the expense of the men at my side.

Though my stomach twisted with anger and my fingers twitched to grab for the blade strapped to my ankle, I put my other hand out, halting Rogan. "Why are you here, Bart? To spit in our faces?"

He frowned. "I would never do such a thing."

I rolled my eyes. Fucking vampires were so literal. "Are you going to tell me who killed my father?"

He smiled, then slowly shook his head. "No. I cannot."

I groaned, annoyed at the impotence of the whole situation. "Then why are you here?"

He fixed me with a stare. "To tell you to keep your nose out of our business. Or you... my dear... will find yourself in an urn, right beside your father."

CHAPTER 2
VINCENT

I zipped through the streets as fast as I could, hating the sting and draining heat of the sunlight on my face.

"You're a fool," I muttered to myself as I wound through the city, navigating my way to the small banquet hall where Sadie was holding her father's funeral.

I should never have let them go alone.

My body ached from being outside at this time of day. The air was thin. The sun was harsh. My skin was going to feel like dried-out newspaper tonight. Not to mention the fact I'd need to sleep most of the night to recover.

But it didn't matter.

All that mattered was finding Sadie and her mates—*my* mates— and making sure they were okay. I had a nagging feeling in my gut that something bad was about to go down.

I began to run. If I moved at my usual vampire pace, I'd be reported for breaking the rules. And no one liked a vamp who broke the rules in this city. Especially a vampire like me, who'd already been ex-communicated for refusing a direct order from a father.

But since running was a typical human activity, I ran at a semi-normal pace.

All the way to the funeral location.

I stopped in my tracks as I entered the parking lot. I inhaled sharply, noting the scent of a father nearby.

"Fuck!" It was a word I didn't utter often or lightly.

There was nothing like the smell of a truly ancient vampire. Well over a thousand years old, they had a tell-tale scent... of age. Of experience. Of murder and death.

I couldn't tell who it was, and it didn't matter. Whoever it was, that level of ancient at Jack's funeral could only spell trouble.

I raced inside and flew straight through the busy main room and then the adjoining open door to where I saw Sadie standing with Fridge and Rogan.

Their faces were twisted into scowls and they were all glaring at a man standing opposite them. A man with long, silver hair who exuded ancient vampire power.

Oh God, no... which one of them is it?

They all look the same.

I gritted my teeth and plunged into the scene, calling myself ten times a fool for allowing them to go out alone. This could have been avoided if I'd been here from the start.

"What's going on here?" I demanded, drawing the attention of the group and assessing the scene quickly.

Fridge was breathing too heavily and Rogan's eyes were slanted and yellow.

Sadie, on the other hand, had smoke practically billowing out of her ears, but she was only a quarter wolf shifter, so she wasn't about to shift on me.

The other two were fifty-fifty bets.

"This... this... vampire," Sadie practically spat the word, lifting her arm and pointing to the vamp, who lifted his head and stared at me.

Double fuck. Bartholomew Jones.

The oldest vampire in the city.

"Just threatened me."

I stepped closer to Sadie and put a hand on her, a frisson of awareness skittering up my spine at the touch, then thought better of it and reached for the men instead. They were the ones who needed calming right now. I gripped each of their wrists and squeezed.

I got almost as much of a hit of lust from Rogan and Fridge, but now was not the time to think about that with Sadie or the two shifters. I shook the thoughts away and focused on the massive task in front of me. I had to keep everyone calm enough so that the father didn't have an excuse to *protect* himself and kill us all.

I leveled my gaze on Bartholomew, though Fridge tugged his arm to get away from me, and I could hear the growl in Rogan's chest rolling up toward me.

I was stronger than both shifters. They couldn't break my grasp that easily.

"Hello, Father." I swallowed hard, trying to keep my cool when I saw the light of excitement in Bartholomew's eyes.

This particular vampire father rarely left the safety of his fortress —a penthouse in one of the most expensive parts of the city.

The fact that he was here, alone, during the daylight, said volumes about how important this meeting with Sadie was to him and the vampire leaders of the city.

I straightened my spine under his scrutiny, determined not to kowtow to him. "May I help you?"

Bartholomew lifted his nose a touch, his anger at my lack of subservience obvious. But I was not about to go down on my knees and kiss his hand in front of all these people, and he knew it.

Especially since my own clan had officially ostracized me because I'd refused to kill Sadie's dad, Jack Williams.

I owed them nothing.

Bartholomew spoke in a derisive tone. "Vincent, Vincent, Vincent. I'd heard you'd become mixed up with the wrong sort of people, but I hadn't realized it was *this* group."

His lip curled up in a sneer, like he smelled something foul, but I was more worried now about Fridge. I could sense his rising heat, causing him to sweat. He was getting hot and angry. And all that hot emotion was making me hard.

Focus!

I glanced across at Sadie, but managed to speak calmly, despite my churning gut. "One can't choose our blood mate, as you know, Father."

The ancient vampire's eyes widened infinitesimally.

I wasn't sure if I'd made the right choice to reveal that Sadie was so important to me, but it would be pretty obvious to anyone who saw us together. No point hiding it now.

Hopefully the vampires wouldn't use her against me in the future, but at this point it was a risk I was willing to take.

"And are these creatures also your mates?" he asked, his gaze flicking around Sadie, Fridge and Rogan. They had all stepped up and now surrounded me.

His eyes settled on Fridge and a smile curled his lips. "The large dragon, I believe?"

"Get fucked..." Fridge hissed in a strange, snake-like voice, and tried to move past me.

I gripped his arm with all my strength and clicked my tongue. "Fridge. Stand down."

I turned and glared at him for a few seconds, not wanting to look away from the father, but also needing to convey to Fridge how serious I was.

I needed him to calm the fuck down.

This vampire could kill all four of us in moments if he so chose.

But I knew Bartholomew was a stickler for the rules, *thank God,* and would not execute us without cause.

We must *not* give him cause.

Fridge's gaze connected with mine and the dragon was on full show. His eyes had shifted to a diamond shape and his skin was rippling with purple and black scales.

I glared at him—hard—willing him to understand.

Please, Fridge. Please. Hold it together.

His jaw clenched hard and his skin began to flicker back to human.

Thank you.

I turned back to the father. "I'm sure Sadie misunderstood you, Father. Thank you for coming by. Can I walk you out?"

"No! He..." Sadie began to argue but I wrapped my free arm around her shoulders and pulled her tightly into my side. "We don't want to keep the father from his important duties, Sadie. Do we?"

Her chest heaved beneath my arm as her breaths huffed in and out. I pulled her in tight and held her against my ribs.

We hadn't known each other long. Would they all trust me on this?

Eventually, the tension left Sadie and she stiffly nodded her head. "Please leave."

Bartholomew obviously couldn't resist a final shot and smiled at her. "Remember what I said. Your father wasn't very smart when it came to the politics of this city, but I hope you will heed my warning. It would be such a shame... if you didn't."

Sadie's breath caught in her throat as she swallowed a sob, but nothing more was said on either side. Finally, Bartholomew bowed his head and swept out of the room.

I raced for the door and shut it behind him as fast as I could, turning around to wait for the expected explosion from my mates. They didn't disappoint.

"What the hell did you do that for?" Sadie screamed at me.

Fridge charged forward with his arms outstretched as though to strangle me. "We could have taken him."

I zipped across the room and out of his reach. Then I decided to let my own feelings explode into my bloodstream, coursing around my body and making me wild with anger.

"What was I doing?" I repeated, glaring at Sadie. "*Saving your life*! Saving *all* of your lives! Do you not know who that was?"

Rogan, who had been the most restrained of the three throughout, began to pace up and down. "It was a vampire. So what? Same as you."

I huffed out a humorless laugh. "Nothing like me. Nothing! That was Bartholomew Jones. The oldest vampire in the entire city. One of the most powerful creatures I've ever met. Also, the most ruthless. He lost his humanity a long time ago, and if you had given him even the smallest reason to attack, he would have taken all three of your heads off and walked out the door without a single person reproaching him. You're lucky I got here when I did to defuse the situation."

Fridge charged up to me, his hands clenched and his nostrils flaring. This time I didn't run away but held my ground and stared up into his gaze.

"What the hell are you talking about? We could have taken him on." He growled at me.

I covered my mouth with my hand but not before a laugh escaped. "Taken him on? Have you lost your mind? You and Rogan could not overcome me... and Bartholomew could kill me with a single blow. Do you seriously think you would stand a chance against him?"

Anger and frustration flashed across Fridge's face and I saw his swinging haymaker punch coming from a mile away. Perhaps he wanted me to see it. Perhaps not.

Either way I ducked and grabbed his fist, twisting him around and slamming him up against the nearest wall. Then I deliberately twisted him back round and got up in his face to make my point.

I grabbed his shirt and put my nose next to his. "Do you think I'm joking? Do you think I'm full of ego when I say this? I am as serious as a seizure. He will kill you... he will kill all of you, if you give him an excuse. I saved your lives just then, and I deserve a thank you, not this nonsense you're dealing out."

Fridge's posture relaxed against me. I was pressing my hard cock into his belly, and as his eyes changed back to human, he glanced down and I realized he could feel it, too.

When he met my gaze once more, there was something else there. Something I'd seen in Sadie's eyes when she looked at me sometimes, but I had never seen it in a man's expression. Something I didn't have time to explore.

Not right now, anyway.

I stepped away from all of them and moved toward the door. I opened my mouth to tell them that I was heading back to the apartment, but then Sadie let out a sob and the others rushed for her.

Rogan and Fridge enclosed her in a hug and held her tight.

Pain split my chest apart as I realized I was once again on the outs of this mating group. I'd been late to the party, and even now, when I was doing everything I possibly could to protect them, it wasn't enough.

Would they ever accept me into their triad? Or would I be doomed to watch from the outside, yearning for more? Yearning for all of it, with Sadie and her men.

I turned and fled, wondering if I'd made a mistake in choosing to follow my heart to this woman and the two men who loved her.

And whether it was too late to undo that choice.

CHAPTER 3
SADIE

I hated tears but I couldn't seem to hold them in right now. I sobbed into Rogan's chest and grabbed tightly onto the comforting hand Fridge offered me.

That had been so close. I could feel it now. The danger that left the room the moment Bartholomew had disappeared out the door. He'd wanted to hurt us. Kill us, even.

His purpose was to threaten me, to get up in my face so that I would react in a way that gave him an excuse to inflict harm.

And we'd fallen for it, hook, line and sinker. Or we would have, if it hadn't been for Vincent.

I pulled myself back and wiped at my wet face. "Oh my God. That was terrible."

"Yeah," Rogan agreed, allowing me to pull away. "Vincent should have stayed out of it."

Fridge crossed his arms over his chest and nodded.

My mouth dropped open. I knew the guys didn't really like Vincent despite everything we'd been through so far together. But were they really that blind? That stupid?

"You aren't serious? He *saved* us." I spun around when I heard the door open, expecting to see Vincent leaving and planning to call out to him to wait, but instead, there it was Lucas, one of the hunters from my dad's workshop.

"Where's Vincent?" And where had Uncle Terry slunk off to? I hadn't seen him leave, but he'd disappeared around the same time Vincent had shown up.

"Who?" Lucas asked, walking in with a bottle of golden-colored whiskey and several glasses.

"My... Never mind."

I took one of the glasses, as did Rogan and Fridge. We accepted the alcohol and drank what was offered. I shared a look with my two mates, promising we'd sort out all our issues after the wake.

"The guys told me to come in and grab you. What's been taking so long?" Lucas asked.

I sniffed and wiped my nose. "Nothing at all. Let's go get drunk."

We were swept into an afternoon of food, too much booze, and wonderful stories of my father's life.

The men in the room knew everything about him. His temper, his power, his graciousness.

It was only afterward, when I was paying the bill and readying to leave, that Terry appeared next to me again.

"Sadie," he hissed. "I need to speak to you."

When I turned to look at him, I was seeing double and giggled.

Damn, I drank too much. Again.

What was wrong with me lately? *Oh, yeah...*

I grabbed Rogan's arm and clung to it to stop from toppling over. "What?"

"Not here," he insisted, and I glanced up at Rogan, who was blinking and looking confused, just like me.

"I got a cab!" Fridge called from behind us.

I looked over to where my dragon shifter mate was falling into the flagged vehicle. It had been a terrible week for us all, and we'd obviously all needed the release.

"Can you call me tomorrow, Uncle Terry? I can barely stand up," I managed as Rogan slung my arm over his shoulders and hoisted me up into his arms.

Terry grabbed my hand. "Sadie. You need to know who killed your dad and why."

I swallowed hard, annoyed that the tears I'd fought so hard to keep at bay all afternoon were now, once again, flowing.

"I know why. They wanted information on my mother's bloodline. But he wouldn't give it up. As for who... it must be one of the fathers. Though exactly who, I don't know." I was almost singing the words now and my eyelids were drooping.

"Sadie," Terry insisted urgently.

I let my eyes close and my head fall onto Rogan's chest. "Tomorrow, Terry. I can't take any more. Not today."

Rogan stumbled over to the cab and Terry watched us go.

That was the last thing I remembered until I woke up the next morning with a dry mouth, a pounding, ear-splitting headache, in a room that stunk of stale liquor.

I gagged as I tried to swallow, wetting my lips. "Damn. Someone needs to open a window. We stink."

"I agree," came a voice from beyond the bed, and a welcome breeze floated through the room as a window was opened. "Vincent?"

"I'm here Sadie."

I tried to open my eyes wider to see him, but the pain in my head only increased. "Damn." I put a hand to my forehead.

"Can I get you anything, Sadie?" Vincent's voice was closer now.

Warm hands ran over my middle, but they were obviously from the two men sharing my bed.

I forced my eyes to open properly and prayed for a painkiller.

Vincent was standing beside the bed, his mouth drawn down at the corners.

I glanced around me. Rogan and Fridge were each side of me. We were all still fully clothed, except for Fridge, who seemed to have gotten rid of his shirt somewhere after the funeral and was snoring happily on the pillow beside me.

I looked up at Vincent once again and said what I'd been wanting to say since he left the wake yesterday. "Thank you for stopping us yesterday. I think you saved our lives."

Vincent's eyes widened, clearly pleased I had seen the truth of the situation, then a gentle smile lifted the edges of his lips. "I did."

I wanted to laugh at his surprised pleasure, but I knew it would hurt too much. "I... ah, need to go to the bathroom. Could you help me up? I'm afraid I'll puke if I move on my own."

Vincent's mouth tightened in a grimace, but he nodded.

I pushed Fridge's possessive hand off my belly and put my arms up to Vincent.

My vampire swooped in and lifted me easily into his arms. I clung to his neck, his cool skin lovely beneath my hot hands.

He carried me into the bathroom, then set me on my feet. "I'll leave you to it."

I nodded. "Thank you. But don't go anywhere. We need to talk, I think." The worry sank into my gut and spread through to my heart.

He nodded, but his eyes were shadowed as he shut the door so I could relieve myself.

I quickly used the bathroom and had a super-quick wash by splashing my face with water, after which I felt marginally improved.

"Yes!" I cried when I found a pack of painkillers in the medicine cabinet above the mirror. "Life saver."

I took two tablets and washed them down quickly with a gulp of water.

I stared at my reflection in the mirror. I was pale, but thanks to the smart move of not wearing any makeup yesterday in case I cried too much, things could have been worse.

Vincent and I needed some time together. We'd only kissed once, despite the fact I desired him and he seemed to desire me, too. I wanted to see what was beneath his conservative suits and feel his beating heart against my body.

Well, vampires didn't have pulses... but that was beside the point.

I wanted to see him out of control. I wanted him to more than kiss me. I wanted to be mated to my vampire... properly.

When I opened the door once again, Vincent snuck into the room, putting a finger to his lips. "I think they're both on the verge of waking up."

Nodding, I lowered the lid of the toilet and sat down.

He handed me a bottle of water and leaned against the now-closed door.

"Oh, thanks," I said, opening the bottle and downing the whole thing in a few short swallows.

Damn, I was thirsty. What was it about excessive alcohol that caused such terrible dehydration?

I wiped my mouth with the back of my hand and threw the bottle in the nearby trash can.

The bathroom was enormous, with a double sink, a toilet and a huge shower with a single glass panel separating it from the rest of the room.

"You wanted to talk," he reminded me.

I nodded. "Yeah... I don't know how to say it, exactly."

Vincent shrugged. "Just say it. There's not much that will offend me."

"Offend you?" Oh... he thought this was a bad talk. "No. That's not it. I wanted to thank you for everything you did yesterday. You faced down Bartholomew with dignity. And stopped us doing something stupid that most likely would have gotten us killed. Or at least, badly hurt. You did all that, Vincent. Thank you."

"It was nothing."

"It wasn't."

He shrugged but didn't say anything more. I could see the unhappiness written across his face in the way he wouldn't look directly at me, only glancing up occasionally from his fixated view on the ground.

Why was he so upset? I had to take a different route. "Why did you leave so fast?"

He shrugged again.

I stood up, feeling uncomfortable in yesterday's clothes. "I mean... I know I burst into tears and we were all being angry dickheads, but you didn't need to leave. You could have joined us at the wake. You'd have been welcome."

This time he did look up and there was pain in his gaze. "Really? I would have been welcome in a room full of bounty hunters? I don't think so. In any case... I achieved what I needed to do."

"Which was what?"

He lifted a shoulder yet again, as though what he'd done was a small thing, when I knew it wasn't. "I had a feeling something would go wrong, and I wanted to stop it. I needed to protect you and your shifter men. So, I came, saved you all—for the moment—from the vampire father's wrath, and returned here to rest."

Oh, the daylight. I'd forgotten about that part. "Did it hurt you to come out into the sun to find us?"

He bent one knee and pressed his foot flat against the door. "Not terribly. I was fine by the time you all staggered back in last night."

I bit my lip. "Was anything bad said to you when we came home?"

He stiffened. "Not really."

I didn't push there, because if something had been said to offend him, it wouldn't have come from me. So, I'd let Rogan, or more likely Fridge, apologize later.

"Well, thank you. Again," I said.

He nodded, finally seeming to accept my words. "You're welcome. You know I would do anything for you, Sadie."

Would he, now?

I reached up under my dress and pushed my pantyhose down, catching a whiff of my overall scent. "Whoa, I stink. Too much alcohol."

Vincent nodded, but didn't move from his post by the door.

I tilted my head to the side. "Would you stay and chat with me while I shower?"

Surely mates could do that... right?

He nodded, and the darkness of his eyes turned molten.

A thrill shot through my belly as my gaze dropped to his crotch. He had hardened at my request. My lips parted as I met his gaze once again.

It was time. Vincent had shown me in so many ways that he was here to support me, to love me, and to follow me into the pits of hell if necessary. I wanted to bond with my vampire; show Vincent he was loved and desired in the way he deserved.

"Tell me about your life before us, Vincent. What did you do every day?" I asked as I unbuttoned my dress, then pulled it off over my head.

I stood there in black cotton underwear. Utilitarian, comfortable. Totally unsexy, and yet Vincent's stare smoldered when he raked his gaze up and down my body.

I didn't hesitate as I unhooked my bra, dropped it to the floor, and pushed my panties to the tiles.

I was ready for my shower, and boy did I need it. Alcohol practically seeped from my pores, and I couldn't imagine that scent was very sensual.

I walked around the glass panel that separated the shower from the rest of the room and turned on the water, conscious of the way my breasts bounced as I moved and the heated stare I felt on my ass.

When I glanced over my shoulder, Vincent was beginning to remove his clothing.

Slowly.

Too slowly.

After making sure the temperature was comfortably warm, I stepped in and tilted my head back under the water and let the heat flow over me. Grabbing the soap, I lathered up my hands before running my fingers over my breasts and torso.

When I looked Vincent's way again, his mouth was open and his hand had paused on his shirt buttons.

I lifted my arms and arched my back, running my soaped-up hands through my hair. Was he going to act on the invitation, or was I going to have to spell it out for him?

When I looked at him again, he was practically salivating, but still wasn't moving.

I sighed and stretched out a hand. "Aren't you going to join me?"

His eyebrows flickered up. "You want me to?"

Laughing, I slid my hands over my body, tweaking a nipple while the other fingers searched out the aching place between my legs.

I wanted to mate with my vampire, and although I had no idea if sex with Vincent would be different than with a non-vampire, I wanted to find out.

"Can't you tell? I want you so much, I ache." I gasped as I circled my throbbing clit with my fingertips.

Vincent was naked and rushing into the shower in a blink. Once inside the cubicle, he lifted me up and I wrapped my legs around his waist.

He pressed me against the cold tile wall and I gasped at the sensation of heat and cold against my skin. Hot water flowed over us as my cool-skinned vampire pressed my back into even colder tiles.

I wrapped my arms around his neck and pressed my lips against his and when he moaned, the visceral sound hit me right in the lower belly, making me want him even more. I was so hot I was ready to cum, and we'd only been in here scant minutes.

I arched against him, seeking out closer contact as his cock thrust up between our bellies.

I broke off the kiss and sobbed, "Take me. Please."

"God, Sadie. You are so fucking sexy." He grabbed my ass and lined up his cock to tease my entrance, just as the door opened and a loud cough broke through my fog of need.

Damn it. I was hoping Fridge and Rogan would stay asleep.

CHAPTER 4
FRIDGE

The sight of Vincent's ass clenched tight, grabbing onto a moaning Sadie, made blood rush straight to my cock.

I expected to feel anger or envy. But instead, I wanted to strip down and join them in the steam-filled space.

Slowly, Vincent lowered Sadie and they both turned around.

It was Vincent's hard cock I noticed first, then the way Sadie took his hand and pulled him out of the shower stall and into the bathroom.

She glanced up at me and bit her lip. I wanted to kiss her nerves away. Hold her.

Fuck her brains out.

"Vincent and I were bonding," Sadie explained.

Vincent grimaced and glanced down at his distended dick. "Well, we were trying to."

Sadie glanced up at him. "Yeah... we didn't really get to start. Or finish." She looked back at us, then raised an eyebrow. "Do you guys wanna join us? Or would you rather wait until..."

"We'll join you," Rogan said before I could decide. Though waiting for them to finish seemed like a terrible idea.

I twisted to look at Rogan and he stared at me, hard. I could almost hear his voice in my head saying, *"Do not fuck this up."*

And he was right. I couldn't go up against Vincent, and I shouldn't. This was our life now. We were a four-person menage... a family. Though admittedly a strange one.

I swallowed hard. "Yes. We'll join you."

The smile that lit up Sadie's face was worth agreeing to the session.

After all, I shared her with Rogan. An extra male that she wanted shouldn't make a difference.

But Rogan doesn't make you want to butt-fuck him.

I groaned and turned around, pushing aside the infernal thought.

I pulled off my shirt, then caught wind of my own scent and turned back around, my dragon's wings flickering inside me.

There was no shift, no need to take flight. Just a growling exchange of my human side with my shifter side. A feeling that knew that my destiny was about to change once more.

I twisted back around. "I think we all need a shower. Can we all fit in there?"

Sadie and Vincent exchanged looks, then Sadie grinned. "We can try."

Vincent led Sadie back into the shower area and flicked the water back on.

Rogan gave me a strange, questioning look, and I shrugged. "What? I stink from yesterday. Don't you?"

Rogan took a whiff of his own shirt and made a disgusted face.

"Exactly," I said.

I undid my pants and pushed them down my thighs, my cock already hard and bouncingly happy to be finally released.

Rogan stripped as well, his cock also at the ready. We stood side by side and watched Vincent with Sadie under the spray of water.

He was taking his time now.

They were both facing us, Sadie's back to Vincent's chest. His hands were on her breasts and his lips were at her neck. Sadie had her head thrown back and she was arching into every caress.

I licked my lips as my hunger for my mate grew. "Want some help, Vincent?"

Vincent lifted his gaze and met my eyes. He nodded. "Sure. Would you like to prepare her pussy for me?"

His words hit me right in the gut and I strode forward, dropping to my knees to taste her wetness.

She cried out as my tongue flicked out and caressed her.

Vincent lifted her up and opened her more fully for me, and I dove in, tasting her flesh, her sweetness. Fluttering my tongue against her clit and along her seam until she was convulsing and crying out to me.

Then she was lifted up and away from me and as the water ran down my back, Vincent turned her around and pushed her up against the tiles, holding her as though she weighed nothing at all.

She cried out as he thrust up and into her, joining them together for the first time.

Floods of pleasure pulsed through my body and I stayed on my knees on the floor of the shower. I couldn't move away.

I could only watch with some sort of sick pleasure as Sadie was nailed against the wall, over and over again, by the strength of Vincent's thrusts.

His ass cheeks clenched tightly as he pounded into her. Sadie's fingernails dug into his back and she screamed out her pleasure.

Vincent thrust one more time, growling deep in his throat and turning his head away from her as he also shuddered in climax.

That's when I saw his fangs in the bright light of the bathroom. I jumped to my feet, my heart pounding and my muscles ready to launch forward and save her if he tried to bite her.

But instead, I witnessed something amazing.

Vincent fought off his need, his hand clenched in a fist against the wall beside Sadie's head. He opened his mouth and threw back his head, tensed as though in pain, then eventually he managed to pull his fangs back in to their sheath.

Sadie's legs dropped from where they'd been wrapped around Vincent's waist and I indicated to Rogan, who had watched the whole episode outside the glass panel, to go next. I was feeling... strange. I didn't trust myself near our mate quite yet.

Rogan grinned and moved into the shower, grabbing the soap and quickly washing himself before reaching for Sadie.

Vincent staggered out of the shower and I caught him before he fell, grabbing onto both of his arms.

He stared up into my eyes like he was drunk and dazed. I knew how he felt. It had been that way for me, after my bonding between Sadie was completed.

I grinned down at him, sharing a moment of understanding with the vampire. Sadie's body was heavenly. Being our mate, being inside her, holding her, kissing her... it was like coming home, every time. But to a home I'd never known before. A beautiful, love-filled home.

Vincent's knees seemed to give out and I clutched him tighter, bringing our bodies into extremely close contact.

Electricity zipped along my skin, similar to the feeling that touching Sadie gave me.

I didn't want to feel anything like that. Not for him. It had been hard enough to accept the whole mating bond idea when it came to Sadie. This must be a leftover from watching Vincent and Sadie together in the shower.

I dropped my hands away and stepped back, causing Vincent to stagger sideways and grab for the sink to stop from toppling over.

I swallowed hard and stared at him as he closed his eyes and swayed. He looked as though he was recovering from a huge hit of alcohol, or a maybe a punch.

I forced myself to focus on what was going on in the shower, where Sadie was being fucked by Rogan.

Their simultaneous groans did nothing to excite me the way it had with Sadie and Vincent.

When Rogan let Sadie stand once more and they both moved beneath the shower, cuddling and kissing under the water, I was in no mood for my turn.

Sadie's eyes came up to meet mine, then dropped down to look at my cock, which had deflated. Her smile wavered, but she bravely walked forward, going up on her tiptoes to kiss me.

I sank into the kiss, enjoying the flavor of Sadie's mouth and feeling the usual zing of desire. Yet this time, I noticed a distinct lack of something.

What? Or who, was the question. And not one I wanted to answer now.

I picked her up in my arms and walked back into the bedroom, needing to get out of the hot, misty air of the bathroom.

I tossed my mate onto the bed and she shimmied up the sheet to lay with her head on the pillow.

I reached down to stroke myself, feeling sick to my stomach at the thought I was about to disappoint my mate. What was wrong with me?

Rogan flopped onto the bed and grinned. "I'll keep her warm for you."

He plumped up one of her breasts and set his lips to her nipple, suckling on her flesh and making her mewl with pleasure.

I groaned with frustration, clenching my jaw and dropping my hand away. I was going to have to pull out of this session. This wasn't going to work.

"I don't think…" I began, then I felt a cool hand on my arm and turned to Vincent.

He was looking serious, his lips thin and tight. "Would you like some help getting your body ready? I can imagine it isn't easy going last."

What sort of help did he mean, exactly?

I glanced down at Sadie, gasping and groaning with pleasure beneath Rogan's mouth. Then she lifted her head. "Oh, yes. Please. I want you too, Fridge."

I opened my mouth, then shut it again.

I glanced at the vampire next to me, my gaze skating over his lean muscles, his strong physique.

I couldn't say the words, but made a tiny nodding movement with my head that I was hoping he would decipher correctly.

Instead of stroking me with his hand as I'd expected, Vincent dropped to his knees and stared up at me. "I haven't done this before, but I've seen it done a thousand times. Let me know if it's all right."

He grabbed my cock in his hand and set his wet, cool mouth to my suddenly burning flesh.

I gasped and moved to get away, but Vincent's hands whipped around and grabbed my ass, hauling me back, deeper into his mouth.

I groaned from the pleasure, my cock responding immediately.

I grabbed his hair, about to pull him off when I heard Sadie whisper, "Damn, that's so hot."

I looked up to see her sitting up, watching us. Desire lit her eyes.

Rogan was sitting with her, looking vaguely interested, but he went back to kissing Sadie's neck while she continued to stare at me. Lust was written all over her face.

Her need fueled mine and I groaned involuntarily.

She nodded at me. "Go for it."

Vincent moaned on my cock and I gasped as pleasure hit me deep. Instead of pulling him off me as I'd originally intended, I threaded my fingers into his hair and held him in place.

Watching him go up and down and seeing my cock slide in and

out of his mouth was one of the most evocative, fucking hottest things, I'd ever seen.

I loved it. And I hated it.

That this vampire... this *male*... a *masculine* vampire, sucking my cock made me feel this good, wasn't something I was comfortable with.

"Stop," I managed, as heat began to tickle the backs of my legs. Pleasure pulsed in every molecule of my body and my balls were throbbing for release.

Vincent came off me with a wet sucking pop and looked up at me, his eyebrows furrowed. "Am I doing it wrong?"

Fuck, no...

"No. I'm just... ready. Thanks." It should have been self-explanatory, but I gestured to my hard cock, glistening with Vincent's saliva.

"Oh." Vincent sounded disappointed.

Sadie slipped to the edge of the bed and stood up in front of me. "Don't stop," she said, her voice husky. "I wanna see you come."

"Like this?" I asked, gesturing to where Vincent still knelt on the ground. "No way."

"Please." She nodded, taking my hand and sliding it between the hot slickness between her legs. "See how turned on I am?"

She kissed me and I took her direction, sliding my fingers up inside of her and feeling her channel clench around me.

Her head dropped back on a sob as I worked her from the inside with my fingers, her pussy gripping me hard.

I stared down into her rapture-filled face, a glow of pride pumping through me.

Then she whispered, "Vincent. Please."

And the vampire's mouth descended on me once more.

This time I didn't fight the feelings, nor the storm of passion that swept me up. This was for Sadie, after all...

I grabbed Vincent's hair with my free hand and held him tight to me while I worked Sadie's pussy and kissed her sweet lips. She began to pant and gasp and squeeze my fingers.

I broke our kiss and groaned as my balls squeezed tight. "I'm gonna come."

I gave the warning for the vampire, so he could pull away, let me finish elsewhere. But Vincent doubled his ministrations, sucking me right down into his throat.

I couldn't stop what happened next. I had no choice.

I threw my head back and roared to the sky, my orgasm ripping through me as I held both mates in the palm of my hands.

One hand gripping Vincent's hair, the other hand deep inside Sadie's quivering body and she shuddered and screamed in yet another release around my fingers.

And for the first time in my whole life, I knew what it was like to feel truly complete.

Fucking hell!

CHAPTER 5
VINCENT

I swallowed down the dragon's seed, relishing the taste and hoping my body didn't reject it.

As a vampire, the only substance I was able to ingest was blood. My stomach rejected all other forms of food, and the effects were not pleasant. But then again... both were liquids from the body, so I would have to see what happened.

I licked my lips clean and stood up, staring directly into the big dragon's face.

Fridge wouldn't look at me. He kept his eyes hooded as though he couldn't keep them open, but I didn't quite believe it.

"Bed," Fridge said and staggered toward the mattress.

Sadie stepped toward me and kissed me, her recent orgasm making her lips that much sweeter and more lush. She tasted like heaven, and I held her tight.

"Are we mated now, too?" she asked.

I blinked at her. "Was that why you wanted me to make love to you?" Had she been as concerned as me about our lack of connection?

She nodded. "Well, one of the reasons. When I was first with Rogan and Fridge, it connected us. Isn't it the same for vampires?"

I swallowed down my immediate response, which was, *"Yes, and yet somehow, I still don't feel complete."* But I had the feeling that had more to do with Fridge, than Sadie.

So, I forced myself to smile and kiss her once more. "I feel connected to you." At least that was true.

Sadie had proven that she wanted me as much as she wanted the other two men, and for now, that was all that was important. "Shall we join the wolf and the dragon on the bed?"

Suddenly Fridge lurched to his feet, muttering, "I need a shower." He quickly disappeared inside the bathroom, shutting the door firmly behind him.

Sadie stared at the door, her eyebrows raised. "What's his problem?"

Rogan burst out laughing and even I couldn't stop the smile that stretched across my face. It was a little humorous.

Sadie, on the other hand, looked affronted, her arms crossing over her naked breasts as though she were annoyed.

Not a look she could pull off when she was so deliciously bare.

"What's so funny?" she demanded.

I gave her gorgeous ass a tap. "Let's go lay down for a little while. Let him have a moment."

Rogan already lay on the large bed and I took the other side, waiting for our woman to join us.

Sadie sighed and crawled over the mattress and into the center position. She lay on her back and put her head on my chest and legs over Rogan. All together, we made a capital H shape.

I stroked her hair and for a moment of silence, everything was as close to perfect as it could be.

Then Sadie whispered, "Did I do something wrong?"

I groaned and rolled my eyes at Rogan, who grimaced.

"Can you explain it to her?" I asked, and the wolf shifter nodded.

"You didn't do anything wrong, Sadie," Rogan said. "But Fridge thinks he's straight. He's going to find what just happened pretty... confronting."

Sadie grabbed for my hand stroking her hair and kissed my finger tips. "Well, I think what you did for him—and me—was amazing. So hot."

I sighed, momentary pain tugging at the place where my human heart once was. "Yes... let's hope Fridge comes around to feeling the same way."

"It's okay if he doesn't though, right?" Rogan said. "After all, he's not gay."

I sighed again, heavier this time. "Nothing is ever that black and white. You mortals and your..." I shook my head. "Definitions on sexuality."

"Us... mortals?" Rogan repeated.

I turned to look at him where he lay with his head on the pillow, a body's length away from me.

"Yes. For me—for most vampires—we don't put such limits on ourselves. It's too restrictive for a person who may live for many centuries. A millennium, even. And with our family—our ménage—I don't see why we must put the same rules on our interactions as we've had in previous relationships. After all, we've never shared a single mate with other men before." I looked away from Rogan's deep penetrating gaze and stared up at the ceiling. "Of course, Fridge is welcome to withdraw and go back to how things were before."

I didn't want it to be that way, of course. I could be honest with myself about that.

Going down on my knees for him, feeling his cock in my hand, in my mouth... knowing that Sadie's beautiful body was connected to me literally via Fridge's body... by God, it had been one of the most erotic things I'd ever experienced.

But if he didn't want me to do that again... then I'd be satisfied with only Sadie's affection.

But knowing what it could be like, if all three of us were involved... Rogan, too, of course, but for some reason it was both Sadie and Fridge that my body seemed to crave.

"I'm starving," Fridge muttered as he barged back into the room, opening the door loudly, a white towel wrapped securely around his waist.

Nothing exposed.

"I am hungry, as well," I said, deciding it was time for me to make myself scarce. "I'll be back in a few hours."

I kissed the top of Sadie's head and quickly dressed, too aware of three sets of eyes watching me.

When I was completely covered, I turned around to face them. "Would you like me to order you breakfast, or can you do it yourselves this morning?"

Sadie slid to the end of the bed and stood up. "Um... we can do it. But we need to talk about what we're going to do from tonight. Technically, we're supposed to be checking out of the hotel this morning, but I'm not sure where we should go. My father's apartment—*my* apartment—is a possibility now that we know who broke in and why." She grinned at me.

I pulled my money clip from inside my jacket pocket. "I'd prefer to stay here."

There was room service for them and pitch dark during the day for me. Not to mention a massive bathroom and bed that would fit all four of us—when Fridge decided to cooperate and join us.

"I'll sort out the bill on my way out to find food. Assuming you're all in agreement?"

Rogan whistled. "Whoa, man. How much cash have you got there?"

I shrugged. "One of the advantages of being my age. I care

nothing for money but have quite a bit of it. Are we in agreement? We stay here a little longer?"

I glanced from Sadie's face, to Rogan's, and finally to Fridge's.

The dragon shifter's face was hard but he nodded, as did the others.

"But I can pay," Sadie said.

I smiled at her. "I've got it. See you all in a few hours."

I left to pay the bill and find a vampire bar nearby.

Although I had managed to keep my composure on the surface, inside I was a mess. A railing, screaming, angry mess.

Why should I feel this way when I'd finally achieved what I ached for? A bonding to Sadie, the woman who was my blood mate.

Our coupling, and the moment of our bonding, was insanely beautiful. It had taken my breath away and made me dizzy with joy. That should have been enough.

And yet, on my journey to completion with her, I'd discovered a loop along the path. A loop that led to Fridge as well as Sadie.

I hadn't expected that. Sadie herself had had to come to terms with more than one mate. Was it possible that I could have also have two mates? Both Sadie, and Fridge?

I had taken a single step along that looped path, and found my paradise in the connection with both of them. Only to be denied minutes later when Fridge refused to face the truth.

What the hell was I going to do now?

Sadie

The atmosphere in the hotel room was tense, and I wasn't sure how to change it. After Vincent left, Fridge refused to talk about what had happened, so I decided to indulge in another shower with Rogan while our breakfast was ordered and delivered.

By the time Vincent returned, we'd showered, dressed and eaten breakfast.

He staggered in, his eyes glazed over from feeding.

I rushed over and grabbed his sleeves to steady him. "Vincent, are you okay?"

He nodded and stumbled sideways, falling onto the couch with a chuckle. "I... overindulged."

He settled more comfortably onto the couch, threw his head back on the headrest and closed his eyes.

Fridge moved away to the other side of the room. I looked at Rogan, who grimaced. I felt the same way and only just stopped from rolling my eyes. Fridge's awkwardness wasn't a good sign. If he and Vincent were at odds, our whole family wouldn't work.

"Are we going into the workshop today?" Fridge asked suddenly. "I told the guys yesterday to take off until noon, but I need to get in there to open everything up for them."

"Sure," I agreed. "Perhaps we need to speak to them about our plan." I sat down on the armrest next to where Vincent was still sprawled on the couch.

"What plan?" Rogan asked, coming to sit opposite us.

"Going down into the blood ring operations again. This time I think we need a full team and who better to hire than the hunters my father trained and trusted?"

I'd been thinking about it yesterday and, as I looked over the men at the funeral, I realized there was no one better to avenge my father's death than the men gathered to pay their respects to his memory.

Fridge finally came closer, dragging a chair from the dining table, turning it around and straddling it. "You think that's a good idea?"

I shrugged. "You guys tell me. You've been down there now. You know what we saw. I'm not sure if they would have increased their security since the last time we went down, since Vincent got the jump on their guard." I tapped Vincent, who slowly lifted his head.

"Yes?" he asked.

"Do you think they would have put more guards on the entrance to the blood ring? You know... since their other guy was stabbed."

Vincent's usually dark eyes were swirling pools of blue. Strange... I'd never seen a vampire with eyes like that. Did that happen to all of them when they fed?

"It's possible. If they believe the blood ring entrance is no longer safe."

I turned back to Rogan and Fridge. "Then we need to act quickly. It's only been a few days since we went, so hopefully they haven't moved anyone, or changed anything yet. Those women need to be rescued. We need to destroy the whole thing."

Just like my mother had done twenty years ago. She had hit the vampires where it hurt... quite literally.

Vincent sighed beside me and reached for my leg, running his hand along my thigh. Tingles of awareness ran along my skin beneath his touch. "Then you'd better organize an army, Sadie, and an escape plan for afterwards. It will be impossible to stay in the city if anyone learns it was us who attempted to take down the blood ring. Father Bartholomew already has his suspicions. I suspect that's why he came to deliver his threat at the funeral."

"Hmm." I bit my lip, thinking. My father owned a house outside the city, many hours away. We'd gone there when I was a child, but it had been years since I'd seen it. "I think I know of a place if we need it, but first we need to decide who at Hunters would help us. Rogan? Fridge? Who do you trust?"

The two men started listing off names and debating which of my father's men would be the best to take with us. Who was single and tough, wouldn't mind going into the hellish underground to take out a dangerous enemy.

Fridge turned to me. "You're gonna have to make it worth their while. Because if we all make it out, and succeed, Vincent's right."

His mouth twisted as he said Vincent's name, but he soldiered on. "They're gonna have to leave the city. At least for a while."

"So, I have to ask people to abandon their homes? Oh my God." I sank onto the couch next to Vincent, and he pulled me into his lap. I felt safe in his arms, and tempted to snuggle in. But I tried to focus on the conversation.

"It's possible we can pull this off without anyone having to change their whole lives... but it will mean killing everyone we see who may identify us later," Vincent said.

I put my hand to my mouth, my brain exploding with this new knowledge.

Vincent went on. "We're with you, Sadie. Because you're right. I cannot ignore what's going on beneath this city any longer. Something must be done, even if it means a change for us. Hell... I'll relocate wherever you want us to, as long as there's a dark room and a vampire bar nearby."

I bit my lip. I wasn't sure there was a vampire bar anywhere near our country property. But blood? I had blood to give him.

The clock ticked around, announcing it was almost noon. "We'd better get going to the workshop if you guys want to get in there today."

I got up and out of Vincent's lap, a sadness dragging at me. Would I be able to live with myself if someone got hurt? If someone died, because of me?

Rogan got to his feet and grabbed my hand. "Hey. Why the long face?"

"I'm not sure I'll be able to forgive myself if something happens to one of you. Or any of the guys from Hunters. This is *my* mission. My... desire to help these women."

Rogan dragged me to the door. "The men at Hunters risk their lives every day. This won't be new in that regard. They all have free will to make their own decisions about whether or not to participate.

Let's go see what they say, and while we're there, you may want to look for that book Shadow was talking about."

I kissed Vincent goodbye and opened the door. "What book?"

"The one the father was looking for. The one Vincent broke into your father's apartment to find."

"The book with your family's details," Vincent reminded me.

Oh. That book.

CHAPTER 6

SADIE

We walked to the workshop and found a man from the Hunters' staff—Travis, I think his name was—hanging around. He was obviously waiting for us to arrive.

"Hey," I greeted him, as Fridge unlocked the door.

"Did you guys hear?" Travis asked, his voice excited to share whatever news he had.

I looked over at him as I walked to the stairs that led to my office on the top floor. "Hear what?"

"They found Terry this morning, at his house. He's dead."

My knees gave way and I grabbed for the railing as I fell onto the stairs. "No."

There was silence all around us, then Travis said, "Yep. His wife found him in the living room."

My breath wheezed in my throat as my ribs crushed my lungs. *Oh my God.*

"A vampire?" *It has to be.* "Uncle Terry said he had to speak to me... I put him off. I didn't think... fucking hell."

He had wanted to tell me something important about my

father's death and I'd been too drunk to listen. What if he'd had the final piece of this puzzle, and now it was gone forever?

Along with him.

Tears burned my eyes and I blinked, causing them to cascade down my cheeks.

I couldn't believe it.

I ran my hands over my head, pressing into my temples, where there was a sudden burst of pain. "They did this to him because of me."

It had to be a warning. For all of us to back off. And Uncle Terry had somehow been the one to pay the price.

"What do you mean?" Travis asked.

Rogan moved over and took my hands, lifting me to my feet. "This is not your fault, Sadie. Terry had his own demons. Do you want me to take you home? Or..."

"No!" I gathered myself and planted a fake smile on my lips. "I want to be here. It's just a... shock. I've known him most of my life."

I swallowed hard and forced some strength into my legs. "I have to do a few things in the office. Check in with my old firm... see you guys later."

I stumbled up the stairs on unsteady legs and managed to get inside my dad's office and shut the door, before completely breaking down.

Oh my God... first Dad, then Uncle Terry?

I grabbed a box of tissues, found a corner and cried for the man who'd loved me. Who'd had something important to tell me yesterday, but I hadn't wanted to listen.

I'd been too drunk, too melancholy. Too annoyed at him for obviously having something to do with the vampire Father Bartholomew, and not necessarily in a good way.

When I was finally cried out, I crawled over to the fridge in my father's office and took out a bottle of water. I wiped my face and blew my nose, and guzzled the water.

Too much loss in too little time.

But now the question was, did Terry's death have anything to do with my father's? Or the blood ring and what we'd done the other day?

Or was it something else entirely?

There was a knock at the door and I hauled myself to my feet.

My eyes were red and puffy, but I called out, "Come in," assuming it would be one of my mates. Fridge and Rogan rarely left me alone for more than ten minutes, especially when they knew I was upset.

But instead of seeing one of my lovers walk in, a familiar face popped his head around the door.

"Hello, cousin," Shadow said, as he slunk his way into the office and shut the door behind him.

He limped to the desk, his long hair brushed back off his face for once. His weird, purple eyes almost glowed as he assessed me, and I smiled in greeting, happy to see him.

"Shadow. What brings you here?"

He frowned as he stared at me, leaning on the cane he'd brought with him. "Are you okay?"

I waved at my red, blotchy face. "Oh. Yeah. Ignore this. It's fine."

"What's happened?" he asked.

I grabbed another bottle of water from the fridge and gestured to him. "You want a Coke?"

The man loved sugar from what I could tell, yet was as lean as a whippet.

"Yes, please," he said and fell into the chair.

"You okay?" I asked, pushing the can across the desk and frowning at the grimace on his face and the way he moved. He was obviously in pain.

He smiled, his skin shimmering with the slight amount of snake in his shifting genes. "I'm fine. It's you I'm worried about. What's going on?"

I shrugged and sat down on my father's executive chair. "My father's oldest friend was found this morning. Dead."

"A vampire?" Shadow asked, cracking the can open and taking a sip.

I nodded. "They believe so. I only just heard, and I'm still in a little shock. I knew Uncle Terry as a kid… he was always looking out for me."

"Terry… your father's hunter," Shadow said, and his voice held an odd tone. Cold.

I frowned. "Yes. Why? Did you know him?"

Shadow nodded. "Sadly, yes. Your father, a few years ago, suspected Terry Morrissen of having dealings with the vampires behind his back. And he asked me to investigate him. Discreetly."

I sat up, leaning forward. "What did you find?"

Shadow pressed his lips together. "That he was betraying your father, in the worst of ways."

I swallowed hard. "And what ways were those?" Although, I could guess. There were only a few things my father would see as betrayal. And they had everything to do with his business… or my mother.

Shadow leaned backwards and lifted his leg to put his ankle over his knee. "The vampires have wanted you since the day they learned of your mother's strength and blood type. But none of the vampires would take you, because they were all repulsed."

Despite the creepy coldness crawling over my skin at his words, I chuckled. My mother had done an amazing thing by making me so unpalatable to the vampires.

Shadow continued. "So, the fathers went to Terry and convinced him to grab you."

My mouth dropped open. "He agreed?"

Shadow glanced away. "I'm afraid so."

I shook my head. "No. Surely, he must have been coerced. They could have threatened him."

The man I'd known wouldn't have sold me out. No way.

Shadow simply looked at me, pity in his gaze. "I'm sorry, Sadie. But they offered him money, and he accepted. He knew what they'd do to you, and he still agreed."

My nose and eyes burned with the threat of more tears, but this time, they were angry tears.

I wiped them away. "I seriously can't believe it."

Shadow nodded. "I told Jack what I'd found, and Terry was retired off. I don't think your dad ever told anyone what Terry had been willing to do, but he made sure the man never worked again."

So that was why Terry had retired at age fifty, when he was still lean and fit and strong. My father had forced him. Wow.

I stared at Shadow as he took another mouthful of the sugary drink and set the can down on the desk in front of us. Was that what he'd wanted to talk to me about?

"What brings you here, Shadow? I assume it was nothing to do with Unc... err... Terry's death?"

Shadow shifted on his seat. "I've come to express my support of your endeavor."

I blinked. "My endeavor? What do you mean, exactly?"

There were so many possibilities whirling through my mind.

He cleared his throat. "I mean..." He dropped his voice to a whisper. "Going into the underground and freeing the women in the blood ring. I want to come with you. I want to help."

My mouth dropped open, then warmth filled my chest. Love for the only family I knew blossomed and strengthened my resolve.

"Shadow, I am... truly... so grateful that you would offer such a thing for me." I swallowed hard against the wave of emotion that batted at me.

I took a breath and continued on, "But I think I've come to the conclusion that I can't do it. I want to... boy, do I want to." I shook my head.

"Then what's the problem?" Shadow asked.

I stared at him for a moment, and raised my eyebrows. "You were one of the people who tried to talk me out of it, remember? You said that for every person we free, they'll just find another to take her place. And after what I experienced yesterday..." I shuddered at the memory. "Meeting Bartholomew and feeling his power, the wrath we would incur if we took him on... It's just not worth it. I can't risk my mates' lives... my employee's lives... in a battle we probably can't win."

Not to mention the fact that even if we succeeded, we'd have to leave the city, the business and the house all behind. It was too shattering to consider, and the risks were just too high.

I'd have nightmares for the rest of my life about what I'd seen in the blood ring, but my father had died to protect me. I couldn't have his death be in vain because I couldn't keep myself from doing something stupid.

Shadow shifted uncomfortably.

I narrowed my eyes at him. "What aren't you telling me? Why do you really want to come with us?"

He had access to the underground, and he was known everywhere according to the boys, for being able to do anything. Find anyone. He was untouchable, and highly sought after for his services.

Why risk his life for us? For me?

Shadow pulled another face and didn't answer.

I rolled my eyes at him. "Oh, come on. You don't usually hold back on me."

In fact, Shadow was always refreshingly honest. Something I loved about him.

"Well," he began, then took a long draw on the cigarette he'd lit. "I recently got into quite the scuffle with an older vamp. I won, by the skin of my teeth. I think if I smelled, or tasted any better than I do, I'd be dead, rather than sitting here talking to you."

Which meant he should be relishing his life, not throwing it away.

"Yeah? So?" I asked, taking a drink of my water. "What does that have to do with joining us in freeing the prisoners of the blood ring?"

Because there wasn't much he could say that would make me change my mind now.

I'd been so determined when I first found out about it. So blind to the danger. But holding my father's funeral and having that damn vampire turn up and threaten me... that had really slapped the silly out of me.

Why throw everything away? Especially now that I had all three of my mates? They completed me, and I completed them.

Nothing was worth risking their lives, and mine.

Not even the blood ring.

Shadow glanced up at me and met my gaze with a look I'd never forget, and spilled the words that would be forged into my memory for the rest of my days.

"Because the vampire that I fought, that is now dead, told me your mother didn't die in the explosion that took down the blood ring twenty years ago. She survived. And as far as that vampire knew, she's still down there."

CHAPTER 7
SADIE

*S*he's been held down there all that time? For years?

My mouth dropped open and I let the first thought in my head fly out of my mouth.

"You've gotta be fucking kidding me."

Shadow flinched, glanced away, then rearranged himself by sitting up straighter and putting his cigarette out in the ashtray discreetly tucked near the corner of the desk. Somehow, I hadn't noticed that before.

Then he looked straight at me so I could see the honesty that was as obvious as the pain on his face. "Your mother could be alive, Sadie. I'm so sorry I didn't find out earlier."

Hot tears filled my eyes and coursed down my face unchecked. I had no idea what to say. What my mother must have endured...

"Um..." I shook my head, speechless for a moment.

Shadow made a strange, growly sound and tsked with disgust. "I wish I'd found out while your father was still alive. We could have re-united them."

I slid forward in my chair, my hand shaking as I reached for the edge of the desk. It offered something to cling to on this cliff top I now found myself teetering on.

The tears kept rolling and as much as I hated showing weakness, I didn't even try to stop them. I couldn't.

She's alive?

My heart banged so loud in my chest I didn't know if I'd hear Shadow if he spoke again, so I forced myself to take a few deep breaths, trying to calm my system.

Don't have a panic attack. That would be embarrassing.

Breathe. Just breathe.

"Okay," I managed at last. "How... how credible do you think that vampire was? Your source?"

Because he could have been lying. That's likely. Especially if they'd been in a fight to the death.

In fact, it was probably more than likely.

Shadow ran his hand over the back of his neck in a thoughtful gesture. Then he looked up again. "I'd stake my reputation on it."

I fell back against the chair. "Holy fuck."

Shadow barked out a laugh. "Ah... yeah. That was my reaction too."

I stood up, needing to move around once my tears had stopped flowing and my anxiety turned into energy. "So... if that vampire is right... we... we..." I couldn't believe I was flip-flopping over this topic. Again.

Shadow shook his head. "You can't leave her down there. It's already been twenty years."

"I know." I shuddered, wrapping my arms around my body as images of the women under the ground swam up in my mind.

Could one of them have been my mother?

Then I stopped pacing and faced Shadow, my mouth dropping open. "Oh my God. Do you think she could have been pregnant down there? Could she have other children?"

Would they be alive?

Shadow stood up so we were eye to eye again. "Don't even think about that, Sadie. One step at a time."

"Which step is first?" I asked, biting on my nails in a childhood habit I'd kicked a long time ago.

"First step... destroy the book."

"Which book?" I asked, then remembered in a flash. "The book! The book with lists... details. The one they've all been looking for?"

Shadow nodded. "Yes. The details of your mother's family. A document detailing the lineage of her witch blood. The book your father was killed for. Although, I have a feeling it was about more than that. But that book was ample reason for the vampires to order the hit."

It came to me in a flash, like my subconscious had been working on the puzzle for hours then pulled the file out of the filing cabinet of my brain, brandishing the answer with an, "aha!"

I knew where it was. I'd seen it before, not that I'd recognized it at the time.

I rushed across the room and pushed open the false wall, revealing my father's safe. I spun the dial around to the digits of my birthday. "I saw this book last week but couldn't make hide nor hair of what the numbers meant. It might not be anything but..."

The safe door popped open and I grabbed the book out from beneath the pile of cash and locked it again, spinning the dial quickly for good measure.

I rushed back over to Shadow and we sat side by side in the chairs on the client side of my father's desk. I handed it over to him, my heart now pounding with excitement. "Is this it?"

He took the leather-bound book and began flicking through the pages.

"I didn't know what it was when I saw it. I just assumed it was a list of bounties, or something to do with work. My dad always preferred paper copies of everything. He hated technology. Computers. Phones." I yammered on, nervously jiggling my knee as Shadow's keen gaze flipped from page to page.

Then he stood up. "We need to burn it."

I jumped up next to him. "This is it?"

He nodded. "I recognize some of the addresses and can see the numbers in a pattern on each page. It would be difficult for most people to decipher, but either way, we need to get rid of this."

I gestured to the book. "Well, you have the matches." That was one good thing about knowing a smoker. Always ready with a light for birthday candles... or when you needed to destroy a priceless book.

He grinned at me. "Where's your dragon? He'd do a better job at disintegrating this than me."

I laughed, loosening some of the tension in my tight chest. "I don't think he has that sort of control over his shifter to be able to just puff out a tiny bit of fire. Come on. Come on." I impatiently jiggled on the ground.

Shadow glanced around. "Do you have a metal trash can? And maybe some water? This is gonna set off the fire alarms otherwise."

I ran for the door and raced into the workshop, finding a large container and taking it back to the office for Shadow.

He grinned at me, flicked open his silver lighter, and opened the book.

I watched with glee and a certain amount of regret as he set alight the pages. That was a list with details of my family. My only living relatives that I knew of.

But better they were safe.

The pages burned brightly in a flare of orange and yellow before he dropped the burning book into the metal container and smoke began to billow out.

"The water," he said, and I grabbed for my bottle, handing it to him.

He doused the flames.

I stared down at the lump of charred leather in the base of the trash can. "They shouldn't be able to decipher anything now."

He laughed. "No. They'd have to be magicians."

I fell back into my chair. "So... one thing done. What's next?"

"Next, we seriously think about whether it's truly possible that your mother has survived all this time," Shadow said, gingerly sitting back down.

I frowned at him. "I thought you said you'd bet your reputation on it."

He nodded and reached for his can of Coke. "I would. I believe that she survived the accident and that they probably got her into the blood ring, but the vampire wasn't sure if she was *still* down there. He couldn't—or wouldn't—say."

I swallowed hard, my heart plummeting. "So, you still think she might be dead?"

I wasn't sure what was worse. Part of me was hoping she'd died quickly. That would be better than a slow, painful death, after years of torture. Wouldn't it? I couldn't think of anything worse.

Shadow clicked his tongue. "I honestly don't know. It would take an iron will... more, to survive that long underground. Especially with blood like hers. I would have thought a father would have drained her immediately. And with her magic... why she wouldn't have escaped before now..." He tsked again.

I sighed and leaned back in the chair, running my hands up and down the armrests. "So, you're saying... what *are* you saying, Shadow?"

I was on a roller coaster of emotions and my nerves were already stretched thin.

He huffed out a laugh. "I guess what I'm saying is... I found out that your mother lived, at least longer than any of us thought. And I... I feel like I owe it to you, and to Jack, to see if it's possible that she or any children she may have had remain in the underground."

I shuddered again but pushed through the feeling. Children... underground...

"I..." I swallowed. "I feel the same way. If you truly believe that there's even a chance that my mother could still be alive."

Shadow nodded. "I do. I hate to say it, and I don't want to give you false hope, but I know people, and that vampire was telling the truth. As far as he was concerned, she's still alive."

My breath caught in my throat.

Then a thought occurred to me. "So... my mother's grave?" I tilted my head to the side. "Who's buried there? *What's* buried there?"

Shadow shrugged. "I honestly don't know."

"That would be a way of finding out if she's alive," I said. "We could check her grave and see if the coffin is empty."

Shadow's mouth dropped open.

I pressed my lips together to stop from laughing at his reaction. "Too morbid?"

He shook his head. "Ah, no. It's clever, I suppose."

There was a brief knock at the door and Rogan walked in. He stopped as soon as he saw my visitor. "Oh, hey, Shadow. I didn't know you were here."

Shadow got up slowly and turned to my wolf mate. "I like it that way." He grinned. "I'll leave you two alone, but I'll be back in two days, Sadie. I'll be ready to go, if you are."

He nodded to us both and limped out the door once more.

I stared after him. "He's so quiet, and yet he really does know how to make an exit, doesn't he?"

Rogan nodded. "Yeah. Anyway... what did he want?"

I exhaled slowly, running my hands through my hair, trying to put together all my scrambled thoughts.

"Um..." I leaned back on the big desk, sitting on the edge. "He thinks my mother might still be alive."

I still couldn't believe it. It seemed surreal to even say the words as a possibility.

"Holy shit," Rogan said, his eyes bugging out of his head.

I huffed out a laugh. "Yeah. We were just discussing whether it's worth digging up her grave to confirm there's no body down there, but surely there's an easier way to find that out?"

Rogan nodded. "Well, yeah. We can talk to the coroner. The cemetery director. See if there is some sort of record."

The coroner was as corrupt as they came. Probably half the people in this city were.

I glanced over at my father's photo still sitting on the desk. "Well, I was planning on burying my dad with her. Perhaps we can ask them to dig the grave up for me to put him down there."

"And while we're down there, open her coffin," Rogan finished for me.

I nodded. "Yeah. I know it's totally horrific. But if she isn't down there and this has been an elaborate ruse, I want to know."

Then a thought struck me, and I looked straight at Rogan. "Do you think my father suspected something? After all, he would have known if she'd been in that coffin or not. And now that I think about it, he never went there to see her or talk to her. Used to say that he carried her with him everywhere he went, and he didn't need to visit a tombstone to talk to her."

And the more I thought about it, the more it seemed possible.

I continued, "But surely he wouldn't have known she was alive and not done anything about it?"

Rogan shook his head. "No way. He believed she was dead. I heard him say more than once that he'd give up everything to have her back."

I blinked rapidly to stem yet another flow of tears and focus on the job ahead.

I cleared my throat. "Shadow also came to offer assistance."

"In what way?" Rogan asked.

"He wants to come down to the underground with us. Be part of the rescue mission. And to be honest, I was starting to think I shouldn't go through with it. In fact, I'd made up my mind not to go. But now—"

"Now we have to go," Rogan finished for me.

Fridge walked into the room. "Have to go where?"

Rogan filled him in quickly about everything I'd said and Fridge's mouth dropped open, just as mine had when Shadow told me the news.

Then he turned to me and met my gaze with dragon irises and a flash of excitement I'd never seen in him before. It bordered on dangerous and I knew he would be a formidable enemy.

"Well, what the hell are we doing standing around then? We have an army to assemble!"

CHAPTER 8
ROGAN

Getting Sadie's mother's funeral plot dug up was simpler than we thought it would be. As her mother's legal husband, Jack had every right to rest alongside her.

The funeral director had counseled us to only make a place for his ashes by her tombstone, but we'd said they both wanted to be in the earth.

So here we stood, staring down into a huge hole, waiting for the emergence of Sadie's mother's coffin.

The guy driving the backhoe had been paid off by Fridge to go on a coffee break when we said to, and when we heard the distinctive thud of him hitting something solid in the large hole, the digger was withdrawn and the guy jumped out with a wave.

"Back in five," he said.

Sadie squeezed my hand tight as we stared down at the dirt-crusted lid of a varnished coffin. I'd assumed it would be practically dust after twenty years in the earth.

"You ready for this?" Fridge asked as he sat down on the ground and swung his legs over, so they were dangling in the hole.

We'd decided he'd be the one to pull back the coffin lid and look, but I had the feeling Sadie wouldn't let the moment go by without looking herself.

Sadie nodded and clung tighter to me. One of her arms wrapped around mine. The other desperately clung to her father's ashes. "Yes. Please. Let's see what's down there."

Fridge nodded and jumped, landing with a thud on top of the coffin.

"Quick Fridge, open it," I urged him. "Before your weight breaks a hole in the lid."

The fucker weighed a ton. I wasn't sure how much weight an old coffin could take. Though six feet of dirt was no small amount.

Fridge dropped to one knee and pulled hard, pushing the dirt away and groaning with the strain of trying to open the lid, until finally... it creaked open.

Fridge looked around the corner of the lid but didn't respond with a noise.

Instead he looked up at us, then with one move, pushed open the lid and revealed... nothing, save the old satin lining.

It was empty inside.

Sadie turned her head into my shoulder and began to sob.

With relief or pain, I wasn't sure. But I nodded at Fridge, who pushed the lid back down again and hopped out of the dirt hole.

"Do you want to bury your father here, anyway? Or..."

She shook her head and tucked the urn even closer to her body. "No. I'm taking him home."

She turned away and walked back to the car.

Fridge walked over to me, brushing at his jeans and tank. "I need a shower now. Ugh."

"When she says home, what does she mean?" I asked him. "Taking Jack home."

Fridge shrugged. "I don't know. But Hunters was the closest thing to a family I've ever known. I'm guessing that's where she means."

And as it turned out, the dragon's guess was correct. We got in the car and Sadie directed us back to the workshop and placed her dad back in the safe, declaring that until she had another home for him, he'd stay where he was most comfortable.

By the time Sadie, Rogan and Fridge arrived back at the hotel from work, I was dying to see them all. With them at work twelve hours a day, I was starting to understand why some vampires chose a more mortal life and gave up the strengths of a paranormal to do so.

I was living an entirely different life from my mates, and it sucked.

"Hello, beautiful," I said, rushing forward as Sadie stepped into the room. I picked her up, sweeping her literally off her feet and carrying her over to the couch. "I missed you today."

I kissed her and tasted the sweetness of her lips, groaning with pleasure as I did.

I felt more than heard the growl of disapproval from the other two in the room.

Too bad. They'd had her all day. I ignored them, running my hands over my mate's lush body, cupping her breasts and grabbing her ass until she was moaning and squirming in my lap.

Eventually she pulled back, gasping and red-faced. "That is a welcome home!"

I shrugged and grinned at her, noticing Fridge out of the corner of my eye staring at us.

I turned to look at him and arched a brow. "Yes?"

"Ssss...Sadie," Fridge said, his voice now containing a strange snake-like tremble. "Tell him what we did today."

Sadie turned back to me with a huge grin. "Well..." And she

launched off on a story I would have thought was fiction if I didn't trust the sources so well.

By the end of it, my head was blown apart.

"Hang on a second," I said, still holding Sadie in my lap. "All of that happened, today?"

I missed one single workday and the whole world turned on its head.

She nodded. "We don't want to waste any time, especially with Shadow on our side now."

I kissed the tip of her nose. "Well, I believe he was always on your side, but to openly declare that he'd go into the underground with us? That's enormous."

She tilted her head. "I agree, but why do you think so?"

"Well, it gives us a huge advantage, for one thing. Shadow can see underground due to his mix of shifters, and he is lethal in a fight." More than lethal. The guy's reputation was staggering based on how many people he'd taken down. "With him on our side and perhaps more of your hunters, we actually have a chance of getting those women out, assuming the vampire fathers haven't changed anything down there."

That was my biggest fear. We'd go down into the underground and be led into a trap, and I'd be there to watch all my mates die.

I shivered and shook myself. "So, you've decided? We're definitely doing this?"

"Hell, yes," came Fridge's response. "I need a shower. Can you order me a steak for dinner?"

He stood and I had to force myself not to turn around and watch him saunter off into the bedroom and through to the bathroom. He had such a nice ass.

I glanced up at Sadie, who was staring at me strangely.

I forced a smile to my face. "I'll follow you anywhere, my love. So, if you want to do this, I will do everything in my power to help you."

Sadie ran her fingertips over my lips. "Would you go sort out your shit with Fridge?"

My eyebrows flicked upwards. "What do you mean? Now?"

Fridge wouldn't like that, me going to him while he was naked and vulnerable.

She nodded and took a sniff of me and smiled. "You kinda smell like you need a shower too."

I frowned at her. "He won't like that, Sadie."

She slid off my lap and grabbed my hand, pulling me to my feet. "For me? Please? Just... make peace with him."

She shoved me toward the bedroom and I glanced over at Rogan for help. He looked as worried as I felt.

I called out to him, "Tell her this is a terrible idea."

He shrugged. "Just don't go in there clothed. It'll make him feel like you have the advantage."

My mouth dropped open. "So, you want me to go in there naked as well? Great."

Two against one wasn't fair.

Rogan shrugged. "Look. We're about to go into a pretty intense, stressful scenario. It would be better if you two were good... or at least on the same page with trust and stuff."

I pinched the bridge of my nose. Damn these young mortals.

"Fine." I walked toward the bedroom and began to unbutton my shirt. "But if he kicks me out, or goes all dragon and smashes stuff, it's on you."

I slammed the bedroom door behind me and grumbled as I tugged off all my clothes. I turned to the closed bathroom door, naked.

Fuck.

I wasn't ready for this.

But considering we had two days until we literally walked into hell and wouldn't necessarily walk out, what did I have to lose?

I opened the door and walked straight into the bathroom, then stopped short, my greeting frozen on my lips.

Fridge was standing in the shower, one arm outstretched, pressing into the tiles and the shower head making water flow down his strong back.

The other hand was working his cock, his breathing coming in pants and gasps.

When he heard the door open, he stopped and turned toward me.

His cock was an angry red, standing straight up against his belly.

His gaze turned vicious as he ground out, "Get out."

I should have. God knows, I should have. But instead of doing what he wanted, I shut the door and slid the lock into place.

Then I turned back to him and tried to stay as calm as possible. "Sadie told me to take a shower and to sort out whatever's wrong between us."

"I told you to get out," Fridge growled, and despite his tension, his erection was still holding, high and hard.

I glanced down at it, then back at Fridge.

I tried a different tack. "If you wanted some help with that, I'm sure Sadie could have stepped up."

Fridge lowered his brows at me but didn't say anything.

I swallowed hard. "You know, it's very possible that we're both going to die in the next two days, so I'd appreciate it if we kept the glaring and fighting to a minimum. After all, we may as well get along until then."

Fridge stormed right up to me and glared down into my face. He was huffing and puffing, and his muscles looked bigger and better than ever.

"Listen, vampire. I don't want you in here."

His cock tapped me on the belly, and I glanced down at the head as it pressed into me.

I'd never wanted a man before. Not sexually. Not like this.

Everything about him was beautiful. From the arrow shaped head of his swollen cock, down to his huge, strong feet.

I looked back up at him and grinned into the face of a very angry dragon shifter. "You might not. But one part of you does. Which head should I listen to?"

Fridge growled loudly and went to grab me. I wasn't going to stand by and let him try to start a fight. He wouldn't win anyway. So, I grabbed his arm, swiped his legs out from under him, and when he landed on his stubborn ass with a grunt, I sat on top of him, straddling his waist.

"Get. Off. Me," Fridge ground out between clenched teeth.

I held him down with both hands pinned to the tiles beneath us and glared down at him. "Why the hell are you fighting me? You could just finish having your shower and leave."

I began to rub my ass along his cock, up and down the shaft, while my own shaft got harder and more difficult to ignore.

Fridge growled again and this time I decided I'd let him up. I didn't really want to mount him on the floor, though it was tempting.

I jumped up and slid toward the shower so he could get to his feet and growl if he needed to.

I stepped beneath the water and grabbed the soap, applying it to my hand and beginning to stroke my own cock.

I groaned as pleasure pulsed through me and Fridge froze a few feet from me, his eyes wide and assessing.

"So, are we gonna sort out what's wrong with you?" I asked him. "Or are you leaving this bathroom angry and horny as hell?"

Fridge stared at me, his green-eyed gaze going down to my groin and back up again to my face.

I tilted my head back under the water, feeling my fangs begin to descend. I was so frustrated with him. With the whole situation. But I was turned on as well. The tingles of my impending orgasm sparked at the base of my spine, making me shiver beneath the hot water.

I didn't look at him when I said, "You better make up your mind, because I'm going to come soon."

I didn't hear him move, but I felt him grab me as he lifted me up and pressed me against the cold tiles behind us.

I didn't open my eyes, I just clung to his shoulders as he grabbed my ass with his hands and growled against my ear, "Not without me."

CHAPTER 9

FRIDGE

I was insane. It was official.

But the vampire was right, about too many things to name. So instead of thinking about how fucked-up my head was, I focused on the one thing that made sense.

We both were probably gonna die in the underground in a few days. And I was angry. Not because we were going to die, but because I wanted to shove my cock inside this guy almost as much as I wanted to do the same with Sadie. When she screamed my name, it caused everything in me to sing.

I had the feeling that hearing Vincent do the same, would have a similar effect. It wasn't natural; it wasn't normal.

But fuck it.

He smelled so good, and every part of me—shifter and human—was crying out for this moment. For Vincent...

I grabbed him and lifted him up against the wall, uncaring of how rough I was, because he didn't seem to care.

His legs wrapped around my hips and I clutched his ass, all tight muscle and cool skin beneath the hot water.

I bent my head, unable to look at him while my body pressed so intimately against his, and closed my eyes and inhaled him.

Every sense went on high alert at the intoxicating scent. At the feel of his skin under my lips as I lowered them to his neck.

Why did this feel so right? I'd counted on it to feel wrong.

But, no... it felt as good as it did with Sadie.

I reached for the soap and slid it over his ass, sliding my cock along his butt cheeks and loving the way he groaned and pushed against me.

There was something about sex with a woman that always reminded me they were fragile. That I needed to take care in how I used my body, where I lay, what I pressed on. But a primal understanding within me knew that Vincent and I could knock down walls together, and neither of us would get hurt.

"Do it. Please," Vincent ground out, bucking against me.

I slid toward his hole.

I clenched my teeth against the wave of lust that slammed into me. There was no going back now.

My arms trembled as I pulled him down onto my cock.

Vincent cried out as I impaled him, his flesh parting easily as I slid up into him and closing around me like a tight fist.

I gasped loudly, clenching everything inside me to stop from coming on the spot.

"Holy. Fucking. Hell," I ground out, breathing hard and leaning forward to drop my forehead onto the tiles next to Vincent's face.

So good.

Pleasure pulsed through every cell in my body, making my muscles tremble and my balls tighten up.

Heat coursed up the backs of my thighs and spread up over my back.

Oh God...

"Fuck me. Quickly. Before I come." Vincent spoke next to my ear.

My dragon roared inside me as I pulled out and thrust back in, fucking Vincent into the tiles over and over again.

Vincent groaned with every thrust and I glanced down, seeing his cock between us, pressed between our bodies.

I stepped back from the wall and held up his body with one hand while grabbing for his thick cock with my other hand.

It throbbed in my grip and Vincent groaned, his ass squeezing tight around me.

"I... oh..." Vincent's eyes opened and met my gaze. I couldn't look away as he began to climax.

His cock spurted between us while he shuddered in my arms, his ass squeezing the head of my cock so hard I had no option but to let go of everything and allow the pleasure to take me.

I grabbed his waist with both hands and fucked him hard and fast, riding through the waves of my orgasm as the hot wave flooded my body, making me cry out loud, and long.

As the wave began to subside, I withdrew from Vincent's body and lowered him down, stepping back under the shower, letting the hot water wash away the scent of our coupling.

The vampire's mouth was open, his fangs extended, obviously in need of his next meal. His eyes were shut, so I stared at him openly.

He rested against the tiled wall, his head back, his chest rising and falling as he panted for breath.

Regret came on swift wings, though why I should care now, I wasn't sure.

I turned to walk away and heard Vincent's voice behind me. "So, we're good?"

I stiffened, not wanting to turn and look at him with his face still ecstatic from the bliss we'd shared.

Especially while my body still throbbed for more.

I spoke without turning around. "Yeah, we're good."

I unlocked the bathroom door, got dressed as quickly as possible and found Sadie and Rogan in the main living area, staring at me with wide eyes and matching huge smiles.

I left the hotel room in the guise of needing a walk.

I promised Sadie I wouldn't be long. After all, we needed to plan the takedown of the biggest vampire syndicate in the history of our city. But for an hour, I needed to be by myself.

I needed to work out how I was going to live with this part of my existence.

I was mated to Sadie, but I also wanted Vincent. I wanted *both* of them with every fiber of my being. They fulfilled very different needs in me—needs that I'd never known existed until now. How was that possible?

Because, at the moment, my dragon and I were at odds.

He wanted Vincent, over and over again. The fool even wanted to *feed* the vampire. What sort of stupid shifter craved that?

And he also wanted Sadie—but that was a need I was much more comfortable admitting with both sides of my shifter soul.

The human, straight male side of me was happier than I'd ever been, with her as my mate. But when it came to Vincent? My human side was disgusted with myself. How could I want them *both* so damn much?

So for now, I walked.

VINCENT

I could barely stand after my first session with Fridge.

I couldn't stop the stupid smile that lifted my lips. I hoped it wouldn't be our last.

I took my time under the shower, slowly washing my body and noticing the parts of me that would have been sore, if I'd been human.

But I wasn't in pain or discomfort. I was so satisfied, I felt like I could sleep for a week. Which was saying something, for a vamp who didn't really sleep.

The bathroom door that Fridge had unlocked opened suddenly. Sadie and Rogan stood in the doorway.

They were smiling at me, though there was also an expectant looks in their eyes, as if they were a little worried about me.

"Are you both all right?" I asked, turning off the shower and grabbing a towel to dry myself.

Rogan crossed his arms over his chest.

Sadie's lips tilted up further. "Ah, yeah... we're okay. Are you?"

I nodded. "Yeah, of course. Why?"

Rogan sniffed. "Because it sounded like you guys were in a fight for a while there, and then, well..."

He shrugged and I knew, despite the running shower masking some of the noise, that they'd probably figured out what had happened.

"Fridge looked pretty pissed off when he stomped out of the bedroom," Sadie said. "We just thought maybe we should check on you."

I burst out laughing. "Um... I'm good. So is Fridge, I think. Don't worry about it. We'll be fine."

Rogan inhaled sharply again, then narrowed his eyes. "So you too did...."

I raised one eyebrow at him, knowing the nose of a full blood wolf shifter would be able to smell the scent of sex on the air. Of our seed. Though most of the evidence was washed away now.

I could certainly still smell it.

Smell *us*.

I ignored Rogan's half statement and stepped forward, still naked. "Would you mind if I got dressed again?"

They parted for me to walk through and find my clothes, though it felt wrong to be dressed again when I was this blissed. This... dizzy with happiness.

I knew the dragon was going to have issues with what had just happened. After all, how could he not?

Our connection would shake his beliefs about himself right down to the foundation.

"Do you mind if I..." *No, don't stay naked. Neither of them would like that.* "Ah, pants perhaps?" I mumbled.

They probably would prefer if I wasn't naked for the rest of the night.

"Is Fridge coming back?" I asked, pulling my pants on and sitting down on the bed, feeling replete and strangely tired.

Sadie walked up to me and took my face in her hands. I loved the feel of her on me, but it was so different to Fridge's touch. They were polar opposites, really. I loved that I was so attracted to both of them.

"Are you really okay?" she asked. "You look like you need blood or something."

I chuckled. That was the last thing I needed. "I'm fine, sweetheart. Though a nap isn't a bad idea. What are the plans for the rest of the night?"

Sadie bit her lip. "We were just going to chat about the attack on the blood ring. Did I tell you that I destroyed the book I found with Shadow? The one you were looking for."

That got my attention. "No. What do you mean?"

Sadie explained about them destroying the link to Sadie's mother's family and I waited for Fridge to return, because he would.

I was sure of it.

Rogan and Sadie's food arrived while we talked, and they began to eat while I watched them, enjoying the run of pleasure through my veins similar to being drunk, or over-indulging in blood.

I swayed where I sat then crawled up the bed, put my head down onto Fridge's pillow and inhaled his scent.

A feeling came over me similar to when I'd first met Sadie and inhaled her scent.

It was settling, and yet exciting.

I closed my eyes. "Can you wake me when you're ready to talk about our next step? I think I might just... rest, for a minute or two."

And I drifted into the best sleep I'd had in over two hundred years.

CHAPTER 10

SADIE

I stared Vincent laying on the bed, my fork halfway to my lips, and my mouth dropped open.

"Um, did he just fall asleep?"

Rogan glanced over at the bed and shrugged, then got back to his dinner. "It was good of him to cover the cost of the room."

I put down my fork and picked up my glass of wine, taking a large sip and enjoying the warmth that spread through my body as I swallowed. "Not just the room cost. He paid for all of it. Last week, the next two weeks, all the food and drinks. Everything."

I still couldn't believe he'd done that. All without any expectation, even without wanting a "thank you".

Rogan's eyes bugged. "Wow."

I nodded, then picked up my fork again, scooping the mushroom risotto and bringing it to my mouth.

I knew how much this room, these meals, cost. It was more than generous.

I dropped my voice to a whisper. "Do you really think they had sex in the bathroom?"

It had sounded more like a wrestling match than anything else, but it was as if something in me just knew. I had a connection to both Fridge and Vincent as well as Rogan, and it had seemed right to leave those two alone to do… whatever it was they needed to do.

"Of course, they fucked," Rogan said. "The scent was everywhere in that bathroom."

I'd had a gut feeling that Fate was playing a hand in Fridge and Vincent's relationship, too. And I couldn't be happier for them. It would make our little family even more connected; more complete.

I eyed Rogan, wondering…

"No. Uh-uh. Don't expect me to turn gay for your viewing pleasure. It's just not in me."

I grinned. He already knew me too well, it seemed. And I knew him, too. He was speaking the truth. For my wolf, there would be no one else but me. For my dragon and my vampire, I didn't mind sharing, as long as it remained between the four of us. If being together made them happy, it made me happy, too.

Rogan chewed and swallowed his steak. "You said you thought they were hot together," he said.

"Well, I do think that. But it raises a few questions in my mind."

Who was the top? Who was the bottom? What position had they done it in? I wanted to know everything!

I giggled when I realized why I was feeling the weight of disappointment in my gut. "I wish I'd gotten to see them together."

Rogan laughed. "I'm sure you will soon."

"But not you too?"

"Nope. I'm all yours, sweetheart. Like I said, I don't have it in me for…" He gestured toward the sleeping Vincent. "That."

"I don't think Fridge thought it was in him either," I whispered again.

Rogan shrugged. "Still."

As if he'd heard his name, the hotel room door opened and Fridge walked in, carrying a pint of blood in a cask. I recognized it from the distinctive marking on the dark box.

My eyebrows rose. "Got a present there, Fridge?"

Was this some sort of post-sex gift?

He glanced down at the table as if embarrassed. His gaze scanned the plates in front of us. "Well, we're all eating. And he always misses out, so..."

My mouth dropped open. *How thoughtful.* It hadn't really occurred to me that Vincent never got to eat with us. But Fridge was right. Why should Vincent miss out just because the hotel didn't serve fresh blood on their room service menu?

Fridge walked over to the bed and stared down at Vincent, sprawled on his belly, fast asleep in the place Fridge would usually sleep.

He placed the blood down on the bedside table and walked back to us, sitting down in front of his dinner and lifting the silver lid.

"Damn, that looks good."

He dove into a massive plate of steak and fries, then grabbed the beer I'd ordered for him on a whim. He downed the whole thing in a few swallows.

My gaze ran over him, looking for some sign of change. What I was looking for, I wasn't sure. But there was nothing unusual, except for the fact he wasn't meeting my eyes. And he always did.

"You feeling better?" I asked. "Did the walk help?"

He didn't glance up, instead shrugging his shoulders and continuing to eat.

I looked at Rogan, then back at Fridge. "You and Vincent sort everything out?"

"What did he say?" Fridge asked, opening a second beer.

"That you two were good," I answered honestly. "Then he passed out."

Fridge glanced over at the bed again. "Yeah. We're good."

I clapped my hands together, happiness coursing through me. I'd ignore the fact that I desperately wanted to know all the details of their sex-capade, and try to focus on our mission.

"Then we're set. We just need..." I laughed. "Everything. Plan A, Plan B. An evacuation plan. A list of people who you think we should take with us."

"And if we succeed, where you'd like to take all the women from the underground," came a sleepy, deep voice from the bed.

Vincent was stretching, sitting up, and rubbing his eyes. He still looked exhausted.

"We can wait until you've rested properly, then talk about this." I told him. "I didn't mean to start the conversation without you."

He stood up and shook his head. "No. I'm feeling much better. Is that..." He inhaled deeply through his nose and looked toward the bedside table.

I nodded. "Fridge brought it back for you."

"Really?" Vincent's gaze sought out Fridge's and I glanced between the two men, watching the flash of something dark in the dragon shifter's eyes. Pleasure filled me. Fridge looked... happy.

"Thank you," Vincent said, his voice now half an octave deeper than before.

Fridge shrugged. "No problem. You want a wine glass or something?"

The tension between them was so delicious, I was desperate to ask more, but Rogan's hand snuck out to squeeze my fingers, and when I looked at him, he shook his head as though warning me off interrupting the fragile peace between the other two.

The development of a new relationship within our foursome.

I searched inside me for jealousy, but there was none. I knew my connection with all three men in this room was strong. Finding further connections—in this case, between Fridge and Vincent— only served to make the four of us closer.

I grinned at them all, feeling like an idiot but unable to wipe the smile off my face.

Fridge grabbed a clean glass from the table and held it out.

Vincent walked over and took it, careful not to touch Fridge's fingers at the same time. "Thanks. I won't drink too much, or I'll be no good as watch tonight."

He retreated to the bed, poured himself half a glass and began to sip at it.

I smiled at him. "You can come closer than that."

He shook his head. "No. I appreciate your tolerance of me, but the smell of this will put the shifters off their meals, I'm sure."

"What do you mean, you won't be able to watch us tonight?" Fridge demanded, ripping through the remainder of his steak as though it were made of butter.

"Hungry?" I asked him with a raised eyebrow.

He ignored me.

I glanced back at our resident vampire, who was sitting casually on the bed, still shirtless. Still hot as hell.

"I don't watch you sleep or anything," he said, attempting to allay some of Fridge's obvious suspicion. "I just mean... I guard you three. I'd never forgive myself if someone snuck in here and hurt you while I was awake and off somewhere else. This hotel is ideal for me to protect you. Minimal entry points. Surveillance cameras. People everywhere."

I swiveled in my chair to look straight at Vincent. "I had no idea you'd been doing that."

It made me care for him even more. "Thank you."

But as usual, he just smiled and disregarded the enormity of his gift.

We all finished our food and ended up sprawled out around the sitting area, me next to Vincent this time, while Fridge and Rogan occupied the two armchairs.

"So, where do we go from here?" I asked. "Should I be shutting down my father's apartment and his business and preparing to flee the city?"

The men exchanged glances and my heart fell. I'd been joking. "Shit."

Vincent put a hand out and ran it soothingly over my thigh. His touch was comforting. "You probably don't need to do that, but you do need a fall back plan. If we do need to leave for a while, someone else should be ready to take over the reins."

"Like who?" I asked. "Who on earth could I entrust my father's legacy to?" Terry was gone. Dad had no close family.

"Shadow," Fridge said.

It was the only answer that made sense. "Yes, you're right. He could do it, and I trust him. But... he wants to come with us, and you said he's a great asset."

Rogan clenched his hands around the ends of his chair arm rests. "Then we disguise him, or make sure, no matter what, he isn't caught. He's a priority to get out."

Fridge nodded. "I'll agree to that, because I know he won't leave without Sadie."

Vincent chuckled. "It's true. I've seen the way he looks at her. If we protect him, he'll get her out."

"Then we're agreed," Fridge declared.

The men nodded as though it was all decided.

I don't think so. I laughed. "Hang on a second. Hold your horses."

They were deciding my future for me, and I couldn't have that. Not if it meant they'd sacrifice themselves for me.

"I'm not living without any of you, so I suggest we all find a way out or... well, let's just say, there's no choice for me."

There was a weighted silence for a moment then we moved on, hopefully with the agreement of my men.

Rogan lifted his head and began listing off names of guys who worked at Hunters.

"Barry?"

"Yep."

"Travis."

"Yeah, maybe."

"Tony? No, he just got married. Wife's pregnant too."

And it went on until they had a list of six guys Rogan and Fridge thought would say yes to our proposal and had the skills and personality to be capable of the trip.

"Anyone else?" I asked, jotting down the last name on the small tablet I'd found on the hotel's table.

I glanced at Vincent. "Anyone you want to invite on this mission?"

He shook his head. "No. I don't trust anyone from my old world not to snitch to the fathers about what we're doing."

I sighed and sat back. "Should we go around lunchtime again? Not tomorrow, but the day after?"

They all nodded, and Fridge said, "We're gonna need to empty out the vault of weapons and protective gear if we want to survive this."

"It's all yours." I grinned at my dragon shifter.

Because I could offer it all to him. It was mine. Everything my dad had ever owned.

Fridge nodded. "We can pay the guys cash from the safe, in advance, tomorrow."

"Okay." Sounded fine by me. At least then the money would get to their families, regardless of what happened.

"And organize whatever you need to do legally for Shadow to take over the business if we need to skip town for a while."

I inhaled sharply. I was a lawyer. "I can do that myself."

The men went on discussing the finer points of the team and the strengths of each man in fighting vampires.

I couldn't help but notice the men they'd left off the list. The ones with wives. The ones with kids.

I swallowed hard, trying to push down the thoughts that swirled inside my head.

Because there was something I hadn't yet told them, and it would change everything if they knew.

I was pretty sure I was pregnant. I could be wrong, of course. The stress of the past weeks could be playing with my normally clock-work-like cycle.

But that part of me I had inherited from my mother... that intuitive witch side, told me I was wrong.

I was going to have their baby.

And I wasn't telling them that. Not yet.

They'd never let me go down there if they knew. And no one was stopping me from rescuing those women. And if all the good luck, hopes and fantasy fairies were with us... maybe I'd be able to rescue my mother as well.

CHAPTER 11

ROGAN

Sadie was looking more tired and pale the longer we talked. "Hey, you wanna get to bed?"

She nodded and stifled a yawn with her hand. "Yeah, but can I ask one thing before I pass out? How are we going to transport those women, and where are we going to put them when we get them out?"

The room went silent once again, as it did each time we talked about this.

The likelihood of us making it out alive—or even at all—wasn't good.

Let alone us getting in, rescuing those women, and getting out again with all of them in one piece.

But I had to indulge the fantasy for a minute. Because if there was the faintest chance we could pull off the impossible, then we had to be ready.

"Well, they'll need a hospital. That's for damn sure."

Fridge snorted. "Yeah, but half the doctors in this city are vampires, and no one is going to believe we just found these starving, pregnant, drained women by the side of the road."

Vincent cleared his throat. "There is a hospital that vampires take their victims to if they go a little far with feeding and don't want them to die."

We all turned to stare at him.

I was the one who broke the silence. "That would be ideal. Though I had no idea such a place existed."

Vincent sighed. "I wish it didn't and personally, I've only been there once. Not for myself, but for a woman I found one night. The vampire and I were friends and he over-indulged accidentally, then we both carried her there. He showed me the way. It is expensive, but very discreet. The staff could definitely help us if we had the cash. Which I do."

I clapped my hands together once, a grin splitting my face. "This plan is certainly coming together better than I thought it would."

Sadie yawned again and I got up out of my chair and reached for her. "I think it's time for bed, beautiful."

She nodded and took my hand, smiling as I kissed her soft lips.

I moaned as lust spread through me. Damn, I wanted her. It had been too long since the last time I'd been inside her. But she truly looked exhausted. I would have to be patient. For now.

As though she read my thoughts she chuckled softly. "Can it wait until tomorrow? I am exhausted."

I laughed and groaned at the same time. "Of course. If I have to."

She suddenly grinned at me, then shot a look toward Fridge and Vincent. "Well, you could always..."

"Nope. I'll wait for you, thank you very much," I said, turning her around and spanking her cheeky bum.

She could keep her teasing to herself.

"What was that about?" Fridge asked, his eyelids dropping to a hooded expression of annoyance as he stood up to join us.

"Nothing. It's all good."

I turned to Vincent, who was still sitting on the couch. Should I invite him to join us?

"Um. We're kinda bed hogs, but if you wanna come…"

Vincent held his hand up as though to say stop. "Thank you. I appreciate the offer, and perhaps one day that will be where we're all comfortable. But for the moment, I'll stay here and think about some of the… intricacies of the plan."

I nodded at the vampire who'd joined our family. Unbeknownst to me, he was quite the team player, and I was glad he was on our side.

"Okay. See you in the morning, then."

"You will, indeed," Vincent said, standing up to smile and nod his head in that old-fashioned way he had.

Fridge hesitated, not following me. So, I walked away and stepped into the bedroom, stripping off my clothes and listening for sounds from the other room.

If something was said between them, even my shifter hearing couldn't pick it up, and by the time I'd climbed into bed with Sadie, Fridge had joined us.

He seemed agitated, but stripped quickly then climbed beneath the sheets.

We fell into a heap, arms and legs everywhere, and even though my mind raced, I dropped into a deep sleep within minutes.

Rogan

The next day we went to the workshop. Vincent asked me to call him if anything out of the norm happened. I think the poor guy was starting to feel left out with us working all the time.

I wasn't sure why he didn't just join us at the workshop, but until this was all settled, it was probably best he maintain his strength. And the way to do that, of course, was to keep being a traditional vampire and only come out at night.

Sadie retreated straight to her office saying she needed to sort out the legalities of what might happen tomorrow.

So, Fridge and I were left standing in the foyer.

"Did you contact everyone on the list?" Fridge asked.

I nodded. "Yeah. They're all coming in around noon."

"Then I better start getting prepared for tomorrow," Fridge said, indicating the vault beneath the stairs. "Start loading up bags and kits for everyone."

I nodded. "Okay." I checked my watch. "We only have an hour, so I'll get to contacting Shadow and checking on today's bounties."

Fridge nodded and we went in opposite directions.

By the time the men we'd invited to the workshop arrived, my gut was in knots.

I couldn't really believe what we were about to do. Part of me didn't believe I'd gone down in the underground in the first place.

Fridge and I would have died without Vincent, and that was only against one vampire. Now we were going down again, and actually taking on the whole blood ring.

I couldn't see how we'd make it out.

"They're here," Fridge said unnecessarily, indicating the foyer, where most of the guys were already congregating.

I nodded. "I'll go get Sadie. Meet you in the training room?"

It was the only space in the workshop big enough for all nine of us.

Fridge nodded and herded the others to the training room. When I got back with Sadie, she and I headed to the front of the crowd and Fridge stood at the back, locking the door so no one else could sneak in.

Sadie stared out at the men, wringing her hands.

I stood just behind her, making sure she knew I was there if she needed me. She shot me a quick, grateful smile.

"Thank you all for coming today at our request," she said.

"Yeah, what's this about?" Travis asked.

"Fridge wouldn't say," Tony piped up.

She huffed out a breath. "I want to hire you for a special bounty. A recovery mission, of sorts."

"For when?" Trav called out.

Sadie glanced back at me and I stepped forward. Probably best we take it from here. I was expecting quite a backlash from these guys, although I trusted every man in the room with my life. That was why we'd chosen them.

"Tomorrow," I said. "And some of you aren't gonna like it."

Tony shifted from side to side, his wolf shifter instincts clearly making him want to run. "How come?"

I sighed. "Because it's dangerous. The most dangerous assignment any of you have ever had. Which is why we have you guys here, and no one else. We need people we can trust."

Max lifted his chin and crossed his arms over his chest. "What's the job?" Max was part dragon, part wolf, part bear. He was as big as Fridge, and more vicious.

"We got word a day ago that it's possible that Sadie's mom—Jack's wife—is still alive."

"Fuck."

"Holy shit."

Curses reverberated right through the group.

"Where?" Max asked.

I glanced at Fridge, who was still standing at the back of the room, standing guard over the exit. "In the underground," I said. "The blood ring."

Every man who had been relaxing, slouching or sitting, got to his feet and yelled.

"What the fuck?"

"No!"

"But... twenty fucking years?"

And a myriad of other negatives.

Sadie dropped to her knees and pulled out the money she had in the bag, spilling it on the floor.

More than a hundred thousand dollars fell everywhere.

The room went insanely quiet all of a sudden, as the men glanced between themselves and licked their lips.

Yes. That was the sort of reaction we wanted.

Sadie stood up. "There's a hundred thousand dollars here. Fifteen grand for any man who says he'll join us tomorrow."

"In advance?" Max queried, stepping closer.

Sadie nodded. "Yes. And I have contracts behind me that will pay out another hundred thousand dollars to every family of anyone who doesn't come back from this one."

The men glanced among themselves.

In the world we lived in, taking our lives in our hands every day, they wouldn't get a much better offer than that.

Max stepped forward. "I'm in. Vampires are my favorite to hunt."

I grinned at him. I knew that about him.

"We're all meeting here tomorrow, nine a.m. We'll rig up with every bit of armor you think you'll need. Any weapon. There's no limit on this one."

Sadie held up a hand and every eye shot to her. "It's my mom. Jack's wife. Don't forget that."

There was a hiss of excitement among the guys. Jack had always placed limits on everything in the vault. To have carte blanche access was a rare thing.

"We go down just before noon."

"What's the objective?" Max asked.

"Rescue the women trapped in the blood ring," I said.

"And any children or babies we find," Sadie added.

"How many are down there?" Travis asked, stepping closer, as did several of the other men, forming a circle in front of Sadie and the money.

"We don't know. At least three," I said. "Could be more by now."

"So, we go down, grab the women, and get the fuck out," Trav said.

Max chuckled without humor. "Yeah, all without the vamps getting us. How far down in the underground are they?"

Fridge walked over to join us. "It's three levels down."

"Three? Fuck."

"Look, this won't be easy," Sadie said. "But I've seen what's down there, and we can't leave those women to face it."

Max glanced at Fridge. "Is it just us eight?"

I closed my eyes briefly. Eight. The men.

Sadie cleared her throat. "I'm coming." There was a glance around the group, but no one said anything. Sadie was, after all, Jack's daughter. "And Vincent and Shadow."

"Vincent? The vampire who saved Fridge the other day?"

I nodded. "Yes. He's strong and fast, and with us and them, I think we can do this."

"Shadow?" someone asked. "Isn't he that weird shifter—"

"He's my cousin, and he's in," Sadie said. Her tone brooked no argument.

After a moment, Max shrugged. "Well, I'm in. You know me. Money is king."

Sadie turned and grabbed the contracts while I bent to pick up the money.

"This way gentlemen," Sadie said, inviting them over to sign their life away.

I stood back with Fridge and watched her hand over the money and get our team together.

"Do you think all six will turn up tomorrow?" I asked Fridge.

I'd had reservations about Davis. He hadn't said a thing since he'd walked in the door, but as he took his money, signed his contract and walked over to us, he stuck out his hand.

"Thanks for asking me to join you guys. You know the vamps

drained my parents a few years ago? I've been looking for a way to get them back."

I stuck out my hand and shook his hand. This was exactly the sort of man we needed.

"See you tomorrow, Davis."

"I'll be here."

The men left with a stack of cash each and a grim but determined smile.

I grabbed Sadie into a hug and held her tight. This next step was going to take us down a path where we had little control out of the outcome.

It scared the shit out of me. But I knew there was no going back now.

No matter what.

CHAPTER 12

SADIE

I worked all day, finalizing contracts for the men from Hunters who were coming with us into the underground, then working on a way to hand over all business control to Shadow while I was gone.

That wasn't easy, and it involved an intense conversation with my reluctant cousin. Shadow didn't want anything to do with my money, business, or apartment, but I convinced him it was necessary.

After all, who else could I trust with everything my father had built?

By the time closing came around, my brain was fried. I collapsed against the back rest of my father's executive chair and groaned. "Fuck, I'm tired."

I pulled the elastic from my hair, tugging at the messy bun I'd twisted my hair into and let the heavy strands fall around my face.

The door opened and my two shifter mates walked in. "Hey," I said, smiling at them both, happy to see them despite the fatigue that dragged at me.

"You okay?" Rogan asked.

I nodded and closed the laptop screen. "Yeah, just tired. It's been a big day." Between the meeting with the men chosen to accompany us, worrying about the consequences of what was going to happen, and setting up the eventualities of the worst happening, I was exhausted.

I ran my hands through my tangled hair and got to my feet, stretching my back as I walked around my desk.

Fridge slid his hand around my waist and pulled me into his huge body. "Hey, beautiful."

"Hi," I returned, going up on my toes to kiss him.

When I drew back, I cocked my head and stared at his contented smile. "How come I feel like I haven't seen you much lately? That's not the case at all." I'd been with him so much, but the usually overwhelming "Fridge" feeling had disappeared. It was nice to have the core of him, without the "bluster".

Fridge's smile instantly fell and he stepped away.

I went straight after him, grabbing onto his hands and squeezing his fingers. "Hey. I wasn't trying to insult you. What's wrong?"

Fridge ran a hand through his hair. "Nothing. You ready to go home?"

I nodded and glanced at Rogan, who shrugged. Something was up with Fridge, and if I had to bet on it, I'd put my money on two things.

Either he was worried about tomorrow and what would happen in the underground, or he was thinking about what had happened with Vincent.

The two of them seemed better. Not as grouchy with each other, but whatever it was between them wasn't fully resolved.

I nodded as we made our way down the stairs. I obviously had to do something to push Fridge and Vincent to be more cordial with each other. The last thing we needed was two of our four at odds when we were about to go into the most dangerous expedition of our lives.

I locked up, then decided we should walk back to the hotel despite my lethargy.

"I could use a stretch," I said. "I've been stuck behind a desk all day."

I took Fridge's hand without waiting for an answer from the guys and we began walking. It was only a few blocks over, and I had to ask Fridge about Vincent. We didn't have a lot of time to sort out the issue before tomorrow.

"Hey, Fridge?" I asked.

"Yeah?" he responded, stopping at an intersection and turning to look for cars.

I shivered at the magic I felt course down my spine. The sense of foreboding and eventuality that was about to happen. "I know you and Vincent had sex?"

He twisted around so fast I almost fell over.

His eyes shifted to their dragon diamonds and his chest seemed to puff up as I stared at him.

"Why would you sss..ay that?" he asked, his shifter voice coming out for us all to hear.

I grinned at him. "Because I was gonna ask if you could do it again. You know... with us there." I gestured to Rogan and back to myself.

"Let's go!" Rogan called out, already halfway across the street.

Fridge and I ran to catch up with him and when we were safely back on the sidewalk, I took his hand again and held it tight.

"Well?" I asked him.

He coughed loudly but didn't say anything.

Rogan was walking ahead, so he was no help.

I squeezed Fridge's hand. "Hey. What are you worried about? I think you two are hot together!"

And I did. Even just thinking about them from yesterday made my stomach tighten and my pussy pulse. Watching Vincent suck Fridge's cock was one of the most erotic things I'd ever seen.

"Why..." He coughed to clear his throat, seeming unable to continue.

I grinned up at him, hoping my approval would be easy to read. "Well, you don't have to tell me any details if you don't want to... but would you do more stuff tonight, for me? I have to admit, I find it a turn-on."

It was my turn to swallow hard. Admitting such a thing was actually difficult.

"You... ah, don't mind that we..." Fridge once again couldn't finish the sentence.

I laughed as I squeezed his hand and grinned at him. "God, no! Takes some of the pressure off me," I joked.

He glanced at the ground and my stomach plummeted from worry.

I stopped walking and pulled on his hand until he faced me. "Hey," I said, cupping his cheek and lifting his head until he looked into my eyes.

His pupils had shifted back to human, though he shivered with a strange sort of tension.

"What's really worrying you? It can't be that you've found another person to have sex with, who's already in our family. It's not like you're off cheating with some other woman, because you know... that would kind of kill me."

And it would. One of the main reasons I'd accepted the Fated Mate bond so easily was the fact it brought with it a certain guarantee that my men wouldn't cheat on me. Nor me on them.

"No... it's not that," he said.

"Then what is it?" I asked. "Because, I don't mean to rush you or anything, but tomorrow is going to be kind of life-threatening in the worst possible way, and I'd really like to make sure that nothing is left unresolved."

Fridge's nostrils flared as he inhaled deeply.

I waited and it felt like an eternity, but finally Fridge said, "I think Vincent's my mate as well as you."

I don't think my mouth hung open for very long, but I'm pretty sure my jaw dropped at least for a moment or two.

I snapped it shut and focused on the solution to his supposed problem. "Um... I don't get it. Aren't we linked already?"

Surely that's how it worked?

He shook his head like a horse brushing off an annoying fly.

I didn't dare look away from his gaze, though I was pretty sure we'd lost Rogan.

Fridge said, "Not through you."

"Oh." What did he mean? "You mean... you two are mates, like... separately?" I wasn't sure what that meant for him and me, exactly. "Does that mean you want to go off alone with Vincent? Without me and Rogan? Because I hope that's not the case."

I'd hate it if that was what he was saying.

He shook his head adamantly. "Oh, God no. I want you just as much. It's just that..."

"You feel connected to him, too?" I asked, trying to make sense of this strange puzzle.

He nodded.

I shrugged. "Well, I don't really see the problem. Isn't a good thing that you two are connected? After all, you and Rogan have been best friends for like... what? Ten years? You and I are Fated Mates. Maybe you're designed to be like... the center of the male trio or something?"

Or the center of all of us?

There had to be a good reason why he felt this way.

Fate didn't set things up without a reason.

When Fridge didn't say anything more, I sighed, kissed him hard on the mouth, then tugged his hand to make him keep walking down the street.

I was starving.

"Look. I'm not sure what you're feeling, but from my point of view, I can't see any negatives to it. If anything, it makes me feel more secure that this family is going to work. And if I fall behind on my affection or sex... or I get sick—" *or pregnant*, "—and can't give you guys everything you need, you have each other. Sounds like a win-win to me."

Fridge shrugged his massive shoulders and sighed loudly. "Yeah, I suppose so."

We were almost at the hotel now, and Rogan was nowhere to be seen. He must have gone on without us. "So?" I asked. "You'll show me some stuff tonight?"

Fridge stared at me, his dark eyes swirling with more emotions than I could name.

Then, he slowly nodded and a small smile played on his lips. "If you want."

I squealed a little to emphasize my approval. "Yay! Oh, I do want to see... let's go."

Because no matter what happened tomorrow, tonight had to be a night we all remembered. Forever.

FRIDGE

I pulled Sadie against my body as we rode the elevator up the single floor to our hotel room, holding her tight against me. It felt so right to have her in my arms. Her scent rose around me and I sunk into it, burying my face in her hair.

And yet, my stomach was in knots at the thought of seeing Vincent again, too.

The dual pull between the two of them made my cock hard in my jeans.

It was such a contradictory feeling, I couldn't work out which was stronger.

"Come on. I'm starving," Sadie said, tugging me down the hall to our room.

"For food or sex?" I asked, stepping up behind her sweet little body and pressing my hardening cock into her butt.

She giggled as she used the swipe card and pushed the door hard to open it. "Both."

Then she bumped her ass back at me before sauntering into the room, swinging her hips like she was on some sort of runway.

Stepping into the room, I let the door shut behind me.

I could smell Vincent from where I stood, though he was still in the bedroom. He smelled like blood and sex, and a fight.

Everything I loved in this world. "Damn it," I said under my breath as I opened the door to the mini fridge and reached for a couple of beers. "Rogan? Sadie? You guys want a drink?"

"No, thanks," Sadie said, then she squealed as though someone had grabbed her, and I knew who it was.

My gut tightened as I sensed Vincent move closer.

I grabbed the two beers out of the fridge, one in each hand. Hopefully that would stop me from reaching for the vampire and kissing him, like I'd been dying to for days now.

"Hey," I said, nodding at him.

Vincent inclined his head, a smile flirting at the edges of his lips. "Hello."

I couldn't stop the grin that lifted my own mouth. He was so proper. So old school. Everything I wasn't.

"You have a good day?" I asked him.

He nodded, and drew Sadie into his side, kissing her lips briefly before looking back at me. "Yes, I did, thank you. I got some rest… mostly."

"Mostly" sounded like he'd done more than simply rest while we were at work, but I wasn't going to push for the information.

Not yet.

Not while my heart pounded and my chest was tight, waiting for the moment that Sadie would ask us to climb into bed together. And I'd get to fuck Vincent again.

I tossed the beer back, swallowing the cold hops as I tried to wash away my dirty thoughts.

Not that it worked, but the beer was good.

Rogan stepped up and took his bottle off me, probably so I didn't drink it.

There was a knock at the door, then it opened without us saying they could come in. "Room service!" the guy called out cheerily.

I raised my eyebrows in question. "But we haven't ordered yet."

A knife flew past my head and I ducked out of the way, diving for Sadie as Vincent flew to the door.

I tucked our mate behind me, my dragon fluttering inside, ready to shift and fly Sadie away.

But Vincent was taking care of the threat, without mercy.

He tore the other vampire's head from his shoulders and slammed shut the door so that no one else could come in.

Blood spattered Vincent's otherwise pristine shirt as he tossed the head onto the silver tray and the thump of the now lifeless body sounded as it fell to the floor.

He growled as though he were part shifter and a laugh bubbled in my chest. God, he was magnificent.

"Damn, you're hot," I said, unable to stop the words from coming out.

FRIDGE

Everyone stilled and stared at me. I wished I could take the words back. But it was too late.

"Um..."

Sadie giggled as she got up off the floor and dusted herself off. "I agree. Nothing hotter than a man who can protect me and our family. Thank you, Vincent."

I got to my feet, my throat thick with emotion.

So much for playing your cards close to your chest. Idiot.

"I actually had ordered your dinner, otherwise I would have acted sooner when he tried to come in the door," Vincent said.

There was another knock on the door. The real room service.

Vincent groaned, indicating the head on the tray. "I'll get rid of this asshole. You guys get your dinner."

Vincent grabbed the body and pushed the cart to the other side of the room, where he opened the window and threw him out.

Sadie stared at Vincent, her mouth wide open. "Ah..."

Rogan slapped me on the arm. "Food. Let's go."

He opened the door and let the cart enter, just as the window slid shut.

"Whatcha get?" I asked, pulling out a chair and sitting down at the dining room table. Or more accurately, what had Vincent decided we were having for dinner?

Should we really trust a vampire's taste in food?

At least I like my steak rare.

Rogan shrugged.

I glanced over my shoulder, then pulled out a chair next to me. "Come join us, Vincent. Tell us what you've ordered."

Vincent moved silently, sitting in the chair next to me without saying a word.

My heart pounded too hard, but I was beginning to feel more excited than terrified, so I grabbed onto those feelings and pushed forward.

"I... ah, ordered a little of everything. Considering how important tomorrow is, I thought you could spoil yourselves a little."

Rogan placed six platters on the table.

"Whoa," I said. "Order enough?"

Vincent nodded and smiled.

I grinned. The man knew us well.

Sadie sat down and began lifting the silver domes to reveal the food. "I'm starving. Wow, it all smells so good."

There was steak, fish, fries, vegetables, risotto and lasagna. Then sides of garlic bread, salads and even a platter of chocolate mousse cake.

I inhaled and moaned at the pleasure that pulsed through my body as the aromas made their way up my nostrils.

"Yum." I licked my lips as saliva pooled in my mouth. "Damn, I'm hungry too."

Vincent took one of the empty plates and indicated the feast he'd ordered and paid for.

"Dig in."

And so, we did. We stuffed ourselves, laughed and chatted about nothing in particular, while Vincent sat back and watched us, a soft smile on his face.

"Did you get the agreement of the men at Hunters today to join us?" Vincent asked.

Sadie nodded, wiping the last of the lasagna sauce from her mouth. "Yes. We have six men who will meet us tomorrow for the trip into the underground."

Vincent's eyes glanced up at the wall where the knife still protruded. "Should we talk about the assassination attempt?"

Sadie stood up and shook her head. "Not yet. It'll kill the mood, no pun intended. Unless you think there will be more coming for us tonight?" She glanced at Vincent.

He stood up and shook his head. "No. I don't think so, but just to make sure…" He dragged one of the chairs to the only entrance and jammed it under the door handle.

Sadie grinned, high on food and likely the fact she was still alive. "Great! We can talk about that shit later, but for now, I want my mates to take me to bed. Assuming, of course, you all want to?"

"Hell, yes," Rogan growled, bumping the table as he stood up and lifted Sadie into his arms. "It's been way too long."

They went off to the bedroom and I glanced at Vincent. Should I warn him of Sadie's plans for us tonight or let her reveal them?

"Come on guys!" she called, and before I could say anything to him, the vampire moved into the bedroom after them.

I sighed and muttered, "Lost my chance there." Quickly I went after them, determined to let the chips fall where they may. At least for tonight.

VINCENT

I'd spent the day super-dosing on the most exotic blood I could afford. Not only did it taste better—from the rarest and strongest of shifters—but it gave a vampire a special buzz, a strength that I was sure I was going to need to protect my mates tomorrow.

But it had backfired in a way, too. I could feel my attraction to Fridge grow, move, change.

There must have been dragon shifter blood in the mix, though I hadn't asked for it specifically.

Fridge stepped up next to me as I stared at Rogan and Sadie on the bed. They were already kissing and touching, tugging at each other's clothes with a desperation that came from not knowing what tomorrow would bring.

But just at this moment, I wasn't focused on the couple on the bed. Every particle of my being was aching for the man next to me. *Fridge.* He didn't touch me, but I could feel the heat radiating off him in a wave.

"Do you like watching them?" I asked him as Fridge crossed his big, meaty arms over his equally large chest. When he didn't answer I risked a look at him. "Well?"

He turned to meet my gaze, his irises doing that weird dragon diamond thing I found truly fascinating.

"Well, what?"

Hadn't he heard what I'd said?

I inclined my head toward the bed, where Rogan had gotten Sadie completely naked and was kissing her soundly.

A gasp from her echoed around the room and lust curled in my belly. "I asked if you like watching them?"

Fridge shrugged, letting his arms fall. "I like watching Sadie receive pleasure. Rogan doesn't do it for me though."

Another gasp sounded, then a cry.

Rogan now had his head buried between Sadie's legs.

She grabbed his hair, her belly shaking with her moans.

She looked up and met my gaze. "Are you two gonna join us?"

I nodded. "Sure."

How we were going to do this, I had no idea. But I unbuttoned my shirt and pulled off my trousers, laying them on the chair in the corner of the room.

Every cell in my body was trained and focused on Fridge. The way he moved, shuffled out of his jeans and tank.

When he finally turned toward me, my mouth fell open.

Damn, he's beautiful.

All bunched, strong muscle. Long cock. Wicked grin, when he bothered to smile.

My tongue went dry and I realized my mouth was hanging open.

I shut it with a snap when I heard Sadie say, "Come on. I wanna watch you guys, too."

She motioned for us to come closer.

I glanced at Fridge, who wasn't moving. "She wants us closer."

His jaw clenched and the muscle in his jaw popped. Then he shook his head slowly. "No, she wants to watch us."

My mouth dropped open. "Us... as in..."

"Us," the dragon said, his whole body shivering as though he was holding everything back.

I glanced over at our female mate who was flipping over and going onto all fours on the bed, Rogan kneeling behind her.

She grinned at me and nodded. "Yeah... can I watch you and Fridge?" She gasped as Rogan slid inside her. "Fuck."

I looked from her to Fridge and back again. "Was that..."

Had she said she wanted to watch us?

Fridge charged over to me and turned me away so that he was pressed up against my back, his arms around my chest, his lips against my neck.

I closed my eyes on a sigh as a wave of lust slammed into me.

Ah... yep. That's what she meant.

"She wants us to fuck. Here, in front of them. You up for it?" he asked, the words sliding into my ear like the hottest, dirtiest, sexiest thing I'd ever heard.

One of my mates wanted to watch me fuck my other mate? Hell yes.

I shuddered, sliding my hands back so I could touch him, feeling his hot skin beneath my palms.

I nodded. "Yes. If that's what Sadie wants."

She cried out as Rogan started fucking her faster. "Yes! Please. Now."

Fridge's hands slid down my stomach, grabbing hold of my cock that already thick. "You need some help there, vampire?"

I couldn't open my eyes, they were so heavy.

I nodded. "Yes, please, dragon."

I could tell that Fridge wasn't going to need any help tonight, though I desperately wanted to suck his cock again. He was already hard, his hips bumping me from behind as he thrust his shaft against my back.

He bit my neck and I shuddered as his rough hand moved up and down my cock.

I turned my head, wanting to kiss him, but he moved away.

"Come on, Vincent. Come... here," Sadie panted, patting the bed in front of her.

Fridge released me and I moved over to the mattress, kneeling on the bed and kissing Sadie's sweet lips as she was bumped and fucked from behind by Rogan.

She gasped against my lips, her eyes a swirl of purple magic and passion.

Fridge's hands were on my back now, pulling me to the edge of the bed, spreading my legs and applying some sort of lotion to my ass.

I glanced over my shoulder, wanting to see the man behind me.

Fridge stilled, meeting my gaze, and hesitated.

Why, I wasn't sure.

Several moments went by and the sounds of Rogan and Sadie's fucking got louder.

I rolled my eyes at the slapping sounds of flesh meeting and the moans that were really getting quite comical. "You gonna let them beat us?"

Fridge's eyes lit up and he grinned as he shook his head.

"Nope."

I turned back around and reached under my belly, palming my own cock and squeezing the engorged head.

Damn, I'm so horny.

Fridge set the head of his cock to my ass and I pushed back, not fearing the burn, only seeking the intense feeling of possession that came with giving myself over to the huge shifter.

Fridge grabbed my hips and pulled me back, thrusting deep inside.

I groaned and let my head fall further onto the mattress.

"You okay?" I heard him whisper.

I nodded my head, reaching my hand out to Sadie and feeling her fingers tangle with mine.

Fridge began to move, riding me with strength and power, not holding back.

I pushed back, wanting him deeper.

Wanting more.

Wanting everything.

Fridge groaned above me and I stroked my cock with my free hand, feeling the tingles of my orgasm already teasing the base of my spine.

I didn't try to control it. Or stop it.

I panted and cried out as Fridge's cock pegged a spot inside of me that filtered pleasure through every nerve in my body.

Over and over again, he struck it, and finally I couldn't hold out any longer. I squeezed the head of my cock as it pulsed in my hand, releasing a cry and meeting Sadie's delighted gaze as I shot cum all over the sheets beneath me.

Fridge fell over my back, pressing me into the sheets as he groaned out his own pleasure and whispered into my ear, "Bite me."

He held his hand up to my mouth, the fleshy part of the base of his thumb calling to me.

I didn't stop to think about it, nor register the shock at such a request.

Fridge groaned as his seed pulsed into me and I sank my fangs into his flesh, the sweetest blood I've ever tasted flowing into my mouth.

I felt Fridge's lips at my shoulder and Sadie's hand still gripping mine.

That was the moment when I truly realized that tomorrow, I'd be risking everything I'd ever held dear.

And they were all in this bed surrounding me.

CHAPTER 14

FRIDGE

"That was sooo hot! Oh my God!" Sadie cried, laughing with happiness.

We all lay in bed, Sadie in the middle, Vincent and Rogan on either side of her.

I was on the edge, not far from Vincent's sexy, cum-filled ass.

I wanted to be closer, to hold him in the aftermath of the hottest session of my life, but something held me back. Something that rode me hard, with anxiety and tension sinking its claws into my skin.

"All right?" Sadie asked, her head lifting off the pillow to look at us all.

When she saw where I was, her gaze narrowed, and she reached a hand out to me. "Come closer, Fridge."

I couldn't deny her and I certainly couldn't deny the fact I wanted to be closer, so I slid up behind Vincent and reached out for her.

Our hands met over his waist and Vincent shifted back ever so slightly, his ass now inches from my stomach.

How much did I want to slide up and spoon him? Feel his cool skin against my overheated balls?

Too much.

I clenched my teeth so hard I heard a crack in my jaw.

"Is that a bite mark?" Sadie asked, lifting up my hand and inspecting my palm.

I flipped onto my back, looking up at the ceiling. "Ah, yeah."

I pushed my palms flat against my chest, not wanting to inspect the proof of the blood drinking, a sexual ritual I'd encouraged Vincent to indulge in.

I still couldn't believe I'd done it. I'd been bitten before. But those vampires had attacked me, either out of hunger or anger. Not with pleasure and care in mind.

Sadie sat up and looked down at us, her gorgeous nipples still erect and crying out for attention. "Vincent, did you bite him? Is that... like... a guy sex thing? You've never done that to me."

Vincent huffed out a laugh, and even though I wasn't looking at him, I could imagine his sweet smile.

I bit my lip and snorted through my nose. My feelings for Vincent were growing stronger every day. Despite initially not wanting to connect with the vampire, he was beginning to become as important to me as Sadie... my mate. And Rogan, my best friend.

Vincent cleared his throat. "I didn't plan to bite Fridge. I never feed on... people."

"So, why did you?" she asked, not letting the topic go.

I sighed, heavily. "Because I told him to."

I sat up and twisted around so I could look at Sadie. The four-in-the-bed thing made the position hard. But I stayed where I was and stared at her, waiting for her to respond.

"Oh," Sadie said then glanced down at Vincent. "You can bite me too, if you want to. Is sex better for you if you do?"

That was something I wanted to know as well. I'd moved on complete instinct when I offered my hand to Vincent.

I'd seen his fangs protrude after he'd fucked Sadie in the shower and when he'd orgasmed with me last time. And a part of my subconscious brain had obviously assumed that he was meant to feed at that time.

Only a guy with a lot of restraint and control would stop his base instincts like that, retracting his fangs when he was ready and needing to feed. And although I respected the strength it took to fight that need, the fact he made the choice not to take the blood made me want to give it to him.

Fucking hell…

Vincent awkwardly cleared his throat, then slid up the headboard, sitting up like we were.

Rogan groaned and arranged himself so he was sitting closer to me, now making a little naked circle.

"Well?" Sadie asked, one eyebrow rising high on her forehead.

"Yes. It made my orgasm much more intense," Vincent admitted. "I wanted to do it with you, too. But I managed to stop myself. I couldn't possibly feed on you, Sadie. You're part witch. I can't guarantee I could control myself and stop if I tasted your blood."

"Which is why it's best he bites me," I said, before I could stop myself.

All three of them stared at me.

"What?" What was wrong with that?

Vincent glanced at me, a nervous smile quivering on his lips. "I appreciate the offer, but I honestly don't want to make either of you my… blood source. I am quite happy to buy it. I have been training myself for many decades to live off the bottled sort."

I pressed my lips into a thin line. Why did I feel rejected?

"Fine," I said, shrugging. "No problem."

I shouldn't have a problem with it, and yet hearing Vincent say he'd happily go back to the bottled crap rather than my blood made me angry.

Like, gut-tightening, fingers clenched into fists, angry.

It made sense that after a great fucking session we'd share such a thing. It might not make sense to anyone else, but it did to me.

"I'm gonna grab a quick shower, then we better hit the hay. We've got a huge day tomorrow. We'd better get some sleep." My voice was grumpy-sounding but I couldn't help it.

I shuffled off the bed and stumbled into the shower, turning on the water and grabbing the soap to scrub clean. I had to gain control over myself, because even I knew my reaction was stupid.

I was angry, and there was no reason to be. I'd just had incredible sex and I should just shut up and be happy.

The door opened and Vincent walked in, looking way too relaxed. His eyes were soft, his movements slow.

"Yeah?" I asked, washing under my arms and smelling sex everywhere I breathed.

"I didn't mean to offend you," he said, staring at me with those big, brown eyes.

I shrugged and washed my cock and balls, hoping to get rid of the feeling Vincent had left on me. "It's cool. Don't worry about it."

Vincent walked closer and I rushed to get out of his way.

I quickly rinsed the soap off and gestured to the still running water. "If you wanna shower, I'm done."

He shook his head. "No. I'm happy to smell of you."

I twisted away to turn the water off, a smirk tugging at my lips. I kind of liked the fact he'd smell of me, too.

"Cool." I grabbed a towel and quickly dried myself, though I could feel the tendrils of desire growing once again.

Damn it. Aren't you satisfied yet?

As my cock began to thicken, I rolled my eyes at myself.

Obviously not.

"Better get to bed."

"Hey," Vincent said, reaching out and touching my arm, stopping me from leaving the bathroom.

"Yeah?" I wrapped the towel around my waist, covering my still-thickening cock.

"Thank you for offering your blood to me. It was incredibly generous of you."

I nodded once. "No problem."

I went to move away, and Vincent grabbed me, his reflexes lightning fast. "I mean... I... I've never had anyone care enough to offer me such a gift and I'm not sure how to be comfortable with it. I've spent a lot of, well, decades, trying to wean off blood entirely. My need for such nutrition repulses me."

I stopped and stared at him. I'd never thought of it that way. That Vincent had not chosen to become a vampire. He was bitten, not born. His way of life was to feed or die.

I grinned and shrugged. "I've got extra. You're welcome to some."

And without looking back, I walked out of the bathroom, pulled off the towel and jumped straight into bed where Rogan and Sadie were still sitting, chatting away.

My heart was pounding too fast, and a nervous type of energy was pulsing through my veins, but I couldn't stop to think about what it meant. Not now.

Vincent, still naked, came and sat on the bed. "Should we discuss the assassination attempt?"

My head came up from the pillow. "Shit, I forgot about that."

Rogan laughed. "Yeah, pretty easy to do when Vincent dispatched him so easily. Wicked moves you've got."

Vincent inclined his head. "Thank you."

"Who was it?" Sadie asked, "Or more importantly, who sent him? Do you think there will be more?"

Vincent shook his head. "No. If they wanted to send more, they would have come together, or already stormed into the room. That was a low-level, trashy young vamp. He could have been here for any of us. Me especially. Since I'm on the outs with my old family and have angered people by taking up a relationship with you, Sadie, I've put a target on my head."

"So, you don't think it has anything to do with what we're gonna do tomorrow?" I asked. Because that's all that really mattered.

We needed to know if they were on to us or not.

Vincent shook his head. "No, I don't think so."

"Great!" Sadie said, clapping her hands. "Then we should probably get some sleep and be rested for tomorrow."

She looked at Vincent and tilted her head. "Are you on watch tonight, or are you going to sleep with us?"

Vincent's gaze slid over to mine and rested on me like a gentle caress.

Was he hoping I'd invite him to sleep with us?

I swallowed hard and opened my mouth to respond, but Vincent said, "I'll stay on watch. Just in case they do send someone else."

Vincent stood up and moved as though he was going to leave.

Every part of me panicked.

To hell with it.

I flicked back the blankets and gestured to him. "Come in for a bit. You can leave when we fall asleep."

Vincent blinked, and although I could feel Sadie and Rogan's gazes on me, I didn't look their way.

Instead, I waited then said, "I don't bite." Though I would, if he wanted me to.

Vincent chuckled at that one, then climbed back into the place between me and Sadie.

He rested his head on the pillow, his back to me.

I lay down behind him as Sadie and Rogan settled also.

Every part of me, human and shifter, hummed with happiness.

These were my mates; my family.

I flicked off the light, closed my eyes and drew Vincent closer. Reaching over him, I rested a hand on Sadie's warm hip.

I couldn't lose them now.

∾

VINCENT

I didn't want to move. I'd never slept in a bed with three other people before. And I'd especially never had my female half-witch's warm curves pressed against my front, and my male dragon shifter lover's possessive arm wrapped around my waist, his cock and heavy balls against my ass.

It wasn't a situation I'd ever thought I'd want to be in, and yet... I seriously didn't want to be anywhere else.

So, I stayed, with my head on the soft pillow and my eyes closed, listening to the heavy breathing of the three people around me.

Sadie twitched and mumbled in her sleep.

Rogan softly snored on occasion.

And Fridge gripped me like a bear and snored like a train.

And it was just perfect.

But I couldn't sleep. Not when the threat of the vampires was hanging over our heads. I needed to keep these beautiful people safe. And when it came time tomorrow, I would get them out of the city and to safety. Somehow.

Because there was no way we were walking into the blood ring, taking away their prized cash cows, and resuming our normal lives soon after.

No way in hell.

CHAPTER 15

SADIE

The night passed too quickly, as it usually did when I slept next to my mates. I rarely woke, and when I did, I drifted back to sleep feeling safe.

When the sun rose, we got up, ate breakfast and dressed. A nervous energy pulsed between all of us, but the silence was hard to break as we did everything we needed to.

"You gonna meet us later, or come to the workshop now?" I asked Vincent. "We still have a few hours until the guys meet us at Hunters."

Though I wanted us all together, I understood that Vincent was weakened by sustained sunlight exposure. And the last thing I wanted was that. Especially on a day when he had to be his strongest.

Vincent frowned. "How many hours until we leave?"

I glanced at my phone to ascertain the time. "About three hours."

He nodded. "I'll meet you there in two. There's something I need to do before we go."

I didn't ask what it was, I just kissed his lips and hugged him tightly. "See you then."

We moved to the front door and Fridge hesitated.

"You coming?" I asked.

Fridge nodded. "Yeah. I... yeah, I'm coming."

Whatever it was, Fridge decided against voicing it, and he walked away from Vincent without even a goodbye kiss.

Or maybe guys didn't do that?

I shrugged. Not my biggest concern at the moment.

My hand strayed to my still flat belly. I had a lot more precious things to think about.

"You okay? Stomach upset?" Rogan asked, glancing down at my hand as we waited for the elevator.

I dropped my hand away and chuckled nervously. "No... I'm okay. Just stressed a bit, I think."

They accepted that as the reason, which it mostly was, and we made our way down in the elevator, through the lobby and onto the street.

"Anything you guys need to do before work?" I asked.

They shook their heads, so we walked the two blocks to Hunters and opened the doors.

I looked around at the pristine polished concrete floors, the timber staircase and the bright, open spaces.

I would miss this place.

I sighed and headed straight up the stairs. I had a few emails to send and some information to gather before we left.

If I was heading into the underground with little hope of coming back, then I was going down wearing my mother's jewelry and as many things sorted out as possible.

I got to work, my lawyer training coming in handy as I finalized my legacy.

Hopefully, I would be back tomorrow, and every little, untrained magical impulse in me said I would return. But not tomorrow.

The door opened and my cousin walked, or rather, limped in.

"Shadow!" I said, getting to my feet. "I just have a few things for you to sign."

He growled with that strange rumble he had, an odd, mixed noise due to the number of different shifters in his blood. "You know I don't want your money, Sadie."

I grinned at him. "I know you don't, that's why I'm offering it to you. I know you're not going to go out and spend it all on booze tomorrow."

He smiled a little at that and I handed him a pen from the desk. "Here, just sign everything and then we can go."

He limped over to the desk and peered down at the paperwork. "What's it say?"

The lawyer part of me wanted to tell him never to sign anything he hadn't read. But the part that just wanted us to get through this next part quickly, brushed over that.

"It's pretty much my will. In the eventuality I die, or don't return, it gives you ownership and control of Hunters, the apartment and all of our bank accounts."

My heart squeezed. A small part of me was nervous about handing everything over to Shadow, but there were a lot more important things than money.

What was the worst thing he could do? Sell the apartment? Sell the business? Spend the money?

I looked over my cousin's raggedy clothes and grinned. Wasn't going to happen.

"I don't like this, Sadie," he said, gripping the pen but not using it.

I rolled my eyes. "Look... if you don't sign it and something happens to me, it goes into a state trust, and the government gets everything. Do you want that?"

"Hell, no."

"Then sign it!"

"Fine." Shadow growled, scribbling his name at every spot and every page I pointed to. "But I'm only doing this because you'll be back here tomorrow and you can shred it all."

"So true," I said, smiling.

When it was all done, I picked up the papers, handed him a spare set of keys, and locked the contracts in the safe. "I'll give you the combination later."

"I already know it," Shadow said.

My mouth dropped open. "Fridge didn't even know it."

Shadow shrugged. "Jack told me years ago."

And right, then, I knew I'd made the correct choice.

I blinked rapidly as tears filled my eyes. "Um... lets go suit up. I'm sure the guys have every piece of ammunition in the armory out."

Shadow grinned. "They do."

We left the office and headed downstairs, my mother's wrist-watch and necklace firmly attached to me and hope in my heart.

Sadie

Shadow had been right. Fridge, or one of the others, had locked the doors, pulled the blinds, and were systematically taking out everything that could kill a vampire.

The room was littered with piles of weapons and armor.

"Sadie. Good. Let's start getting you kitted out."

I groaned. "This is like... my least favorite part."

Vincent walked over. "Well, our least favorite part would be you being drained by a vampire, so let's cover you up a little, huh?"

I laughed as I smiled at my vampire mate. "When'd you get here?"

He kissed my lips, the coolness of his skin making me shiver—in the best way. "About ten minutes ago."

I turned toward Fridge, who was coming at me with a Kevlar

suit. It was heavy, but obviously a good idea for where we were going.

"Okay. Let me just take this sweater off."

I'd worn a long-sleeved t-shirt and leggings today, knowing that I was about to be burdened with a whole lot of heavy, protective gear.

Fridge slipped the Kevlar body suit over my head then attached the arms to the body.

"You, beautiful girl, are the most precious thing going down there."

So not true, I almost said. But I supposed it was technically correct, since it was likely I was carrying a precious thing.

I let them suit me up and gathered my hair into a low ponytail, watching as the other men shared the remaining body armor between them.

Some, like Vincent and Fridge, ended up with none. Though when Rogan saw Fridge had nothing to cover even his neck, he took the Kevlar off his arms and gave it to my mate.

"You know the vamps always go for you," Rogan said. "At least cover up your carotids."

Vincent nodded and stepped up, bending and twisting the small loops until Fridge had at least some protection around his neck.

Next was the weapons.

I grabbed as many silver stakes and knives as I could find, attaching them to my thighs, my ankles, my lower back and my forearms.

I couldn't shoot a gun straight, but I could throw a knife.

Then I stepped back and watched the men work. Rogan loaded up, Fridge packed bags, and even Vincent grabbed my father's knife and a few wooden stakes for the trip.

The other men we'd hired to come with us all seemed calm, though there was a nervous excitement in the air. I could only put it down to the threat of death.

Finally, around noon, the eight bounty hunters, one vampire, and Shadow, faced me.

"Let's go."

I opened the door for them, set the expensive alarm system and closed the door.

Before I turned around to them, I kissed my fingers then pressed them against the front door of my father's workshop.

His operation had begun as a venture of one. Himself. And he'd grown it into a multi-million-dollar business. It was impressive and yet was mostly due to a hell of a lot of hard work, sweat and tears.

And a little blood. I couldn't count the number of stitches I'd sewn into my dad over the years.

I sniffed, the memories flooding my brain. "Time to go."

Fridge picked up two of the bags, while Rogan and Vincent grabbed the rest.

I walked next to Shadow, down the road, and toward the hole in the earth that would lead us to the underground.

We made it there in record time, or perhaps that was just because I was too busy looking around and absorbing everything around us.

The trees, the lights, the fresh air, the people.

Because too soon we were standing outside a vampire blood bar, which marked the entrance to the underground.

"This it?" Max asked.

Fridge nodded. "Yep. But it's heavy. Let Vincent get it."

I grinned over at my big dragon shifter as he proudly watched Vincent open the grate.

He was falling in love with my vampire mate, and it was kind of amazing to watch.

The grate creaked open and Rogan walked over to the hole. "It's time."

He slung the bag over his shoulder, and put his night vision goggles on his head, ready to pull them down once he stepped into the darkness. "Remember," he said. "There's a one-floor drop, a road, then another drop into the level we're going. The mission is get in, grab the women, and get out."

The men around me nodded and I shivered with a horrible premonition that made my stomach curl. Most of them weren't getting out alive.

I forced myself to say something. I had to. "Th-thank you all. I really can't tell you how much I appreciate what you're doing here today. For me. For my dad."

The men, like most men, just nodded or grunted at me with acknowledgment.

I sighed, grabbed my goggles and followed Rogan into hell.

CHAPTER 16
VINCENT

I held the grate open to the underground and had to watch as my female mate, Fridge, and Rogan descended the ladder until I couldn't see them anymore.

It made me sick to stomach and desperate to go after them.

What if there's a team waiting for them in the tunnels and I can't get to them in time?

But no one else had the strength to hold the grate open, so I clenched my teeth and stood like a statue.

Shadow, then the other six men followed, all of them armed to the teeth and calmer than I'd expected. Obviously, Rogan and Fridge knew what they were talking about when they'd recommended these individuals.

I only hope we're not leading them to their deaths.

As soon as the last man went down the ladder, I climbed in and closed the grate, anxious to be close to my mates once more.

Although Fridge and Rogan were very capable fighters, vanquishing vampires took a whole lot more strength than they naturally possessed. Especially the older vamps, like the fathers. They were lethal.

I shuddered at the thought and hurried past the six men from Hunters. I caught up to Fridge, who stood next to Sadie, looking hilarious in his night vision goggles.

I tried not to laugh and I managed it, however a smile may have snuck out. They looked like strange beetles down here, although I could understand why they needed the goggles.

It was dark. Unnaturally so, in the underground, which was designed for vampires, and shifters like Shadow, with serpent and nocturnal creatures like the fox mixed into their blood.

Shadow limped up to me, strangely void of all protective gear.

I didn't ask why he would choose not to wear even a vest to safeguard his vital organs. The man was a legend amongst all creatures. And he didn't smell appetizing to me; quite the opposite. It was no wonder vampires detested biting him.

"Everyone's here?" I asked the group.

Fridge glanced around. "Yes. Do you think they would have replaced the guard on the entrance door?"

I nodded. "I do. Which means we need to attack as a group." It had taken the three of us—Fridge, Rogan and me—to kill the last guard they had stationed at that door. If there were two of them or more, we'd be in for a fight.

Fridge indicated one of the other huge guys. "Travis, you stick with us. The rest of you guard Sadie. The entrance to the vault is an extremely heavy metal door and it will probably have a guard. Vincent, Rogan, Trav and I will take him out and force open the door. The rest of you keep Sadie safe."

"Where's the door?" Max asked suddenly.

Fridge indicated down the tunnel. "We've still gotta go down another ladder and another level, but it's not far. Stay close."

I saw a couple of the men shudder at the mention of going further into the earth.

I didn't mind it myself. It was dark and slightly warmer than this level. But for a human, to be trapped so far beneath the fresh air made many of them nervous.

"Let's go," Fridge said, taking Sadie's hand and tugging her along the corridor toward the entrance to the second level.

I stuck close behind him, with Rogan and Shadow at my tail.

We reached the grate and I lifted it up, allowing Fridge to go down the ladder first. The hairs on my arms stood on end as I watched him go. He was so precious to me now. If something happened to him...

I shook myself and forced a grim smile to my lips for the benefit of the rest of the group. There was no going back now, no matter what.

The troop descended to the next level and we walked past the bar and towards the entrance to the blood ring.

I glanced around, looking for signs of life, but the tunnels were strangely vacant. I hadn't even seen anyone in the bar when we passed, which was strange and disturbing. Although, this was the most likely time of day for the vampires to be home, resting. It was why I'd recommended it.

But something didn't feel right.

Then again, when would it? In a month? In a year? If Sadie's mom really was down here, could we leave her even another day?

I hurried past the half dozen from Hunters again to join the front group, where Fridge was convincing Sadie to stand back.

"Please, go and stand with the other guys while we sort this out."

"But I..."

I walked forward and smiled at her, ready to cajole our mate for her own safety.

"Stay here, and hopefully we won't be long. If we get around that corner and there's a whole coven of vampires waiting to take us out, I'll yell 'Run,' and I need you—no matter what—to do as I say. Do you understand?"

I was trying to be calm and patient, but this was important. "Sadie?"

She crossed her arms over her chest, and I was sure she was pouting behind all that gear.

I reached out to her and squeezed her arm. "Sweetheart. You need to promise us, that if we tell you to run, you'll run. We'll hold them off as long as we can. You have three men who are willing to die for you, but we can't be worrying about you. It's dangerous for us. Do you understand?"

Surely, appealing to her in this way would work.

When her arms fell away and she nodded, I grinned. "Good girl." I turned back around and said to my team, "Let's go."

And with Fridge, Travis and Rogan, we rounded the corner and came up against... nothing.

"What the..."

I stopped and looked at the men next to me.

Travis grinned. "That's a good thing. Right?"

I looked at Fridge, fear eating at my gut.

"What do you think, Vincent?" Fridge asked.

"I feel like we're walking into a trap." There, I'd said it.

I backed up and hurried around the corner to meet Sadie and the guys once more.

"What happened?" Sadie asked, running up to me.

"There's no one there," I said. "I think we're about to walk into a trap."

Max said, "How do you know?"

"Well, I don't. But it feels like one. It's too quiet down here today. There's no guard. I just... I don't like it."

Max laughed. "The vampire's scared of the underground. A bit tragic, dude."

Fridge growled from beside me and I wanted to grin with happiness at his natural defense of me. Though it was hardly necessary. I could rip this shifter in half.

Plus, now wasn't the time.

"Look. I might be wrong, but I had to say something. I'm worried we're walking into a trap here."

Sadie reached out to me, gripping my fingers. "If you think we should go back, we will. But when is it going to be safer to return, do you think?"

"I don't know." *Never* would be an appropriate response.

"I think we should just... go. Maybe we lucked out today with the guard," Max said.

I glared at the shifter. He was really starting to annoy me.

"Why are you so determined to push us into going now?" I asked, narrowing my gaze at him.

He laughed. The idiot laughed! "The money, of course. I'm assuming we don't get paid unless we go in there."

That was true. But money wasn't worth dying for. "I'd be happy to compensate you."

Sadie squeezed my arm again. "I'd really like to proceed, Vincent. I don't feel like we'll get another chance if we don't go now. Unless, you absolutely believe it's the wrong choice."

I couldn't say that. Not for sure. There was no evidence that I was right. It was just... a feeling.

"No," I said, shaking my head. "I don't have any proof that I'm right. So, if you want to go ahead with the plan, let's do it."

And to hell with the consequences. I hadn't expected to get out of here alive anyway.

"Okay. Thank you. Let's go together, then."

Sadie led the way this time and we all made our way to the huge iron door. Last time we needed a key.

"Do we still have the key?" I asked, realizing there might not be another way in.

Rogan dropped to his knees and rummaged through the bag at his feet. "I pocketed the last one. And I brought it with us. Hang on... Here."

He brandished the key and my heart fell. *Damn it.* I'd been hoping that would stop us.

I took the key and tried it in the lock, wistful they had changed the combination.

But no, the lock twisted and clicked as it unlocked.

This was getting to the "this is too easy" stage.

But the group huddled around me, breathing down my neck, wanting to move forward.

"Fridge, help me with this," I said, and began pulling at the heavy door. This part was not so easy. It took Max and Rogan stepping up to help us in order to finally open it wide enough for our team to get through.

And hopefully we'd be coming out carrying the women.

By the time we'd finished opening the massive door, we were all panting and sweating and I was beginning to feel the pulse of adrenaline.

Maybe we *could* do this.

I took over. "Fridge and I are on point. Everyone, get your weapons out, eyes open, and work together. It's the only way we're getting these women home."

And it would be. There would be guys who needed to fight, men who needed to carry women, and those who would need to grab Sadie and run. Probably.

Fridge took out a large knife he carried at his waist, the silver glinting even in the intense darkness. "Vincent and I are lead. Follow our instructions."

We crept in, moving into the darkness then surfacing in the first room. It was dimly lit and furnished with chairs and a few beds. And there they were. The victims of the blood ring. Three women attached to IVs, being siphoned of their blood.

There was a pregnant young woman and two who appeared older. All looking pale and drawn and barely alive.

To my horror, my fangs descended at the smell of the fresh blood in the air.

The women all turned toward us and their mouths dropped open.

Sadie ran to them and whispered, "We're here to rescue you. Quickly. Let's untie you."

I forced my lips over my fangs to hide them and began pulling the IVs out of the females' arteries. I'd done some medical training a hundred years ago. One of my many occupations.

The women gasped. "He's a vampire."

Sadie nodded. "Yes. And he's here to help." She turned to the men. "Tony. Travis. Come and grab these women."

Shadow suddenly appeared beside me, growling a strange sound. "I'll take this one."

He swung the pale woman that lay in the bed in front of me up into his arms and she moaned in pain.

He was shaking in the strangest way, one I remembered vividly.

Shadow had found his Fated Mate. And it was a woman who'd been in the underground for God knows how long.

"Take her and go," I said to Shadow. "You two." I pointed at the two closest guys. "Pick up the women and follow Shadow. He knows the way to the hospital."

The men carefully picked up the women, the pregnant one groaning and grabbing for her belly.

"Go," I said, then Sadie jumped in their path. "Hang on. Please. Can you tell me if there's anyone else down here? Are there more women?"

The pregnant woman nodded her head, her neck as weak as a baby's.

Tony raised her higher on his chest so she could rest against his shoulder better.

"Through there. To the left, more."

"Go," I said, and Shadow led the group through the door and back toward the surface. Hopefully they weren't stopped, although by the look on Shadow's face, he'd die before he let anyone near the woman he was carrying.

I turned back and watched Sadie shoot off in the direction the woman had directed, through the left door.

I ran after her, Rogan and Fridge hot on our heels.

The smell in the room was intoxicating in the worst possible way. Blood. Exotic, incredibly beautiful blood that I'd never smelled before.

It had to be a witch. A powerful witch.

I saw her before she spoke. A woman. In the corner, hooked up to one of the machines. But this woman wasn't just connected, she was tied down, ankles and wrists bound to the chair she sat in.

We crept forward, then Sadie let out a strange sob and fell to her knees in front of the woman.

"Mom? Mom? Is that you?"

The woman lifted her head, and there in the dark, I saw a spark of recognition.

She lifted one of her hands but couldn't reach out.

Then she spoke, "Sadie? You can't be real."

She then sobbed so hard I could barely understand her, but she was saying something like, "Help me. Please."

Rogan rushed forward and began tugging at the rope she was bound with. "Fridge, I need your knife."

Fridge came forward and gave Rogan his knife. He began sawing at the ropes, freeing her arms and legs.

I went to work on the IV needle in her arm, my stomach dropping with disgust at seeing all the different needle marks marring her flesh.

She coughed. "They're on my legs, too. They've run out of veins."

She was probably right. Next it would be to tap her carotid artery, and then she'd be done for.

"Let's get you out of here," I said, bending down to lift her, then I heard a thud and a cry from the other room.

"They're here," Sadie's mom gasped.

There was another groan and a scream. That was two down. We'd brought six from Hunters with us. Two were on their way back to the surface, so hopefully we still had two more left to fight with us.

I handed her to Rogan. "Take her. And if you get a chance to run, do it."

I was the strongest of our group, and I bolted for the exit to the room.

Fridge was just behind me as we charged into the fray. There were four vampires in the room, attacking our guys.

I went straight for the vampire closest to me, who was draining the blond shifter we'd brought with us. I ripped at his throat with my fingers and punched him hard in the head, snapping his neck.

He fell to the ground, along with the guy we'd brought with us.

Fridge cried out. I turned around and Fridge had disappeared, dragged off somewhere. Two of the vampires were now missing too.

"Fuck." This was not good.

The final vampire came at me and I grabbed the blade at my waist, gripping the black rubber handle, then driving the silver stake straight through his heart.

Then the whole room went cold and Max stepped out of the shadows, a grin on his stupid mouth.

He'd managed to get around the vamps pretty easily.

"Here he is. As you requested," Max announced, indicating to me.

The smell of an ancient father was like no other and, as Bartholomew glided into the dim light of the draining room, my heart sank.

We were fucked.

I straightened up, assessing the strengths and weaknesses of the room in a heartbeat. If I could get Rogan to run with Sadie and her mom, I might be able to hold off the father long enough for them to get away before he killed me. Maybe.

I was super-dosed on blood, but then again, the father probably was as well.

"Rogan. Bring the ladies out here please!" I called out, and I waited for them so I could put my plan into action.

Sadie

"Oh my God. Was that Max?" I asked, glancing over at Rogan. "Did he bring the vampires here?"

Rogan's nostrils flared as his eyes shifted to wolf yellow. "Yep. Fucking traitor."

He'd sold us out. One of my father's own had sold us out, on a mission to rescue Jack's wife. I couldn't believe it.

Rogan hoisted my mom higher on his chest, holding her tightly.

I glanced from him to the door when Vincent called for us. "What do I say?"

Rogan grimaced and lowered his voice. "We're in trouble in here, there's no way out. If Vincent wants us out there, he might have a plan."

I called toward the door, "We're coming!" I trusted Vincent with everything inside of me. I could only pray Rogan was right and my vampire mate had a plan.

My mother's hand suddenly grabbed my arm, quicker and stronger than she appeared.

"What's wrong?" I asked her, then almost slapped myself upside the head. "Um... apart from everything, of course."

A smile trembled on her thin lips. "Come closer."

I bent my head over my mother, turning away so I didn't poke her with my night vision goggles.

She whispered into my ear. "I knew you were coming for me. I felt it days ago. I have some magic left, so if we need to fight them... if there's no other choice... I can take them out."

I gasped and stared at her, shocked. "Really?" Then why hadn't she done it before?

She nodded, then pulled me down to her again. "But I might need your help. Your dormant magic can amplify mine. Are you willing to do that?"

I nodded and gulped. "Of course."

"It will hurt," she warned me.

I shrugged. It couldn't be worse than dying down here. "Anything, Mom. Anything."

She smiled at me then went back to cuddling into Rogan's chest like she was as helpless as they thought she was.

"You ready?" Rogan asked me and I nodded.

Would I ever be ready to walk into a room with a vampire father, a traitor, and my vampire mate? All of them ready to fight to the death?

Nope. But here goes.

I walked in front of Rogan and glanced around for signs of Fridge.

I couldn't see him anywhere, but as I searched inside my heart, I knew he was still alive. Somewhere. He wasn't dead yet. I'd know if he was. I'd feel it. And I was pretty sure Vincent would, too.

I walked up next to Vincent, forcing myself to stay calm despite the way my heart pumped frantically in my chest.

"So... traitor. What did you get for turning us in?" I spat at Max, who stood next to the vampire father, Bartholomew, still wearing the protective armor my dad had paid for, the night vision goggles I now owned.

He grinned at me. "A lot more money than you were offering."

Then he turned to Bartholomew. "So, where do I pick up the rest of what you owe me?"

Vincent began to chuckle. "You don't think you're actually getting out of here alive, do you?"

Max took a step back. "What are you talking about?"

I reached for my knife that was strapped to my thigh, pulled it from its sheath and flung it with as much strength as I had. With all the anger and pain in my heart.

There weren't many spots on Max's body that weren't covered in my protective gear, but that made my aim true.

The knife slid into his throat, in the gap between his chin and the Kevlar covering his chest.

Max staggered backwards, gasping as blood gushed down his chest. He fell against one of the chairs they'd kept the pregnant woman tied to, and I watched with a great sense of satisfaction as he bled out on the ground in a big, spluttering mess.

Then I remembered Bartholomew was in the room and glanced over at the vampire father. "Oh... I hope you didn't mind me killing your source."

I meant it sarcastically of course, but when Vincent chuckled, I glanced over at my vampire mate who was staring directly at the father.

"The vampires value their sources—" he began.

"But value nothing above loyalty," the father finished.

"So...." I started, "You're glad I killed him?"

Bartholomew smiled in the darkness. "Well, you did save me the effort. And you seemed to take a lot more pleasure in it than I would have."

I snorted. "I certainly did."

The father inclined his head. "I'm glad. So now that you will die, you can do so with a smile on your face and happiness in your heart."

ROGAN

I gripped Sadie's mom with both hands, trying to figure out what the fuck we were going to do. Vincent surely wouldn't have called us out here unless he had a plan.

How were we going to get past the vampire father? Vincent had said that he was so strong he could rip us in half before we realized he'd moved.

So why hadn't he already?

Was he savoring our demise?

And then the reason he hadn't already killed us came to light. "Put the witch down and step away," he said, looking straight at me.

He wants Sadie's mom safe.

"No," Sadie said, stepping in front of her mother. "You've had her long enough. I want her back."

He chuckled, the sound as ominous and poisonous as I could imagine.

Suddenly, Fridge came charging back into the room, covered in what I had to assume was his own blood.

But he was in full flight, his skin dark and scaly, his hands transitioned into claws.

He ripped into Bartholomew and I watched in awe for a moment as Fridge attacked without losing control of his shifter.

"Run!" Vincent screamed at me and pushed at Sadie. "Go. We'll cover you."

He launched at Bartholomew, joining Fridge in battle.

I didn't think; I just ran, pumping my legs as fast as they would go, Sadie hot on my heels.

We flew through the drain room, into the hallway and past that solid steel door.

That's as far as we got.

There was a group of vampires waiting for us on the other side of the door.

"Go back. Go back!" I yelled at Sadie, doubling back into the long hallway. "Is there another way out?" I asked her mother.

Sadie's mom shook her head and I backed into the corner of the strange room, pulling Sadie with me. My heart was pounding and my wolf was howling.

With two walls at my back, I only had to protect the front. But how the hell were we going to get out of this now?

*S*ADIE

We were trapped.

And worst of all, I could hear someone moving toward us once more. But it was Vincent, dragging his leg and gripping the side of his neck where he was bleeding.

"Oh my God, are you all right?" I asked.

Vincent shook his head, looking dazed and confused. "He let me go."

"Who?" I asked, then I heard it. The chuckle of the ancient vampire as he glided his way across the room toward us again.

"Sadie… I'll ask you again. Please. Put your mother down and leave her where she belongs."

Rogan's growl from beside me and my mother's gasp had my hands curling into fists at my side.

I forced myself to inject some levity into my tone, though sweat ran in my eyes and I could barely see through the night vision goggles now.

"Bart," I addressed the ancient vampire. "So nice of you to join us."

Fuck it.

I tore the goggles off my head, wiped at my face and eyes to clear some of the heat response, cleared the screen, and pulled them back on my head.

"That's so much better," I said, though a shudder ran through my body at the scene before me.

I could see so much better now, and that meant I could see the anger in Bartholomew's face. And the truly frightening number of vampires that had now infiltrated the room where we were trapped.

Suddenly, it hit me with the force of a thousand knives. One simple truth. We were all going to die unless I could work something out.

"Found this one in the corner," said a vampire to my right as he hauled Fridge's body along the ground and threw him at us.

He fell to the floor with a heavy thud and I rushed forward, with Vincent at my side.

"Fridge! Is he all right?" I asked Vincent, who was running his hands over Fridge's body.

He was unconscious, and bleeding from every body part I could see. His face, his neck, his arms, his chest. His arm was broken too, if the angle it hung at was any indication.

Vincent dropped his head and pressed it against Fridge's massive chest. "He's still alive."

Vincent looked up at me and stared me straight in the face, and

the message was clear. Fridge was alive, but barely. We had to get out. And we had to find a way to carry him.

Fuck. The odds of us getting out of here in one piece just got smaller.

I straightened my spine and stood tall, staring at the old vampire father. "What do you want?"

He smiled with a look made me shiver from head to toe.

"Simple. I want you and every other witch in the state, bound and bleeding for me."

I shuddered again. "I don't know any other witches. I've never even met any of my mother's family."

I stared straight at Bartholomew and I was proud how steady my voice remained.

But I was telling the truth, and from the way his lips suddenly pulled down, he knew it.

"Then I'll just take you. Grab her," he said.

"No!" Rogan gripped me and tugged me back to my mother.

Vincent put his hands under Fridge's arms and dragged him back into our corner.

So, there we were, our backs pressed, quite literally, against a wall. Shadow had gotten out and taken some of the women with him. And us... we were together. All four of us.

Five, if you counted my unborn baby.

My hand went to my belly and pressed flat. *I'm so sorry.*

I put my other arm out and yelled, "Stop! I'll go with you. Just let my mates leave."

Bartholomew chuckled. "I don't think so. We'll hook them up to a machine and drain them. Shifter blood is highly sought after, especially a dragon."

His eyes lit up with pure malice and my neck tingled with a warning as anger pooled in my blood.

"Except for Vincent, of course," he added.

I swallowed hard, willing my anger to grow, to flicker, so that I could feel the magic my mother had spoken about only moments earlier.

"What will you do with Vincent?" I asked, glancing down at where he squatted next to Fridge's body.

Damn, I hope he's still breathing.

"He needs to die for his treason, that's obvious," Bartholomew said, like it wasn't someone's life he was talking about. "But how much pain we should inflict beforehand will be the question. Do we torture him for the information he has? Or simply tie him in the desert and let the sun turn him to ash?"

My mouth ran dry and my heart began to pound in a totally different way.

"I said I'd go with you willingly. Just let them go." Why the hell wouldn't he take that deal? "Surely I'm worth more to you than them?"

When he shook his head slowly, my heart sank. I was going to have to try something else.

Then a thought occurred to me, and I wasn't going to get a second chance at this one. "Can I ask you one question before you kill us all?"

Bartholomew inclined his head as though he would grant me this small favor.

I clenched my teeth and blew out a breath through my nose. "I need to know who killed my dad."

I heard my mother's gasp from beside me and ignored it the best I could. I had a mission. I would explain everything to her later.

Bartholomew frowned. "The vampire assassin that carried out that assignment has been dispatched since that night."

A sense of triumph filled my heart. *I hope it was painful.*

"Okay. Well then, tell me who ordered the hit. Was it you?" I asked, as gently as I could, hoping he would admit to it, and I would, with pleasure, help my mother kill this creep.

Bartholomew met my night vision gaze, the ghost of a smile lifting his lips.

I waited, my heart beating so hard I was afraid I'd miss the words when he said them.

"Please. Just tell me," I asked again.

The vampire father sighed. "If you must know... yes, it was me. We kept your father alive to raise you to adulthood, to become a new donor. But when the time came to take you, he kept getting in the way. And he wouldn't help us with information on your mother's line, no matter how much money we offered him. It was time. Long past it, to be frank. But the years go by so fast..."

I inhaled sharply against the pain stabbing at my heart.

He'd died for me, like I always feared he would.

I reached for my mother's hand and she pressed closer to me, whispering in my ear. "If I can use you as my base, I might be able to do it."

I knew what she meant, and so did Rogan.

And from the sudden fury I saw on Bartholomew's face, he'd heard her, too.

"Get her."

"No!" I yelled, squeezing my mother's hand tight. "Now."

The light hit first, like in a lightning storm. The blast of white filled the room.

I screamed at the pain in my eye sockets as I was momentarily blinded.

I wrenched off my night vision goggles with my free hand.

Then, like the thunder, the noise hit. But instead of the roll of storm clouds, the sound came in the form of my scream inside my head, and then in the room around us.

The pain was so intense, I could barely stand, but I forced my knees to lock and stared at the vampires in front of me. They were flinching in the face of my mother's magic, but they weren't dying, nor were they running away.

In fact, Bartholomew was slowly, inch by inch, step by step, moving closer.

"Turn it up!" I yelled at her, though the burn in my blood, in my skin, was so intense I wanted to curl into a ball and rock myself to sleep.

She glanced at me, her sallow skin quivering with the force. "It's gonna hurt," she said, trembling.

I wasn't sure if she meant her or me, but the answer didn't matter, though it would probably be both.

I glanced down at Vincent and Fridge, feeling Rogan's hands on me.

I wasn't letting them die. Not for me.

Not here. Not now.

I extended my free arm and held out my palm, willing my untrained magic to curl with my mother's and blast these fuckers to hell.

"Do it!"

She twisted my wrist and shot her magic harder at the vampires, and they began to die. Screaming in pain, their skin evaporated. Their bodies turned to black dust.

Bartholomew trudged through the white light as one would move through a snowstorm.

I took all my anger, all my hate, all my protective instincts and focused all that into my hand.

White magic shot out of my palm directly at him.

It forced him back.

"More!" I screamed, at my mother, or myself, I wasn't sure.

Their screams and my own were ringing in my ears, but I couldn't stop. I wouldn't. Not until we were safe. And free.

We blasted the whole room and beyond. Pain, like fire, stripped my bones, my skin, all the way down to my toes until finally, Bartholomew began to wilt like a flower under the hot sun. His skin and flesh melted away and he too, joined the pile of ash on the floor.

The vampires were dead, and my mother fell to the ground beside me.

The pain inside me stopped, but there was nothing left to hold me up.

I crawled to her.

I did what Vincent had done with Fridge and pushed her frail body over, placing my ear on her chest.

My own breathing was too loud, and my heart hammered like it was racing to the finish line. I held my breath, and there was the faintest of sounds.

Lub-dub. Lub-dub.

I pushed myself up a little so I was still lying down, but no longer on her frail rib cage.

I looked up at Rogan, who was staring down at me. "I think she's still alive."

He crouched down and put a hand to her neck. He nodded. "There's a pulse. It's faint, but it's still there."

I was feeling dizzy. Beyond dizzy. I was going to faint or vomit. Or both.

I glanced up at Rogan. "Get us out of here."

And then the whole world went black.

CHAPTER 19

ROGAN

I stared down at my mate, unconscious, lying next to her mother.

"God, they were incredible." I glanced around the room, where there was nothing left of the vampires who had been set on murdering us.

Nothing but piles of dust and ash.

Vincent grabbed my arm. "We need to get them out of here. I can carry Fridge. Can you carry Sadie and her mother?"

It would be a stretch. One over each shoulder, perhaps? "I think I can. You sure you got him?"

Fridge had to weigh a hundred pounds more than Vincent, and I knew Vincent had taken a few injuries in the fight. More than a few.

He nodded. "I can do it." He grabbed Fridge's arm, knelt down, and pulled Fridge over his back in an old-fashioned fireman's carry.

"Get the women," he said, his face a grimace of pain.

I didn't stop to ask if he was okay. We'd only be okay when we got out of here.

I picked Sadie up first, putting her over my left shoulder, then very carefully put her mother over my right.

I wasn't sure how fast I'd be, but I had them both. "Let's go."

We moved along the tunnel, stepping over the ash of the fallen vampires and moving through the now-empty blood ring draining center.

Shadow had gotten the women out. There was no one left.

We kept moving, finally reaching the ladders to get back to the surface. I couldn't climb with two women over my shoulders and no arms to hold the rungs with.

"I'm going to have to do this in two trips."

Vincent turned and looked at me, then nodded. "I'll go first. And I'll help you lift them up through the hole."

I nodded, and we did exactly that. Somehow, Vincent, with all his vampire strength, carried Fridge up the ladder and pushed him up through the grate, then put him down on the first floor.

Panting with exhaustion, he reached through the hole and I set Sadie down to carefully carry her mother up to Vincent.

"God… she practically weighs nothing," he said as he took her from me.

I nodded and went back for Sadie, who was still unconscious. "You shouldn't have risked your life with that magic. It could have killed you," I said, even though she couldn't hear me. I shook my head.

I carried her over my shoulder, up the ladder, climbing one rung at a time.

Vincent took her and pulled her up to the next level. "Yes, but she is our Sadie," he said in answer to what I'd said below. "Fierce and protective and loyal. That's why I love her."

I nodded. That was why we all loved her so much.

I glanced around, looking for anyone or anything that might attack. But there was no one to be seen.

We rested for a moment, then heard footsteps running down the tunnel. I jumped to my feet and reached for the knife at my waist, finding it missing.

Ah, well. I clenched my hands into fists. We didn't get this far to die now.

A wave of relief washed over me when I saw one of the Hunters, Travis, running down the tunnel toward us.

He'd come back for us.

"Holy shit! You made it out!" he yelled, getting closer. "You all okay?"

I glanced at Vincent. "Define okay."

Vincent grinned at me, though he was as pale as a stale bottle of milk, and swaying slightly. He needed blood, and the rest of us needed medical care.

"Can you carry Sadie's mom?" I asked Travis, gesturing to the tiny woman lying next to Fridge. "I can't carry them both up the ladders and we've got one to go."

"Of course," Travis said, scooping her up into his arms. "Let's get moving, though. I sense movement in the tunnels, though I'm not sure how many."

I nodded and picked Sadie up, then glanced at Vincent. "You need help with him?"

I didn't know how I'd help, but we could swap for a bit.

But Vincent shook his head. "No. I've got him."

I grinned at the vampire as he pulled the huge dragon shifter up and over his body, groaning under the strain. "You really love him, don't you?" I asked.

Vincent stared at me for a moment, then shot me a grin. "Hell yes. Now let's go."

With the help of Travis, we managed to get our precious cargo up out of the underground, and into the daylight once more.

We collapsed onto the sidewalk, panting and sweating and swearing profusely. "Fucking hell. I can't believe we made it out alive."

Travis hailed a cab and pulled open the door. "Get in. All of you. You shouldn't stop. Just keep moving."

I glanced at Vincent. "To the country house?"

Vincent nodded. "You got the address?"

"Yeah. I do." Sadie had given it to me before we left this morning, just in case.

We climbed into the cab and Travis looked at Vincent then said, "Just wait two minutes, okay?"

He hurried over to the vampire bar across the road, went inside, then returned quickly with two quarts of blood.

He passed them into the cab and the driver groaned. "No blood in the cab."

I rolled my eyes. "Trust me, we've got money to cover any damages."

"Go, and don't stop until you're safe," Travis said.

"Thank you for all your help, Travis," I said, then glanced up at him. "Did you get the women to the hospital with Shadow?"

Travis nodded. "Yeah. We did. They're being looked after by some magic guy."

I grinned at him. "Good luck Trav."

He patted the top of the cab. "Take care, guys." He limped back into the shadows from whence he'd appeared.

I re-adjusted Sadie, who was lying across my lap and looked at Vincent. "Time to go?"

He nodded. "Yes. Let's go."

I gave the address to the driver as Vincent began to drink from the casks Travis had bought for him. He had one hand resting on Fridge's still form.

I kissed Sadie on the forehead and held her close.

It was time to take our mates home.

SADIE

Damn... everything hurt!

I opened my eyes and pressed both hands to my temples, trying to stem the throb of pain. My arms ached, my skin burned, and the world around me spun.

But I was alive!

And if I was lucky, so was my baby.

"She's awake!" I heard someone call at my side, then turned my head to meet Rogan's intense gaze.

His hand slid over my arm and interlinked our fingers. "Sadie, my beautiful mate. How are you feeling?"

I swallowed hard, my throat sore and my mouth dry. "Thirsty."

Rogan didn't move, but called out, "Bring some water."

I glanced around the room, trying to get my bearings. "Where am I?"

Then I saw my mom lying in the single bed next to me, pale as a ghost. "Oh my God. Is she all right?"

Rogan gripped my hand and Vincent walked in the room, looking strong and healthy. "Sadie... I..." He didn't seem to know how to finish that sentence, so instead dropped his head and kissed me on the lips. "It's so good to see you awake."

He stood straight again and handed me a glass of water. "How about you sit up?"

I nodded and tried to push against the mattress, but my muscles hurt too much. "Damn, not sure I can."

Rogan carefully lifted me up and placed pillows behind my back. I leaned against the headboard.

I took the glass and put my lips to the rim, taking grateful sips to wet my mouth and swallow.

"How long have I been out?" It had to be more than a day the way I was feeling. And to put it nicely, I felt like death warmed over.

"Two days," Rogan said.

My mouth dropped open. "Whoa."

"I was going to put an IV in tonight if you didn't wake up on your own. Dehydration was becoming a problem."

"And that's why I need to pee so bad," I said, and pulled the sheets back.

I gasped at the pain that shot through me.

Rogan swept me up into his arms. "Allow me to escort you."

I gripped his neck and let him carry me to the bathroom, where I went to the toilet and splashed some water on my face.

The house we were in was neat and had a country-type, old-fashioned feel.

When I staggered back out of the bathroom, Rogan handed me some tablets. "For the pain."

I didn't ask what they were, I just put them in my mouth and swallowed them down with some water.

I took a step and my legs shook. This time, Vincent hoisted me up and carried me back to the bed.

"How's my mom doing? Where's Fridge?" I asked, then a streak of horror shot through me. "Please tell me he got out."

Rogan grinned. "He's in the next room. He's still unconscious. He was pretty badly drained by the vamps, but Vincent carried him out."

I glanced at my vampire mate. "But he's like... three hundred pounds."

Vincent shrugged and I glanced over at Rogan, who looked proud.

"Damn... wish I'd seen it."

Vincent chuckled. "You and your mom saved us all. You didn't need to see me carrying an unconscious Fridge. It wasn't pretty."

"What wasn't pretty?" Fridge grumbled from the doorway.

"Fridge!" I cried out as I gazed upon his gorgeousness. He was wearing a pair of thin black joggers and nothing else.

He was pale and had more scars than I could count, especially on his arms now. But... "You're a sight for sore eyes."

He staggered over to me and kissed my lips. "So are you." His grin was crooked but genuine. He headed back to the doorway and leaned against the frame for support.

Vincent didn't say anything, he simply walked slowly to the doorway, then wrapped his arms around Fridge and held him tight.

Fridge frowned, looking confused, but then he hugged him back, cupping the back of the vampire's head gently. "You okay?" he asked Vincent.

Vincent broke off and huffed out a laugh. "Me? You're the one who's been unconscious for two days."

"Yeah, feels like it," Fridge said, swaying on his feet.

"Come sit down," Vincent said, taking Fridge's hand and pulling him to sit in the chair by the bed,

"Is my mom okay?" I asked, "Has a doctor been by?"

Would they have risked calling one?

Rogan shook his head. "No. Vincent has some medical training so he checked you all out, went out to the local hospital and stole some supplies, and he's been looking after you."

Vincent nodded solemnly. "You, I've mostly just been watching, Fridge needed some repairs, and I considered a blood transfusion, but he didn't need it in the end."

"And my mom?" I asked, my gaze furtively shooting across the room to where she lay quietly.

I swallowed hard. She looked almost dead, she was so still.

Vincent squeezed my shoulder. "She needs rest. I hooked up an IV the first day we got here, and I gave her an iron infusion. We'll see what else she needs when she wakes up."

"Great." I leaned my head back, sliding deeper into the mattress and under the covers once more.

My hand slipped to my belly, cradling the life I hoped grew there.

"Are you okay?" Vincent asked. "Would you like something to eat."

I smiled, thinking that now may be the time to tell them my news. "I would, but now that we're all together and awake and alive... I want to tell you guys something."

They all waited, staring at me. My wolf mate, my dragon mate and my vampire mate.

Three men to love me, and hopefully, whatever children came along.

"I don't know for sure, because I haven't seen a doctor yet, but I think I'm pregnant."

Vincent froze, Fridge's mouth dropped open, and Rogan grinned like a Cheshire cat. Or in his case, a satisfied wolf.

"It's not certain," I added. "But I'm late, and considering us all being Fated Mates, and all the sex... well..."

I shrugged. Surely it didn't take a genius to add those numbers up.

"This is fantastic news," Rogan said, reaching out and rubbing his hand tenderly over my belly. "How are you feeling?"

"Fine at the moment," I said. "Other than... you know, half dead from my mother using me as a booster for her own magic."

A growl came from Fridge. "We would never have let you go into the underground if we knew."

Vincent suddenly snapped out of his statue-like state. "And that's exactly why she didn't tell you."

Then he looked at me, his eyes sad. "I know the baby is not mine, but as your mate, I hope you will include me also. I can certainly help with all the night feedings."

Rogan laughed. "Dibs on the non-night stuff."

I reached out to Vincent and grabbed his hand, pulling him close. "Don't say that. All three of you will be this baby's daddy. And hopefully we'll have a lot more children. I grew up as an only child, so I want this one to have at least one more sibling, maybe two or three."

I wanted a family, a big one. And with three mates, surely more than one baby wouldn't be a problem.

"If that's what you want."

I pulled him down for a kiss. "I do. As I'm sure Fridge does too."

I glanced over at my dragon shifter mate whose eyebrows were still tugged low. "Hey," I said. "Did you know that Vincent carried your big butt up two ladders? From the blood ring rooms, all the way to the top?"

I hoped that was right, but that was the impression I'd gotten from Rogan.

Fridge's uncertain expression cleared immediately as he stared at Vincent. "Is that true?"

Vincent nodded.

Then Fridge grabbed for him, pulling Vincent onto his lap. "So, I owe you my life, again, huh?"

Vincent grinned this time. "I suppose so."

Fridge cupped Vincent's jaw and kissed him.

I bit my lip as tears swam in my eyes. I was surrounded by love, and this baby would be, too. I pulled Rogan onto the bed with me and cuddled into his broad chest.

My father's murder had been avenged, and we'd gotten those women out of the blood ring.

And somehow, miracle upon miracle, I had my mom back.

I closed my eyes and sighed. I had to wonder, what would tomorrow bring?

EPILOGUE

SADIE

Six months later

The spark I'd been trying to create with my hand died, like I'd blown out a candle on a birthday cake.

"I'll never get this," I muttered, snapping my fingers on my right hand and trying to bring it back. I was getting so frustrated at the lack of magical ability I had, even after six months of training.

My mother laughed and walked toward me, where I sat on the swing in the huge backyard. "You're seven months pregnant, Sadie. Your energy is elsewhere at present. Stop expecting the world of yourself."

I rubbed a hand over my large belly and sighed.

Mom bent over and spoke directly to my bump. "And how is my grandbaby today?"

I grinned at her affectionate tone. Never in my wildest dreams had I imagined I would have my mother here with me, alive and well, for the birth of my first child.

"He... or she, is good," I said, rubbing the spot under my ribs where my child liked to kick me. "Active, but good."

"Active is a sign of good health," Mom said, and led me over to a couple of chairs we had set up on the patio that wrapped around the house.

I sighed and listened to the men inside, banging and hammering away. "Do you think they'll be done by the time the baby comes?" I asked.

They were building an extension onto the house—a nursery—for our little one.

Mom nodded. "Yes. But whether or not we'll have time to decorate it... well, that's another question."

I sighed and stretched in the chair. "How'd you sleep last night, Mom? Any better?"

Mom winced a little, then smothered it with a smile. "You heard me?"

I nodded. "Yeah, we always do. I was just hoping it was getting better."

Mom still had terrible nightmares. She was a land mine of emotional trauma and scars. We had to be so careful about what we said or did.

Vincent walked on egg shells around her, and wouldn't feed on the property at all, choosing to drive two hours to another city to get blood.

I wasn't sure she'd ever fully recover.

Mom sighed. "I am, so much better. I can sleep now. I can see the sky." She glanced up.

The guys had put a massive sky light over Mom's bed so anytime she wanted to, she could reassure herself she was no longer trapped underground.

"And your mates are just beautiful, Sadie," Mom said, smiling. "They make me feel a lot safer. Just like your father did."

I rubbed my belly thoughtfully. "I heard from Shadow yesterday. He wants us to come back and take over again. The business, the apartment. I think he feels guilty for living our life, or something."

Mom bit her lip. "I can imagine he would, but really, he's doing you and all of us a favor keeping everything running, keeping your father's business alive."

"That's true. I'll send him a message to thank him for everything he's doing, and that we won't be coming back for a year at least."

"Are your mates happy with that?" Mom asked.

I nodded. "For the moment. I know they miss the city and their jobs a little. But the baby and I are more important to them, and until we know it's safe, we're staying here."

Mom excused herself to go inside and make herself a pot of tea, and I stayed on the patio, talking to my baby and singing softly to myself.

We had money, a house, and a family none of us had ever dreamed was possible.

Shadow could take on the blood ring and hold court for all the paranormals in the city.

I was staying here for now.

Mated to three men—two of whom were also mated to each other—pregnant and happy. Life didn't get any better than this.

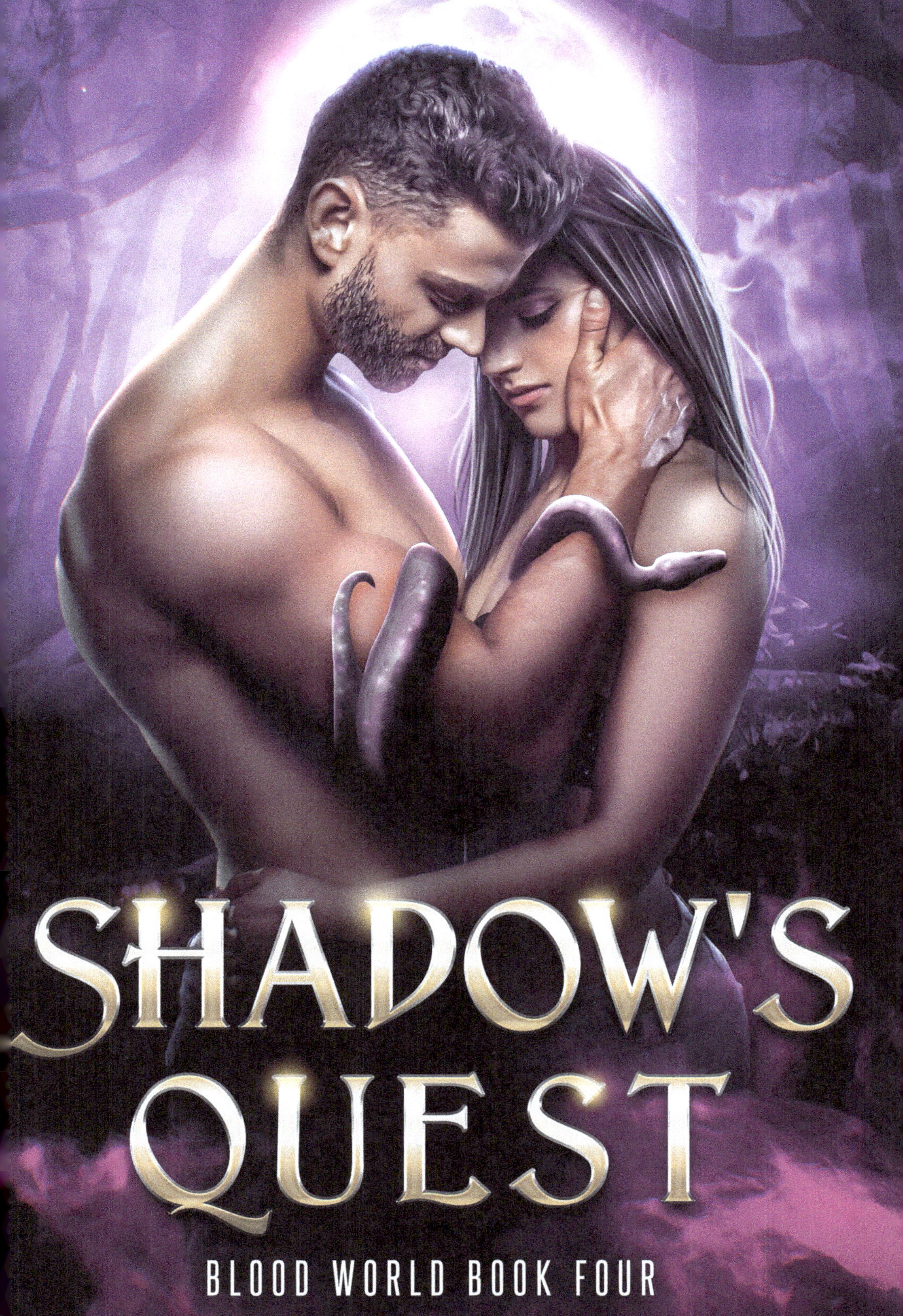

SHADOW'S QUEST
BLOOD WORLD BOOK FOUR
TAMSIN BAKER & AMELIA SHAW

SHADOW'S QUEST

THE PARANORMALS BLOOD WORLD BOOK 4

SHADOW

The blood ring's underground operation was like walking into hell on earth. Dark, disgusting, and loaded with the metallic tang of blood in the air.

I went into the depths of darkness willingly, because my cousin Sadie had asked for my help. And my aunt, Sadie's mom, had been held prisoner down in the underground for almost twenty years.

Twenty *years*. We'd only just learned she might still be alive. That fact was nothing short of a miracle. Bringing down those vampire leeches was worth anything to me. Even if it meant my life.

I followed Sadie and her bounty hunter team down the manhole, past the vampire bar I often frequented with my clients, then kept going. Past the point I'd ever gone; past the point of no return. We climbed down into yet another level of darkness. Then, after killing a vampire and breaking into the blood ring's guarded rooms, we stepped through the huge door designed to keep everyone out.

I crept along the hallway like a rat, quiet and quick, and kept a lookout while Sadie and Vincent rushed forward, speaking in hushed tones to the women we'd come to save. Witches, who'd been kept down here by the vampires and hooked up to machines and tubes so they could be drained to within an inch of their lives, and then drained again. Over and over. Unwilling blood donors for the wealthy vampires' tastes.

I rounded a corner and the hallway opened into a chamber where there were three women. None in this chamber were my aunt. But then my attention snagged on one of the women. She was lying on a bed, strapped to a machine that was syphoning her magical blood from her veins. She was so pale she was practically the same color as the once-white sheets, and even in the dim light of the room, I could see the weakness in her body. The frailness in her muscles.

How long had she been down here? And what had she endured?

I could barely take my eyes off her. The pull toward the woman was so strong; so all-consuming.

Sadie was untying the pregnant woman on the next bed. Vincent stepped over to my woman...

I shuddered.

My woman.

Yes. She was my woman. My *mate.*

No! I'm not meant to have a fated mate.

My abomination of mixed genetics should never have created a person such as myself, let alone allowed Fate to hand me a woman as precious as this one.

Surely, Fate could not be so cruel to this poor damaged soul as to shackle her with *me* as her mate?

I took a step closer, watching as Vincent withdrew the needle from her arm. I felt it again—an undeniable desire to grab her and hold her close. I would kill anyone who threatened to hurt her.

My body trembled as I walked forward on unsteady legs, desire coursing through me. Every instinct in me was fighting the urge to snatch her from Vincent. My various shifters snarled and hissed. I could barely stand the buzz in my mind.

But they were all in agreement about one thing. They wanted— no, they *needed*—the woman lying on the bed in front of me.

She was dying a slow death, and if we didn't get her out of here and to medical help soon, she wouldn't make it. My mate was in danger of dying before she and I ever introduced ourselves.

"I'll take this one," I growled out once Vincent had detached the needles from her skin. I bent over her and didn't hesitate as I lifted the woman into my arms.

She moaned softly as I transferred her from the rancid bedding and encouraged her to lean against my chest. The stench of waste filled my nostrils.

I held my breath, my shifters flinching at the smells of the room. But when she turned her head and pressed closer to my shoulder, nuzzling in like a small kitten, a deep shudder of happiness pulsed through me.

Damn it all. I was never meant to feel any of this.

"Tony and Travis. Take these two, and go with Shadow. He knows the way to the hospital," Sadie said, and I nodded as I turned back toward the exit.

I did know the way. Taking the injured women to the hospital had been my idea. And there was nothing—literally nothing—I wanted more than to get my mate out of here and secure medical help to ensure she could recover.

The two beefy bounty hunters Sadie had brought with us picked up the other two women who had been on the draining machines in this room. One was extremely pregnant, and the sight of her belly made my heart pound and anger pulse through my gut.

What sort of monster would do this to a helpless woman? Rape her until she was pregnant, then steal her baby for its blood? All the while draining her of vital blood, too.

Vampires...

I held my mate tighter to my chest and clenched my teeth. "Let's go."

I forged forward, back the way we'd come. Tony and Travis joined me, and we headed down the dark tunnel and through the iron door, making our way up toward the light. Ahead of us in the tunnel, three vampires suddenly loomed.

"Oh, fuck," I said, slowing my steps and considering options.

"What is it?" Travis asked, staring ahead.

The two hunters wore night goggles to help them see in the dim light. My shifter genetics included both fox and hare, so my nocturnal vision made the need for goggles redundant.

"Vampires."

The woman in my arms was barely conscious, and yet she whimpered when I lay her down near the wall, as if she couldn't bear to be parted from me.

"I'll be right back," I whispered to her, then stepped back into the firing line.

"You two stay with the women," I told Tony and Travis. "I've got these guys."

Three vampires were going to test my skills. Probably to the point of breaking them. But no matter what happened to me, I'd never fought for anything more important than the mate a few feet away from me.

I took a breath and clenched my fists, determination pulsing through me. They would not get to her.

"Here," Travis said, pressing a gun into my hand.

I lifted my arm and fired at them, relieved to see my aim was true for at least one of the vampires. The silver bullets hit the central vampire in the chest.

I squeezed the trigger over and over. One, two, three, four.

The other two vampires darted out of the way as the middle one went down, turning to ash.

I threw the gun to the ground as the remaining vampires launched at me. I slid to the side, pulling my knives from the sheaths strapped to my thighs.

I sliced through the air. A sharp bite sank into my lower leg. I slid out of the way of whatever that was.

One of the vampires swung at me. I dodged, coming up under him to land a good jab into his throat. The other vampire leapt at me as I twisted, but he managed to wrap his arms around my chest from behind. He bore down.

I cried out as my ribs broke, the bone-cracking pops sounding like death popcorn in my head.

I threw back my head, hitting and dislodging the vampire, then took a swing at him with my silver knife. I scored a direct hit and he crumbled into ash behind me.

I panted hard, sweat forming on my forehead.

My leg was bleeding, and already infected from what I was pretty sure now was a vampire bite. I wouldn't die from that—I'd built up a pretty good tolerance to them—but it burned like hell.

The third vampire lunged at me and punched me in my already-broken ribs. Excruciating pain rolled over me. I dropped to my knees, clutching my ribcage. The world around me swayed. The vampire slammed his fist into my head. I rocked to the side, stomach churning, and slumped forward.

Maybe I wasn't going to win this fight after all.

The vampire stepped in front of me. He opened his mouth and exposed his teeth, triumph in his feral eyes.

Travis and Tony darted in from both sides. They grabbed the vampire, yanking him back. The vampire twisted and thrashed in their hold, but they tightened their grip on him.

"Stab him!" Travis yelled.

With effort, I pushed to my feet. I staggered forward and, using the last of my strength, slid my knife directly into the vampire's eye socket.

He crumbled into ash. I stumbled backwards, my head swimming.

"Thanks, guys," I panted, reaching for a lighter in my pocket.

I flicked the lighter, a huge flame rising from the silver square I'd carried with me for over a decade.

"You seriously stopping for a smoke?" Tony said.

I chuckled, not surprised they couldn't see my injuries.

"No. I need to cauterize the bleeding from my leg, or I'm not gonna make it."

There was deathly silence as I held a silver dagger to the flame, got it red hot, then took a deep breath. I'd used a lot of mental tricks over the years to deal with the chronic pain my birth condition gave me. But this was going to sting like a mother fucker.

"Want me to do it?" Travis asked, walking over.

"No... I..."

Maybe it would be easier if he did it.

Travis read my hesitation correctly, took the blade, squatted down and pressed the blazing hot metal against my leg.

I swallowed the scream that rose and clenched down on my jaw while swimming through the levels of consciousness. I refused to pass out.

"One. Two. Three." Travis pulled the blade away and stood. "And I thought the stories about you were exaggerated."

He chuckled before patting my shoulder. "You're the toughest bastard I've ever met."

"Thanks," I managed to say, the pain beginning to recede.

I reached down and touched my leg, and my broken ribs reminded me of why that wasn't a good idea.

At least the bleeding had stopped.

I tried to take another breath.

Shit.

Small, slow breaths. One foot in front of the other.

"We've gotta get out of here before any more come." Tony rushed to pick up his witch.

I limped over to my mate, but Travis bent over, picked her up, and deposited her into my arms.

I opened my mouth to thank him, but he was already picking up his witch. "You're right. We better go."

I nodded, sealing my pain barriers into place inside my mind. This was going to hurt, but once out in the fresh air, I'd feel better. No matter what.

"Okay. Let's go."

My mate put a hand on my neck, and that small warmth and attempt at comfort made the walk to the first ladder almost bearable.

"Back up the ladders," I said, as I stood at the bottom of the entrance and glanced up. "We're gonna have to work together to get them all up safely."

Travis nodded as he hoisted his very pregnant witch up his chest. "I'll need help."

I didn't want to hand my mate off to either one of the shifters again, but for her safety, it would be smarter to have them help. "I'll climb up first, then lift the women through the hole."

"You sure you're all right to do that?" Travis said, nodding at my chest. "You took quite a beating before."

I shrugged, ignoring the screaming from my broken ribs and the blood soaking my clothes. "Pain and I are old friends. I can do it."

Tony walked closer. "Do you want me to pass her up to you?"

I gripped my mate tighter in my arms. Putting her in a fireman's carry, then hoisting her up through the hole probably wasn't the best option for her.

"Ah, yeah. But can you hold yours as well?"

"I can stand a little," my mate whispered, my wolf shifter senses keen enough to hear her.

I glanced down. "Are you sure?"

She nodded. "As long as I can lean on him."

I didn't like that idea. What if she fell? "No. If you're strong enough for that, I can carry you over my shoulder, and you can crawl through the hole when we reach the top. Okay?"

She nodded. "I can do that."

Her voice was sweet, but so broken it made my heart ache.

"Let's go then, beautiful." I gently maneuvered her over my shoulder, which would free up my hands to climb the ladder.

A loud bang sounded from the direction we'd come. I turned toward it, staring into the darkness.

"Should we go back and help?" I asked, speaking my thoughts aloud.

Travis grunted, shifting his witch. "We can. But we'll have to leave these women here."

The three women began to sob. Including my mate. That settled things. Sadie and her mates would have to look after themselves now. I turned toward the ladder.

"They're on their own. The goal was to rescue these women, and we're doing that. Let's get going."

I re-settled my thin, fragile mate over my shoulder and began to climb, one hand at a time, dragging my bad leg up each iron rung. Pain splintered through my back and I clenched my jaw, refusing to let the agony win.

I'd taken some hits, sure, but nothing that wouldn't heal.

I reached for some of my limited magic and found only a tendril curled inside me. I focused on the warlock within me and pushed the healing magic through my body, soothing some of the breaks and hoping the internal bleeding would stop, or at least slow down.

My breathing became a little easier and the sharp edge to the pain dulled. Then the magic was gone, depleted. I had nothing else left to give.

I reached for the next rung and pushed up with my good leg. Three more to go. I hauled my mate, whose name I didn't even know, up the final rung, until my head was through the hole.

My lungs strained as I heaved in a breath.

"Can you... get onto the floor?" I asked as I climbed up the final step.

She rolled to the side, landing beside the manhole and curling up into a ball.

I groaned as I surfaced through and sat down on the concrete floor, breathing hard. I would have been seeing stars if the small amount of magic I'd used hadn't reduced the pain to a reasonable level.

"Bring her up," I called to Travis, who held the pregnant woman.

I dragged my legs up through the hole so I would be able to reach down and pull her up.

My broken ribs would hate me for what I was about to do, but I would deal with that tomorrow. For now, I had people to protect.

"Are you okay?" I asked my mate, then shook my head. "I'm sorry. That is the most ridiculous question."

She unfurled, like a flower in the sunshine, then wiggled around so that she was still lying down but was no longer in the fetal position.

"I'm Katie."

My mate had a name.

I smiled despite the pain that rolled through me. "Nice to meet you, Katie."

"Thank you for saving us... I don't know *your* name."

"Everyone calls me Shadow."

"Hmmm... but that's not your name."

I opened my mouth, but I wasn't sure what to say. I never used my real name. Ever.

Travis hauled himself up the ladder, one rung at a time, barely holding his witch since he needed two arms to climb. She clung to his neck while he tried to hold her in place with his elbows.

"Just a little bit more," I called, as I reached down to grab onto her.

She extended her thin arms up to me and I grabbed a hold and pulled her up as gently as I could. She weighed less than Katie, but looked nine months pregnant. That could not be a good sign for mother or child.

Travis groaned and came up through the hole after her.

"I'll help Tony," he said to me as I wheezed through the pain in my lungs. "You wanna start moving?"

I nodded and pushed myself to a stand. "Yeah, I can do that. I'll carry Katie to the entry point, then we can all climb out together."

I picked up my mate once more, and the pain began to ease. Was she working a spell on me? She was a witch, after all. Or was it simply the feeling of holding her against my body that was working its own magic?

I limped past the vampire bar, sticking to the shadows as Katie buried her head in my neck and trembled.

"Don't worry," I whispered to her as we grew closer to the final ladder. "No-one's going to hurt you now."

And no-one would. Ever again. I'd make sure of it.

We reached the entrance point and I leaned against the ladder, closing my eyes as exhaustion washed over me. "We'll wait here for Tony and Travis. They won't be long."

"Thank you for saving us," Katie whispered.

I pulled her tighter against me. "I'm sorry it took us so long to find you."

I had so many questions I wanted to ask her, about how long she'd been down there and what she'd been through, but now wasn't the time. If she really was the mate I believed her to be, in the long term I would find out everything, and hopefully I would be able to help her heal.

The sound of footsteps met my ears and I straightened up to better see the people who approached us.

It was Tony and Travis, carrying their witches.

"You okay?" Travis asked me. "You want me to take the lead?"

I shook my head. "I'm fine. This is the easy bit now. We just need to get up into the sunlight, where most vampires don't dare to tread, then make our way to the hospital. It's about three blocks down."

"You don't think we're gonna be spotted?" Tony asked. "The three of us are carrying women covered in dirt and blood."

I grunted as I lifted Katie against me. "There's no choice. We have to risk it, and we need to move fast, because once the Vampire Fathers find out what we've done, they'll be after us."

Katie moaned and quivered in my arms.

I straightened. "No more talk. Just follow me."

Somehow, I managed to get up the final ladder and into the sunlight, hauling my emaciated mate through the hole. She gasped and rolled onto her belly the moment we surfaced, shielding her face from the light with her hands.

Shit. I'd forgotten about the fact that Katie probably hadn't been in natural sunlight for a very long time.

I stood over her, in the direction of the light, creating some shade. "Are you all right?"

She nodded. "Help the others. I'll be fine."

I got to work lifting the other women up through the hole, and then, as an unlikely group of six, we hauled ass through the city. We made our way past a throng of people who stared openly at us. At least they didn't try to stop our progress.

"Not long now," I whispered to Katie, whose face I could barely make out under the layers of blood and grime.

She clung tight to me as I carried her through the crowds to the only hospital in the city the vampires didn't own.

It was run by warlocks, who were the most hunted species in the city.

CHAPTER 2
SHADOW

"So, you'll help me, Shadow?" Sadie had asked, only a few days ago.

I'd looked her straight in the eye. "To find the people responsible for your father's death? And have the chance to maybe rescue your mom?"

She'd nodded. "Yes. I want to kill the ones responsible, and if they're part of a corporation, take them down too. Are you interested?"

I'd grinned. "Abso-fucking-lutely."

Now look where that fateful conversation with my cousin had gotten us. Sadie and her three mates were fighting for their lives somewhere down there in the underground, and thanks to her inviting me on this do-or-die mission, I was running—well, limping—through the streets with my newly found mate in my arms.

I shook my head. Who would have thought it? Sadie had three strong, paranormal mates. A wolf, a dragon and a vampire. Who'd have thought that would be possible? Not that she'd had a choice about it. Fate had decided for them.

Fate was a fickle bitch. Probably why I was still single.

Or had been, until now. What had the gods been drinking the day they decided I, with all my screwed-up hodge-podge of genes, should have a mate as beautiful as the one I held in my arms?

"In here," I said as we ducked down an alley that had magical wards engraved into every door and brick.

Travis and Tony faltered, but then followed me.

The wards kept vampires out and could detect ill-intent. I was happy to see the two bounty hunters passed the tests of the warlock who'd set up the wards.

I stopped and turned when we came up against a steel door with a shimmer of magic passing over the handle.

"Where are we?" Katie asked. "I can feel... familiar magic..."

"Somewhere safe for you." I pressed my hand to the metal panel in the wall.

The door slid open and a man I knew well stood on the other side. He'd put me on my ass in several scuffles, and patched me up when I'd been close to death. I owed him.

"Nathaniel," I said, black spots forming at the edges of my vision. Now that we were nearly done with our mission, I was about ready to keel over.

I gritted my teeth to concentrate on staying with it. There'd be time later to fall apart from the pain.

"Shadow. Who have you got there?" Nathaniel sounded as if he were discussing the weather. He wore a pristine long purple jacket and black leather pants that made him look like a magician.

I cocked my head at him and groaned. I didn't really have time to explain before I passed out, but Nathaniel was one of the most powerful warlocks in the state, and could kill us all with a flick of his hand.

I had to find the energy to speak, or we weren't getting the help we needed.

I drew a deep breath, ignoring the warning beats of my heart, and squinted at him. "Tony and Travis are bounty hunters. They worked for Jack—now they do the same for Sadie. We rescued these witches from the underground, and they all need medical care."

Nathaniel's perfect face didn't even flinch, but his eyes widened ever-so-slightly.

I'd surprised him. That was a first.

He stepped back and waved his hand theatrically. "Then you better bring them all inside before the vampires smell you." He wrinkled his nose as though disgusted. "You all reek of the sewer."

"Well, guess where they were hiding them?" I asked, stumbling forward, my vision beginning to fade. I swayed on my feet. "Nathaniel. You need to take her. I'm going to..."

My eyes slid shut and I clamped down on the last reserves of energy as Katie's weight was lifted from my arms, before I slid into the beckoning oblivion.

KATIE

I didn't want to leave Shadow's arms, but when his eyes closed, I reached out for the nearby warlock. He lifted me just as Shadow crumpled to the floor.

"Oh, no," I whispered. I hadn't meant to whisper. I wanted to shout, but I literally couldn't. I coughed to try and clear my throat.

I hated how weak and soft I sounded. I wasn't weak. I wasn't soft. But I hadn't spoken in... too long.

The women down there with me didn't want to talk. We barely had enough energy to stay awake, let alone chat.

"Is he okay?" I asked as the other men came inside with the women I'd shared the underground prison with.

The warlock who held me grimaced. "I've never seen Shadow go down like that. Even after fights that would have killed most men. What happened down there?"

The man who carried a very pregnant Nadine, stepped around Shadow. "He took on several vampires alone. Saved our asses."

The warlock nodded. "Come with me. I'll send someone for Shadow."

I squeaked out a rejection. I didn't want to leave him.

"Don't worry," the warlock told me, holding me tightly in his arms. "We'll come back for him. I promise."

The warlock held his head high as he carried me along a brightly lit tunnel and into a room with a bed and medical equipment. He didn't show any sign of emotion, but I could tell he didn't want to carry me. And I didn't blame him. I was disgusting.

"I can have a shower, if you have one," I whispered.

He shook his head as he put me down onto the white sheets, the softness strange against my skin.

"No. First you need fluids and food. Then you can shower, or I will have one of my nurses clean you." He glanced over his shoulder. "Would you like Shadow in here with you?"

I stared at him, not sure why he'd asked such a question. But there was only one answer that felt right. "Yes, please."

I needed Shadow near me. I wasn't sure why, but I felt bereft when his arms weren't around me.

He nodded and went about setting up a second bed. "I'll help the others, then I'll be back."

The other men lingered in the doorway with Nadine and Sasha. "Thank you. All of you. For getting us out."

I couldn't create long sentences, and my breathing wasn't great, but I wouldn't give up until I had my strength back.

The two men nodded at me, then followed the warlock out.

I was propped on my elbows, with my neck straining. I took a steadying breath and lay back, the softness beneath my back foreign, and yet familiar from my childhood.

"Knock, knock," a woman called from the open door. "I'm Josie, one of the nurses here. Can I come in and set up your IV?"

I nodded, looking the woman over. She had long blond hair and a bubbly personality that made me like her straight away. She also had a ripple of magic around her that hinted at some witch in her. So why hadn't *she* been captured by the vampires like I had?

"Thank you," I said, as she brought in two clear bags and began setting up the IVs.

"This one is for fluid mostly," she said, then *tsked* when she saw the gashes and scarring on my arms from the blown veins. "I think we're going to need to be creative with you."

She managed to find a vein in my foot that wasn't damaged by the vampires and slipped the needle in so gently I didn't even feel it. Which, after all the blood draining they'd done to me, was heaven.

I sighed as she started the first IV.

"And this one has a whole lot of glucose to try and get that body of yours healing, though I'm sure Nathaniel will be in here to do some magic on you soon."

I leaned back into the pillow. "So... he *is* a warlock. And you're a witch. My instincts aren't failing me." That's why the magic felt familiar.

I was beginning to relax, slowly, beneath the bright lights and the warmth of the fluids seeping into my veins.

There was a groan from the doorway and I glanced in the direction of the noise, a new warmth spreading through me, closer to my heart than I wanted to admit.

"Get in the bed, you stubborn bastard." The warlock growled at Shadow, who leaned against the doorframe, one eye open.

"Get off," Shadow said, shaking his shoulder. He lifted his head, and a tremor of a smile tilted up his lips as he stared at me. "Hey. You okay?"

I nodded. "I am. Thanks to you. Are *you* okay?"

"Yep." He heaved himself across the room, his back bent, and his limp even more pronounced now.

When he reached the bed, he let out a pained groan as he rotated and fell onto the blankets. Then he closed his eyes and a soft moan left his lips.

I hated seeing him in so much pain.

I opened my mouth to tell him that I wished I was better; that I could heal him.

Back in the day, when I was well, I had great healing magic. But it was gone, and I had no idea if it would ever return. So, instead, I glanced at the nurse attending me.

She grinned back. "I'll set Shadow up with some fluids. Nathaniel, this gorgeous girl needs some of your magic."

Shadow's gaze flashed to me, both eyes open again.

"Just keep your hands to yourself," he snapped at Nathaniel.

My mouth dropped open, horrified he'd speak to the warlock like that. Nathaniel just cackled with laughter.

"Well, well, well, my old friend. It's like that, is it?" he asked, though it sounded like a rhetorical question.

Josie attended to Shadow, while Nathaniel walked over to me and smiled. "I'm going to do a little repair work. I can't do anything for your memories, I'm afraid. My magic doesn't work well with mental scars. But I can heal your flesh. The scarring on your arms. Speed up the rebuilding of your strength, and muscles. And these damaged veins."

I bit my lip. Part of me wanted to keep the scars in my flesh, a vivid reminder of the war I'd participated in and survived. But they would call the attention of the vampires to me, and that was the last thing I wanted.

"Do you have a way of disguising my scent?" I asked. "I don't really care about the scars, but I want to make sure the vampires never find me again."

I was proud of the way my voice barely trembled as I spoke.

But tears burned my eyes and the back of my throat.

"I can't go back." I swallowed hard. "I'd rather die. So, if there's anything you can do…"

There was a silence in the room, then Nathaniel smiled. "Wait right here."

He disappeared and I glanced over at the weird shifter lying in the bed opposite me. He was staring at me like he was afraid to blink in case I disappeared.

"I'll never let them take you. I give you my word. Never." His voice had a strange vibration to it, almost like a hiss.

I nodded, not sure if Shadow had the power to make such a declaration, but he certainly seemed confident.

Nathaniel hurried back into the room, purple coat waving in the breeze. He reminded me of my Uncle Larry. My very gay Uncle Larry.

"Drink this," Nathaniel said, un-stoppering a small bottle and handing it to me. "This is a potion that will disguise your magical scent."

I glanced over at Josie, who grinned. "We all take it. Tastes like moldy blueberries, but hey, better than the alternative."

I put the bottle to my lips and tipped it back. The potion slid down my parched throat, the taste just as Josie had described. But with dirt.

"That was... interesting," I said, with a swallow. "Thank you."

My stomach gurgled loudly and I pressed a hand to my belly to stifle the noise.

"I hope I don't vomit it back up. That would be a real waste."

"You shouldn't," Nathaniel said with a frown. "There's nothing poisonous in it."

I waved my hand. "Oh, no. I didn't mean there was anything wrong with the potion. It's just that..." I swallowed again, my throat aching from all this talking. "They didn't really feed us. I haven't eaten proper food for a while."

They'd kept us alive through IVs, similar to the one I had attached to my foot.

As though she'd read my mind, Josie whisked over and detached the IVs that were already half empty.

"Then how about I get you some nice soup, and we start rebuilding that body of yours?" she said, her voice light, though I could hear the sympathy behind it.

"That would be great," I said. "Thanks."

She bustled off and Nathaniel stepped forward. "Close your eyes and rest, Katie. I know you're tired and in a lot of pain. Let me see if I can help with that a little."

He raised his hands and the magical white glow of a powerful warlock's magic shimmered in his palms.

I closed my eyes and let his healing powers wash over my body.

"It's okay," I said, quoting Shadow, but it felt appropriate. "Pain and I are old friends."

CHAPTER 3
SHADOW

Despite the seriousness of the conversation to which I was listening, I couldn't help the smile that flirted at the edges of my mouth. She'd quoted what I said in the underground. It seemed that we had more in common than I realized, though bonding over a mutual need to deal with chronic pain was hardly something to be happy about.

Nathaniel finished making Katie glow with white light, and at the end of it, she looked better. She seemed fuller in the face, and her skin was a healthier color.

Nathaniel turned to me and rubbed his hands together. "Your turn."

"No, no, no." I waved my hand in his direction. "You know I'm not up for any magical healing."

Nathaniel dropped his hands and frowned at me. "There are no medals for being tougher than everyone else, Shadow. You know I can help you with your pain."

I rolled onto my side and heaved myself up to a sitting position. "It's good training for when I need to put up with more."

I hated how Nathaniel's magic felt. It was fake. It made me weak.

My gaze slid over to where Katie was now peacefully snoring away. Poor woman probably hadn't had a proper night's sleep in ages.

Not that many of us did.

"Thank you," I choked out to Nathaniel. "For helping us."

Nathaniel's gaze slid over to Katie, then moved back to me. There was a gleam in his eye. "Does she know?"

"Shh…" I whispered. "And know what?"

He rolled his eyes. "Relax. She'll sleep all day now. I put a touch of sedative in that potion so she could catch up on a little rest. She needs sleep so that she can heal."

I nodded. "Good."

"Does she know that she's your mate?" Nathaniel asked.

I stared at him.

How was I going to bluff my way out of this one?

A lot of people thought I could read minds, but I couldn't. I just read people's body language and facial expressions. If I was related to them, the way I was with Sadie, by blood, then I could get a little more from them. A word or a thought here and there.

"She's not my mate. What are you talking about?"

Nathaniel stepped closer and pressed a hand to my shoulder. "You're not the only one who can read a room, Shadow."

There was a light breeze against my cheek and suddenly I could breathe better again.

"Hey!" I said, shaking off his hand. "I said no magic."

Nathaniel grinned as he strolled to the door. "I own this place, Shadow, not you. Don't tell me what to do." He stopped and turned back to me. "Seriously, though, if the vampires come for her, don't you want to at least be able enough to put up a decent fight?"

I opened my mouth to reply, then slammed it shut again.

He was right. Now was not the time to be stubborn. "Thanks."

He shook his head. "Will wonders never cease? Rest up, my friend. I have a feeling this rollercoaster ride is only just beginning."

I lay back on the soft, clean bed, enjoying the sensation of no pain for the moments it lingered. Nathaniel's magic was strong and it would get me through the next few days. But soon my twisted spine would start to ache and I'd be thrust back into my world of pain once more.

Damn, I needed a smoke.

"No smoking in the hospital!" Nathaniel called from down the hall.

That guy definitely had mind-reading powers.

"Fine. A shower then."

I hauled myself up to my feet and stretched. God, he was good. My ribs felt great, and all my bleeding had stopped.

I walked toward the ensuite bathroom and even my limp wasn't as pronounced. I opened the door, glanced back to check that Katie was still sleeping, then ambled inside the small white room.

Nathaniel's hospital was more like a swanky hotel, with soft lighting, plush pillows, and rather decadent bathroom facilities.

I shook my head as I stripped off all my clothes, dropping the blood-covered rags on the floor. Then I turned on the shower head, adjusted the water, and stepped beneath the spray. "Oh. God."

The heat against my muscles was utter bliss, and as I reached forward, I pressed my hands against the tiles and bent my head, letting the water flow over me.

I hadn't stopped to enjoy a shower in too long to think about.

I was always moving, always chasing, always hiding. My job as a P.I. meant that someone always wanted me dead. That didn't allow for a lot of long hot showers where I could close my eyes and not think about who was on their way.

Nathaniel's hospital was one of the only places I could do that. The magical illusions were strong enough to keep this place, and its patrons, safe.

I picked up the soap and started scrubbing. I was caked in the scent of the underground.

By the time the door opened, the underground scent was washed away and the smell of fresh soap permeated the air. I assumed it must be the nurse Josie, come to deliver clothes, meds, or food. But when I turned, I met a set of gorgeous blue eyes, with a magical purple swirl. I froze.

"Katie?"

"Oh, I'm so sorry. I just..." She wrapped her arms around herself and shivered.

"What's wrong?"

She turned away, obviously disgusted by my nakedness, then glanced back. "I heard the shower... I don't know. I'm freezing. Could I jump in when you're done?"

How was she awake when Nathaniel said she'd sleep through the next several hours?

"Of course!" I said, grabbing a nearby white towel and winding it around my waist. "I'll leave the water on for you. It's nice and hot."

She smiled as I grabbed another towel and began to dry my hair and upper body. My cock, despite my best intentions, rose in greeting of my beautiful mate.

"I'll get out of your way," I said as she dropped the thin chemise she'd been wearing onto the pile of dirty clothes I'd left.

She wore nothing but a pair of dirty panties now, and my throat ran dry.

"Please, don't leave," she said. "I know I'm disgusting to look at, but I don't want you to go. I don't want to be alone."

"You're not disgusting. You're beautiful." The words fell out of my mouth.

She glanced down and shook her head. "I was once, but the vampires destroyed me."

I shook my head, moving over to lean against the sink. "Nathaniel's magic is healing you. You're looking healthier by the minute. Look."

I pointed to the mirror and Katie stepped up in front of it.

She lifted her hand and traced the outline of her ribs and her gently rounded breasts.

She was still very thin. Her legs looked more like bones than actual thighs, but still, she was bigger than she had been an hour ago.

"I still don't want you to go."

"All right. I won't." I shook my head. "Not if you don't want me to."

"I feel safer with you here." She wobbled her way to the shower and put out her hand.

She gasped as though the water pained her.

I inhaled sharply as she pushed her panties down her legs, then once again put out her hands to feel the pressure of the shower.

"Do you want me to turn it down?"

She nodded, stepping out of the way so I could reach the tap. "Yes, please."

I steeled myself against the desire pouring through my veins. The last thing I should do was lust after a woman who'd just been through hell. But the fated mate bond knew no such boundaries.

I walked into the shower alongside her, and she swayed on her feet like an exhausted reed in the wind.

I held my breath as I twisted the dial and adjusted the shower head to reduce the pressure, not wanting to touch her, intensely grateful for the towel wrapped around my waist.

The water changed from a downpour to a light rain, and I felt Katie's sigh on my back.

"Oh, thank you."

I nodded, not trusting myself to speak when my various shifters were all snarling inside of me. My wolf shifter, the strongest of all, howled with passion.

Instead of succumbing to my baser instincts, I forced myself to march across the bathroom and sit down on the toilet lid to avoid any accidental touching, or worse. This woman had been through so much. The last thing she needed was someone like me groping her.

"Can I ask you a personal question?" Katie asked into the silence.

I had to drag my gaze off the tiles to focus on her face. She was completely naked, all soaped up, and something melted inside me at seeing the beauty before me.

"Of course," I said, though generally the answer to that sort of question would be 'hell no'.

I ran a hand through my tangled, wet hair and continued to wait for her to ask what she wanted.

I had so many questions myself.

What was it like down there in the underground? Who were her parents? How much witch blood did she have? How long had she been there? How had they taken her?

Could she feel the attraction between us that shimmered and purred like a finely tuned engine?

"What sort of shifter-warlock mix are you?" she asked, then bit her lip in a self-conscious way that hit me way below the belt. "I know that's probably quite rude, but if you wouldn't mind sharing it with me…"

I would normally care very much. The information wasn't something I revealed to many people.

"I'm a mix." I crossed my arms over my bare chest. I really needed to get dressed, but she'd asked me not to leave her alone.

A soft chuckle sounded. "I know. That part's obvious."

I glanced across at her. She was carefully cleaning her skin, inspecting every puncture mark and hole those asshole vampires had made in her flesh, frowning at every mark.

I had to distract her.

"Wanna guess?" I asked her. "I'll tell you if you hit the right combination."

Most people couldn't see the warlock blood in me, unless I told them, like Sadie. But Katie had picked it up straight away.

A ghost of a smile shimmered in her eyes. "Sure. I can sense the warlock, that's obvious."

I laughed at that. "To you maybe. No-one else has ever sensed it. Not even my own cousin."

She shrugged as she rubbed some shampoo in her hands, then applied it to her waist-length hair. "I haven't washed my hair since they took me. I wonder if it would be better just to cut it all off."

She rubbed her hands through her hair, then her arms dropped.

She groaned, tried again, then let her arms fall. "Yeah, I think shaving it off and starting again might be easier."

"What's wrong?" I asked.

"I can't hold my arms up. The muscles are... you know. Too weak."

I stood up. I wasn't having her shave her head if she didn't want to.

She was beginning to tremble from standing. Of course, she didn't have the energy to wash her hair.

I walked back over to the stall and pulled a shower chair over with me, that had been resting against the wall. "Sit. I'll wash your hair for you."

She stared at me with wide open eyes, her vulnerability as obvious as the quiver in her lower lip.

I gave her half a smile. "Though I warn you, I've only ever washed my own."

And not that often, either.

She sank into the chair with a grateful sigh and picked up the shampoo bottle for me. "Here you go."

I stood behind her and tilted the head of the shower so it warmed her thighs. "Is that all right?"

She nodded and said quietly, "Yes. Thank you."

I took a deep breath and got to work.

CHAPTER 4
KATIE

I didn't know how long I'd been down in the underground. There had been no daylight, no clocks, no way of measuring time.

I ended up counting how many times they took away bags of my blood.

There had been three hundred and seventy-two bag changes, give or take a few.

Did that correlate to days? Weeks? I didn't know.

But it had felt like an entire lifetime. In the end, I'd craved the sleep, and the pain-killing IVs they put into my body. I'd wanted to be dead. Every day. I'd prayed for it. Begged the vampires who drained me until I passed out, to kill me.

That was until the door had opened and Shadow had rushed toward me, picked me up in his arms, and carried me away from hell.

At the time it had felt like a dream, part of a fantasy I'd conjured up in my drugged sleep. After all, how many times had I envisioned a savior? A man who would do exactly what Shadow did: walk into the hell hole I was being kept in, kill all the vampires, and carry me away.

Well, he hadn't killed *all* the vampires, but I was sure he'd killed more than a few in his day. He had the strength and cunning for it; he'd proven that when he fought three of them at once. He also had the scent of one who'd taken a life, or twenty.

"Tilt your head back a little if you can," Shadow said, as he rubbed some of the rose-scented shampoo into the top of my head.

My neck started to ache, weak in all upright positions.

"And back to normal."

I moaned as I shifted my head back into the right spot.

"Sorry," I mumbled, embarrassed to be groaning over such a small thing.

Shadow moved his hands over my hair, from the ends to the crown, then set his fingertips into my scalp and began to massage my head the way a hairdresser would.

"You never need to apologize," he said, his voice barely above a whisper. "I don't know how you survived down there, but I'm glad you did."

Tears prickled in my eyes, and I swallowed hard. "Yeah. Me too."

I closed my eyes and let Shadow wash the dirt and grime away.

Then he leaned over me, took the head of the shower off the handle, and gently rinsed away the suds.

I didn't open my eyes. I didn't want to see the black water that I knew would be washing over my skin and down toward the drain.

A moan erupted from my throat. "That feels like heaven."

He put the head of the shower back, the water beating a steady rhythm onto my legs. Then he repeated the shampooing, massaging, and scrubbing, then washing it all away.

Then he did it again, and I sighed. "Three shampoos? That's a first."

He chuckled. "Yeah, well... I like to be thorough."

A tingle of something akin to excitement fluttered inside my belly. But that wasn't possible, surely? How could I be feeling anything even close to desire when I was in this sort of physical state? It didn't seem right.

I shook the feeling away. "Is that necessary in your job? Not the hair-washing. The thoroughness?"

"Yeah. I'm a P.I. A private investigator."

I grinned. "A Sherlock Holmes, huh? Why don't I believe that you're snooping after cheating wives or embezzling money clerks?"

Shadow washed the suds away once more. This time, I opened my eyes and was happy to see relatively white bubbles, floating down over my skin.

"My work is a little different to that," he admitted, then grabbed the conditioner. "How should I do this? Is there a brush, or…"

I shook my head, black spots beginning to twinkle at the edges of my vision. "Just slap some in. I think I need to lie down."

Shadow squirted a handful of conditioner into my hair, rubbed it in, quickly washed it out, then swung me up into his arms just as I was beginning to sway on my seat.

I let my head fall onto his naked chest. It felt so comforting, to be in his arms.

"Thanks for that." I closed my eyes, shame washing over me. "I can't believe how weak I am."

We stepped out of the bathroom and into the bedroom just as the door opened and Nathaniel walked into the room.

He froze, mid-stride, his lips quirking up at the edges as though trying not to laugh. "Am I interrupting something?"

I smiled at him, too exhausted to lift my head. "Shadow was helping me shower, but I got too weak and almost fainted."

That wiped the smirk off Nathaniel's face. "I need to do some more healing for you, I think. And perhaps, get you some clothes."

I glanced down at my still-naked body. It meant nothing to me. "Yeah, sorry. Modesty isn't really a priority after what I went through."

Shadow emitted a soft growl, before turning and looking at my blackened sheets. "She needs fresh bedding."

I almost laughed at the sound. He had wolf shifter in him. That was nice. Good for night vision, speed, and strength.

I wonder what else there is.

"I'll find Josie and come back in five," Nathaniel said, before disappearing.

I patted Shadow's chest, enjoying the amount of energy rolling off him. I wasn't sure if he was protecting me, or jealous, or what. But it was nice to be near someone who felt so much. Especially after being around vampires for so long. Their aura was that of death, indifference, or evil.

I shuddered.

Josie bustled into the room, stripped my bed, and re-made it with crisp, clean, white linen.

"Thank you."

She smiled at me, then bent over and retrieved a hospital gown from one of the drawers next to my bed. "How about we put this on you, and I'll go in search of something comfortable for you to wear."

I nodded and Shadow set me on my feet. Josie put the gown on me, tied it up, and folded back the blankets for me.

I slid between the covers, my body aching from all the standing. "That's so much better, thank you."

I lay back on the pillows, unable to hold up my head any longer. That shower had taken everything out of me.

"You need some hot soup," Josie said as she folded up the dirty sheets and carried them out of the room.

Shadow turned around, still wearing his wet towel, then looked at his bed. "My bed's gross as well."

"There's more dry towels, or these lovely... fancy gowns," I managed, though my eyes were beginning to close.

"I'll get Josie to change my bed, too."

I let exhaustion drag me down into sleep.

I could hear people moving around, and talking softly, then the warmth of Nathaniel's magic on me once more. I smiled and lay still, letting him do whatever it was he wanted to do.

Shadow was right. I *had* looked better in the mirror than I'd imagined. My eyes were still sunken, my ribs protruding. But every time Nathaniel did his magic, I felt my body strengthen.

When he was done, I opened my eyes. "Thank you for that."

Nathaniel stared down at me. "How are you awake? That spell should have knocked you out for the whole day."

I shrugged, staring up at him. "Why are you trying to drug me?"

I wasn't really worried about his motives. For him, like most doctors, he probably thought that making me sleep would help me, but I'd been sleeping for most of the time in the underground, and I didn't want to sleep anymore.

"It's not drugs. I just..." Nathaniel's pale cheeks flushed a little. "I need to get something. I'll be back in a moment."

He left the room and I glanced across at where Shadow was grinning.

"What's so funny?" I asked him.

He rolled onto his side where he lay, shirtless, in his new clean sheets. "Nathaniel is one of the most composed people I know. Nothing ruffles him. And you just shot him to smithereens. Well done."

I rolled onto my side to face him, but kept my head on the soft pillow. "I didn't mean to."

"And that's what's so beautiful about it."

A long moment of silence passed, then I decided to start up our conversation again.

"So," I said, "you're part wolf shifter then? How much? Almost half?"

Shadow nodded, his dark eyes flashing with the yellow of his wolf, then a touch of purple. "My father was mostly wolf shifter, so yes."

"What was the other part?" I asked. "Let me guess. It's another shifter."

I looked at him, assessing his body. He walked with a slight limp and his shoulders curved into a hump when he was in pain.

It had to be an animal that didn't fit well with a warm-blooded mammal.

I glanced up at his face, where, in the light, I could see his skin properly.

Scales.

"You're part reptile, aren't you?" I asked. "What sort?"

His nostrils flared. "Yes. Snake."

I grinned. "That's amazing."

He snorted. "Hardly. It gave me this skin, but... you're right. There is some good in it. My snake genes hide my magic from the vampires."

I tried to sit up, but found no strength in my arms, so lay back into the pillow.

"What do you mean?" Now that was something I needed.

"Reptile genetics cause a scent in a person's skin that can mask warlock or witch blood. My cousin Sadie... the woman who was with me when we rescued you... her mother cast a spell that imprinted Sadie with snake blood. My blood actually, not that I told her that," he said with a twist of his lips, but I could see the pride behind his eyes.

"And that... saved her?" I asked, amazed.

Was it really that easy?

He nodded. "Yes. The spell must be done by a witch of vast power, which Sadie's mom was."

"Was?"

"Is. Hopefully. Everyone thought she died in the underground a long time ago... though, I heard rumors that she may still be alive. I transferred those rumors to my cousin, which is what made Sadie organize the rescue party."

A memory surfaced through my brain. "There was another woman down there. Older. They kept her isolated. In her own room."

Shadow's eyes opened wide. "That could be her. If she was still alive after all this time, that would be a miracle."

I didn't want to think about it. To have survived what they did to us was bad enough. But to spend a lifetime down there...

No. I'd rather be dead.

Nathaniel bustled back into the room, holding a crystal and a string.

"May I?" he asked.

I nodded and rolled onto my back, nausea spreading through my belly. I wasn't sure I wanted to know the answer to the question he was about to ask my body.

The warlock hung the crystal over my center and moved it up and down, murmuring to himself. When he got to my lower abdomen, the crystal turned cloudy white and began to hum a song I hadn't heard before.

Nathaniel snatched the crystal back into his hand, then slid it into the pocket of his jacket. "Katie, I'm afraid I have to tell you something."

My stomach twisted and I wanted to cry. I met the warlock's gaze and nodded, my eyes filling with tears. *No... please. Not that.*

"They succeeded, didn't they?" I whispered.

He glanced at Shadow, then back at me, pity clear in his eyes. "I'm sorry to tell you this, Katie, but yes. You're pregnant."

CHAPTER 5

SHADOW

My heart stopped.

Nathaniel's words circled around and around in my head. *She's pregnant.* How was that possible? She'd been in the underground for so long...

Then it hit me—the truth of her impregnation—just as the sound of Katie's sobs cracked open my heart.

I got up from my bed, and without thinking, picked her up, rearranged the blankets, and sat back down on her bed with her in my arms.

"It's okay. It'll be okay." I rocked her on the bed, Katie's sobs ringing in the room.

I dragged my gaze up to Nathaniel, where he stood staring down at us.

"It's okay," I said again on automatic, cupping Katie's head to me.

She pushed up from my chest and glared at me. "It's not okay!"

She struggled against me, so I turned her around and sat her on the bed next to me so she could talk to Nathaniel.

"Can I get rid of it?" she demanded.

I shuddered at the thought of how such a baby had been conceived, and how Katie must feel about it. A baby conceived in rape must be an incredibly hard thing for the mother to process.

I opened my mouth to say something, but Nathaniel cut me off. "It depends on how far along you are. Do you know?"

She shook her head. "Time doesn't move normally in the underground. I can't even tell you how long I was down there."

Nathaniel and I exchanged a worried glance, then he started backing toward the door. "I'll go and find an ultrasound machine. I won't be long."

He disappeared again.

I stared after him. I'd spent a decade trying to ruffle that man's feathers, to no avail. I'd seen him more shocked today than in the ten years I'd known him.

I glanced at Katie's tear-stained face, then started to slide off the bed so she could lie down. She grabbed for me, her warm hands clinging to my biceps.

I shivered, the feel of my mate's hands on me almost too good to name.

"Don't leave."

"I won't," I said, grateful for the clean jeans I wore thanks to Josie finding them in a cupboard somewhere. "I was just moving so you could lie down."

I grabbed a chair and dragged it close to her bed, while she slid down onto her back and sighed. "Not exactly the way I pictured my first baby's ultrasound."

I looked at the floor. As a man, and one who had sworn never to have his own children due to my genes, this wasn't a moment I'd ever thought about for myself.

"Are you sure you want to destroy it?" I said, preparing for a slap to the head I probably deserved.

Instead, she pressed her lips into a thin line. "I don't know."

She covered her face with her hands, so I had no way of reading her anymore. Was she ashamed of the fact she might want to keep a baby bred for the vampire's purposes? Did she remember the event that caused it? So many questions, none of which I had the right to ask.

I reached out for her hand and squeezed hard. "I'm here if you need me. Okay?"

She nodded, breathing deeply through her nose.

Nathaniel came back in, dragging a primitive-looking machine with a screen.

I glared at him. "I'm not sure she wants to see it."

He nodded, and set up the screen facing away from Katie. "But I do have to see what's in there, I'm afraid. Katie, could you please lift your gown up and I'll put some gel on your skin?"

She reached down and pulled up the hospital gown she still wore, showing her flat belly and protruding hips.

"How..." I shook my head. "Sorry. Ignore me."

How had someone so unwell, so unhealthy, managed to conceive at all?

As though hearing my question, Katie turned her head toward me, her eyes sad. "The man who impregnates the witches trapped in the underground is a warlock. I've heard from the other girls that his magic is so strong it allows his children to grow, practically anywhere."

My hands tightened into fists where they rested on my knees. "Anyone I know?"

She sighed. "It's not his fault."

"It's not his... *what?*" I exploded.

"He's kept prisoner in the underground just like we are. They drain him, too, then force him to inseminate us."

"Inseminate? So that means..."

She shook her head. "I wasn't raped. He can't... do that, I don't think. He's too weak. And I don't even remember them doing it."

She put her hands over her face and I sank back in my chair in relief. Although still terrible, it was so much better than the version I had created in my mind.

The version most of my clients and associates believed.

I glanced over at Nathaniel, trying hard not to look at the black and white screen he was staring at. "How are the two other women we brought here?"

Nathaniel didn't look my way. He was too busy tapping on keys and moving the little wand around. "They're doing well. I'll keep both of them here until we can find a safe place for them. Especially Nadine. She's due to give birth any day."

He turned toward Katie, his eyes showing a sympathy that made my stomach drop. "Katie, this is a tough call. You are weak, and your child is very strong. If you tell me that you'd rather die than go through with this pregnancy, I will help you abort it. The fetus is on the cusp of being too old to terminate, but it will come down to your will on this one. I will do as you instruct."

I glanced at Katie's face. Emotions warred in her eyes. Then she looked at me as if for guidance, and my heart practically broke in my chest.

"How can I help?" I asked her.

She inhaled deeply, her nostrils flaring. "I don't know if I could raise a child, when I don't even know if his father is alive or dead, or who he even is."

I squeezed the hand I still held. "You can do anything you set your mind to. The only real question is, do you want this child?"

Because if she did, I'd... I'd... I had no idea what I was thinking. My thoughts were in turmoil.

Katie blinked and tears coursed silently down her face. Then she glanced over at Nathaniel. "Can I see it?"

"Of course, you can." Nathaniel turned the monitor around so that both of us could see the blank screen, then he set the wand back on Katie's lower abdomen.

"Oh, my..." Katie whispered, before she placed her hand over her mouth.

There, on the screen, was the most perfect little baby. Rounded head, a string of white pearls for a spine, and tiny arms and legs moving slowly around.

"He... She... They're beautiful," Katie said, tears welling in her eyes for an entirely new reason now.

That baby was half-Katie. Something shifted inside of me as I stared at it, a long-lost hope springing to life like a buried plant amongst the ash.

"Too early to know what it is," Nathaniel said, "but from what my limited experience tells me, the baby is strong and healthy."

I nodded and dragged my eyes away from the screen.

"I'll help you," I said, my throat choking with emotion. Even though she didn't know it yet, this woman was my mate. And I would take on this baby for her.

Her gaze flew to mine. "What do you mean?"

"I mean... that if you want to keep this baby, I'll help you. Stay with you. Protect you."

Love this baby like it was my own.

Katie's lip trembled. "I can't ask you to do that."

"You didn't. I'm offering. But if you don't want to go through with it, I'll stay here and help you while you regain your strength."

Part of me wanted to reveal all to her right now. That I was her mate. That I couldn't, and wouldn't, have children of my own.

I lived with chronic pain, a lifelong smoking addiction, and the weirdest mix of shifters growling, snapping and slithering inside of me. I wouldn't pass that on to a child. So, if Katie accepted me as her mate, this child may be the only one she ever had. The only one I would ever have.

Just like that, my mind was made up. But it wasn't my decision to make.

Katie held her breath, then said, "Can I have a day or two to think about it?"

Nathaniel smiled. "Of course."

He handed her a towel to wipe away the gel, and as soon as she was done, her hand slipped back to her still-flat belly, cradling her child.

Warmth spread through me like melted honey. She'd keep her baby, who'd be magical and strong... and hunted like nothing else by the vampires who'd bred it for its blood.

Fuck.

Katie and her baby needed my protection. More than anyone.

Nathaniel cleaned off his instruments, packed up his machine, and gave me a pointed look. "I'll leave you two alone to talk."

I glared back at him.

"Talk? About what?" Katie asked.

Neither of us answered as Nathaniel slipped out of the room and shut the door.

Katie reached out and squeezed my hand. "What's he referring to?"

I shook my head. "It's nothing. Nathaniel's just being an interfering pain in the ass."

Katie frowned at me. "You have something you need to tell me, don't you?"

I clenched my jaw. Then I exhaled slowly. This wasn't how someone was supposed to find out they were fated to be mated to... me.

She narrowed her eyes. "You're married, aren't you? Or you have like... ten kids dotted around the city?"

I burst out laughing. For the first time in my entire life someone had truly surprised me.

I laughed, and coughed, then laughed again. "Oh, my God. I need a cigarette so badly."

My hands were beginning to shake from the withdrawal, but at least due to Nathaniel's healing magic, I wasn't in much pain.

She crossed her arms over her chest. "Smoking's not good for the baby."

I opened my mouth, then closed it again. How was I meant to fight that logic?

Then I sobered. "I'm not married. I don't have any children." I shrugged. "I never expected to."

"Why not?"

"Well, I never thought I'd have a fated mate, nor find anyone who would fall in love with me."

"A fated mate?" Katie repeated. "Like, a soul mate?"

I nodded, absorbing the fact that she didn't know what that was. Which meant she was mostly human and witch.

"Yes, shifters can have a fated mate, if they're lucky. A person designed only for them. My cousin Sadie has three."

"Three?" Katie said, her eyes goggling out of her head. "How does she manage three?"

I chuckled. "I don't really know... and I don't want to think about it, to be frank."

Katie lowered her gaze and glanced down at her hands. "You don't have a fated mate?"

She began twisting the white sheet between her fingers and my stomach tightened.

I could do this. I could. I had the balls to be honest with her.

"I do, actually."

Katie's head shot up, her eyes round and big. "You do? Who?"

My heart began to pound in my chest as I swallowed hard against the fear racing along my veins. How was she going to respond to finding out she was probably stuck with my fucked-up, chain-smoking ass forever?

I straightened my crooked spine and looked her in the eye. "You are, Katie. You're my fated mate. I'm so sorry."

CHAPTER 6

KATIE

"You're sorry?" I repeated, dumbfounded. "Why would you be sorry?"

Had I heard him right? So much had happened today that part of me was convinced I was having some long, elaborate dream.

Everything that had happened so far was definitely within the realm of a dream. I'd been rescued and cared for by a man I found far too handsome to put into words. I was pregnant… okay, not exactly a good thing. But now this man said I was his soul mate, and wanted to look after me and the baby?

What the actual fuck? How was any of this possible?

Shadow, whose real name I still didn't know, looked at me like he truly was sorry.

I reached out and grabbed his arm, loving the shivers of sensation that I always got every time I touched him. "Tell me again. What are you sorry for?"

"I'm sorry that you might be stuck with me when you could do so much better."

My mouth dropped open. "Are you serious?"

He stared at me, but didn't say anything more. How did I explain to him that I found his strength amazing? His bravery intoxicating?

I leaned forward and reached out for him, cupping his face and pulling him toward me. I hadn't kissed anyone in so long. I don't know how I got the courage to even attempt it in that moment, and yet somehow, it felt like the perfection action to take.

As his eyes widened, and we got so close I could feel his pulse thudding beneath my fingertips, the rightness of this moment swept over me.

I closed my eyes and lifted my chin, hoping he would take over from me, and he did. His hands slid around my body, holding me gently around the waist as his lips pressed against mine.

I moaned as pleasure washed over me, lighting me up from the inside. He pressed deeper, spreading my lips apart so he could sweep his tongue into my mouth.

I began to topple forward, wanting to be closer. I let out a little squeak as I lost my balance.

He pulled back and grabbed my hands, pushing me back, steadying me. "Are you okay?"

Heat flushed into my cheeks. *How embarrassing.*

"Yeah... I just don't have my balance back yet."

I began to sag, my muscles trembling from being upright for so long.

"Lie down," Shadow said, getting to his feet and easing me back until I was lying against the pillows.

"What's your real name?" I asked, pulling the blankets up over me, feeling cold when I wasn't folded in his embrace.

He frowned down at me, but then a tiny smile flickered at the edge of his lips.

I lifted my hand and pressed my fingers to my mouth, savoring the delicious taste of him.

He tilted his head, assessing me. "I don't usually tell people..."

"But you'll tell me, won't you?"

If I was who he said I was—though I still hadn't wrapped my head around the whole 'fated mates' concept yet—surely he'd want me to call him by his true name?

He swallowed hard, his throat working as though he was struggling with what he needed to say. "Yes, I will."

"I won't tell anyone, if that's what you're worried about."

He glanced at the floor. So, that *was* what he was stressed about. Perhaps his reputation would be affected? Or it would give away some of his power. There was always power in a name, whether or not you held magic inside.

I opened my mouth to say he didn't have to tell me if he didn't feel comfortable, but then he blurted it out.

"It's Phoenix," he muttered.

"Phoenix?" I repeated, unable to see anything embarrassing about it. "As in, Arizona?"

He lifted his head and stared at me, the swirl of his magic showing purple in his eyes. "As in, rising from the ashes. My mother never thought she'd have any children, and she probably shouldn't have."

I gasped. "Don't say that." Was that really how he saw himself? As a person who shouldn't exist? "You can't mean it."

He stared at the white floor. "But I do." He lifted his head and stared hard at me. "I promise to protect you, and your baby, if you want me to. And if you decide you would prefer to never see me again... I will disappear."

My throat tightened and swallowing became difficult.

"I don't want that," I whispered.

He stilled. "You don't want me to protect you..."

I clutched at his hand, drawing it over to me. "God, no. I meant, I don't want you to disappear. *Never*. I don't know what I'm feeling, and I'm not familiar with the fated mate bond, but I know I don't want you to leave. But asking you to take on me, with all my scars, *and* my baby... the danger we would be in constantly... it's a lot to ask of anyone. Too much."

I stopped talking to swallow the sob that rose in my throat. We were screwed on so many levels. The vampires would find me. Take my baby. Kill me. Hurt Shadow.

The tears overwhelmed me, and I couldn't stop the sobs from pouring out.

Gut-wrenching, wanna-vomit sobs.

Shadow swept me up in his arms, which only made me cry more. This man was so beautiful. Limp, smoking habit, scaly skin, and all. He was everything. My hero. And by me wanting him to stay near me... I would put him in the worst sort of danger.

"I can't... I can't..." I wanted to tell him everything I was feeling. Hurt, regret, love. But it was all too much.

So, I just cried, and let Shadow hold me, until I ran out of tears and could barely sit in his lap any longer. Every part of me was exhausted.

Josie came back into the room, glanced at us, and walked out again.

I wiped my face with my hands, then reached for the sheets on my bed to dab at my eyes. "I'm sorry. I'm such a mess. You wouldn't know it... but I was pretty cool, once."

And I had been. I'd been... alive. And fun. And happy.

Shadow grunted. "You're the most amazing person I've ever met, and I'll keep telling you until you believe me—you never have to apologize. For anything."

Nathaniel walked in at that point, and sighed like we were a nuisance. "I think I'm going to need to put your beds together. You don't seem to want to be apart."

Shadow growled, but there was a strange bark beneath now. Another layer.

I glanced up at him. "Is there a fox in your shifter mix?"

Shadow stared down at me, his eyes a bottomless pit of emotion and turmoil.

Then he nodded. I smiled, and for a moment, everything was simple.

"Hey. How come she gets to know what sort of mix you are, and no-one else does?" Nathaniel asked, his hands planted on his hips.

"Because I'm his mate," I whispered, and snuggled into his chest, rubbing my face on the exposed part of his neck so that I could feel his skin against mine and smell his beautiful scent rising to encompass me. "You're not."

Nathaniel's arms dropped and a soft smile tugged at his lips. "You told her."

I glanced up at Shadow. "He knew?"

"Of course, I knew." Nathaniel scoffed. "It's as obvious as the smitten look on his face."

Now I was embarrassed.

"Should we stand up?" I asked. "So you can push the beds together?"

"I was kinda joking," Nathaniel muttered. "But yeah, sure."

I stood up on legs that wobbled and excused myself so I could go to the bathroom, another luxury I was supremely happy about.

When I returned to the room, the beds were now one, and had been remade with clean sheets and blankets once more. Josie stood there with a tray of food.

My stomach rumbled at the sight. "Oh, thank you."

She grinned. "Get in, and you can eat."

"And I'll do some more healing," Nathaniel said, following me around the bed and standing by my side as I slid beneath the covers.

Shadow stood off to the side, staring at me with his intense gaze.

"Again?" I asked.

Nathaniel nodded. "You're taking it so much better than the other two. They've both been asleep since their first treatment. I don't know if it's your pregnancy, or your resilience, or..."

I shrugged. "I'm a healer myself." I lay back and closed my eyes. "Or I used to be, when I had magic. Before they drained me dry."

As Nathaniel's magic worked once more, heat flushed my body. I stayed conscious through the whole session, loving the sensations that bordered on pleasure, my hand slipping down to cover my still-flat stomach.

My child would benefit from this healing, I was sure.

I internally groaned at the happiness I felt at the thought of my child being stronger.

I was keeping my baby. I couldn't get rid of it now that I'd seen how healthy, big, and strong it was. I didn't really care how I'd gotten pregnant; I had a child who needed me to love them... protect them. And I would.

When I opened my eyes, Nathaniel was staring down at me, interest clear in his eyes. "How much of a witch are you?"

I stared at him. "What do you mean?"

"What percentage are you? Most of the magical people I know are fifty percent, most are less."

"Oh..." I swallowed hard. I didn't know that was a thing. "My mother was a witch and my father was a warlock."

"With no shifters, or humans, in the mix? What about your grandparents?" Nathaniel pushed.

I stared at him. "I don't know. I don't think so."

"Where have you been living?" Shadow asked, approaching the bed with wide eyes. They both seemed shocked at what I'd just revealed.

"Before they took me?" I clarified, a little surprised by his question.

He nodded.

"Up near Whitehorse, northern Canada. I came here to study, and was taken within days of arriving." I pushed past the lump in my throat.

"You mean to tell me you're a full witch? The most sought-after magical blood there is?" Shadow asked.

I sniffed, struggling not to cry at the look on his face. "I suppose. We don't have vampires where I come from. Not like the ones here."

I was from a small town in Canada where, during summer, daylight lasted twenty-three hours a day. The vampires, even the daylight-walking ones, didn't like living anywhere near us.

Shadow sat down on the bed with a huff. "We have to get you out of here. This city. We can't stay."

"I agree," Nathaniel said, his gaze darting to the door. "I think I'm going to go and check on the security we have set up around the building."

He hurried out of the room.

I reached across the bed toward Shadow, gripping his arm and squeezing. "What's he so worried about?"

Shadow turned to me with a tight smile. "Everyone in this city is under the impression that witches and warlocks are gone. Hunted by the vampires to extinction for their blood."

"But Nathaniel..." I gestured to the healer who'd left the room.

Shadow nodded. "There are some of us who still possess some magic, but we're diluted with other shifters, or human. You... if your blood is as pure as you say, they'll come for you. And for the baby. We need to keep you safe, and get you out of the state as soon as possible."

I nodded and withdrew my hand, wishing more than anything the same thing I'd wished every day I'd been down in the underground with the vampires.

That I'd never come to this horrible city.

CHAPTER 7
SHADOW

As soon as I explained how important it was for us to leave, Katie withdrew into herself. She closed her eyes and curled up into a ball on the bed.

I wasn't sure what had distressed her so much. I leaned over the large bed and pressed a kiss to her forehead. Then I stood up and began to pace around the room, my mind a whirl.

I'd assumed Katie to be, maybe, one-quarter witch.

Sadie's mom had been a full witch; Sadie was half. That in itself to me had been amazingly rare. But this... wow. None of my family were full bloods. They'd all bred with shifters to decrease the magic in their genes for the advantage and safety of their children.

But Katie had grown up somewhere where there wasn't such a threat from the vampires. Not like we had here. Where was Whitehorse exactly? And could we get there by car?

"Shadow," Nathaniel whispered from the hallway, and I paced over to the door, loving the temporary lack of pain in my back, legs, and ribs.

It was going to be a shit moment when Nathaniel's magic wore off and I didn't feel this good anymore.

"Yeah?" I asked, sticking my head out the door.

Nathaniel gestured for me to come out and I did, after glancing back at my mate to see her still cuddled into herself on the bed. The food Josie brought had been forgotten.

Nathaniel's hair stuck up at odd angles.

"What's wrong?"

"I can't keep her here," he said. "I'm sorry, Shadow. But I can't. They're going to come for her."

"They'll come for all of them. You can keep them safe," I said. "You've always protected those the vampires are after."

Nathaniel ran a hand through his hair and it was obvious that was how he got to looking so bedraggled. "I have six injured shifters, and three hurt witches in this hospital at the moment. I can't protect them all if the vampire blood ring finds us. She is more powerful than me. That's how she stays awake through every healing. I don't think the vampires knew how valuable she is... or they would have accidently killed her long ago. You need to get her out of the state. I'll do everything I can to help you, but you need to go as soon as possible."

I groaned and thrust both hands into my jeans pockets. "Seriously, Nathaniel? You finally find one witch who's more powerful than you, and you kick her out? Insecure much?"

Nathaniel punched me in the arm. "This isn't a joke. It's nothing to do with that. These girls will be missed, Shadow. The vampires will tear the city down around us looking for them. My wards can only handle so much before they'll crumble and fall. I am responsible for everyone in this place. I can't risk her staying here for long."

I tilted my head to the side. "She's really more powerful than you?"

He nodded once, with more a jerk of the head than a purposeful nod. "Yes. And speaking of which..."

He grabbed me by the arms and sudden heat burned up my shoulders and into my back.

"Hey," I said, pulling away from him. I staggered to the side of the hallway and leaned against the wall.

Nathaniel stumbled back, so hard he landed on his ass in the hallway. So much for the always calm, charismatic warlock I used to know.

"What the hell did you do?" I asked, squeezing my eyes shut as waves of ecstasy flowed over me.

Nathaniel pushed up from the floor and stood. He straightened and flicked his jacket to square it up.

"I just shot you with every bit of healing magic I have. I'll be drained until tomorrow now, so let's hope the vampires don't attack tonight… but if they do, you'll be the one fighting them off. Not me."

I stifled the moan of pleasure that swam through my veins, making me feel drunk, in the worst way. My tongue was loose, my eyes were barely open. I wanted to crawl into bed with my mate, and devour her whole.

And I just might do that.

I pushed away from the wall and began to drunkenly swagger back to my room.

"Why did you do that?" I asked around the thickness in my throat.

Nathaniel stared at me, the usually swirling purple eyes now a dark flatness I'd never seen before. "Because you need it, Shadow. You're good… one of the best fighters I've ever seen. But you're gonna need more than your cunning to get Katie out of here, and to safety. You're going to need a miracle. I've given you everything I've got. Use it wisely."

He walked away and I was left staring after him.

What had he done to me? I could barely think straight.

I staggered back into the room, stripped off my clothes, wanting to be out of the cloying, hot layers, and slid between the cool sheets.

"Oh, that's better." I groaned as I lay down, though the room still spun around me.

"Are you okay?" my mate whispered next to me.

I reached for her, and pulled her across the bed and into my arms.

"I am now." I dropped a kiss on her clean hair, loving the way she flattened her hands against my bare torso.

"What did Nathaniel say?" she asked, stroking my skin in ways that made every part of me throb with desire.

"You need to stop doing that." I grabbed one of her hands that was circling my nipple.

She gasped and pulled her hand back.

"Oh no!" I turned onto my side and arranged us so I could stare at her while we lay with our heads on the soft pillows. "Don't misunderstand me. It felt good."

"Then why did you ask me to stop?"

I laughed.

"Because... well, because..." I couldn't find the words, and my eyesight was failing me. I could barely see her through my drunken vision.

Bloody warlock.

"It's okay. I understand," she said, then she dropped her gaze.

I groaned in frustration. "You don't understand, or you wouldn't look so miserable."

Oh, fuck. My filter is totally gone.

I shook my head. "I want you to touch me, but I'm trying not to offend you."

"What would offend me about that?" she asked, glancing up and meeting my eyes.

As with so many moments in my life, the answer was in actions, not words.

I reached for her tiny hand and pulled it down to my groin, where my cock was already thick and hard for her. I put her hand near it and let go of her wrist, so I wasn't forcing her to touch me when she most likely didn't want to.

"This is the problem," I said. "I want you, desperately, but you're in no state to accept me. And not to mention the fact that you may find me repulsive. I don't know."

I shrugged and let my eyes close, not even sure how I got myself in this situation.

"I don't find you repulsive. I..." As words seemed to fail her, she wrapped her hand around my cock, squeezing gently.

I gasped and jerked back.

"Did I hurt you?"

I laughed, settling back into position again. "No. But I almost came all over you. And that would just be..."

What? Disastrous? Disgusting? I didn't even know the right word.

Then her hand was back, wrapped around my shaft and stroking me up and down.

"What did Nathaniel do to you?" she whispered. "You seem so... different."

"Different?" It was hard to talk with her hand sending waves of pleasure right through me. I opened my eyes and managed to focus on her face. "What do you mean?"

She smiled and there was a seductive element to the way her lips lifted. "Relaxed."

"He... uh..."

She kept up the stroking, a kiss to my sternum adding up to the most seduction I'd ever had to face.

"Katie!" I ground out the words. "If you keep doing that..."

"When I came to this city, I'd hardly ever been with a guy. I wanted more than anything to fall in love, and finally feel... *this*."

Her eyes were wide and she was staring at me with all the love, and lust, I could every wish for.

Could it be true? Did she really feel *something* for me? Something that was more akin to love, than hate or disgust?

"This?" I asked, biting off a groan as she changed the angle of her wrist and began pulling me in exactly the right way.

"Yeah… like this," she repeated. "Like how I feel when I'm with you. As if I never want to let you go."

I leaned forward, pressing my forehead against hers, unable to stifle the moan of pleasure rolling up from my throat. "I'm going to blow soon, Katie. If you don't stop…"

But she didn't stop. Quite the opposite. She moved her hand harder, and faster, and I let go of my control.

I reached for her chin and tilted up her face. Then I crushed my lips down onto hers, kissing her hard as my orgasm rushed through me.

I wrapped the sheet over the top of my cock, moaning into her mouth as my hot seed pulsed out of me. Wave upon wave of pleasure jerked my body and I melted into the pillow and mattress, feeling more replete than I had ever felt in my life.

I groaned as I nibbled on her bottom lip, then slowly withdrew from her still clutching fingers.

I glanced down at the sheets, now wet and scrunched. "Looks like we both need another shower."

Katie sighed happily. She pushed the sheets off our bodies until they hit the floor, then reached for a clean blanket piled up on the dresser next to her. "No. I wanna stay here. Wrapped up with you in our warm cocoon."

She flicked the blanket over us and turned over so I could cuddle behind her. She bumped her pelvis back into my belly, and I chuckled as I wrapped an arm around her and tugged her close.

"I wish I could pleasure you in the same way," I risked whispering to her.

"Me too," she said, just as quietly. "Maybe soon. If you want to."

I kissed the back of her neck. "I would love to. Whenever you're strong enough, you tell me. I want to give you all the pleasure in the world."

She nodded, her fingers toying with my hand.

I closed my eyes, relaxing into a post-orgasmic bliss. We likely had a few hours before we would need to leave. I could get in a small nap.

Katie took my hand and pressed it to her belly. Where once there had been only flatness, was now a soft, rounded curve.

Exhaustion dragged me down, but I cupped her belly with my palm and held Katie and her child through the darkness into sleep.

CHAPTER 8
SHADOW

"Wake up, Shadow," Nathaniel whispered urgently, pulling me from my slumber.

"What is it?" I mumbled. Maybe it was his magic. Normally I would wake in an instant.

"They're here."

Oh, fuck!

I growled as I rolled over and attempted to get to my feet. I staggered and shook my head, still half-drunk with pain-killing magic. Was this how a normal person felt every day when they didn't have to smoke like a chimney to battle the crippling pain in their body?

Then I realized I was naked. "Shit."

I reached for the pile of clothes Josie had brought for me. I pulled on the jeans and picked up a gray shirt to pull on.

"The vampires from the blood ring?" I asked. "How could they possibly find us so fast? I mean, Katie drank the snake potion. Shouldn't that provide some protection?"

He shrugged. "It should, and I would expect it has kicked in by now. But they must have tracked her here from the scent trail she left on the way here. Whatever the reason, they're here, and they're attempting to get in through the wards I have stationed around the hospital."

"Won't the wards kill them?" I asked, as I buttoned up the shirt.

I glanced over at my mate, who was discreetly getting out of bed and going through the drawers for clothes of her own.

"I don't have any magic left," Nathaniel hissed at me. "My wards are strong, I admit. I built them well. But if they get through, we're done for. You have to lead them away."

I groaned. "Why can't we stay here; wait it out? Surely, they'll leave eventually?" Even as I spoke the words out loud I knew it was a ridiculous sentiment. The vampires would not give up that easily.

Not to mention the fact that they were here for the other witches too, not just Katie.

"Nadine and Sasha are barely a quarter witch. Katie is a full blood magical being. There is no way they're after the other two. Not with this much urgency."

I glared at him. "You're throwing us to the wolves, Nathaniel."

"I have given you every hope I can. Katie's had three healings, and you have all my strength, Shadow. I have to protect my staff, and my patients, and... look, I'm sorry. But you need to leave."

Nathaniel turned on his heel and stalked out.

"Bastard," I spat, running my hands through my hair, then tugging on the ends in frustration. Though part of me knew he was doing the right thing. He did have others to look after, not just us. "I thought we'd be safe here."

A twang of guilt shot through my heart. I'd been right to bring the women here. I'd been wrong to think Nathaniel was invincible. He wasn't. He was still a mortal man, with magic that could heal, and help the sick. He'd protected me in the past, but it seemed that when the power of the whole blood ring came to bear, even the perfect warlock faltered.

I turned to face my mate, a lump in my throat. "I'm so sorry."

She pulled a warm sweater over her head that was three sizes too big and tugged it down over her thin frame. "I'm going to use your words and throw them right back at you. You never get to apologize, Shadow. For anything to do with this. You saved my life, my soul, my baby. It's not your fault, and it's not Nathaniel's either, that the vampires want me so much."

I narrowed my eyes. "Did you know that your blood is considered one of the rarest in the world—at least, for vampires?"

She stared straight back at me. "I didn't even know vampires *liked* witch blood until I was in the underground, or I would never have come to this horrible city! Because, from the moment they bit me, they went bananas. They almost killed me, so many times, because they took too much from me. I never really knew why they did it so much to me and not the others. But they killed other girls they brought into the underground too... so no, I didn't realize. At all."

I could see it in her eyes—those gorgeous blue eyes that were beginning to swirl with purple magic—that she was now realizing the full truth.

"So, what do you want to do?" I asked her.

She glanced down at her bare feet. "I want to grab a pair of shoes, preferably a pair I can run in, and I want to make a break for it. We have to do what Nathaniel asked us to do—lure the vampires away, and hope it's enough so they leave the hospital alone."

I nodded, absorbing everything she was saying. "There are a lot of magical people here."

She snorted. "There are. A practical buffet for the vampires."

"Now you've had the snake potion, that might make our escape faintly easier," I said, hoping I was right.

She nodded. "Exactly. So hopefully they won't smell me like they did before."

I checked my watch and sighed. "It's just gone six. We've got about two hours of daylight left, then the city will be swarming with vampires."

Vampires could day walk, as they'd adapted to the modern world well, but there was a payment for such a thing. They were weaker, and the strongest vampires were those who adhered to the night-time routine they were designed for.

"Then we need to leave as soon as possible," Katie said, rounding the double bed and standing before me.

She was looking better than I'd seen her so far. Her cheeks were flushed and full, her eyes sparkling with magic and health. But she was still very thin, and seemed fragile.

She put both hands on her hips and glared at me. "I'm not as weak as I look. And we need to go, for the sake of all the others."

"We need weapons," I said. "We need—"

"I've got some for you," Nathaniel said from behind me.

He was standing in the doorway, arms full of knives and guns.

I lifted an eyebrow at him. "Feeling guilty about throwing us to the wolves?"

It was a low blow considering the man had saved Katie's life, but I didn't like being told we had to leave the only safe place in the city.

Nathaniel shrugged. "Yeah, I am."

He dumped the weapons on a nearby gurney and marched off.

I sighed and pressed two fingers into my forehead, forcing myself to think, and fast.

Where could we go?

My place? Too dangerous, and it was partly underground, which Katie was sure to hate. Sadie's apartment? Not safe enough.

The workshop?

I shook my head. There was only one safe place, and that was wherever Katie had come from.

I whirled around. "Where's your home again, Katie?"

"Canada, up near Whitehorse."

I grinned at her. "Where there's sunlight twenty-four hours a day."

"In summer, yeah. In winter its practically twenty-four-hour darkness."

Yet the vampires didn't go there. Interesting.

"We need to get you out of this city, out of the state. And get you home."

She took a step closer. "You're coming with me though, right?"

I grinned at her. "Yes."

How did I tell this woman I was never leaving her side? It still sounded like a completely foreign idea to me, and I was a shifter who believed wholeheartedly in the fated mates concept.

"Let's get suited up then."

From the collection of weapons Nathaniel had dumped for us, I strapped knives to my thighs and put a gun holster over my shirt.

When she didn't move, I handed her a dainty little dagger. "If you aren't comfortable carrying a weapon, at least strap this to your ankle. Just in case."

I hated the idea that we were going to have to fight our way out of the city, but it would be worth it to get Katie to safety.

She took the dagger and strapped it to her calf.

I grabbed a jacket from the wardrobe and pulled it on over my gun holster, leaving it unzipped in case I needed to get to the gun easily. I checked the bullets before I loaded up. Silver, with a core of wood. Perfect vampire killers—presuming there weren't too many of them coming after us.

I grabbed her hand, my heart pounding like a bongo drum in my chest. "Come on. We better go."

We exited the hospital room, looked left and right down the hallway, and headed toward the main exit.

Nathaniel darted from one of the rooms, cutting us off. "They're trying to break in. I suggest you head out the staff exit, then I'm going to lock the place down for as long as I can."

I didn't ask any questions about the why's or how's, or if there was enough food for them to survive if he did manage to hold them off for a while. I just said, "Show us where it is and we'll leave now."

Nathaniel nodded, pushed past us, and started running in the opposite direction. Through the hospital, down a hall and up some stairs.

We followed him through a maze of hallways I'd never seen before, then through a thick door that led into a house. We were suddenly surrounded by exposed brick walls, windows that looked out on a normal city street and a nice, homely hallway.

"Where are we?" I asked, confounded. This did not look at all like part of the hospital.

"My home," Nathaniel said. "Which I fully expect them to find, and destroy very soon, but at the moment, it's the only way out other than the main entrance where they've congregated."

A wave of gratitude washed over me. If this was the last time I would see Nathaniel, I couldn't leave things as they were. Angry. Hostile.

I extended my arm and shook his hand. "Thank you, my friend. I won't forget what you've done for Katie. For us."

He grinned at me. "God speed, Shadow. If you ever come back to the city, look me up."

I nodded. "Will do."

I grabbed Katie's hand, and Nathaniel pointed up the hallway. "The front door is that way. As soon as you get out of here, start running north, and don't look back."

Katie launched herself at him, hugging him tight. "Thank you for everything. I'm so sorry I brought so much trouble with me."

Nathaniel glanced at me with an apologetic look in his eyes as he pulled out of Katie's embrace. "I am assuming that you don't need my help with your pregnancy anymore? You're going to keep the baby?"

She glanced at me, then nodded. "Yes. Shadow told me he would look after us."

Nathaniel's grin was big and bright. "He will. He's a good man. I'm glad you found each other."

A loud crash came from behind us, back down in the maze of hallways where we'd come from.

Nathaniel jumped. "*Fuck*. I better go."

"Hold on," Katie said, grabbing for Nathaniel's hand. White magic flowed through their shared grip.

Nathaniel's eyes widened, then he tugged his hand back. "You need that for yourself."

Tendrils of purple magic moved through Nathaniel's eyes again.

"You need it, too," Katie said with a smile. "And thanks to you, I'm growing stronger by the minute."

There was another loud bang from behind Nathaniel, and he started to back away.

"Go!" Katie urged. "Seal yourselves in. We'll see you when everything settles down."

Nathaniel nodded once, turned tail, and disappeared back the way we'd come.

I grabbed for my mate's hand again, and tugged her toward the entrance to Nathaniel's house. "That was good of you, to give him some of his magic back."

She shrugged. "Without him, I'd be dead."

I pulled open the large wooden front door and we burst out onto the street. It turned out we were right in the middle of downtown. That meant we had about ten miles before we'd be able to reach the edge of the city, which we wouldn't be able to do on foot, not in two hours, and not with a swarm of vampires chasing after us.

"Do you have enough magic to get yourself out of the city?" I asked, hoping she was one of those witches who could teleport.

"No."

"Then let's start running," I said, pulling on her hand. We started jogging down the street. "I'll think of a plan on the way."

She didn't answer me, but she was right beside me as we hot-footed it through the city. I knew every street, every alcove, every shadow in this damn place.

But as the sun began to lower, and red hues cast themselves across the sky, the snarl of angry vampires reached my ears.

We were about to be in a hell of a lot of trouble.

CHAPTER 9
KATIE

My chest tightened with fear as the sky grew darker. My body hurt like it had never hurt before. We'd run for what felt like miles, and we were still within the darkened streets of this seemingly never-ending city.

We stopped at a crossroad and I bent over, pushing my hands against my thighs as my legs wobbled. I had the worst stitch in my side. Every breath I took was agony.

"I can't keep running like this." I panted, pushing myself to stand up and inhale as deeply as possible. My heart was going to give up at this rate. "I've barely moved from a bed in... years. I can't..."

Shadow nodded. "I know. We need a place to hide until morning."

He looked around us—I assumed to get his bearings and work out where we could go.

"I think I have a place. It's about two blocks over. Can you make it?"

If it was guaranteed I could lie down at the end of this run? *Absolutely.* "Yes. I think I can."

I could feel the magic coming back, and my baby was safe within me. That in itself gave me the strength to keep going. I would rebuild myself into the person I'd been before, but even stronger.

We just had to survive this night.

"Follow me," Shadow said, and I did. Just as I had been for the hours we'd been running through the city.

Shadow's spine was straight, his limp unnoticeable as he continued to run down the street, turn left, then bolt across a road.

He looked strong and healthy, which according to him, wasn't normal. Which also meant that whatever Nathaniel had given him, magic-wise, was working. And it also made me think about what *I* could do, long term, to make him feel like this. Strong. Free of the pain that had obviously plagued him all his life.

When we finally reached an old, ramshackle house, we stopped.

I wheezed through my aching throat. "Is this it?"

He nodded, breathing hard. "It's abandoned, and protected with magical charms like the hospital. I've hidden people here before."

"Okay," I panted. "Let's go."

Before I fall down and can't get up again.

As Shadow pushed open the gate in the white picket fence, it fell off its hinges.

He sighed and dropped the gate to the ground.

"Come on." He grabbed my hand and tugged me down the beaten path and up to the front door.

"There could be other people in here, hiding or whatnot. Just ignore them, and we'll find a corner for ourselves."

I nodded, not knowing anything about this world, so I decided I was one hundred percent going to trust Shadow on everything.

He opened the door, which was unlocked, and closed it loudly behind us.

Inside, the house was a mess, with threadbare furniture and the smell of urine permeating the air.

It was a familiar scent, unfortunately. The vampire lair had been pungent with the smells of the women around me.

"Let's try the bedrooms," Shadow said, leading me through what used to be a lounge room, and down a hallway.

He seemed to know the layout well, and I could feel the tingle of magic in the air. It wasn't strong, and I didn't believe it would stop a vampire if they came to attack us now, but it was ever-present and I had to believe Shadow when he said we would likely be safe here. At least for a short time. He hadn't led me wrong yet.

The first bedroom we opened had several people inside, huddled on the bed. Their eyes glowed in the dark room and my heart leapt.

Shadow shut the door again without saying anything and tried the next bedroom. There was a bed shoved into one corner, and little else.

"Hello?" Shadow called out, but when no-one moved to indicate there was life in the room, we stepped inside.

Shadow shut the door behind us, then crept around the room, checking under the bed and behind the curtain.

I put my hand to my stomach, worried about the baby. The pregnancy made me more of a target for recapture, but the more I considered it, the more I was determined to protect my child.

But... did protecting my baby mean getting rid of it before the vampires could take and torture it? My thoughts were all confused. I had to talk to Shadow about it, given he had offered to support us. "Do you think the baby will be safe, where we're going? If the vampires catch us, the baby has no chance—except to live a life of torture, pain and terror. Should I... would it be better to just... get rid of the baby? Now?"

Shadow stopped his investigating and whirled around, his eyes flashing silver in the darkness.

I tilted my head, wondering about his shifter mix. "You never answered my question fully. You're part wolf shifter, snake shifter, and warlock. What else is in there?"

He inhaled sharply. "A small amount of fox shifter, and some hare as well."

"A hare? Like... a wild rabbit?"

His nod was more of a jerk. "Yes. I think the hare, in combination with the snake, is what gave me my spinal deformity, so I'd wish it away if I could. But... back to you. What do you mean get rid of the baby right now? Isn't that dangerous?"

"No more dangerous than waiting for a vampire to come here and kill us... or capture us, which would be even worse. When they find out I'm pregnant, they'll wait until I give birth, then take the baby to steal its blood, too. They might even kill him or her, but not before they torture it. Hurt it. I heard that happens a lot with vampires that can't control themselves. I can't have that. Wouldn't it be better, just to end it now?"

I didn't know where I got the confidence or strength to say such a thing, but the adrenaline was pumping hard. I didn't want to be the reason Shadow was killed, and if I wasn't pregnant, I could fight.

Shadow held out his hand, "Come here."

I walked forward on legs that were like jelly, took his hand, and leant against him.

"Can we sit down?" I asked.

He groaned, falling onto the mattress. "Let's lie down."

I nodded and lay with him on the cold, thin blankets. The smell was musty, but I didn't care. I had Shadow's warm arms around me and my body could finally rest after our dash through the city.

"Now," Shadow began, tracing a pattern on my arm. "What were you saying?"

I took a deep breath and sighed. Did we really need to go through it again?

"I have enough magic to end the pregnancy, I think. It will leave me pretty weak, but at least if they catch me, they won't have my child, too."

There was quiet in the darkness as Shadow absorbed my words.

"So, you want to protect your child?"

Tears burned my eyes and I took another slow, deep breath,

willing them away. I didn't need to be crying again. That didn't help with anything.

"Yes. Of course. It's a precious gift."

He pulled me closer so I was lying half on him now, my head on his chest, hearing the steady sound of his heart beating beneath my ear.

"It sounds like you want to keep your baby safe, not lose it, Katie."

The burning in my eyes was back, but I refused to pay it any heed. "Of course I do! But it's not safe, Shadow. To keep it isn't safe, for any of us. And what are we going to do, even if I can get to safety? Find my family after all this time? Who's going to look after us? Protect us from the vampires that will come looking for us? I can't go back. And I won't let them take my baby. I won't."

I shook my head, biting my lip painfully to stop any tears from falling. Nathaniel had said that my child was still young enough to terminate successfully. I didn't have much time before we crossed over the line and the spell would surely kill both of us.

I sat up, determination gripping my insides. I'd do this for my baby, and for Shadow. He wouldn't have to raise a baby that wasn't his. If he still wanted me at the end of all this, then at least I'd only be one person to look after. Not two.

Shadow's hands clamped down on my arms like a vice.

I glanced his way. "What's wrong?"

"Can you really do it yourself? Anytime?" His voice wavered, as though he was upset about something.

"I can now that I have my powers back."

Shadow didn't reply. I couldn't work out what had gotten him so upset.

"I'll be okay. The most important thing is that my baby won't end up in the vampires' hands, and that you will..." *Be happier if I get rid of this thing that isn't yours.*

I hated thinking about my baby like it was an unwanted parasite growing inside of me. But I steeled myself against the softened feelings.

"I will... what?" His voice was low.

"Well, you know." I swallowed hard. "This baby isn't yours. That has to be hard for any man to accept, especially one with our connection."

He rolled on top of me, pressing his hands down into the mattress on either side of my head, his heavy weight bearing down on me.

"I can't tell you what to do with your body," he said, groaning as though he was in pain, his face twisting.

He could; I'd do anything for him. But I didn't understand his point.

He rolled off me, but stayed pressed against my side, one arm slung over my waist. "Do you actually want to get rid of the baby, or are you doing it because of the vampires? And because it's what you think *I* want?"

"You don't want that?"

"I want what makes you happy, Katie."

"You make me happy," I whispered. I still didn't understand this conversation, and I wanted him back on top of me. I needed the closeness to push away the lonely, cold feeling swamping me.

Shadow growled, his wolf obviously becoming impatient. "I'm just going to say it, out loud. I don't want you to get rid of the baby. If you need to, that's your decision, always. But you should know that I don't want you to."

"You don't?" I gaped at him. Had I heard him right?

He glanced down, avoiding my gaze. "And you should know that I, well, I can't have any. Which means, I can't give you another child if you lose this one."

"You can't?" I repeated, my heart feeling tight in my chest.

"I got myself fixed a long time ago," he said, though it looked like the last thing he wanted to admit. "My genetics are too twisted. The pain... I couldn't inflict that on a child of mine. I couldn't."

I swallowed hard. "I'm sorry you felt like that was your only option."

He pressed his lips into a thin line. "I never thought it would really be a problem. I never expected to have a fated mate, nor find anyone who would fall in love with me."

I turned on my side and reached for his face. It was probably too early to tell him how much I already loved him. I was still getting used to the idea myself.

"So, you want me to keep the baby? Even though it's not yours?"

He nodded fiercely. "I do."

"And when it's born? What if you hate it? Hate me for birthing it?"

He leaned down and pressed his lips to mine. "I could never hate you."

CHAPTER 10
SHADOW

How could I make her understand? The words I was saying were being wrenched from my lips. I had no control over them. But I had to get them out. If she destroyed this baby, she would destroy herself. I could tell. She was already in love with the tiny being, and I was as well.

"I'll love the baby like my own," I swore against her lips. "You have my word."

To prove my point, I slid down the bed, pulled up the over-sized shirt from the hospital, and pressed my lips to her belly.

I felt, more than heard, Katie's sob, and I hoped it was one of relief, rather than sadness.

I trailed my lips up her flesh, taking a moment to nuzzle at her small breasts and lick her tight little nipples.

She gasped and arched up into my mouth, her hands threading into my hair. So many doubts and worries wove through me, and yet I couldn't stop touching her.

"Is this all right?" I asked, after a minute or so when she didn't push me away.

"God, yes," she whispered. "The only place the vampires touched me was my veins. It was calculated and cold. I ache to feel like a human again, Shadow. Like this. Warmth and passion."

"Are you sure..."

She pushed my head back down to her breast. "Will you make love to me?"

"I'd love to." I thrust against her. "Are you strong enough?"

She nodded. "Definitely."

She opened my thighs and I settled between them. She was so horribly thin, and I didn't know how her starved body would react to me, but I wanted to be as close as possible to this beautiful woman. My future... hopefully.

And yet, what would she think of me when she found out about all the things I'd done in the past? When she learnt the reason they called me Shadow, was because I lived in the shadows? A creature who didn't dare step into the bright sunlight for fear of complete rejection. I didn't fit in the real world. I didn't fit anywhere really.

I'd spent my adulthood alone.

"Shadow, please..." Katie whispered, as she held my head to her breast, thrusting the flesh up into my mouth.

Now this perfect woman had crossed my path, and I knew I didn't deserve her.

Her, or her child. But I'd be damned if I was going to waste another moment of loving her, because who knew what tomorrow would bring? For either of us.

I suckled on her nipple like a starving man, exulting in the way she gasped and held me to her. I used my right hand to unbutton her jeans, and slid my hand beneath the waistline and covered her.

She jerked and cried out, opening her legs wider.

I took my time, allowing us this small moment to enjoy one another, and I was determined to make it as good for her as possible.

I circled her clit with my middle finger, flicking the little bud from side to side as she clawed at my hair and shoulders.

I moved up her body, kissing her neck, then her lips as she turned her face to mine and grabbed for me. I slid a finger down her wetness and into her body, loving the way she gripped me and bucked against my hand.

I groaned, my own desire building, my cock hard and straining against my jeans. Katie thrust her tongue inside my mouth and I met her passion with my own, moving my finger deeper, then adding a second, stretching her tightness and building her pleasure.

She arched her back and moaned, sinking her nails into my shoulders to hold me to her. But I wasn't going anywhere.

I kissed her deeply, then withdrew my fingers to circle her clit once more.

She broke off from my lips, panting. "Get naked. Please. Now."

She pushed her jeans down her thighs and began to wiggle out of them.

I slid off the mattress and pulled the shirt over my head, unbuttoned my jeans, and awkwardly pushed them down over my straining cock.

Then I stopped and stared at her. She'd gotten her shirt off as well and lay on the bed, on her back. Her legs were open and she reached for me.

How did I get this lucky?

I glanced up toward heaven, calling on the saints to help me get through this without coming in two seconds flat.

"Fuck, you're hot," I said as I climbed toward her, kneeling on the bed, then lowered myself onto her.

We groaned in unison as our flesh met, hot skin against hot skin. My wolf howled inside me and I shuddered, every part of me exulting in happiness.

I turned my head away, afraid that one of my lesser shifters would rise up.

"Come here, my beautiful one," Katie whispered, wrapping her arms around my neck and pulling me down to her.

I chuckled, the tension forgotten. "You're the beautiful one, Katie. Now and forever."

I reached between us and set my cock at her wet entrance.

I didn't want to rush. I wanted her to need me as much as I needed her. So, I took my shaft and used the throbbing head to paint her pussy with her own juices, dipping the head into her body, then moving the wetness around to her clit, then up and down her slit.

Katie bucked up. "Stop teasing me. Please. I can't stand it."

"Then let's find heaven together."

I sank into her pussy, letting her body stretch and her wonderful heat surround me.

I lowered myself onto her, taking her lips in a kiss as she gasped against my mouth.

"Are you okay?" I asked, halfway inside of her.

She was so tiny, so tight; so perfect. I didn't want to hurt her.

She lifted her thighs and wrapped her legs around me. "Please, don't stop."

I surged inside, moaning out my pleasure as Katie kissed me deeper.

I paused, until I felt her quicken around me. Then I couldn't stop myself from thrusting forward until I was deep within her.

I shivered at how perfect the moment was, how perfect *she* was.

"God, I love you," she whispered.

She loved me? My heart broke, and remade itself twice as big.

I kissed her mouth as I surged back, then thrust forward again, unable to speak. I would love her forever. Every one of my shifters needed her. But she couldn't possibly love me. I'd saved her from the underground, sure, but that wasn't love.

I pushed the thoughts aside and focused on the feel of her around me. The clench of her pussy tightening. I rode her slowly, then harder and harder, until the room was filled with the sounds of our meeting bodies, and groans of pleasure.

Then the heat began to consume me and my snake slithered up within me.

I groaned. "No."

"What's wrong?

"My sssnake…" I hated that part of me. The scales. The slithering. The sounds as I spoke.

She tilted her pelvis up and smiled at me. "Please, don't stop. I love all of you. Especially the part that protects you from the vampires. Maybe you can share some of your blood with me one day."

Just like that, my passion exploded, even as I felt my skin shift, and scales sprout over my face and back.

Katie didn't falter. She leaned forward and sank her teeth into my shoulder, the heat of my impending orgasm tingling in my legs.

"Please come with me," I whispered in her ear, taking her in long, deep strokes.

She squeezed tight around me. "Don't stop."

I thrust once more, and for the first time in my life, buried my cock deep inside my woman and pulsed my seed into her.

Katie came with a gasp, her pussy squeezing me, milking my seed. Shudders of pleasure rolled over me, again and again. I growled, and hissed, and carried on in the most embarrassing way, and yet my mate clung to me.

She held me to her with her arms and legs. Held me until the shudders stopped, my shifters had receded, and there was nothing in the world except the two of us.

I collapsed on top of her, breathing hard. She stroked my hair and held me to her breast, and I didn't try to move away.

"Did I hurt you?" I asked, lifting my head.

She laughed, a soft, breathy sound.

"Not unless you count the out of body experience I just had. That was amazing. Thank you."

She tugged on me to lie down again, and I let myself rest on her.

I'd never been able to relax around anyone before. Not like this.

We were in the middle of a warzone, trapped in a house by the darkness and the vampires that hunted us, and yet, I'd never felt so free. So... at peace.

I let my eyes close, and settled into my pain-free body in a way I could never usually do. A part of my brain was always working on shutting down the pain in my spine or in my leg. A part of my brain always wanted to be somewhere else.

Not this time.

Every part of me was happy, totally in accord with this person we were sharing the moment with.

"Did you really mean what you said about the baby?" she whispered, sounding almost afraid to ask the question. "That you want to keep it?"

I nodded against her. "I do."

Her whole body hummed with a happiness I could feel as if it were my own.

"I'm so relieved," she said. "I really want this baby. I love it already."

"I know. I could sense that," I said. "And I'm glad."

She kissed my head and I lay my hand against her belly, which was beginning to swell with a subtle curve.

"Do you want a boy? Or a girl?" I found myself asking.

She chuckled, hugging me tight. "I don't care. As long as they're happy and free. Powerful too would be nice, so they can blast the shit out of anyone who tries to hurt them."

I laughed at the imagery and propped myself up on my elbow so I could look down at her.

"I hope they have your face," I said, sweeping my fingers down her cheek. "Your heart."

I pressed my hand to her chest, over the beating organ we gave claim to driving the tender feelings in a person.

I swallowed hard as emotion clogged my throat. "Thank you for dealing with my shifters coming out like that. I usually have more control. I'll try to make sure it doesn't happen again."

She shook her head and reached up to cup my face. "Whatever your ancestry, I love you. Your scales, your howl, your insane feelings that you aren't good enough. I accept all of it, just as I hope you'll accept me for all the things I bring with me, too."

"Of course, I do."

She smiled up at me. "You've never had anyone love you for just you, before, have you?"

Her question took me aback. "Well, my parents were pretty good people, but I never really felt like I fit in with them, so I moved here. To this city. And my Uncle Jack, Sadie's dad, gave me a job. And my life just kinda went from there."

She shook her head. "You didn't answer my question."

I regarded her for a long moment, then, in a rare moment of clarity, answered her honestly. "No. I haven't."

She smiled up at me, then rolled onto her side, sticking her ass back so I could spoon her. I cuddled into her back, and held her tight against me.

She pulled the old blanket up over us and sighed as we settled together. "Well, you have now."

I closed my eyes, but didn't allow sleep to claim me for a long time after Katie fell asleep.

I'd never been afraid to die. I'd always believed no-one would miss me when I was gone, and with death would come a peace I'd never known in life.

But not now.

I didn't want to die. I was actually afraid to leave this beautiful creature and the child she offered me. The future that beckoned.

I had to get her out of the city. Her life, and mine, depended on it.

CHAPTER 11
KATIE

Waking up, wrapped in the heat of my mate, was a dream come true. No, it was even better. I'd never even dared to dream that a moment like this could exist, not even before the underground.

I took my time, absorbing the moment. Heat rushed to my eyes, and for once, I did not fight the emotion.

Only a few days ago I'd been lying on a bed in my own filth, strapped to a machine that literally drained the blood from my body. They left me with only just enough to survive.

The pain had gone a long time ago. But the weakness, the depression, was ever-present. I'd wanted to die. Prayed for it.

Now here I was, my lover's hand pressed against my growing belly. A man who claimed I had been sent to him by Fate. His soul mate! A man who was doing everything in his power to protect us.

He was mine. To say I was grateful, would never be enough.

Shadow shifted on his side of the small bed, rolling even closer. He wanted me. He needed me. Just as I needed him.

The other thing that had me excited this morning, was something I hadn't felt in so long. My magic was truly returning. Yesterday, I'd felt its presence, but only after Nathaniel had worked on me three times.

Part of me had assumed that once his magic wore off, I'd be like a used battery in need of a re-charge; unable to power up on my own.

But I'd been wrong! This morning I felt strong. Stronger than I could remember being, even before the vampires had taken me away. I wasn't sure if that was my memory playing tricks on me, or if the small amount of magic I felt this morning was giving me some sort of high.

"Good morning," Shadow whispered into my ear, before rolling over to groan and stretch out his body.

He was so beautiful. I loved everything about him. The way his hair fell over his eyes. The shine of the faint scales on his skin in the light.

His tenderness. His strength. His courage. His patience.

I was one lucky woman.

"We'd better get moving," Shadow said. He gave me a quick kiss on the lips, then slid off the bed to grab his clothes from the floor.

"I can't believe we were safe here all night," I said, following his lead and reaching for my own clothes.

I still wasn't particularly self-conscious about my nakedness. It just wasn't a concern for me. But as we became more intimate, I wanted Shadow to think well of me.

I pulled on the huge shirt Josie had given me, and the jeans that were baggy, but at least they didn't fall down when I ran.

Which I assumed we'd be doing a lot more of today.

"So? What's the plan?" I asked, the nerves working their way back into my belly.

"We need to jack a car, and get out of the city, and across state lines if we can."

I nodded. Great. Committing a felony was on my to-do list today.

"Do you think getting to your parents is the way to go?" Shadow asked.

I shrugged. "I have no idea. It's been years… I think… I still can't tell how long I've been down there, since I saw them. I honestly don't know. And it's a long drive. It will take us a week to get there by car."

I'd flown down for college, then been kidnapped within two days. I had no idea how we'd get there if we had to drive.

He pressed his lips together. "I think it might be smarter to head home to my parents' place then."

My heart jumped in my chest. "You wanna take me home to your parents?"

He grinned. "Of course. They live in a community where there are a lot of witches and warlocks still around. They are mostly masked to vampires because of the mix of reptile shifter genes within our lines, but I think you'll be comfortable there."

"But your work… your business?"

He'd built a life for himself here. Wasn't he worried about leaving any of it behind?

He shrugged. "The only important thing to me, is you. And your baby."

I wanted to correct him and say, 'our baby', but until the child was born and I could hand him or her to Shadow, it would be my baby.

"Okay. Let's do it."

Shadow nodded, pulled on his boots, and looked out the window. "It's still early. By looking at the position of the sun, I'd say it's about seven a.m. We should get going before it gets busier."

We snuck out of the room and headed to the front door. Shadow pressed his ear to the door, and stayed there.

"Hear anything?" I asked, though I wasn't sure what he would be listening for.

He pulled away. "No. I think the wards are still in place, so we should be all right to leave."

I clapped my hands, my gut twisting. "Let's go steal a car."

He rolled his eyes, but grinned at me. "Let's go."

He opened the front door and kept me behind him. Then, once he'd looked left and right, he took my hand and we hurried along the path.

"Don't run," he said. "We don't want to attract attention."

"Like yesterday?" I asked.

He nodded. "It was busy then. There's no-one around at the moment, and we'll stand out like no-one's business."

We made it one block before a vampire walking down the street spotted us. He had bright red eyes and stopped walking to stare at us.

Shadow froze, tensed up, and then pulled me across the road and down an alleyway.

We came to a dead end. "What do we do?" I asked, looking back in the direction we had come.

He opened a door I hadn't even seen, hidden in the brick work. "In here."

He got in first, then pulled me inside.

The space was tiny and dark, but as Shadow pulled the door shut, I pressed myself against his chest, closed my eyes, and tried not to think about the fact I was locked in a room smaller than a jail cell.

"What is this place?" I whispered, not sure if anyone would be able to hear us from the outside.

"It's a hiding hole," Shadow said, and I wanted to laugh. Did people just name exactly what something did, rather than come up with anything original or fun?

Shadow continued. "They're all over the city. Strongly warded against vampires. We'll stay here for a little bit, then we've gotta find a car I can steal."

I nodded.

Shadow's hands shook as he stroked my hair.

"Are you okay?" I whispered.

"Yeah. It's just the nicotine withdrawal. Normally I'd be a shaking mess by this point, but since Nathaniel took all my pain away, I don't really need them."

So, he used smoking for pain management? Good to know. Just another reason to use my magic in the future to keep him healthy, and out of the crippling pain he'd endured all his life.

"I'm glad you're feeling better."

Shadow chuckled. "I keep waiting for it to wear off. I've never gone this long without pain. It's strange, to say the least."

I nodded, but didn't say anything.

I reached down into myself and felt for my magic. It was there, deep down in my soul, growing stronger with every passing minute.

Shadow pushed open the door behind me. "Hopefully he's gone by now. Let's take a look."

I turned around.

The vampire wasn't gone.

He stood a few feet away down the alleyway, staring straight at me. He grinned when we appeared, his wickedly sharp teeth making my stomach twist.

Shadow slipped around me, and with deadly efficiency, pulled the knives from his thigh holsters and cut the vampire's throat.

The vamp froze in place, swaying on his feet as he stared blankly at us while black oozed out of his wound. Then Shadow swung the blades once more, decapitating the vampire.

My mouth dropped open. *Wow.*

"Let's run," Shadow said, and we bolted along the alleyway. "Where there's one, there'll be more."

We rounded the corner and ran straight into a swarm of vampires. Four of them. The creatures spun around to face us, eyes glowing red.

"Holy shit." I stared as they circled around us, their eyes wild, their movements deliberate.

Shadow nudged me. "Katie. Run!"

But there was nowhere *to* run, except back the way we'd come.

"Leave the girl and go," one of the older vampires said to Shadow, his English accent similar to one of my captors.

I shuddered.

"Not a chance," Shadow said.

Without warning, the vampires lunged at us.

Hands grabbed me. Shadow yelled out. They dragged me away. I fought against their hold, twisting and squirming as I screamed. They pulled me farther away from Shadow. I reached for him, until the vampires closed around me, blocking my view of him.

My magic surged up inside of me, then it was dark. One of the vampires had thrown something over my head.

I was suffocating. I couldn't breathe.

Hands dragged at me, pulling me down and away from Shadow.

I tried to fight them, but my arms wouldn't move. I couldn't even scream now.

When I heard Shadow's pained cries, I knew they'd hurt him. But how bad was it? Could he survive an attack of this magnitude? I reached for my ankle, wanting the knife I had strapped there. I was picked up and swung over someone's shoulder.

Then they were running, carrying me away.

Away from Shadow. Away from freedom.

"No!" I sobbed, pulling at the sack on my head, but it wouldn't come off. So, I tugged at it long enough to create a bubble in front of my face so I could breathe.

I beat at the back of the man holding me, but he didn't even seem to notice.

I was captured once again. I was going to be thrown into the underground, and my baby was going to be stolen from me. Killed, or drained. Just like I would be.

I swallowed the sob that rose. No-one was going to save us now.

And if they'd killed Shadow, I'd find some way to escape, and then I'd channel all my rage right back onto those vampire bastards. I was done lying back and being a victim. The first chance I got, I was going to save myself, and my defenseless baby. And then I would exact revenge for whatever they had done to my mate.

CHAPTER 12
SHADOW

Teeth ripped into my flesh, but soon enough the vampires began to choke, and cough, and spit out the blood they'd sucked into their mouths.

Not only was my scent off-putting to them, but from what I'd gathered from the few vamps I'd talked to over the years, my blood was practically poisonous to them.

"What the fuck are you?" One male vampire growled as he spat my blood onto the pavement beneath his feet.

I staggered sideways, getting a wall behind my back. "You don't want to know."

I held tight to the hilts of both knives.

The vampires narrowed their eyes at me, sizing me up.

I darted forward, slashing at the vampire who'd taken a chunk out of my arm. He ducked, then slid sideways.

This guy was fast. Or was I too slow? I couldn't tell.

"Let's go," one of the other vampires said, and all of a sudden, I was alone.

They were gone, and they'd taken my mate with the

I sagged against the wall, blood dripping down my shirt and running along my arm.

I glanced down at the wound in my leg, pain throbbing through me. "Shit."

The fucking vamp had taken my flesh down to the bone.

I put a hand over the wound and limped to the road. I needed help. Now. I put up my hand, and one cab drove right on past.

"Fine then," I muttered. They wanted to play it like that, I didn't have time to wait my turn.

I stepped onto the road and turned toward the oncoming traffic.

"Stop," I said, though the driver wouldn't be able to hear me, and the cab ground to a halt a few feet from my aching legs.

His beeped his horn loudly and hung out his window. "What the hell are you doing?"

I limped around to the passenger side and pulled open the door. "I need your help."

"There's a fee for bleeding all over the back seat," the cab driver said, a snarl written all over his face.

"Take me to Hunters. I'll pay the fee."

Jack's business was the only safe place I could think of.

Sadie was hopefully now out of the underground, safe and secure. One of the last things she'd said to me before we went down, was that she'd left everything to me. Her dad's business, his apartment. Everything.

I'd been totally unprepared for such a thing when she'd announced it, and I'd told her I didn't want it. I wasn't someone who really cared about money, or luxuries. But in this moment, I was grateful to my cousin. At least I had a place to go that would provide me enough time to stitch up this wound. Then I had to work out how to get Katie back.

The driver and I sat in silence for the twenty minutes it took to get to Hunters.

I threw too much cash at him as I got out of the cab, but I knew how hard the smell of blood was to get out of small spaces like cars. "Thanks."

I stumbled out of the car and found Hunters locked. Of course, it was; it was still early. I used the code Jack had given me years ago to open the digital combination lock and pushed open the glass door, practically falling into the foyer.

Then, I went straight for the first aid room, stumbling through the door and looking for something to stem the bleeding. And fast.

"Hey!" a male voice called out from the direction of the front door. "Is anyone here?"

Shit. Should have thought about locking that when I came in.

I considered hiding, then threw caution to the wind. "I'm in the first aid room, and I could use some help."

A guy, about twenty-five years old, stood in the doorway. From the smell of him, he was some sort of wolf shifter—Jack's favorite.

"You're Shadow, right?"

I nodded, pulling bottles off the shelf, then finding what I needed. "Yep. That's me. Can you help me out?"

"Um... yeah. Of course. What do you need?"

"Pour this onto my wound, then help me stitch it up."

The guy came closer, took the bottle, and whistled. "This is gonna hurt like hell."

I clenched my teeth and grabbed hold of the bench. "Do it."

A credit to him, the young guy didn't hesitate; he just poured the solution over my arm and shoulder.

I groaned and inhaled sharply through my nose as a wave of pain swept over me, making darkness flash behind my closed eyes.

I forced my eyes open as the pain began to recede.

Then he threw the rest of the solution on my leg. I almost passed out.

Harden up, you pussy.

"Do you know where everyone is?" he asked.

I forced my eyes open. "What's your name?"

"Joseph. But you can call me Joey."

"Fine. Joey. Sadie's left me in charge until she gets back. She and her mates have left for a while."

"Really? How come?"

I shook my head, staggering over to a chair so I could sit down. My legs weren't holding me up very well at the moment. "You don't want to know. Just trust me when I say, I'm in charge. And I need your help with this."

Joey cocked his head to the side, as though assessing me for my trustworthiness, then he shrugged. "Okay."

He stitched me up, finding more bites on my arms than I'd realized, and dosed me with a different potion.

When I'd finally stopped bleeding, I staggered to my feet. "I need some food, and I need a plan to get Katie back."

The pain in my body was already disappearing, which was plain strange. I had to assume that Nathaniel's magic was at work again.

"Who's Katie?"

The front door opened. I hobbled over to the hallway to see three more guys come in.

Fridge and Rogan must have assumed they'd be back working today, and hadn't told any of their guys that the workshop would be closed.

"Hey, Shadow!" One of the hunters called out, and as he got closer, I recognized him.

"Hey Taylor." I held out my hand to the wolf shifter, but instead of shaking it, he only gaped at my blood-covered arm.

"What the hell happened to you?"

"Vampires."

Taylor tsked. "Bastards." He looked around the room, and frowned. "Where's Sadie and Rogan and Fridge?"

I took a deep breath. "They left me in charge."

Taylor's eyebrows flicked up. "Are they okay?"

"We broke into the underground yesterday."

"You what?" another guy asked, walking up to our group.

I didn't like crowds and I didn't like to be in charge. There was a reason I worked for myself. *By* myself. But Sadie had wanted me to look after my uncle's business, and I would help her if I could.

"We broke into the underground, and rescued the witches they had locked down there."

The guy who'd joined us, another wolf shifter with orange-red hair, ran to the door, shut it, and locked it. Then he ran back and stared at me with an excited look on his face. "So, what happened?"

I swallowed, hating the way they were all looking at me, but knowing I had to step out of the shadows and into the spotlight for this. For Katie. For my mate.

"Travis, Tony, and I grabbed three of the witches and took them straight to a secret hospital I know. But the vampires came and took my witch off me." I swallowed the acid that rose in my throat, anger eating at me.

"What about Fridge?" Joey asked. "And the rest of them."

"I don't know," I said honestly. "Sadie told us to leave. She stayed to look for her mom."

"Her *mom*?" Joey repeated, his mouth dropping open.

I nodded. "I don't know if they found her, or if they got away."

The red-headed guy pulled out his cell phone. "I got a message this morning from Fridge, but haven't checked it yet. Hang on..."

He tapped on the screen then grinned. "They made it out. They're hiding. And... he said Shadow's in charge."

He lifted his gaze to mine, and I held up a hand. "I'm Shadow."

"I'm Dakota," he said, "but you can call me Dax if you want."

I nodded. "Great. Well, Dax, I think I need your help."

A plan was beginning to form in my head, but I couldn't do this on my own.

Dax and Joey nodded. "Watcha need?"

Taylor crossed his arms over his chest. "We're with you."

I took a deep breath, then blew it out in a rush. "I need to find Katie, the witch they took from me."

Dax narrowed his eyes. "You want to look for the vampires that took her?"

"Yes. And I don't even know where to start."

Dax shook his phone. "Want me to call Fridge and find out what happened with them? Maybe they could give us a clue into how to find her."

"That's a great idea," I said.

Dax grinned and headed off to the workout area to make the phone call.

"What do you want me to do?" Joey asked, his eyes bright and alert.

"You're okay with hunting the vampires?" I asked him. "Most of the people who've gone after the blood ring haven't come back."

"Oh, I'm in," Joey said with the confidence of youth. "I know a lot of the guys would be happy to join us. If there's money in it."

I frowned. "I have money."

Quite a lot, actually. I didn't have many expenses, even with the regular amounts I sent home to help out my parents.

Joey stuck out his hand. "Then consider your bounty hunters hired."

I reached out and shook his hand, noticing the way his gaze ran over my scaled hand and face.

But the smile didn't dim; in fact, there was another light in his eyes now. "I've heard of you, you know? The best P.I. in the city. The strangest of all the shifters. I heard you can kill anyone, even the oldest vamps, because you're so fast. Is that true?"

I chuckled, then coughed to clear my throat. "No. I just stick to the shadows. People don't know me."

He stared at me, then he shrugged. "Well, it's still an honor, man. I mean, you're kinda a legend around here. You and your silver cigarette case." He frowned. "You need a smoke? I've got some."

Did I? I probed my mind, then shook my head. "Nah. I'm okay for the minute. Thank you, though."

Thanks to Nathaniel's magic, even my new injuries weren't bugging me now. "Do you think you could contact other hunters and see who's in?"

Joey nodded. "A few of the older guys won't wanna take the risk, but I'm sure I can rope in at least a dozen."

A dozen would be amazing.

"Great. Get them here as soon as possible to suit up. We're raiding the vault."

I had access to everything, thanks Sadie. And we were going to need all the knives, guns, and stakes we could get.

Joey clapped his hands together. "Yes! I'll go make some calls."

He pulled his cell out of his back pocket and saluted, before heading off to do his own research.

Dax jogged back into the room. "You'll never guess what happened!"

We all turned toward him and Dax grinned as he began his tale.

"Sadie found her mom and, together, they practically blew up the underground yesterday. Killed one of the vampire fathers too. And I'm happy to report, they all got out safely. Just."

Sweet relief coursed through me. My aunt, my cousin and her mates were safe. And they'd taken out one of the most powerful vampires in the state. That could only mean good things for us.

"So that means they can't take Katie straight back to the underground. It's gone."

Dax nodded. "Yeah. And Fridge said that his vampire mate, Vincent, knew of some places we should check out. Where the vampire fathers live. He's messaging me a list, though I didn't quite get that part. Since when does Fridge like guys?"

I laughed. Dax was too young to understand the mate bond.

"A fated mate bond isn't something you can fight, though I'm pretty sure Fridge fought that one pretty hard. He's mated to both Sadie and Vincent in equal measure."

Dax tilted his head, then shuddered like he couldn't think of anything worse than a fated mate.

My heart twisted in my chest. That was exactly how I'd felt a few days ago, though secretly the loneliness would have slowly killed me.

Dax's phone dinged and he lifted it up, turning to stand side by side with me so I could see the list of places Fridge recommended we check out.

I forced myself not to move, though the close proximity of the other man made me a little nervous. I wasn't used to people wanting to be so near me.

I scanned the list, then tapped the screen. "I know that place. One of the fathers lives there. In the penthouse."

"Then I'd say that's the first place we should look," Dax said, sliding his phone into his pocket. "You got a team?"

"A team?"

"Yeah, its gonna take a whole fucking special ops unit to attack a vampire den. And if you expect to walk away with your witch, then we're gonna need men."

I indicated the first aid area, where Joey had wandered off to make his inquiries. "I think Joey's calling in some of the other hunters."

Dax crossed his meaty arms over his meatier chest. "We're gonna need a lot more than that. Don't you have friends? People you've worked with? Anyone who can fight, who'd like to take the vampires down?"

My mouth dropped open. Did I dare? I'd worked in this city for a decade. I did have contacts. People who owed me.

Powerful people.

Dangerous people.

Did I dare call in every favor I was ever promised? For Katie–yes. I wouldn't hesitate.

I nodded. "I do. Give me a few hours and I'll get our army together. If we can attack before sundown, we'll have an advantage."

"Sounds good to me," Dax said.

I walked upstairs to use Jack's computer and landline phone. I had an army at my disposal, and I'd never even recognized it.

After tonight, the vampires would give me my witch mate back, or I'd burn the blood world city to the ground.

CHAPTER 13

KATIE

I was more furious than I'd ever been in my whole life. I wasn't scared like last time. Instead, I wanted to pound these vampires' faces into pulp with my fists.

Thanks to Nathaniel's magic, and his potion, none of the vampires who'd grabbed me had tried to bite me. They'd taken a whiff of my skin, and shrunk away like I was poison.

Good!

That gave me more time to rebuild my strength, and my magic. Shadow wasn't dead; I could feel it. I didn't really know how that was possible, but I could sense his presence, deep inside me. Or at least, that was how it felt. I was sure I'd know if he was dead.

I just had to stay alive long enough for him to rescue me. Again.

Unless I could figure a way out of this by myself.

"Where am I?" I asked, glancing around the fancy room they'd put me in. When they'd taken the hood off my head, I'd been shocked to find I was in a temperature-controlled, darkened bedroom.

I could smell blood in the air. There were vampires around. But I wasn't back in the underground. In fact, from the looks of things, I was in a swanky hotel many levels up.

"Shut up," one of the male vamps said, and turned his back on me.

My stomach ached.

"Could I get something to eat, please?" I asked, as gently as I could.

Feigning fear was the best way for them not to see me as a threat, though I was. I really was, now. My baby, and my love for Shadow, gave me every reason to fight these vampires.

My life was not forfeit. They would not tie me up and take my blood ever again.

"I said, shut up!" The vamp whirled on me, his eyes angry and red.

I sniffed and sobbed a little. "Please. I need some water, and some food. Please."

The guy groaned as though I pained him and marched to the door, then slammed it shut once he left.

I jumped up off the chair and raced to the window, throwing open the curtains. It was dusk over the city, the sun setting and casting hues of orange and red over the landscape.

I couldn't see much from up here. The cars below looked like tiny ants zooming around the streets. We were definitely in a high-rise building.

"Looks like I'm going to be a meal for one of the fathers," I mused aloud.

I hurried back to my chair, just in time, as the vampire stormed back in with a bottle of water and a sandwich he'd obviously pulled from the hotel room fridge.

"Here." He shoved both at me.

He wrinkled his nose as he got close to me and I sent up a prayer of thanks to Josie and Nathaniel for their potion that made me smell like I had reptile blood. I was going to have to buy that by the truck load when I got out of here.

And I would.

I'd thought that when the vampires got me again, I'd be looking for the closest sharp object to throw myself upon, but now that I was in the situation, it was the opposite. I had a future to look forward to.

A man who wanted me. A baby who needed me. These vampires had stolen years of my life, and they weren't going to take any more.

I sipped my water and ate the gross sandwich, because I needed my strength when the moment came. The one I never got the last time they took me.

When they'd grabbed me from the street last time, I'd frozen, terrified. I'd been bitten and drained to the point of passing out. When I'd woken up, I was underground, attached to tubes, and was too scared to fight back. When I finally realized that I needed to fight for my life, I was too weak.

That wouldn't happen this time.

The door opened and an old vampire glided into the room.

He drew close to me, then glared down. "You smell odd."

I dropped my head and stared at my hands clasped in my lap.

"Give me your wrist," he said.

I didn't move.

He grabbed for my hand and lifted it up to his mouth. I tried to fight a little, but I could feel how strong he was. He'd snap me in two if I fought too hard.

He ran his teeth over the veins at my wrist, then bit down.

I flinched, hating the tugging and pulling at my arm.

I looked away, disgusted by the sounds he made. Moaning, thirsty, gobbling sounds.

Then he detached and dropped my hand like it had offended him.

I pressed my other hand into the two puncture wounds, hoping to stem the flow of blood.

"You taste tainted. I can tell you're a witch, and a strong one at that. But your blood has been washed with something... wrong. I will wait another day, then drink again."

He turned and disappeared out the door.

I gaped after him. That was it? He was testing me for my sweetness? And when he found that my taste appealed to him, what then?

I glanced up at the vampire who'd given me the sandwich. "What happens when he comes back and likes the taste of my blood?"

He stared at me, his eyes cold. "The father will choose your path."

I pushed to my feet so I was eye to eye with the blood sucker. "But what are the options? Will he keep me here for a regular snack? Or what?"

Why wasn't I being transported straight back to the underground? What had happened to their operations down there?

The vampire glared at me. "The father will choose."

I turned and walked away, because seriously, that was just a crap answer.

The vampire didn't budge from his post. He was probably my bodyguard.

"Can I have a shower?" I asked, then pointed at a door off from my room. "Is that a bathroom?"

He nodded.

"Thanks," I forced myself to say, then sashayed to the bathroom and shut the door.

Once I was inside, my composure started to crumble, but I steeled myself against the feelings.

"No," I whispered to myself. "You can fall apart after Shadow rescues you. Not now."

I stripped off the dirty clothes and had a long shower. After all, it was going to take Shadow a while to find me, and the vampire father wasn't coming back for a day.

What else should I do?

I washed my hair by myself, aching for Shadow as I did it. Having him wash my hair and shower me had been so necessary at the time, and yet so sensual. So beautiful.

I'd never thought a man could be so tender, and tough, all at the same time.

I scrubbed my hair, then found a brush in the pile of hotel-style bathroom products. It took me forever, or that was how it felt, to detangle my hair.

In the end, I asked the vampire for some scissors and chopped half of my long hair off. It really was a caked, disgusting mess.

When I was finally done, I swiped my hand across the steam-covered mirror and stared at myself.

I looked better than I had yesterday, and the fact I'd been able to have such a long shower and was still standing, was testament to how much stronger I was.

My cheeks had filled out, and my eyes were no longer pools of dead nothingness.

I clenched my jaw and ran my hands through my now-shoulder-length hair. When we got out of here, I'd get a real hairdresser to fix it up, but for now, I felt so much cleaner and healthier. But I was exhausted.

I wrapped one of the huge, fluffy towels around my body, then ventured back out into the bedroom and sat down on the bed.

My bodyguard was still standing in the corner, looking as bored as ever.

"Should I go to sleep?" I asked. "Or is there something else I need to do?"

The vampire grunted at me, then nodded and left. He obviously found watching me a waste of his time.

As soon as he left, I scoured the room for some clothes, finding only the complimentary robe. I wrapped myself in its fluffy depths.

Oh, my God, it was luxurious, which confused my body no end.

I should be in full-on survival mode, and yet I found myself falling into a deep sleep, content with the knowledge that I would be safe soon enough.

Shadow will be here soon.

I woke to loud bangs and screams. My heart pounded and fear raced around my body.

It was time. My mate had arrived.

CHAPTER 14

SHADOW

I'd called in every favor, every marker, every debt. I had a menagerie of shifters, hunters and humans at my back, ready to fight to the death to find my mate.

We decided to go straight to the place on Fridge's list I recognized—the hotel where one of the vampire fathers lived. I had to hope that's where they had taken Katie.

If they couldn't use the underground to hide her, it stood to reason that they'd put her in the other safest place in the city.

A high-rise building with an army of vampires to keep her from getting taken again.

We stormed through the main doors and took out the security guard at the elevator. Then, as the two women behind the reception desk jumped to their feet and exposed fangs, Dax took them both out, too.

I hurried over to the elevators where the comatose security guard lay on his side. I lifted his lip to see the fangs protruding from his jaw. "All vampires. I think we've got the right place."

Dax hustled up next to me. "The whole place could be crawling with them."

I nodded, touching the silver stakes at my waist, ready and willing to take out as many as we needed, to save Katie.

"Hey Shadow," Thomas said, creeping up next to me. He was part fox also, and had a super-fast mind.

I'd saved him years ago from a group of vampires. He owed me, and he had a vengeful streak a mile wide. Perfect for this mission.

"Yeah, Tommy?" I asked, watching our army pile into the ground floor, twenty-six of them in total, awaiting my command.

"I can work their computer system. Might be able to find the father for you."

I nodded at him. "The father will be in the penthouse, but if you can lock every door on every floor to keep all the other vampires trapped, that would be handy."

"And unlock all the doors on the penthouse floor?" he asked, his eyes bright and alive with the excitement of the chase.

I shoved at his chest and grinned at him. "Yes! Smart ass. Thanks."

Dax grabbed the security vampire's tags and handed them to me. "This should open the doors, elevator, and stair wells. I think."

I grabbed it and went over to the pair of elevators. "Some of you stay down here. Make sure no-one comes in, and for God's sake, don't let anyone out."

A couple of the hunters I'd brought with me grabbed two of the shifters. "We can hold the fort down here."

Dax headed to the elevator doors. "Let's go to the penthouse. You sure she'll be up there?"

"No. I don't know. But it's my best guess."

I knew the fathers. I'd studied them over the years. Avoided them, fought their hired help. This wasn't going to be easy, but if we were fast, we might be able to get in and out with little to no injuries.

"Let's go," I said, swiping the card over the silver reader.

The doors opened.

"We're with you," Dax said, as multiple hunters and shifters piled in.

I swiped the card again and pressed Penthouse One. But there was another button. Penthouse Two.

Shit.

The doors started to close. I slammed my hand between the doors and darted out to stop the other elevator.

"We need the card as well. The elevator won't work at all without it," Taylor said, holding out his hand.

I handed him the card and said, "You go to Penthouse Two. We'll go to Penthouse One. You're looking for a witch, about twenty-two or so. Super thin."

Taylor nodded, grabbing his gun. "We'll see you afterwards."

I rushed back to my elevator, and the doors dinged shut.

I shuddered as we moved up, up, up. I hated these things. It was unnatural to be so far up in the sky. My hare shifter, my wolf shifter, my fox, and my snake, all hated it. And that was most of my blood.

I closed my eyes and focused on the mission. What I was here to do. Save Katie. Kill vampires. That was all that mattered.

The elevator climbed higher, the numbers above our heads growing, until finally, the elevator rocked to a stop.

"I have no idea what's out there," I said to the eight guys who'd piled into the elevator with me. "Be ready for anything."

I pulled the silver stakes from my thigh holsters and gripped them hard. My heart pounded, and the magic in my veins thrummed to the forefront.

The elevator doors dinged open on Penthouse One.

I launched forward, stakes raised, ready for action.

There was nothing.

We stood in a small empty foyer with a single door.

The guys piled out behind me. I crept forward, until I was right in front of the door.

"I don't like this. One single point of entry and exit," I said.

Dax called out. "There's the emergency stairwell, if we get stuck."

"Yeah, and need to run down thirty flights of stairs," Alex said. "Fun."

I nodded. "At least there's a second escape route, and with Tommy blocking all the other floors and doors, hopefully that means we won't be met with anyone on the lower levels."

There was a soft thump from beneath my feet and I realized the other guys had already breached level two.

We needed to go.

"Come on." I reached out for the handle, only to have the door swing open in my face.

It was a vamp, not even looking our way, as he chatted to someone on the inside of the room. Then he turned to see us, and his mouth dropped open. "What the…"

I didn't hesitate. I slammed the silver stake straight into his heart.

He burst into flames, then crumbled to the carpet in a pile of ash.

Screams erupted from within the apartment, and we stormed in.

Human women sat in a row on the couches, ready to be fed from. Three vampires stood around watching them.

My army attacked like a swarm, using their knives and silver bullets to kill the three vampires.

They corralled the screaming women who had all jumped up at our entrance, and now stood in a tiny circle flapping their arms.

"Do you ladies want to be here?" I demanded. "Or are we rescuing you too?"

"Well, yeah… sort of," one of the blondes said. "We chose to be here."

I nodded at my guys. I didn't have time to process that. "Leave them. I've gotta find Katie."

I dashed to a door off the room, to find a bedroom. It was empty.

I went to the next room. Also empty.

"Looking for this?" a man said as he walked out of the next bedroom holding Katie against him, a knife to her throat.

Fucking hell.

I went still and quiet. This vampire held my life in his hands. My future. I would do anything he said if it meant saving Katie.

But I also knew how to deal with people. Bullies especially. And showing weakness, or fear, was not an option.

"Let her go, and we won't kill you," I said.

The men around me moved in to circle the offending vampire.

The vampire pressed the knife into her throat, making blood well and trickle down her neck. "No closer."

"Stop," I said to the guys.

They froze in place.

Katie didn't say anything. In fact, she was so still, she didn't even look like she was breathing.

Then she flicked her gaze toward me, just for a second, and I saw something that surprised me. Anger. She was still alive, still fighting to be free, even if it didn't look like it to her captors.

Thank Christ.

The relief made me sag, and I slid the stakes back into their holsters. I'd tried not to think about it, but I'd been terrified about Katie's mental health and how she'd dealt with the fact that the vampires had captured her again.

I'd been afraid she would hurt herself, or worse. She'd always said she'd rather die than go back into the underground.

"Let her go," I repeated, in my strongest voice. "And you can leave."

The vampire grinned. "Once the fighting starts, mongrel.... You're mine to kill."

"What..."

Then I felt him. *The father.* The hairs on the back of my neck prickled and I turned to see him on the other side of the room. He moved into the room like a disease. Fatal, slow. A destroyer.

He stared at me with all-knowing eyes. They glowed red in his weathered head, his long silver hair flowing over his black robes.

He looked like some aged, helpless priest. He wasn't. He was the deadliest person here, and we needed to act fast.

The time for games was over.

"Get him," I yelled.

The hunters launched at the father vampire, daggers and knives drawn.

The father moved like only an ancient vampire could, with lethal speed and perfect strength.

He killed two of the men right in front of me, then moved around dispatching the other five. I couldn't just stand there.

The father had Taylor in his grasp. Taylor tried to get away but the father's hold was too tight. He leaned down and chomped down on Taylor's throat.

I swung one of my silver stakes into the side of the father's neck.

The father growled and threw an arm out, sending me flying across the room and into a wall.

The remaining hunter shot the father in the head, but the vampire took him out, too.

I groaned as I staggered to my feet and glanced over at my mate. The vampire still had her in his grasp, knife to her throat.

How on earth was I going to save her now?

I sucked my magic into my core, using it to strengthen my resolve. I gripped the remaining stake I had strapped to my thigh with my left hand and pulled the silver knife from my belt with my right. My fastest weapon.

When the vampire father came for me, I was ready. And he was injured. Black blood poured from his neck, and the hole in his face spoke of the gunshot wound. He needed to feed and I dared him to come for me.

I dropped my arms, feigning fright. He grabbed me by the shoulders and pulled me toward him.

I braced for the pain of his bite and exulted in the groan of disgust as he tasted my tainted blood.

He pulled up, his mouth open, my blood pouring from his lips like an open wound. "What are you?"

"Not yours to eat," I growled, and sliced his throat with my silver knife. As he gasped for air, I plunged my silver stake deep into his heart.

The father fell backwards, but as he fell, he swung at me, his talon-like nails slicing through my face.

There was a loud thump as he hit the ground, but the damage had already been done.

I screamed out from the burning pain and pulled away. I needed to kill him. He wasn't ashes yet. So, I reached for another stake I'd stashed at my calf, but as I gripped the hilt, I didn't get time to use it.

The vampire who'd been holding Katie threw her to the floor and lunged at me, knocking me to the ground. I could barely see, thanks to the poison in the vampire father's claws working through my system.

The vampire pounded into my back, forcing me further into the ground. Then he kicked my ribs and I heard them break. He slammed his foot into my back again and again.

I couldn't cry out. I could only reach out for my mate who looked like she'd fainted away on the floor.

When the vampire pulled my head back to reveal my throat, Katie's eyes popped open. She was on her feet in an instant, her eyes flashing with rage. Silver glinted near her hand. She'd grabbed the small dagger I'd given her.

The vampire stood up and turned to her. With one smart, fast move, she shoved the dagger into one of his eyes.

The vampire screamed. I slid my second silver dagger along the carpet toward Katie.

She ducked down, grabbed the dagger, and thrust it straight into the vampire's heart.

My heart pumped so fast it sounded like a steam engine, but at least I got the satisfaction of seeing him turn to dust before us.

"We need to get out of here," she said, glancing down at the dead bodies around us.

I nodded, pushing my hands into the carpet and forcing myself to my feet. "We do."

The father I'd staked began to crawl along the carpet, hauling himself to his feet.

"Oh, my God," Katie whispered, then started pulling me toward the door.

"Go," I told her. "I'll catch up with you."

The pain in my body was indescribable. So much worse than anything I'd experienced before.

"Go, Katie. Please." I waved at her as I hauled myself along the furniture, dragging my broken body toward the entrance.

I wasn't going to make it, but I wouldn't give up trying. "Go!" All that mattered was that Katie and her baby got out of here.

Her eyes flashed, and I knew she wasn't leaving me.

"No," I whispered, dragging myself a little faster and swallowing the scream of pain as I moved.

There was a cold breeze on my neck. The father was up, and he was close.

"Leave him alone," Katie yelled, then charged at me.

"Who's going to stop me from killing him, little one? You?" the father asked.

I turned just far enough to see him looming behind me.

"I wouldn't tease her, if I was you," I said, blood spilling out of my mouth and onto my shirt.

Fuck. I wasn't going to make it. I just had to stay conscious for a little longer. Help Katie in any way I could.

"Why not?" The vampire father tilted his head at me. "What's she going to do? Stop me before I take your head from your body? I don't think so. Then I'm going to drain the witch, just for vexing me."

He reached for me, his cold, undead fingers grabbing onto my shirt.

I couldn't move. Couldn't respond, and yet everything began to change, moving in slow motion.

The vampire grimaced, his sharp teeth flashing in the dim lighting. Then white light hurtled past me, meeting the vampire's flesh like the beam from a fog lamp.

His flesh peeled off his bones, leaving little more than a skeleton. And then that too, was gone.

My mouth dropped open. The father had disappeared before my very eyes.

I turned to see Katie standing beside me.

Her arms were outstretched, fierce determination on her face. She glowed with a magic more powerful than any I'd seen before.

I stared in wonder. In love.

Then I hit the ground with a thump that felt like it cracked my skull.

I was in a world of trouble.

"Go. Please. Save yourself," I whispered at my mate.

She placed her beautiful hands down on my back and shushed me.

"Be still," she said. "Breathe. And I'll heal you."

I was far past healing, or magic. And yet, there was no choice but to lie still and let Katie attempt whatever she was trying to do.

Save me, obviously. But how did she even have any magic left after dealing with the vampire father? That should have wiped her entirely.

The pain in my ribs began to lessen, a soothing warmth spreading through my joints and bones.

I was dying. I couldn't feel my body any longer.

"Katie," I said, turning my head to try and see her one more time. "I love you."

Everything went black, and I died.

CHAPTER 15
KATIE

"Don't you dare die on me!" I yelled at Shadow as he took a final breath.

I screamed, standing up and forcing my arms out in front of me. This was not the time for my lover to die.

No.

I closed my eyes and drew on every bit of magic I had. I gathered every tiny shred of strength and love I had for Shadow, and I poured it all into the spell I worked over his broken body.

I screamed as I dropped to the floor, pressing a hand to Shadow's back and feeling the softest amount of breath rising and falling from him.

"Help!" I yelled, though to whom, I didn't know.

Everyone around me was dead, and I couldn't lift my arms now. The spell I'd used to kill the vampire father, followed by my attempt at healing Shadow, had taken every bit of magic I had. I was done for now.

I let myself collapse, lying half across Shadow's back, my hand snaking across to lay over my rounded belly.

Hopefully I hadn't taken too much of my body's energy. It was still needed for my gorgeous little baby. But if I couldn't stand up, nor move from this spot, we were probably done for anyway.

At least we're here together.

The door flew open, and men piled in.

"Holy fuck, what the hell happened here?"

I lifted my head and stared at one of the men. He looked mostly human.

"Help," I whispered, trembling.

The guys converged on me.

"Are you the witch Shadow was looking for?"

I nodded and one of the big guys lifted me into his arms. "We've gotta get you out of here."

I let my arm drop, pointing to where Shadow lay. "He's alive. Get him. Please."

"Alex, grab Shadow," the guy said, his voice booming in the room. "Check every man, carry who you can. But we're leaving in three minutes."

There was a rush around the room, and my head started to spin. I made sure that the guys grabbed Shadow, then closed my eyes for the elevator ride down.

We collected more soldiers who had been camped out in the basement, and headed out.

"Where to?" one of the guys asked as they carried me through the streets.

"Where's safe? The workshop?" another man offered.

I had no idea what the workshop was, but if Shadow had brought these men with him, I had to trust them.

They carried me to a cab, ordered the guy to take us to an address, and before I knew it, I was sitting in a large room with a whole lot of gym equipment. They placed Shadow in front of me on a red gym mat.

His face was healed and he was no longer bleeding, but he wasn't waking up.

"We better set up a perimeter and stay here with them tonight," one of the men said.

"What about food?" another asked.

"Get some for the whole crew. Get some sleeping bags and shit too, if you can."

The words were rolling around me, and yet I didn't really understand what was going on. I crawled over to where Shadow lay on the floor mat and lay down beside him.

I stroked his face, pushing the hair out of his eyes. "Please wake up," I whispered. "I can't do all this without you."

Shadow didn't respond and I pressed even closer, reveling in the beat of his heart. His breath on my face.

He was alive. That was all that mattered.

I'd find a way to get him well.

I may have run out of magic for the moment, but I would recharge. I would grow in power again, and then I would heal him. I'd bring him back to me. And our baby.

"Katie..." Shadow's whispered plea came out of nowhere and had me sitting bolt upright.

"Shadow? Did you say something?"

He still wasn't moving. Was it my imagination? Or was it really possible that he was waking up?

Then I saw it. The smallest of movements. His eyelids fluttered, then his lips pulled tight as he groaned and tried to move.

"Shadow?"

He nodded.

"Oh, thank God!" I cried, throwing myself at him and pushing him onto his back so that I rolled on top of him.

I had no magic left to help him, but I still couldn't help myself from asking, "Are you okay? Are you hurt?"

His arms moved slowly around me and I pushed up with my weak arms to smile down at him. "You're alive."

He nodded slowly, staring up at me like he couldn't believe I was on top of him, and we were both still breathing.

"What happened?" he asked.

I lifted a hand to wipe at the tears that were falling from my eyes, with no regard to my preference not to cry.

"I killed the vampire father, which felt so good, by the way." I slid down to sit beside him, but kept a hand on him at all times.

It *had* felt amazing to kill that vampire. So good. I'd dreamt about being strong enough to kill them for so long. And now I was.

"I think I remember that part," Shadow said, one side of his mouth quirking up into a weak smile. "Then how did we get back to... the workshop?"

I grinned at him. "These guys came storming in and carried us both home."

Well, this place wasn't exactly home, but all the feelings inside this place were good, and I was comfortable to stay here. Maybe even forever.

I kind of liked the idea of living in a place with weapons and an alarm system connected to the police.

"But..." Shadow stopped, then inhaled sharply. "I thought I died. I felt... dead."

I shrugged. "I wasn't ready to let you go."

Shadow dragged himself up to sit next to me. "You used all your magic to bring me back to life?"

"Well, I'm not sure you actually died." I hadn't checked his heartbeat, or his breathing. I'd just launched at his healing like a starving dog at a bone. "But yes, I used my magic to heal you. How are you feeling?"

Shadow raised his arm and looked down at the flesh that had been mauled by a vampire.

There was scarring, and the flesh looked raw, but he still had an arm. And that was all that mattered.

"Did we really survive?" Shadow whispered, then looked up at me. "I didn't think I'd get out of there alive."

My heart skipped a beat. "But you came for me anyway."

"Of course, I did, Katie," Shadow said.

"God, I love you." I leaned forward to kiss him.

He sighed as our lips met and I drew him even closer. We had survived an enemy that no-one else in the city would have been able to vanquish.

I felt quietly confident now, that we would be able to do anything together.

EPILOGUE

SHADOW

Six months later

I leaned forward in the director's chair and hung up the phone, mystified by Sadie's conversation.

I shook my head. "Another year? Really?"

"Hey sweetie!" Katie called through the door, just before she waddled in, her hand on her lower back. "How's your day been?"

"You shouldn't be up and walking around." I scowled at my mate, before rushing around Jack's huge desk and grabbing for her hands.

She lowered herself into the chair and rubbed her belly. "I was due a few days ago, Shadow. I want this baby out of me. Now."

I wanted to tease her and tell her we needed to give her more orgasms to get the labor going, but I'd been working double time on that for the past month, and daily sexual sessions were not helping.

"Who was that on the phone?" Katie asked. "I thought I heard you talking to someone as I came up the stairs."

I leaned back against the desk and crossed my arms over my chest. "It was Sadie, actually."

"Oh? How is she?"

"Very pregnant as well."

Katie's eyebrows flicked up. "And? When are they coming back?"

I got up from the desk and moved back to the director's chair, from where I'd been running Hunters in Sadie's absence for the past six months.

"She said another year or so."

Katie blinked, then ran her hand over her belly. "Really? Well, that's... unexpected, I suppose."

"I told her that we wanted them back to run the company, but her mom isn't doing so well, and they've decided to stay in the country."

Katie flinched, but I assumed that was her back, as always. She'd been uncomfortable for months now.

"Well, I can't say I blame her," Katie said. "I can't imagine what Sadie's mom suffered being in the underground for almost twenty years. That's just... insane."

I nodded, my fingers aching for my small silver cigarette case. Thanks to my mate, who regularly used her magic to help me with my pain, I didn't need the hand-rolled cigarettes anymore. But sometimes I missed the habit.

"Are you okay?" I asked my mate, who only nodded and waved for me to go on. "Well, she said we should stay. Keep running the business, living in her dad's apartment. The whole lot."

"Did you tell her we preferred to live here?" Katie asked with a grin.

I shook my head. "No. But that doesn't really matter. The most important thing is you and the baby are safe. I've had Jack's old apartment cleaned and renovated. Everything is super-bright, and light, and the windows are unbreakable. Even against a vampire."

Katie grinned, then inhaled sharply.

"You sure you're okay?"

Katie jerked to her feet, a wet patch forming on her light-blue maternity jeans.

"Uh…" I stared at her. Had she just wet herself?

"My waters just broke." She gasped. "I've been having cramps all day, but I didn't think it meant anything."

"Oh… *oh!*" I jumped to my feet and raced around the desk. "You sure you want to go to Nathaniel's hospital?"

She nodded, breathing hard. "Definitely. I owe that man a lot. And I feel safe around him."

I was glad Nathaniel had moved into new premises. After he'd survived the vampire attack, he'd set up in a new part of town. A safer part, with even more magical back-up.

The other great thing that had changed about the city was that a lot of the vampires had moved on, and I hadn't heard anything about a new blood ring being set up.

Between Sadie and Katie, two vampire fathers had been taken out, and no-one could tell me if there were any others around.

Without that protection and structure, a lot of the vampires had up and left, leaving us with a safer city, especially for my magical mate and her unborn child.

"You got your bags packed, right?" I asked her, knowing the answer, but having a broken-brain moment.

She nodded, beginning to breathe deeper and slower. "Yes. It's in our room."

"I'll get it." I raced out of the office and into the room next door.

It had been an office once upon a time, but we'd reinforced the window with vampire-proof glass and set up our bed there.

Neither Katie nor I needed a lot of space or material possessions, but we needed security, and a window so she could see the stars.

I grabbed the bag on the bed, already stuffed full of clothes and baby things. On top of the bag was a little potion bottle, and I palmed that to give to my mate. She still took the elixir Nathaniel provided, so that she smelt like a snake to the vampires.

Nothing would get rid of her fear of being taken again, but the elixir helped, as did living at the workshop.

I raced back to my mate, who was waiting patiently at the top of the stairs for me.

"Shall we go?" I asked, and she gripped my hand, hard.

"Yes!"

We hurried down the stairs, and took a cab the three blocks to Nathaniel's new clinic.

Within hours, a mewling, blood-covered, perfect human being lay in Katie's exhausted arms.

"She's so beautiful." Katie sobbed, kissing her baby daughter's wet dark hair.

The baby cried, her tiny hands flailing for purchase.

I kissed Katie's sweat-covered forehead. "You were amazing, sweetheart."

"You were," Nathaniel re-iterated, taking off his gloves and throwing them in the trash. "Welcome to the world, little girl."

He grinned at me, reaching out to shake my hand. "Congratulations, Shadow."

I nodded back. "Thanks, man."

Katie lay back on the bed, smiling brightly. "Do you want to hold her?"

Did I? I had no idea how to hold a baby.

"Let me help," Josie said, stepping between us. She wrapped the baby in a thin pink blanket and handed her to me.

I ended up cradling the infant in my arms without meaning to. She just fit in my arms, against my chest. Like she was always meant to be there.

I stared down at her. She had stopped crying, and instead, opened her eyes and stared up at me.

"She's looking at me," I said, rocking her back and forward.

Katie laughed happily and I looked at my mate.

"Of course, she is," Katie said. "She loves her daddy already."

My nose tingled with an emotion I dared not name, and I stared down at my baby daughter.

"She's the most beautiful thing I've ever seen."

Josie chuckled. "That's what all the new dads say. I'll be back in just a moment, Katie. You rest."

I carried my little girl over to the window and showed her the city. A place people had once called Blood World, but not anymore.

Now it was a place I was happy to raise a child in, with my mate.

"Happy birthday, beautiful girl."

THE END